NIGHT TIDE

By

Michael W. Sherer

Michael W. Sherer

NIGHT TIDE

Cover Design: Anita Elder Design and Michael W. Sherer

Night Tide

For Valarie

Praise for the Blake Sanders Series:

NIGHT DROP

"Looking for an adrenaline rush? You'll find that and more in *Night Drop.* Blake Sanders is back, and that means the action is non-stop!" —Alan Russell, author of *Multiple Wounds* and *Burning Man*

"I LOVED this story. *Night Drop* is a fast-paced, tension-filled thriller that will grab you by the throat until the very last page. Blake Sanders is one of the most intriguing characters I've read in years. This is definitely Sherer at his best." —KT Bryan, author of *Team EDGE*

NIGHT TIDE

"A great, great read! Even better than *Night Blind*, and that's not easy." – Timothy Hallinan, author of *The Fame Thief*

"...a cracking good story and a first-rate thriller." – J. Carson Black, *New York Times* and *USA Today* bestselling author of *The Survivors Club*

"A tight, well-constructed story and characters that leap from the page. I'll definitely be back for more." – Robert Gregory Browne, author of *Trial Junkies 2: Negligence*

NIGHT BLIND

"An appealing, empathetic lead..." —*Publisher's Weekly*

"This is an exciting, well-crafted thriller and most certainly a satisfying one." —*Mysterious Reviews*

"Thriller writer Sherer renders a sympathetic lead character and an engaging...story line in his latest..." — Allison Block, *Booklist*

"Loved every page of it."
—Brett Battles

"A tightly paced page-turner that's impossible to put down. Terrific!"
—Allison Brennan

"Pay attention. You won't want to miss a word."
—J.T. Ellison

"...rich, complex, and deeply satisfying."
—Bill Cameron

Michael W. Sherer

NIGHT TIDE

CHAPTER 1

The smell of gas hung on the porch of the ramshackle house like a bookie's leg-breaker, heavy and oppressive, full of menace. I backed away cautiously, nose full of the rotten-egg odorant in the gas. Finding a spot where polluted air left off and fresh air began was tough. I tucked the paper I'd been holding under one arm to dial 9-1-1, told the operator about the leak and gave her the address.

"What's your name, sir?" she asked, her voice clipped but polite, all business.

"What difference does it make?" With four more stops to make and a waiting bed after that, the thought of hanging around to answer questions didn't thrill me. Besides, for all I knew Caller ID had put my name on-screen in front of her anyway.

"I need your name, sir."

"Sanders. Blake Sanders."

"Are you the homeowner, sir?"

"No. I was just passing by. I smelled gas. I called you."

"But the leak is at the address you gave me?"

"Yeah, I'm pretty sure. That's where the smell's coming from."

"Is there anyone in the house?"

"How would I know?"

Odds were pretty good someone was home. No one had stopped newspaper delivery. Unless people planned on being gone only a day or two, they usually put a vacation hold on their paper.

"Sir, I'm reporting this to dispatch now. They'll have the fire department on scene as fast as they can. In the meantime, it would help to know if anyone's in immediate danger."

"I'll see what I can do."

I disconnected before she could think of more suggestions, dialed information and asked for a listing for the gas utility. I punched my way through the prompts to report a gas leak and finally got a live person on the line. He took me through the same rigmarole without much enthusiasm, his voice flat and disinterested, and said they'd send someone.

Pocketing the phone, I stared at the house in the gray, pre-dawn light, debating what to do next. The house stared back, the broken slats on the porch rail giving me a snaggletoothed grin. Dew on the tall grass in the weedy yard soaked through the mesh tops of my athletic shoes, spurring me to action. I sucked in a deep breath and held it, climbed the few steps to the porch and pounded on the front door. No answer. I pounded harder. This time I thought I heard a faint voice inside telling me to hold my horses.

"You need to get out of there," I yelled, expelling the breath I'd been holding.

I dove off the porch, gulped down more air, and went back to banging on the door with the heel of my fist.

"I'm coming!" said the gravelly voice, muffled by the door. "Keep your pants on!"

The entry light blinked on and the door opened mid-swing. On the other side stood a disheveled man in baggy sweat pants and a worn bathrobe rubbing the sleep from one eye. An ample beer belly pushed a cotton undershirt out between the open folds of the robe. In the yellowed light the sweat-stained shirt appeared several shades off-white. Scuffed, dirty slippers covered his toes, but his bare ankles were mapped with blue veins. Long, greasy gray hair hung in ropes to his shoulders. Several days' growth of beard in matching gray covered his face. He dug two fingers into it and scratched, scowling.

"What the fuck do you want?" he said.

"You can't smell that?"

"Smell what?" He took a step toward me, stuck his head through the doorframe and sniffed.

"You've got a gas leak. You need to get out of the house."

He peered at me suspiciously and sniffed again. This time, his eyes widened in shock.

"Jesus, mister, you weren't shittin' me, were you?" He stepped onto the porch.

"I called 9-1-1 and the gas company. Fire department should be here any minute."

On cue, a siren's wail drifted over the rooftops and down the city's grid of canyons between houses and buildings. Absently, he wrapped the robe over his belly and cinched it tight. Dazed, he shuffled down the steps onto the walk. I followed him down and steered him toward the street with an arm around his shoulder.

"You're Mr. Donato?" I said.

He glanced at me. "Yeah. Phil Donato. That's me. How'd you know?"

I held up the paper and put it in his hand. "You're on my route. Is there anyone else in the house, Mr. Donato?"

He shook his head, matted locks barely budging. "I live alone."

The sirens grew closer, burped once and went silent as an SFD engine and a squad vehicle pulled onto the block with lights flashing. The engine's crew jumped down and busied themselves running out lengths of hose and climbing into their gear. A lieutenant got out of the squad car and walked over to us. His nametag said "R.F. Hinckley."

He looked at us both and settled his gaze on me. "You the one who called it in?"

I nodded.

"And this is the homeowner?"

"Mr. Donato," I said. "He says there's no one else in the house."

He wrinkled his nose. "Lucky you came by."

Donato stared at the house as if he hadn't heard us.

Hinckley leaned toward him. "It's all right, sir. Gas company is on the way. Soon as they find the leak and fix it, you can go back to bed."

There was no response. The lieutenant shrugged and turned away to check on his men. I watched them set up, antsy now, wondering when the utility would show up. Then again, I'd done my part. I had no reason to stay.

Before I made up my mind, a gas company truck rolled up, nosed in to the fire engine and parked. As the driver got out, one of the firemen yelled over the low rumble of the engine, diverting my attention.

"Hey! Don't go in there! Hey you!"

I turned to see Donato partway up the walk, already a dozen yards away.

"My cat!" he said. "I forgot my cat! She's in there."

"Wait," I said, taking a step. "You can't go back inside."

He didn't stop. As soon as he spotted me moving toward him he broke into a shambling run, losing a slipper on the way up the walk. I went after him with a burst of speed that elicited a groan from the titanium and ceramic joint in my hip. I hooked an arm around his stooped shoulders as he reached the steps and changed direction, dragging him aside toward the bushes fronting the house. Planting his feet, he bent at the waist, and my looped arm suddenly held air, not his shoulders.. The abrupt lack of resistance sent me over the edge of the porch arms churning like a wind turbine in a steady breeze. As the bushes rushed up to meet me, I twisted to avoid a branch in the eye and saw the old man disappear into the house.

Something inside—furnace or water heater, maybe an old thermostat—sparked and ignited the gas with an ear-splitting *whump* and ball of orange flame that blew out the front windows. Shards of glass rained down as a blast of hot air rushed over me, sucking the oxygen out of my lungs. I lay in the dirt, dazed and blinded, the sudden shock turning the whole world black.

CHAPTER 2

Perry Langford stepped outside the visitors building at the federal penitentiary in Marion, Illinois, and tasted freedom for the first time in more than twenty years. Even the air smelled different to him than it had on the other side of the fence, a hundred feet away. He raised his arms and stretched, lifting his face to the April sunshine, then climbed into a waiting cab. As it pulled away, he looked back one last time at the hellhole that he'd called home. *Never again.*

From downtown Marion he took a bus to Carbondale, ate lunch in a diner near the station and wandered around town until the time came to board an Amtrak train to Centralia. The train arrived in Centralia two minutes behind schedule. After disembarking, he walked a mile through town to the house where he'd grown up. It stood empty, his parents having died years before.

The next day, he met with his parole officer, applied for several jobs around town, and spent the afternoon cleaning the house. Neighbors looked out their windows and offered grudging smiles, glad to see someone finally taking an interest in the place. They watched, nodding appreciatively, as he placed full trash cans neatly at the curb. They waved at him the next day when he mowed the overgrown yard and trimmed the scraggly bushes covering the windows. They beamed on the third day when he put a fresh coat of paint on the front porch.

On the fourth day, the neighbors saw him leave the house dressed in an ill-fitting gray suit. He never came back.

* * * * *

She sat in the rented car, cocooned in the dark. The list of names lay in her lap, pencil in her hand resting on it lightly. She tried to remember how long she'd called strange hotels and executive apartments home, how long it had been since she'd driven her own car, cooked a decent meal in her own kitchen. At

11

least it wasn't raining. Seattle had maintained its dreary reputation during her first week in town, but recently had put on a sunnier face. She could see a swath of light blue painted over the tops of the buildings to the east, and stars glowed faintly in the dark sky overhead, promising another cloudless day.

She stifled a yawn, circadian rhythm thrown off by the hours she'd been keeping lately. Not just because of what she had to do. She hadn't been sleeping well. Good, old-fashioned insomnia. Hormones, maybe. Stress, more likely. Soon, though, it would all end. She sensed she was close. A muffled blast half a mile away rattled the car and lit up the sky behind her. She drew a line through a name on the list, set paper and pencil on the seat next to her and turned the key in the ignition. She sat several minutes longer with the engine running until she heard the sound of passing sirens fade away somewhere far behind her and die with a squawk.

Exhaustion rolled over her like a runaway truck as she navigated the dark city streets to her next task. She didn't know how people could work nights. The months of travel had taken their toll, but not like the past two weeks. It was the crazy hours. Who in their right mind turned their lives inside out and stayed up all night except vampires? Then again, who in their right mind would give up nearly everything in pursuit of answers to something that happened twenty years ago? Answers to questions that supposedly had been answered already? A man had been tried, convicted and gone to jail. Why was she still convinced he wasn't the only person who had been involved? Because others, like her contact, believed the same thing.

She'd spent nearly twenty years trying to forget what had happened, but she'd been drawn back in until it had become an obsession again. And now it had cost her a marriage and maybe her sanity. Certainly, she'd lost sleep. She laughed at the thought, startling herself in the dark. Her smile quickly faded as she sat up and looked through the glass, head swiveling to get her bearings. She'd arrived. She took in the entire street, suddenly anxious, wondering if she might have missed him.

She was in it for good now. She'd spent nearly eighteen months tracking down the first one on the list for them. As much as she wished she could convince herself that she didn't know what would happen once she found the man, she wasn't naïve. They'd told her what to do to take care of the problem. It wasn't as if she'd taken out a gun and shot the man. It wasn't like that. But she knew the man was dead. The explosion not long before confirmed it. And this one, the man she waited for, was supposed to lead her to the others. He wasn't on their list, but she wondered what would happen to him anyway.

God, she was tired. So tired. She shut her eyes for just a moment, and her head nodded until her chin nearly touched her chest. She lifted it halfway, fighting the exhaustion, but it was so heavy that sleep pulled it back down, dragging her thoughts with it into dreamland. Images swirled and collided in her subconscious as she drifted from one uneasy dream into another. *No, no, no!* She had to be alert so she didn't miss anything.

She woke with a start, forehead and nape of her neck damp with perspiration, and peered out the windshield to get her bearings as tendrils of the dream slipped away. The sky outside had lightened considerably.

Not long now. She shifted on the seat to get more comfortable, remembering now why she had to see this through. Her sister...

Michael W. Sherer

CHAPTER 3

After getting a once-over from an SFD paramedic, I gave a statement to one of the beat cops who showed up. I traversed the remainder of my paper route uneventfully, though unsteadily, ears still ringing and hair a little singed, and stopped for coffee at my usual spot, a restaurant on the south end of Capitol Hill. The place suited my temperament. The customers—a swatch of humanity most of middle-America encounters only at the circus—provided a source of free entertainment. The coffee was strong, the restaurant warm and dry.

Charlie Jones and Craig Downing already claimed a table in a far corner. Craig seemed to have adopted Charlie's aversion to sitting with his back to the entrance. I didn't know anyone besides cops and crooks who seemed to care much. Seattle beat cops, the pair worked Three-Charlie in East, which meant they covered the Charlie sector of East Precinct during third watch. I didn't think Charlie appreciated the irony of working Charlie sector half as much as I did. The two cops had been friends since Downing had been a rookie, partly because of their shared experience in Iraq—Downing's tour, though, during the war started by "W," Charlie's courtesy of Bush the Elder.

Charlie waved me over, a magnanimous gesture from him. Jones had been one of my buddies in college, a fraternity brother at UW. Pre-law as an undergrad, he dropped out senior year to enlist in the Army shortly after Iraq invaded Kuwait. By the time they launched Desert Storm, Charlie was trained and ready. He happily shipped out to serve his country, the allure for Charlie "giving those camel jockeys a wake-up call." After his tour, he went back to school but switched majors to criminology and became a cop instead of a lawyer.

We'd drifted apart over the years. For a while we half-heartedly kept in touch, but by then I had a wife and kid, and Charlie's career took him in a different direction. I stood up for him at his wedding. He came to a couple of Christmas parties

Molly and I threw when we were still married. Otherwise, we didn't have much contact.

That had changed when I took over the paper route. Our paths tended to cross more. Literally, since we worked the same shift in the same area of Capitol Hill. And a few months earlier I'd found myself at odds with SPD over several murders, including a sweet nonagenarian friend of mine. Investigators thought I'd committed them. Loyal to the badge, Charlie sided with SPD. Until the truth came out. But Charlie had always been quick to form an opinion and stick to it.

A few inches shy of six feet, with an athletic build he'd managed to keep trim over the years, Charlie had always seemed big to me. Something about the way he carried himself, along with that unerring self-assurance that he was always right, inflated his presence, giving the impression that he took up more space than he really did. And as I approached him now, I realized the passing years had done little to change him other than salt his temples with gray and add character to his boyish face.

"Buy you coffee?" Charlie said. He was still trying to make amends.

His voice sounded as if it had dug its way through several layers of cotton by the time it reached my auditory nerves. The rumble of timpani that had accompanied me since the gas explosion made my head ache.

"Hey, Charlie." I eased into a chair and nodded to Craig. "*Officer* Downing." The pair had been sitting a while judging from the amount of coffee remaining in their cups.

Downing grimaced. "Morning, Legs. I'm off duty, remember?"

I gave him a tight-lipped smile at the mention of the old nickname. I wasn't feeling all that sociable after the morning I'd had. I'd always hated to lose, and though grateful beyond words for being upright and breathing I still couldn't figure out how I'd lost Donato.

Charlie ran his fingers through wiry hair that was only a tad longer than a military cut. "You work at the restaurant last night?"

The paper route barely covered rent and utilities. I washed dishes at a Mexican restaurant on weekends. "No, why?"

He shrugged. "You look more beat than usual. You okay?"

Reluctantly, I related the early morning incident that had thrown me off my normal routine.

Charlie's eyebrows arched. "So *you're* the big hero. Heard the call come over the radio."

"You'd have done the same."

"Not hardly. They don't pay us enough."

Downing drained his cup, then tipped and rolled it, eyeing the inside to see if any coffee had somehow eluded him.

Charlie eyed him briefly, and changed the set of his jaw. "The old man make it?"

I swallowed hard, a video replay of the fireball running though my head. "No."

Charlie held my gaze and finally nodded. "Tough break. I know you did what you could."

Downing set his cup down, cleared his throat and stood. "I'm heading home."

"Okay, partner. Be safe out there." Charlie idly toyed with his cup, tearing little pieces off the lip as he watched Downing leave. "He's a good kid."

"Hardly a kid, but definitely a good guy."

Charlie swung his graying head my way like an old ram. "You're still coming next weekend, right?" He saw my hesitation. "Memorial Day? Cookout with my folks? Any of this ring a bell?"

"Oh, right. Sure, I'll be there."

He frowned. "You better be. I swear I'll go nuts if I don't have someone to talk besides my old man. Christ, you have the attention span of a minnow. Write it down, will you?"

"Lay off, Charlie! I don't have to write down *every*thing. I'll remember, okay?"

I didn't see dead people. I wasn't a vampire. Or a zombie-hunter. I wasn't a dream catcher, and I couldn't cast spells or work magic. I didn't have a physical deformity or disability— unless you count being just shy of six-foot-nine. I didn't have a readily identifiable condition. I didn't blurt out obscenities, bark like a dog or stutter and tic like someone with Tourette's. I wasn't narcoleptic, though I sometimes wished I could fall asleep that easily. I didn't smell colors or hear emotions like a synesthete. I couldn't claim the wild mood swings of a manic-depressive, but wouldn't have been surprised if a shrink categorized me as mildly bi-polar. Who isn't?

What I had was a little more insidious and pervasive. A disorder hard to diagnose accurately and so loosely defined that lots of folks scoffed at the suggestion it was real or debilitating. Most people thought pediatricians and child psychologists made it up to help parents and teachers get better control of energetic or unruly kids. Adults who have it were dismissed as whiners who just wanted a convenient excuse for bad behavior. But brain scans didn't lie.

Many of us with ADHD appeared perfectly normal. Even the symptoms of our disorder—inattention, impatience, inability to finish tasks, chronic lateness, disorganization, risk-taking—were all within the realm of normal behavior taken individually or even in small clusters. People who witnessed my tendencies to interrupt conversations, make nonsensical statements or appear not to be listening just found me rude or arrogant. They didn't suspect an underlying organic flaw in my brain circuitry, a chemical imbalance, a comparatively smaller mass of gray cells in the parietal cortex. Why should they? I was just like them in most ways. Sort of.

So I forgot things occasionally. Which is why I kept lists. Even then, I forgot things. But Charlie could have given me a break since I'd almost been blown up a few hours earlier.

"Babs will be there, won't she?" I said, lightening my tone some to alleviate the tension.

"Sure, but she'll be making girl talk with Connie. I need a buffer between me and Clayt."

Charlie's use of his parents' first names sounded discourteous, even cheeky. Manners had been my mother's bailiwick, but my father had insisted on respect, which meant using titles when addressing one's elders. My father had been "Sir" most of the time, "Dad" some of the time, and someone I still feared, though he'd been dead for more than twenty years. Charlie's parents were aging hippies who'd treated Charlie and his sister Sarah more like miniature adults than children growing up. They'd called their parents by name since they could talk.

"And Craig...?" I said.

"Has family obligations," he finished for me. "And no, I don't have any other buddies on the force that are free."

"So you're stuck with me."

His face lightened. "Bring Molly. Then we'll have an even number of guys and girls."

The thought tempted me. My ex-wife could beguile an Inuit out of a sealskin coat. "You know that dog won't hunt, Charlie. Besides, I'm sure she's busy. She's a popular girl."

"How do you know unless you ask?"

My resolve wilted under his stare. "Fine. I'll ask."

"Good." He swept the bits of paper strewn on the table into his empty cup with his hand and got to his feet. "I'm heading out."

He left me alone nursing a bitter cup of burnt coffee, old memories, creeping exhaustion and a sense of gratitude for whichever Fates had conspired to delimit flying glass and flames to the night air, not flesh.

Michael W. Sherer

CHAPTER 4

A figure sat on the stoop of the house in Madison Valley where I lived, lowered head resting on knees hugged tightly together, face obscured. Gravity pulled the straight short blond hair down toward the blue-jeaned thighs so it splayed out like a dust mop. A Raggedy Andy gargoyle guarding the entrance. I didn't believe in ghosts. What haunted me in the dead of night were memories, emotions unexpressed, thoughts left unsaid. Those bitter siblings, regret and remorse, whispering in my ear. Ice water ran down my spine and filled the hollow space in my chest, making me wonder if I should rethink my beliefs.

"Cole?" I wasn't sure I actually spoke the word aloud.

The shaggy head rose. A delicate hand brushed aside the fringe, revealing the face of an attractive doe-eyed woman with a heart-shaped mouth. Ann, not Andy. A pixie face, like Twiggy's or Hepburn's—Audrey, not Kate—that didn't come close to resembling Cole's. A burning sensation erupted from the raw, red scar that remained where he'd been ripped out of my life.

The pain turned to sudden annoyance, anger directed at the elfin lawn jockey perched on the porch. For a brief moment she'd made me think Cole had pulled off a trick no one's managed for a couple thousand years. I rubbed the back of my neck. The early morning blast must have rattled a screw loose to make me see ghosts like that. The woman's large blue eyes flitted over my face impassively, perhaps mirroring the exhaustion that always hit me around that time of day like a leg-whipped roller derby queen. Life flickered in their Caribbean depths like silvery fish, and the corners of her mouth softened. She didn't smile, but she looked less grim.

"Blake Sanders?" Her voice didn't match her appearance. It sounded deeper than I expected, carrying more timbre.

A process server, maybe. Who else would camp out on my doorstep at such an early hour? Some customer intended to sue, no doubt, because I hadn't placed his paper in the right spot, causing him emotional distress. I looked for signs of paper near her hands. They were empty, devoid of even jewelry. She pressed them on her knees and rose to her feet. Standing on the second step gave her a height advantage over me, slight but reassuring, her stance said.

I stopped short. "And you are ...?"

"Keely Radcliffe." She said it with the kind of off-handed ease of someone used to getting what she wanted, someone accustomed to directing traffic—household retainers, maybe, or office staff.

"I'm sorry. Who?" She repeated the name. It meant no more to me the second time, but the repetition might help me remember it. "Whatever you're selling, I'm not buying."

"Please. I just need a moment of your time."

I waved her off and cut across the grass toward the walk by the side of the house. Technically, the doorstep and the house that went with it belonged to Peter Stabler and his partner Chance Reno. I rented the in-law apartment below them, the entrance around the back.

"I really need to talk to you," the woman said, louder this time and with a hint of plaintiveness, the pitch of her voice rising.

"I don't need to talk to you," I said over my shoulder. "I need sleep."

The concept of eight hours of uninterrupted sleep, a visit from the Sandman, a mid-winter's (or mid-spring's) nap, some shut-eye, rest and repose, a little Rip Van Winkle, presented a paradigm about as real as life in a Norman Rockwell painting. People who work the night shift would give eyeteeth—hell, their first-born children—for a decent snooze.

"It's important," she called. She stood her ground, either not desperate enough or too proud to follow me. Or beg.

"Can't be more important than my date with a pillow."

My headache threatened to morph into a migraine, and stiffness had settled into various extremities from the rough landing in the bushes earlier. Through the ringing in my ears I heard my bed calling my name.

She said two words that changed everything. "Perry Langford."

I stopped and faced her, wondering if she saw the palsy shaking my knees as if they were made of Jell-O. "What about him?"

"He's out."

I braced myself as the words torpedoed the concrete wall repressing all those memories, waited for the flood I'd never confronted. Only a rivulet of muddy guilt trickled through the hole cratered by her bomb. Too much water over that dam in twenty years. There wasn't much left except silty recollections.

"That's nice." I started to turn away.

"I don't think he did it."

I cocked my head. "Twenty-plus years? That probably doesn't mean a whole lot to him now." I shrugged. "I'm happy for him. I hope he makes a life for himself."

She stepped off the porch and pushed an unruly strand of hair out of her face with the same gesture she used earlier.

"You're not making this any easier." She tried a smile, but the accusation was clear.

I frowned. I kept telling Jeri, the leader of a support group I attended, that sleep, not anger, was really the issue I needed to work on. Keely Radcliffe appeared attractive enough that in other circumstances the thought of asking her out for coffee may have entered my stream of consciousness. As things stood, neither her looks nor her play to my sense of guilt had worked for her so far. A more direct route seemed in order so she didn't string this out all morning.

"What do you want?"

She recoiled but recovered quickly. "I'd like you to help me find him."

I shook my pounding head, pain, lack of sleep and the absurdity of her proposal clouding my thoughts. "I haven't seen or spoken to Perry Langford since he went to prison. I don't know where you got my name, but you're barking up the wrong tree. I don't have a clue where he is, and don't know that I care to."

"Please." She took a faltering step, her eyes beseeching me. "Hear me out."

"Keely, was it? Where you come from maybe it's perfectly acceptable to call on people at this hour of the morning. But in my world it's bedtime. I get cranky and just a little bit testy when I'm up past my bedtime. A holdover, I'm sure, from my childhood and no doubt one of my many failings. Whatever, you'll just have to excuse me. I think you've mistaken me for someone who cares. Good luck to you, whoever you are."

I spun on my heel and left her standing there. On the way down to my apartment, I wondered when I'd skewed my priorities so far off-kilter that I preferred a down pillow to the company of a pretty woman.

Not long after, I dreamed of a skinny kid with dirty blond hair, a nose that looked as if had been flattened by the smack of a nun's ruler and eyes the color of a hazy summer day in L.A. flecked with yellow smog. His wide mouth perpetually turned up at the corners in a "He-e-re's Johnny" smile, the accompanying glint in his eye either mischief or madness. I could never be sure which.

He picked up a two-foot cylinder of polished aluminum from a worktable in the garage. About three inches in diameter, it gleamed in the dim light, almost as if lit from within. Half the six-bay garage—formerly a small barn on what had once been the outskirts of town—held a workshop, the other half an odd collection of antique cars. A treasure trove to young boys, filled with tools, gadgets, car parts, dingbats and widgets, whozits and whatchamacallits, the shiny cylinder just one more toy in a fantasy playground.

Grease-stained canvas tarps hung haphazardly over a Model T and a horseless carriage that predated the Ford by two decades. An old woody wagon, cherry as the day it came off the assembly line, sat in one corner, hood up. Wires sprouted out of the engine compartment, curling over the fenders like vines. A big lathe and drill press stood in one corner. Wooden worktables and benches lined the walls, covered in wood and metal shavings, small pyramids of gunk, oil spots and hand tools. Dust motes floated in the sunlight that angled inside an open garage bay door. A puff of air redolent of oil, solvents and newly cut grass stirred them lazily.

The kid tipped the cylinder on end, resting the butt on a bench. The cylinder sported a half-inch hole on top, a dead-center black bull's-eye ringed with silver. He picked up a dented can containing black powder and poured some into the hole. Using a metal rod tipped with a square of stained blue cloth, he tamped the powder down into the hole. He centered a clean circle of white cotton over the hole and shoved it inside with the rod. From another can on a shelf, he tipped a single stainless steel ball into the palm of his hand. The metal marble gleamed in the light, heavy in his hand, but so shiny it appeared clear and weightless. Grinning, he held it up between his thumb and forefinger and dropped it down the hole. It disappeared with a soft rasping sound. He tamped another cloth round in after it.

He set the cylinder into a vise bolted to one end of a wooden sawhorse, and gently cranked the jaws closed. With a wave, he signaled me to take the other end of the sawhorse, and we carried it outside and placed it in the driveway. He inched his end around until satisfied with where it sat, and then ducked back into the garage. A moment later, he lugged a bag of cement back out into the hot summer sun and leaned it up against a leg of the sawhorse, then went back inside and got another.

When he finished, he pulled what looked like a piece of string from one pocket, and a wooden kitchen match from the other, a gleam of triumph in his eyes. He poked the string down into a small hole in the side of the cylinder I hadn't noticed before. Slick as you please, he bent down and struck the match against the concrete drive. He touched it, still flaring, to the fuse. We watched it spark and burn down into the hole.

A second later, the cylinder spat fire with a resonant *boom* that rattled my teeth and made me jump. Fifty yards away, the half-inch steel ball ripped a chunk the size of a melon from the trunk of a big oak tree. Despite the forty-pound sacks of concrete mix, the sawhorse flew ten feet behind us. Blood trickled down one of my shins where it had clipped me on the way.

"Per-*ry*!" A woman's voice called from the house. "Perry-winkle Langford, what on earth are you up to?"

With a grin, Wink grabbed one end of the sawhorse and quickly dragged it into the garage.

CHAPTER 5

Langford pushed himself, finishing his last taekwondo *pumsae* with as much exertion as he could muster, his bare torso glistening with sweat. He pulled up and walked around the clearing with his hands on his hips, breathing heavily. He took in the woodsy scents of fir, spruce and cedar and the salt air coming off the water in front of the cabin. The flat expanse of water reflected the light blue sky of early morning. An eagle chattered high in the topmost dead branches of a nearby Douglas fir.

"Good morning to you, too," he said with a small smile.

The eagle's high-pitched piping cleared the last of the cobwebs from Langford's brain. He'd slept like the dead for the first time in years. In prison, he'd learned to sleep with one eye open. In prison, he'd learned a lot of things. His first year inside he'd spent in a SHU—single housing unit—in " D" unit in East Corridor. Not the worst, but housing reserved for really violent offenders. The egregiously brutal—the hard-case murderers and those with revolutionary tendencies—got locked down in "H" unit, otherwise known as "the hole." The solitude had nearly killed him. Twenty-two hours a day in a space only twice the size of a grave. But good behavior and a sympathetic warden had earned him a cell in "C" where he'd had more freedom—a communal mess hall, more recreation time, access to the prison library and the commissary.

He'd made a point of not risking a return to the SHUs, keeping his nose clean, working hard at the various prison jobs he'd held over the years. He'd found ways to manage prison life without succumbing to its degradations. But he knew solitary confinement would have slowly driven him insane. And then a few years earlier, just like that, the entire prison had been converted to a medium-security facility.

He stretched, grateful to the old man who'd taught him *tai chi* in the exercise yard every day. Distance learning, he'd called it, watching and emulating the man's movement from two enclosures away in silence, since talking was a punishable infraction. Demonstrating or practicing martial arts had been a "high severity prohibited act," but the old man had convinced the assistant warden that it was a form of meditation integral to his Buddhist religion. Langford had recognized it for what it was— slow-motion self-defense skills. Skills that had warded off the few attempts others had made to turn him into their bitch, teach him respect, or simply put him at the bottom of the prison pecking order. All he'd wanted was to be left alone, and it hadn't been long before most of the cons recognized he was no threat and steered clear. Later, with the Internet privileges he'd earned, he'd studied the *tae kwon do* forms he now practiced.

The lack of fences and bars, barbed wire and guards still seemed otherworldly to him. He wasn't used to the lack of a schedule, and he'd automatically been waking early, keeping prisoner's hours. He didn't mind. Mornings here on the outside were glorious, quiet and peaceful. Sunrises, which happened early this time of year, were the most gorgeous things he'd seen in twenty years. He'd spent his first few mornings at the cabin sitting on the shore, watching the sky lighten and turn pink, orange, and finally a brilliant turquoise as Earth inexorably spun on its axis toward the sun.

He put thoughts of prison out of his mind. No sense dwelling on the past. Besides, he needed his head clear to accomplish all he'd set out to. There was more work to do on the cabin, and he needed supplies. All that could wait, though. Breakfast first. After his workout, his stomach growled.

* * * * *

A second boom echoed in my ears as Wink's smile faded along with the dream. I frowned in my sleep and slowly drifted up to consciousness, the noise finally registering as someone pounded on my door.

"Keep your damn shirt on," I yelled. "I'm coming."

I yanked on a pair of blue jeans, ran my fingers through my hair, and trod barefoot across the cold wood floor to the door. A man in a suit appeared on the other side of the peephole. I didn't recognize him. Sensing my presence, he raised a badge in front of the peephole. The sight of it jump-started my heart, sending a surge of adrenaline coursing through my veins like a hit of cocaine.

"FBI," the badge said. "Open up, Mr. Sanders."

My palms grew damp and clammy. "What do you want?"

"Don't make us kick in the door, Mr. Sanders."

I could have told him to go away, but he'd probably come back. And if he made good on his threat, it would take an extra shift at the restaurant to pay for the damage to the door. The bright aqua numerals glowing on the microwave in the small kitchen dog-paddled into focus—11:22. At the rate my pulse thrummed in my ears, going back to sleep was out of the question. With a sigh, I swung the door open and padded into the kitchen to make a pot of coffee.

The first suit through the door stood in the middle of my small apartment, alert but relaxed, eyes following my movements. A close-cropped nap of tightly curled, steel-gray hair framed a face the color of my usual morning latte. A grill brush in matching gray covered his upper lip. He wore the suit with practiced authority, radiating a presence larger than his slight stature. A collar pin in the freshly- starched, snowy white shirt pushed the knot of a regimental tie into the room like a signal flag.

"Mr. Sanders, I'm Special Agent Drucker," he said. High cheekbones and crow's feet around his eyes suggested he'd known how to smile once. Maybe he'd forgotten.

Drucker, rhymes with "f__er." Too early to think in those terms, but mnemonics and forced concentration helped me remember names a little better at least some of the time.

"And what makes you special, Agent?" Chalk it up to nerves; I heard the words at the same time he did.

The small sigh and curled lip said he'd heard it before. "This is Special Agent Taylor." He waved a hand without taking his gaze off me.

A second man had followed the first inside, much younger and not as comfortable in a suit, though it hung well on a body that looked chiseled from a slab of granite. His bullet-shaped head sprouted without benefit of a neck directly from broad shoulders that rippled under the material as he moved. A shadowed area, like the stubble against his dark complexion, outlined male pattern baldness. *Mr. Clean, in those white pants, like sailors' pants; Taylor rhymes with "sailor."* He stepped to one side, sizing up the place as if casing it, and examined the books and magazines strewn on the coffee table. He hadn't given me more than a glance since he'd entered.

The coffeemaker burbled behind me. I took a step toward Drucker, arms outstretched, wrists pressed together. His expression went from curious to scornful.

"What, no warrant?" I said. "Guess you wouldn't have kicked in the door after all." I watched Taylor riffle through some papers on the small dining table that doubled as a desk. "Find anything interesting?"

His attention didn't even flicker.

Again my mouth moved before my brain had a chance to edit. "No one likes The Donald's comb-over, but I don't get how shaving your head hides the fact that you're bald."

Drucker tensed, one of his hands balling into a fist, but the corners of Taylor's mouth turned up, and he looked at me for the first time, face spreading into a grin.

"You must be out of it, man. Shaved heads have been 'in' ever since everybody wanted to 'be like Mike'—even Bruce Willis. Jordan made hairless as macho as hirsute, if not the epitome of cool."

He came over and stuck out his hand. "Bob Taylor. I saw you play once when I was a kid."

Why people still remembered the two seasons of ball I played at UW always managed to mystify me. I'd been good, not great. I'd used the fact—and the few resultant sports connections—as leverage, when necessary, for clients of the public affairs firm I once worked for. But I'd spent most of the intervening years trying to forget.

I met his firm grip, trying to swallow a mouthful of foot.

"You got sick or something, came down with some weird—"

"Osteomyelitis." The word sent a twinge through the muscles around my artificial hip. I clamped my jaw shut.

He nodded. "Yeah, that." He raised an eyebrow, but I didn't enlighten him further.

Drucker's face puckered as if he'd bitten a lemon. "Can we move on?"

Taylor shrugged and stepped back in deference to his partner. I got a sudden sense of who was who if they decided to play good-cop-bad-cop.

"Perry Langford," Drucker said to me. "Name ring a bell?"

They noted my surprise. A little voice told me I'd probably be smart not to let them know why. With the hundred other thoughts and questions rebounding off the inside of my skull like pinballs it wouldn't be tough.

"Sure," I said. "We were friends when we were kids." They knew that or they wouldn't be standing in my apartment.

"Have you seen him?"

I shook my head. "Not since he went to prison."

"Has he tried to contact you at all?"

"Why would he do that?"

"You just said you were friends."

"A long time ago," I said. "I haven't seen him or been in touch in twenty years. Why would he try to contact me?"

Drucker considered me. Instead of answering he asked another question. "Why *didn't* you ever visit, if you were friends?"

I shrugged, hoping the heat I felt creeping up from under my collar wasn't evident.

"I was in school out here, a couple of thousand miles away. Kind of hard to visit, if you know what I mean. I never went back. There didn't seem much point in writing."

"You knew that Langford was released from prison." It wasn't a question.

"No," I said. Not really a lie. A few hours earlier I hadn't known. "When?"

"Several weeks ago."

I looked from Drucker to Taylor. "What does this have to do with me?"

Drucker hesitated. "He's disappeared."

"Free country, right? He did his time."

Drucker frowned. "He was released early, on probation."

"I still don't see what this has to do with me."

"We have reason to believe he's in the area. We thought he might get in touch since you two were buddies once."

I shrugged again. "Sorry I can't help."

"But you'll let us know if he *does* contact you?"

"I suppose."

Drucker cocked his head half an inch.

Taylor shifted his weight and looked at Drucker uneasily. "We need to tell him."

I glanced from one to the other. "Tell me what?"

Drucker didn't acknowledge him, but something behind his eyes clicked into place. He loosed a soft grunt. "Langford might make an attempt on your life."

It wasn't just my palms sweating now. "Why?"

"Good question. What's he got against you after all these years?"

I could have sworn I saw a bright yellow feather sticking out of the corner of Drucker's mouth before he turned and walked out.

CHAPTER 6

It had started out as a joke. A stupid college prank. But pranks inevitably lead to trouble. I just came along for the ride, a bad idea unless you're willing to pay for the gas.

Wink had sketched out a simple plan: get in; take the stuff; get out.

Getting in was easy. The building always remained open. Before Columbine, before 9/11 and Virginia Tech, classroom buildings had no security cameras, no magnetic-stripe key cards. Everybody got along. Well enough, anyway, to be a little more trusting, a little less paranoid. The '60s—Vietnam War protests, riots in Watts, campus shootings, lynching of civil rights volunteers—were ancient history. At the time, the Iron Curtain was about to succumb to the onslaught of capitalism, if not democracy. And students in that narcissistic decade of the 1980s were far more interested in crass materialism than making social statements or scoring political points.

Finagling our way into a chemistry lab proved only moderately more difficult—keys were easy enough to come by if you knew the right grad students, according to Wink. Wink was an undergrad, a junior, starting his third year of engineering, but with a minor in chemistry. A security guard might question our presence, if we actually ran into one in a lab after midnight, but Wink could probably bluff our way out of trouble if it came to that.

The chemical supply locker had been the most difficult part of Wink's plan. Not even graduate students would relinquish a key unless they were supervising an experiment. Wink used one I cut for him in my father's hardware store, from a duplicate he'd fashioned out of a soda can. That made me implicit, an accessory. I didn't ask how he'd managed to get the impression of the original key. I still thought of myself as a passenger, not a co-pilot.

We got in; Wink got the stuff; we got out.

A hot breeze stirred the leaves in the campus woods, their rustling canceling out the loud percussion solo my heart thumped against my ribs. But the air did little to dry the sheen of sweat that coated my skin, plastering my shirt to my chest. The heavy blanket of late August heat and humidity pressed down as though tucked in too tight. Not even the breeze could throw it off.

"One more stop," Wink said.

I looked at him blankly.

"Come on, Legs." Wink said. "Let's go."

I hurried to catch up, falling in step as he hustled down the walk. Our shadows lengthened and melded with the darkness as we moved away from the building. We crossed the road toward another large classroom building. As we drew closer, white letters engraved in a stone marker announced the engineering building.

I slowed. "What do you need here?"

Wink stopped a few paces ahead and turned. "Tubing." When I didn't move, he said, "The stuff in the chem lab is all rubber. I need latex tubing. Surgical tubing."

"From engineering?"

Darkness hid his face, but I knew his perspicacity painted it with disdain, pity, amusement. I felt his withering gaze even if I couldn't see it. With Wink, amusement always won out. I think my obtuseness entertained him.

I shook my head. "You go."

"Scared?"

"Hey, I was right beside you back there."

He smiled. Watching him steal a few yards of latex tubing didn't frighten me. I wasn't even all that afraid of getting caught. I feared what my old man might say when I lost my scholarship if we did get caught. He couldn't actually say anything, of course, since he'd keeled over from a heart attack two years earlier, a few weeks after I'd been offered a near full-ride basketball scholarship to college. That didn't prevent the sound of his disappointment from reaching for me from the grave.

"I'll stay out here and keep watch," I said.

He shrugged. "Suit yourself."

Hooking a thumb under the strap on his backpack, he hitched it up higher on his shoulder and strutted down the walk to the entrance as if going to class at two in the morning was customary. The brightly lit doorway delineated his wiry figure for a moment before he disappeared inside. The glass and steel door closed softly behind him as if hermetically sealing him off from the rest of the world.

I melted into the shadows under the trees lining the path, the black velvet night caressing me. I felt drawn to the dark side even then. Not criminality, though the adrenaline rush caused by the danger Wink's foray put us in excited me. Rather, the quiet and peacefulness of the sleeping world and comforting cloak of darkness appealed to me. Nighttime's lack of sensory input stilled the thoughts that by day caromed around the inside of my head like billiard balls on a break shot.

The metronomic chirp of crickets, the sweet far-off call of a whippoorwill and the oppressive heat lulled me into a stupor. I sank onto my haunches and let gravity take me all the way down until I sat cross-legged on the grass, feathery blades cool under my fingers. Pain radiated from my left hip down my leg. I straightened it and stretched. The pain had gotten worse and more consistent recently. I shrugged it off. Stiff, no doubt, from a long run earlier.

Headlights in the distance flashed and winked out as a late-night reveler pulled into a dorm lot and parked. One of the black squares on the third floor of the building in front of me turned white, spilling light from within. I lifted the old watch close to my face. It was one of the few things handed down to me by my father that I'd had any interest in keeping. The luminescent green tips of the hands glowed dimly. Two-seventeen in the morning.

The lighted window went dark again. Nothing stirred. My shirt stuck to me damply. Even the breeze had died, another hint that most of the world blanketed by night had gone to sleep. Three more days before I headed to Seattle for my junior year at UW. Killing time until then, hanging out with Wink.

The lights in the entryway suddenly winked out, too. Two dark figures emerged a moment later, paused and darted away, disappearing into the night. I blinked, wondering if lack of sleep had me hallucinating. A third figure emerged dressed like the first two, in black from head to toe, despite the heat. A man, from his size and build. I shrank back farther into shadow, fingers and toes tingling, blood singing in my ears. Now a fourth man appeared and conferred with the one already outside the building, their low tones barely audible. The third man trotted up the path toward me, the opposite direction of the first two. I held my breath as he passed not more than ten yards away; he didn't pause.

I'd told Wink I'd keep watch—for campus security, not people coming *out* of the building. I froze. The last man strolled a few yards from the door and stopped. He turned and tipped his head back as if inspecting the upper floors. Taking a quick glance around, he raised his wrist toward his face, and suddenly raced back to the entrance, hugging the building.

Seconds later, an explosion on the top floor shattered the stillness, lighting the night with a blinding flash. It ripped a chunk of roof off the building and blew the wall apart, the blast spewing chunks of brick masonry, mortar and broken glass all the way out to the street. Little bits of building whizzed past like angry bees. The trees protected me from most of it, but a few stung me, drawing dots of blood, black against my skin. When the last of the debris rained down, the night fell deathly silent again, insects and nocturnal creatures temporarily hushed. For a moment, I heard nothing except the ringing in my ears.

Sudden screams let me know the detonation hadn't deafened me. Long, agonized shrieks of a human in mortal pain rose and faded to a moan. The black shadow detached itself from the side of the building and slipped back inside. Numbed by the explosion, I sat rooted to the spot.

Where was Wink?

The screaming began again, shrill and high-pitched. This time, a loud *pop-pop* ended it abruptly. Quiet reigned once more.

The figure in black emerged through the door moments later, running now. Stripping off the mask as he ran through the night, he gave me a brief glimpse of his profile, a streetlamp carving sharp features out of the surrounding ebony. And then he was gone.

Where the hell was Wink?

A siren wailed distantly. Unsteadily, I got to my feet and took a few tentative steps toward the building, willing the door to open. But it remained sealed. Another siren joined the first from across campus somewhere.

I turned and ran, forgetting the pain in my hip, the screams still echoing in my head.

Michael W. Sherer

CHAPTER 7

The long gravel drive meandered through a quiver of old - growth Douglas firs aimed at a cloudless cerulean sky, then dipped through a wash and climbed a gentle rise. Around a short bend, crackling tires went silent as the surface changed from gravel to concrete, the drive widening and spilling into a large clearing like the mouth of a river. A modern rambler spread out across the delta, living quarters to the left and a four-bay garage flowing off to the right. The tailgate of Charlie's pickup peeked from behind a far corner of the house, parked on the grass.

I pulled up in front of one of the garage bays next to a silver Prius. Stickers on the back bumper supported a state referendum (YES TO I-1000!), opposed Big Oil (NO ANWR DRILLING), and gave a nod to political affiliation (AL GORE/MOTHER EARTH '12). I parked and walked to the house. Rhododendrons laden with pink and magenta blossoms shielded the windows from prying eyes. Sunlight dappled the front porch through the branches of a flowering dogwood and danced across the door in ripples of light and shadow. The sensation of reaching for the knob almost felt like swimming underwater.

The door swung open before my hand touched it, revealing a handsome woman with a long plait of gray hair wound on top of her head and a broad smile on her round face. She wore a simple white peasant blouse with flowers embroidered on the lace yoke. A teal cotton crepe skirt hung below her knees. Dangling from a thin leather cord around her neck a small sterling peace symbol rested in the hollow of her throat.

"Blake!" She pulled me inside and wrapped her arms around my waist for a quick hug. "It's been such a long time. Good to see you."

Holding me at arm's length, her eyes roved from my feet to my face. "Are you getting enough to eat? Big boy like you."

I laughed. "Nice to see you, Mrs. Jones."

"Connie, please," she said firmly. "How many times have I told you? Goodness, I feel old enough as it is."

I nodded. "I eat just fine, thanks. How are you?"

"Good, good." Her head bobbed. "Come in. The boys are back in the kitchen."

She led the way, bare feet softly whisking the hardwood floor. The loose fabric of the skirt swayed from side to side with the roll of matronly hips. She followed my progress with a glance over her shoulder. "You haven't been out since we moved here, have you?"

"No. First time. It's a beautiful property."

"You'll have to take a tour. No trouble finding us?"

"Your directions were perfect. And I can't imagine a better day to take the ferry."

The house on the Kitsap Peninsula was about a twenty-minute drive from the Southworth ferry terminal, a forty-minute ride across Puget Sound from West Seattle. Signs of encroaching development in the rural area had cropped up—new, large houses and real estate signs offering land or subdivided five-acre plots—but forest dotted with small farms still dominated. Sparsely populated despite the growth, the area attracted horse farms and meth labs.

"How long have you lived here?" I said.

"Must be five or six years now."

"Then it *has* been too long since I've seen you."

"Not like the old days when Charlie brought you home from UW during the holidays."

No, not like those days—at least a decade had passed since I'd last seen Charlie's parents. But he and I hadn't socialized much in those years until recently.

Connie led me down a short hallway and started her tour in the garage, part of which had been converted into a woodworking shop. On the way back through the house, she showed me a small home office, and an expansive formal living room with large windows overlooking the back yard. Male voices drifted down the hall, the confluence of words a bright plume of heat fueled by passionate beliefs. Connie followed a narrow path through a large family room toward the kitchen. She worked her way around a large worn leather recliner, an oak end table covered with magazines and knick-knacks, and an overstuffed sofa, ignoring the two men. Keeping my head down, I stayed on her trail, registering Charlie's voice in passing.

"… so you're saying if Clay, or Sam, wanted to enlist and serve our country that makes me a bad parent?"

Connie faced me across the island in the kitchen and rolled her eyes. "They might be at it a while," she said. "Can I get you something to drink? Iced tea? Lemonade? A glass of wine?"

"Lemonade sounds good, thanks."

I turned and watched Charlie and Clayt in the next room, Charlie on the edge of a brown corduroy chair, leaning forward, earnest and tense. Clayt relaxed, one arm over the back of the beige velour sofa. One the spitting image of the other, but a mirror image, like matter and anti-matter. Charlie's hair, graying at the temples, cut short, Clayt's thin and hoary, pulled back into a short wispy ponytail. Charlie clean-shaven, Clayt sporting a goatee. The same patrician nose and prominent high cheekbones on both.

Mismatched furniture crowded a room filled with well-thumbed books and magazines, rumpled newspapers, opened mail and scraps of paper penned with notes, and pottery vases. A blocky Scandinavian entertainment center housed a bulky television and component stereo system. Old photographs and more books crammed the shelves, an eclectic range of titles reflecting varied interests and voracious curiosity. A glance at the spines nearest the kitchen—*The Oxford Book of Essays* next to copies of A.A. Milne's *When We Were Very Young, Shakespeare Complete Plays and Poems, Das Kapital, Silent Spring* and a worn Bible—showed a complete lack of any orderly sort of catalog system. Framed posters of '60s bands and original art covered the walls, a braided rug the floor. A lighted sand candle on the low coffee table separating Charlie and his father emitted a faint scent of strawberries. Their voices rumbled on as the argument continued, but the words didn't register.

Clayt finally glanced up and saw me standing just inside the room. "What do you think, Blake?"

I shook my head. "Uh-uh. I'm not getting in the middle of this."

"I can't believe we raised you," he said to Charlie, then called into the kitchen, "Can you believe he spent his formative years with us, Connie?"

"Let a kid express his opinions and call you by your first name, what did you expect?" I said, keeping my tone cheery.

Clayt's face darkened briefly, but he matched my smile with one of his own.

Charlie swiped a hand over his face and stood, looking like he had a bad case of heartburn. "I need a beer. Join me?" This last bit he directed at me.

Without waiting for an answer, he stepped through double doors leading to a patio off the back of the house.

I glanced from Clayt to Connie. Connie shooed me toward the door with a small smile. I went gratefully. As much as I'd hoped a holiday barbecue would provide a welcome respite from the insanity of the past week, I also wanted to corner Charlie and get his take on the visit I'd had from Drucker and Taylor and what I should do about Wink. I didn't like the idea of Wink being in the wind out there somewhere, not knowing what he was up to or what grudges he might hold. Charlie might have advice on the best ways to find out.

CHAPTER 8

Outside, Charlie stood stiffly next to a gas grill on the far side of the patio, fingers curled into his palms. Bending down, he fished in an ice-filled cooler, brought up two brown bottles dripping moisture, and tossed one at me. I managed a one-handed grab without spilling any lemonade. Charlie twisted the top off his and took a long pull, throat muscles rhythmically working the cold liquid down his gullet as he gazed out across the back yard. The terrace extended twenty feet out, ending in a low stone curb to keep people from tumbling down a small embankment. In the center, the pond of slate drained down a set of wide shallow steps into a broad lawn that climbed a gradual rise to the edge of the forest a long wedge shot away.

I looked for a way to ease into the conversation. "Where's Babs, and the boys?"

His answer was muffled by the breeze, but distinct enough. "Down in Portland. At her mom's."

"That's a surprise."

He faced me. "To you, maybe. Where's Molly?"

The sword cut both ways. "Up in Friday Harbor with her latest. A doctor. Jane set them up."

"You don't approve, I take it."

"She's an adult," I said. As much as I might have wished it, I no longer held any claim on Molly. "You changed the subject. Why is Babs in Portland, not here?"

He took a few steps and sat heavily in a patio chair, absently rubbing a thumb against the label on the bottle in his hand. I ducked under the umbrella unfurled over the table and sat opposite him, uncapped my beer and poured half into my lemonade. He wouldn't meet my gaze.

"I'm taking the sergeant's test," he said.

My eyebrows rose. "You've been a beat cop for fifteen years."

"That's right." He thrust out his lower jaw. "A damn good one. I did it for Babs and the kids. You work a beat, you go home, simple as that. After a while, you pick your hours. I worked it so I could spend a lot of time with the boys. Pick them up from school. Coach their ball teams. Help with homework." He fell silent.

"But ...?"

"They're growing up. They don't need me around as much."

"Bullshit. What are they, sixteen and fourteen? They need you more than ever."

"You know what I mean." He paused. "Okay, so I'm doing this for me. It's time. I deserve it. And the boys are old enough to understand that. Besides, I can still work out my schedule so I spend time with them."

"And Babs?"

He drew a long breath. "She's not happy about it. It means more responsibility. And more pay. I don't get why she can't see this is good for her, too."

I shrugged. "It means change. Besides, don't cops' wives worry about everything?" He didn't answer. "You guys are okay, right?"

He looked stricken for a moment, then seemed to shake it off. "Who knows?" He stared at something over my shoulder. "I *need* this. I didn't spend all that time in college just to work a beat. I swear I can feel my brain atrophying as we speak. Fifteen years, the same thing, day in, day out. Christ, I feel like I'm sleepwalking most of the time."

"There's more, isn't there?"

Like a tug on a marionette string, the question jerked his head around. His eyes narrowed.

"Babs wouldn't freak out over a promotion," I said. "I'm sure she's glad for the extra money."

He grunted. "I'm taking the detectives exam, too. Putting in a transfer. Homicide, if I can get it. More hours, and less predictable ones when you're on call."

"But less likelihood of getting yourself shot out there on the street. I'd think Babs would be thrilled."

One of his shoulders rose and fell. "Go figure. Seventeen years married to this woman, I still don't know what makes her tick." Before I manufactured a suitable response, he gave my shoulder a nudge. "Time to put you to work. There's a cooler in the back of the truck. Go get it while I fire up the grill."

"What're we having?"

"*I'm* having baby-back ribs. You're welcome to share, or you can have the tofu dogs Connie's got planned." He glared at me. "What? It's not like I don't eat right at home. You see any spare meat on these bones?" He did a decent runway turn. "Just once, I'd like a serious cholesterol fix. And what's a Memorial Day backyard barbecue without barbecue?"

I raised my hands in surrender and headed for his truck.

"Grab the oven mitts off the front seat," he called.

I waved and nodded, already lost in rambling thoughts. The mid-afternoon sun blazed hotly, hurting my eyes, colors so bright they shimmered surreally like animated cells flickering on a movie screen. The darkness of the world I normally inhabited leached the color from everything. In the light of day, the surroundings took on hundreds of shades of green—celadon, emerald, sage, evergreen ... *Kermit green.* Blossoms and flowering shrubs splashed the tableau with Kool-Aid hues of pink and purple, filling the air with fragrance. *God, I loved the scent of Molly's neck after she showered. How long had it been?* Somewhere in the treetops overhead, a bald eagle trilled and cackled, answered by the whistles of her chicks. *Bee, again. Busy, busy. Tofu dogs? Wonder what Molly's doing now? Why doesn't she dump that dog of a boyfriend?*

I reached over the side of the truck bed and hefted the cooler. *Ribs—pig for the Pig. Bright out here. Wish I'd brought shades. When had my future stopped being so bright I no longer had to wear them?* Ten steps past the hood of the truck I stopped dead. *Damn, forgot the mitts.* I set the cooler on the grass, backtracked, pulled open the driver's door and leaned in. *There they are.* I scooped them up with one hand and raised my head, Charlie visible through the open passenger door window, fiddling with the grill. Beyond him ...

45

"Gun!" I shouted, the word still reverberating in my head at the sight of it.

A figure all in black rounded the far corner of the garage— black fatigues, black boots, black ball cap, black bandana pulled tight across his face just below black-lensed sunglasses, black assault rifle. The color of *my* world.

The man's head jerked toward the sound of my voice, giving Charlie time to dive over the low embankment behind the grill. The barrel of the rifle swung toward me. I lowered my head and pulled my torso out of the truck as a short staccato *brat-at-at* from the rifle spit lead into the passenger door panel with metallic *thunks.* The sharp, deep boom of Charlie's handgun answered the burst from the man's AR-15. The man returned fire, and now the sound of another assault rifle joined in from a different direction. I raised my head just far enough to peek through the rear window of the cab. A second black-clad figure advanced slowly from around the other corner of the house, hugging the wall.

For an instant, a memory of other figures in black froze me with indecision. *This is different.* The crystalline bubble of memory burst and disappeared, replaced by something else. The suicide survivors support group therapist, Jeri, had warned me: the rage could swell like magma under a lava dome, the pressure increasing until it broke through and spewed, hot and destructive. It churned in my gut, harsh and acidic.

These two didn't belong here.

"Under the seat!" Charlie said over the din, a note of desperation in his voice. "A little help here, Blake!"

I ducked down and groped under the seat, fingers closing around the cold, hard butt of one of Charlie's back-up pistols. I freed it from its hiding place, slid it out of its holster, and took slow, deep breaths, willing my heart to stop trying to jump out of my chest. Poking my head up for another look, I racked the slide to chamber a round, mentally ran through the checklist Charlie had taught me. The second man hesitated, head swiveling. He hadn't seen me, didn't realize who Charlie was yelling at.

Hit ratio. My mind paused for a millisecond to consider the notion. I was spending too much time with Charlie at the range. *Miami cops, 15.4%; Baltimore, 49%.* My heart beat faster, and my peripheral vision turned dark as if a tunnel closed around me. *Take your time. Don't rush it; you might miss. Teach that bastard some manners.* Muffled shouts came from inside the house. The popping sound of gunfire outside receded as my focus retreated inward. Time and motion slowed. *Breathe. Dirgha pranayama.*

Guns belonged in children's games of cowboys and Indians, where no one died and the only blood spilled welled from skinned knees. *Camp Menominee. The shooting range.* My mind flashed on the pleasure of hunkering into a prone position, butt of a .22 rifle snugged up tight against my shoulder, blocking everything out of my head except the black concentric rings painting a sheet of paper twenty-five yards away, focusing on slow, even breathing, then holding it and squeezing the trigger. *Focus. See the target on his chest.* More memory clips whipped by—the weight of a target pistol in my hand, the solid pressure of recoil traveling up my arm each time it fired; the glow of satisfaction in peppering the rings of those targets in ever tighter clusters; and pride in taking home high marksman ribbons at the end of the summer. The grudging admiration I'd seen on Charlie's face occasionally at the range.

Don't think, move!

I stood and extended the semi-automatic over the roof of the truck cab in a two-handed grip, the hot sheet metal searing the tender flesh on the underside of my forearms. Sounds faded until the only thing I heard was my own *ujjayi* breath. *Cowboys and Indians.* Shifting slightly, I put the added metal of the roof pillar between me and the gunmen. Sensing the motion, the second man turned, eyes widening above the neckerchief that covered his features. *Now!* I sighted down the barrel and steadily squeezed off one shot, then another. *Breathe. In and out.* I squeezed in rapid succession, quickly losing count, watching each shot slam into the target, its energy rippling outward, twitching the man's torso until he went down.

Dim shouting slowly registered on my consciousness again. The tunnel constraining my vision widened and grew lighter. Three sharp whistle blasts pierced the air.

A voice shouted from the other side of the house. "They're not here!"

"Fall back!" another one said. "Pull out!"

"Shit!" A third voice, closer. "Shit! I'm fucking shot!"

Charlie! The top of his head was visible over the edge of the patio, rocking back and forth. Beyond, the other gunman was gone. The roar of an engine and squeal of tires on pavement floated over the roof of the house, and quickly faded away in the distance. Through the sudden silence I heard my ears ring from the repeated concussions of gunshots.

I crossed the grass at a run, cut the corner of the patio and leaped down the embankment, landing at his side. He sat with one leg folded under him, the other splayed out, both hands clasped tightly against a spot high on his chest just below the collarbone.

"Charlie?"

His head tilted up, eyes slowly traversing the ground between us until they met mine.

"Bastard fucking shot me," he said, eyes wide, his breathing raggedy. "It fucking hurts!"

Under his hands, a spreading claret stain muddied a yellow parrot on his shirt. I pried his fingers away. With each irregular breath, bubbles frothed around the edges of a dark hole centered in the stain.

My heart skipped a beat. "Jesus, Charlie! That doesn't look good."

"Nicked the lung, I guess," he said, "but missed the heart."

"What, you're a doctor now?" I pulled my shirt over my head, folded it, and quickly placed it on the wound, pressing his hands on top of it.

He winced. "That's why it's bubbling, Sherlock," his wry voice raspy now as blood seeped into his lung. "And why I'm still breathing."

"Shut up and keep pressure on it."

I frowned, bent over him and looked at the back of his shirt. No exit wound. I didn't know if that was good or bad.

"Okay, okay," he said. "Now, would you call it in? Before I die would be nice."

Michael W. Sherer

CHAPTER 9

Langford checked his mirrors for traffic. Seeing no one on the road behind him, he slowed as he drove past the entrance to the property looking for signs of life. He'd cased the property several times before, and this was his second pass of the day. He knew he'd have to go in on foot to get a real sense of the activity within. At the end of the road on the left, just before the T intersection, stood a pasture in which a couple of horses grazed. A rutted track led to a gate in the fence at the corner of the pasture. He turned in and parked. Anyone passing by would likely think his old truck belonged there. His frayed jeans, muddy work boots and oil-stained Cargill ball cap with a creased brim added to the effect.

He shut off the engine and patted the dash. The International Harvester Scout had been up on blocks in the shed by the cabin when he'd first arrived, and though it hadn't been driven for twenty-five years it was practically brand new. After filling it with oil, inflating the tires and installing a new battery, it'd started up on the first try.

He got out and locked up. Skirting the corner of the pasture, he walked along the fence line until he was well away from the road. A chestnut mare lifted its head, ears perking and turning toward the sound, eyes following his movements. It broke into a trot toward the fence and nickered softly. Langford smiled and pulled an apple from the pocket of his nylon windbreaker. He'd come prepared this time. Holding the apple out on the flat of his palm, he let the mare wrap its lips around it and pull it away. He raised his hand and stroked the patch of white on the mare's forehead as it crunched the fruit between large molars, then he turned and disappeared into the woods.

Quickly making his way back up the hill toward the property, he moved among the trees, avoiding the road, taking pains to move as quietly as possible. On his first exploration of the woods around the property he'd almost run into one of the video cameras guarding the drive. Working his way carefully around the perimeter of the grounds that fronted the road, he'd spotted the infrared sensors and remaining cameras. But he didn't know if the property owners had wired the surveillance equipment for sound, too, so he took no chances. On subsequent trips he'd covered almost every inch of the property, using the county parcel viewer as a guide. The extra work had been worth it. He'd made a discovery that he bet few people, if any, knew besides the owners.

Stealthily, he worked his way from tree to tree toward the house set back from the road. When he drew close enough, he saw an unfamiliar car parked next to the Prius in front of the garage. And someone had parked a pick-up truck on the grass beyond the corner of the house. *Visitors.* He wasn't surprised. It was a holiday, he reminded himself, something they didn't pay much attention to in stir. One day was pretty much the same as another there. Langford nodded to himself and quietly stole back the way he'd come. *Patience.* When he learned their routine better, he'd do what he'd come for, not before.

When he reached the pasture, the other horse had joined the mare at the fence line and stood with its muzzle over the top strand of wire. It nickered expectantly. Langford pulled another apple from his pocket, offered it up and remained where he stood for a moment, watching the horse quickly masticate the crisp, juicy treat, pink froth bubbling from one corner of its mouth. *Simple pleasures.* The horse stretched its neck and nuzzled him, looking for another sweet. Langford smiled and patted his cheek and rubbed his muzzle. With no snacks forthcoming, the horse quickly lost interest and swung its head back over the fence and down to the ground to nibble some grass. Langford wiped his hand on his jeans and strode back to the truck.

The interior was already hot from being closed up in the sun. He stripped off his windbreaker, opened both doors and rolled the windows down, letting some air in before he settled into the driver's seat. He backed out onto the road and slowly cruised up the rise toward the property for one more pass. As he drew even with the drive he heard a series of rapid explosions. *Fireworks.* A *rat-tat-tat* was answered with a *boom*, and another *boom. Gunfire!* Someone didn't care whether there were visitors or not. But maybe the unexpected presence of visitors had bought the occupants some time. Somebody was putting up a fight.

Fury filled him like molten metal poured from a crucible. *Damn it! Twenty years of searching and planning, and someone else was about to fuck it all up and take it away. But not if he could help it. He knew something they probably didn't.*

He pressed his foot to the accelerator, putting as much distance as he could between the Scout and the property entrance before the shooters barreled out of there. A quarter mile up the road he took a right at the intersection, away from Port Orchard, where responders from the sheriff's office would most likely come. Checking his mirrors, he watched his speed, careful now to appear normal, like nothing had happened. He tamped down the anger burning inside and slowed his heart rate with deep, even breaths.

Movement up ahead caught his attention. Off to his right, a small SUV was hurtling down a dirt track toward the road in front of him, a small cloud of dust billowing up behind it. Langford kept his eye on it, aware that at his present speed, it'd come close to ramming him if it didn't slow when it reached the road. He let up on the accelerator just a hair, and bore down. The SUV didn't appear to slow at all as it approached, but at the last minute, the driver slammed on the brakes, fishtailed, then yanked the wheel and accelerated onto the road just yards in front of Langford.

He barely caught a glimpse of the two people in the vehicle, driver bearded and grim, a female passenger clutching the dash, white-faced with fear. It was enough. He pressed the gas pedal to stay behind the fleeing vehicle, his mind hard at work formulating a new plan.

Michael W. Sherer

CHAPTER 10

The blades of a medevac chopper whirled gently then slowly gathered speed as the whine of twin turbines built to a deafening roar. The downdraft flattened the grass into a crop circle pattern. Inside, Charlie raised an arm off the stretcher and waved weakly as they shut the wide door. The fuselage lurched and rose gently, pulling the wheels off the ground, and the fantail rotor swung in a wide arc until the copter's nose pointed east. The chopper rose swiftly, nose dipping as it cleared the treetops, and zoomed out of sight, a giant dragonfly in search of prey.

A Kitsap County sheriff's deputy waved me over to the patio table, face alternately tinged blue and red, even in the bright sunlight. Strobes flashed atop the emergency vehicles circled haphazardly on the grass around the yard. I counted five—two county cruisers, a Port Orchard cop car, a South Kitsap Fire & Rescue van and an aid unit. Several more sat in the drive in front.

A small platoon ranged the property, an overpowering 9-1-1 response to the magical words, "shots fired, officer down." Patrol deputies festooned the stakes they'd pounded in the ground with crime scene tape, delineating a perimeter around the truck and patio. One of the county's two crime scene deputies directed placement of numbered markers next to the shell casings and snapped photos. Strewn across a wide swath of slate and grass, the little bits of brass winked in the sunlight, lending the macabre circumstances a festive air.

A paramedic knelt on the ground by the man next to the house, zipped a black body bag closed around him. The coroner hadn't arrived yet, but he wouldn't dispute the cause of death. Nine rounds were missing from Charlie's back-up piece. Four flattened slugs had embedded themselves in the Kevlar vest under the man's black fatigues. One round had hit him in the pelvis, another in the shoulder; two missed him entirely. The head shots, probably. At the range, they taught to shoot at center mass first, then in a pattern—two at center mass, a head shot, two to center mass, one to the pelvic girdle, then back to center mass, etc., until the target goes down. The training paid off—one of the few things I'd found I was really good at since giving up basketball. One of the nine—the last?—had slammed into his rib cage under his left arm where the armor provided no protection. A lucky shot when he raised his weapon to fire.

Two more medics chatted nonchalantly at the back of the EMT bus, one sitting inside the open doors, the other standing outside, a foot on the bumper, hand resting on his knee. I caught a bit of it as I passed by.

"Looks like a fucking war zone. Those are five-fifty-six by forty-five casings. Assault weapons."

"Guy was lucky the bullet didn't fragment."

Both Charlie and I had been lucky. I assumed Clayt and Connie had been, too. They were simply gone, whether before or during the firefight was anyone's guess.

As I approached, the deputy waved at an empty chair, as cavalier as the medics.

"Have a seat."

I surveyed the faces around the table. "Didn't know I'd be playing to a packed house."

"We take it very seriously when a member of law enforcement gets shot," he replied.

"I don't? Bastards ruined a perfectly good picnic. Pissed me off." I heard the rising pitch of my voice, and took a deep breath. "I defended myself and Officer Jones to the best of my ability. Now I've got a death on *my* conscience, detective. You kill anyone yet today?" My hands trembled. I slid them off the table into my lap before anyone noticed.

"Simmer down," an older cop said, his voice friendly. "We can imagine what you've been through. It can't have been easy."

"Then what's all this?" I drew a circle in the air with a finger.

"Like Deputy Roberts said, we're taking this seriously," the older cop said. "We want to find these guys, whoever they are. The more departments we have looking, the faster we get results. What you've got here," he circled his finger around the table, imitating me, "is the core investigative team. Lead detective Roberts and his partner Hartson both report to me, Lieutenant White. Officer Boyer there, with Port Orchard police, will help us locally. And Detective Lewandowski is our liaison with Seattle on this, since your friend Jones is an officer with SPD."

My gaze lingered on Lewandowski. "You got here fast."

"Badged my way to the front of the ferry line," he said. "Lights and sirens from Bremerton." He gritted his teeth. "He's one of *ours*. Chief, assistant chief, maybe a dozen guys or more have been waiting for him at Harborview since we got the call. You gettin' the drift yet?"

I regarded the faces again. Clenched jaws, furrowed brows and flushed skin mirrored my own. I nodded.

Roberts took control again. "Take us through it one more time."

I recounted what I remembered. No, I didn't know who the men were or where they'd come from. I had no idea how many there'd been, but in addition to the two I'd seen, I'd heard at least two more voices. No, I didn't know what they wanted or why they opened fire, but they seemed to have been looking for someone. When they hadn't found whoever it was they wanted, they left. No, I didn't see their vehicle or get a license plate number. I'd been too busy shooting at a man who'd seemed intent on killing me.

"Attempted kidnapping?" Hartson said to his partner.

Roberts turned to me. "What, exactly, did these people say?"

"The two out back here? Nothing. I heard shouting from inside the house. Didn't understand most of it. Someone said, 'They're not here.'"

Roberts squinted. "'They're not here?' You're sure? Not, 'They're gone?'"

My fingers curled into my palm. "I'm sure. Right after that someone else yelled an order to fall back. The guy who came from over there—" I pointed toward the far corner of the garage. "—he fired a couple more rounds and split. A few moments later I heard a vehicle take off."

"Could be someone has a vendetta against Jones," Lewandowski said. "He's got a wife and two kids. Someone may have come looking for them."

I leaned forward, the sudden movement causing a couple of them to recoil. "Charlie's parents are gone! That doesn't seem like 'attempted' anything. Seems like the real thing to me."

Before I'd pulled out my cell phone to dial 9-1-1, Charlie's second thought had been Clayt and Connie. Charlie was bleeding out, but he'd made me run into the house to check on his parents before calling for help. I'd searched, yelling their names, yanking open doors and upending furniture, but after wasted minutes scouring every inch of the house and garage, I came to the same conclusion that still echoed in my ears—*they're not here.*

"They didn't just vanish," I said. "How would anyone know Charlie was going to be here? And why would they think his wife and kids would be here, too? If they followed Charlie, then they'd know Babs and the boys weren't with him. It doesn't make any sense."

The cops exchanged glances. No one ventured a guess. Or maybe none of them considered my questions worth answering. Hartson looked at me and rolled his eyes, but Lewandowski frowned, eyebrows knitting as if he doubted his own suggestion.

"Who was he anyway?" I jerked my head in the direction of the body.

"We don't know yet," Roberts said quietly. "No ID."

A patrol deputy hurried across the patio from the house. "Lieutenant, Detectives, we found something. You need to come see this."

The three county cops rose and headed for the house. Lewandowski and the uniform from Port Orchard followed. I didn't wait for an invitation, and no one told me to stay put. I brought up the rear as they trooped into the house. The young deputy led us to a small security panel on a wall in the kitchen.

"There're a few more of these panels in the house—one by the front door, one by the door to the garage, another in the master bedroom," he said. He pointed to a small screen on the panel. "We found cameras around the property, tripped by motion detectors. There's one out by the road. Like an early-warning system when visitors show up."

Wordlessly, he turned and led the way down a hallway. We fell into single file to avoid more deputies and another crime scene detective, moving from room to room dusting for prints and collecting evidence. The group fanned out inside the master bedroom and clustered around a small linen closet next to the bathroom door. I stood up on the balls of my feet behind them to get a good look over their shoulders at a gaping black hole in the bottom of the closet. Propped against a wall inside the closet, a section of flooring held back a flap of carpeting.

"What the hell?" someone said.

"It's a tunnel," the deputy said. "Tedesco's down there now checking it out."

"How long's he been gone?" Roberts said.

The deputy glanced at his watch. "Close to ten minutes."

"How'd you find it?" Roberts asked.

"A corner of the carpet was loose, sir. Looks like it's designed to flop back in place when the trap door's closed, but it wasn't quite flush."

"Good eye, deputy," Lieutenant White said.

Silence fell over the assemblage as if the men had been called to prayer. The seconds ticked by glacially. Minutes later the hole lightened almost imperceptibly, slowly turning from black to brown. The yellow beam from a flashlight flickered on the dirt walls below. A moment later a man's head popped into view. He blinked a few times, breathing heavily as he gazed up at the faces sardined into the space. An arm reached for him and helped him out, and the cops made room. I backed up quickly, toes barely avoiding the tread of a steel-toed black brogue.

"What've you got?" White said as Tedesco stepped into the circled space they'd cleared for him.

"Tunnel leads south, sir." Tedesco brushed dirt from his uniform. "About three hundred yards. Comes up in a shed big enough for a large vehicle. Dirt track leads south into the woods from there then turns east. I'm guessing it probably dumps out on Banner Road."

The men glanced at each other, as if waiting for a cue. White looked pointedly at Roberts.

Roberts didn't hesitate. "Check in with crime scene," he told Tedesco. "See if they can spare someone. Burke, maybe. Then go around and see if you can come in at the shed from the east, and tape off the scene. We may be able to get tire track impressions or something else that can help tell us what happened. Could be the Jones couple managed to get out this way."

"It's like they were expecting it," Lewandowski muttered. "What the hell were these people into?"

I wondered the same thing.

CHAPTER 11

After another hour of questioning, they let me go without charging me. They kept Charlie's back-up gun, of course, and admonished me not to stray too far from home.

My paper route took more than an hour longer than usual that night. I couldn't get the shooting out of my head and ended up missing several stops. I retraced large portions of the route to make sure the right people got the right papers, the scene playing like an endless film loop in my imagination. Several times, involuntary tremors quaked so badly I had to wrench the wheel and pull over until they subsided, leaving me drained and short of breath.

Not even the magnificent sunrise that bloomed on the horizon like a peach blossom opening against a pale blue sky seemed to hold much promise. I knew I wouldn't even be able to get close to Charlie's room for all the cops, so I drove home and fell asleep in my clothes.

* * * * *

Craig Downing was just leaving when I went to see Charlie later that morning. He stopped me in the hall with a somber wave.

"Hey, how's he doing?" I said.

Downing shoved his hands in his pockets. "Good. You know, under the circumstances. He got lucky, man. Docs pulled a bullet out of his scapula. The word is that forensics says the shooter made a mistake. Round was a mil-spec M-one-nine-three, but an FMJ."

I held up a hand. "English, Craig."

His face pinked. "Sorry. It was a full metal jacket bullet, so it stayed intact. Did much less damage than if it had been a round like the hollow point boat tail SWAT uses. That bullet fragments in a zillion pieces. Would have killed him for sure."

"They looked like pros to me. How could they screw up that bad? Not that I wish they hadn't."

He shrugged. "Guys use FMJs for target practice. Maybe the shooter just mixed up his magazines. Grabbed the wrong one. Like I said, lucky."

I nodded.

He shifted awkwardly in the silence. "Thanks, by the way. You know, for being there. Most folks would have ducked and covered. I heard you took one of them down."

"Sure."

"Well, I'll see you around, then."

"Yeah, see you."

I watched him walk down to the elevators, then I entered Charlie's room, knocking on the door as I went. Charlie's chalky face barely stood out against the white hospital pillow, his expression vacant, eyes dull and slow to pick up on movement. A corner of his mouth turned up in recognition—not a smile exactly, but an indication he was lucid.

"You look like shit," I said.

He licked his lips. "Feel like it," he said in a scratchy voice. "Told you I'd live."

"If you call this living." I looked around. "I can't tell if this looks more like a florist shop or a mortuary."

He managed a full-fledged grin this time. It didn't last. "You did good."

I hesitated. He stared at me, brows knitting in concentration. His eyes went out of focus and despite his effort to hold it steady his head bobbed from the drugs dripping into his IV tube. When I finally nodded his eyes shuttered and he relaxed, head lolling back on the pillow.

"What happened out there, Charlie?" I wasn't sure he heard me.

He struggled to raise his eyelids. "Been trying to figure it out." He winced, and pressed a hand against his side. "Hurts to breathe."

I squeezed his forearm. "Don't talk."

Gratitude washed though his eyes. We'd have to play Twenty Questions.

"Any idea who those men were?"

He shook his head.

"You never saw them before?"

His mouth was a grim line, lips white at the corners.

"Did they tell you about the tunnel?"

He nodded.

"Did you know about it?"

A headshake.

I sighed. "I don't imagine there's any possibility Clayt and Connie decided to augment their retirement account? Open a meth lab? Grow sinsemilla out in the woods?"

The headshake was vehement this time.

"Fine. I'll take your word for it." I stared at him. He blinked first. "They expected trouble, Charlie. People who expect trouble are usually the ones stirring the pot."

That elicited a grunt—acknowledgement, I guessed.

"You knew about the security system?"

"Helped them put it in."

"Seems like overkill to me."

"They're city people. Out in the country. They worried a lot."

"Or they expected it, like I said." I paused. "You have no clue?"

"No," he said. "Couple of middle-aged hippies. Harmless."

"And no idea where they might have gone? Who was after them? Nothing?"

"They're my parents." He winced and raised a hand in helplessness, the effort draining him. He didn't have to say more.

"Where's Babs?" My head swiveled reflexively as if she might have snuck in without me noticing.

Charlie grimaced at the mention of her name. He squeezed his eyes shut, a tear leaking from one corner. His face reflected pain greater than any he'd shown so far.

"She's not here? This is serious."

He opened his eyes and peered at me. "You think?"

I rubbed my shoulder as if kneading out the sting. "Sorry. Man, that's cold."

"She's scared. I don't blame her."

His head turned at the sound of the door opening. A willowy brunette walked through, pushed by a sense of purpose, her ponytail a standard streaming behind her.

"Damn doctors are worse than auto mechanics," she said.

"Sarah." I stared, but remembered to close my mouth.

The scowl on her face softened when her gaze swung toward my voice. Age had carved more angularity into her features, harder planes and angles. The maturity added subtlety to her attractiveness, the difference between a head-stopping Ferrari and a more carefully appraised Continental GT.

"Blake," she said softly. "It's been so long."

She moved in to embrace me and rose on tiptoes to kiss my cheek. The heather cashmere turtleneck under my fingertips felt soft, the body beneath it firm, athletic.

"Hey! Hey!" Charlie piped up from the bed.

Sarah pulled away with a smile.

"What are you doing here?" I said.

"Where else would I be?" She looked up at me expectantly. "Tim and the kids can do without me for a day or two."

"You're staying at Charlie's?"

Her smile broadened. "Don't even think of offering, Blake. I know your place is a lot closer than the house in Renton. College was a long time ago; crashing at your bachelor pad just doesn't sound as much fun anymore. Besides, I'll be here at the hospital most of the time. Until his doctors say he's out of the woods, I'm okay in that chair."

She nodded toward an easy chair in the corner that pulled out into a flat futon. It might have accommodated about two-thirds of my frame.

"Bachelor pad?" I said weakly. "Monk's cell, you mean. And how do you know it wouldn't be fun? My landlords upstairs are a hoot. You'd love them."

"I'm sure I would." She smiled. "Some other time, maybe."

"Good girl," Charlie said thickly. He tried to wet his lips.

Sarah quickly stepped to the side of his bed and handed him the cup of ice water sitting just out of his reach. She smoothed the hair back from his forehead while he sipped through a straw.

"Always my protector, right, big brother?" The words sounded strained, despite the upturned mouth.

Charlie rolled his eyes up to look at her face above his and smiled wanly, unspoken history passing between them. I knew some of it—ancient. Didn't want to know more.

She turned and sat on the edge of his bed. "How've you been?"

I hesitated, not sure how to answer. "Not bad."

Her neck and cheeks turned crimson. She let out a nervous laugh and waved, as if to dissipate an offensive odor.

"Sorry. Dumb question."

"No, it's fine." I leaned against the windowsill, braced myself with my arms. "Other than getting shot at? I've been good, actually. You?"

An infectious laugh erupted from her throat at my earnest attempt to sound normal. Tenseness in her shoulders melted, the twenty-year-old college girl appearing under the well-turned suburban soccer-mom façade. The chitchat flowed freely after that, light-hearted banter catching us up on each other's lives. Superficial enough to avoid touching off potential landmines. Cheery enough to keep Charlie grinning.

When the grin disappeared and his head lolled on the pillow, I made excuses and told him to get some rest.

"I'll walk you out," Sarah said. "I need some coffee. Need anything, Charlie?"

Charlie shook his head slowly. "Just need to get out of here."

I patted his good shoulder. "Do what they tell you. You'll get better faster."

He clapped a hand on top of mine and struggled to lift his gaze. He opened his mouth, but nothing came out. Questioning eyes searched my face.

"It's okay," I told him. "It'll all be okay."

He nodded gratefully and closed his eyes.

In the hallway outside, Sarah took my arm as we walked to the elevator. "Buy you a cup of coffee?" There was nothing coy in her expression.

"Sounds like a fine idea." I needed to ask her the same questions, but not in front of Charlie.

CHAPTER 12

We sat on hard plastic seats of uncomfortable steel-framed chairs in a deserted corner of the hospital cafeteria. I offered to splurge on better coffee somewhere else, but Sarah didn't want to stray too far in case Charlie needed her. So we settled for the remains of an air pot that tasted as if they'd been brewed hours before and took our paper cups to a small table covered in plastic laminate made to look like maple veneer.

Sarah toyed with the stir stick in her cup before raising her chin. Tiny pearls of dew seeded her lashes. Turning her head, she blinked them away. Looked at me again with a tentative smile and a sniffle.

"That was just so close, you know?"

I reached across the table and gave her hand a gentle squeeze. "Take a lot to get rid of Charlie."

The corners of her mouth moved higher. "It would, wouldn't it?" She grew somber. "Thank you. For being there. I mean being there for Charlie. Not for having to go through that. It must have been ... you know ..."

I nodded.

"Are you really okay?"

"Hard to say." I shrugged. "I think so. Doesn't feel like I had much of a choice."

She sucked in her lower lip. "It's all so bizarre, so unreal. What are we going to do?" Baleful eyes glinted with tears again.

My lips pursed. "What do you know about your parents, Sarah?"

She straightened, blinked. "What do you mean?"

"I mean how well do you know them? You call them by their first names. What about their friends? Where'd they grow up? What were their parents like?"

"What's that got to do with anything?"

"Those weren't duck hunters, damn it. If you and Charlie don't know what those men were after, then you're going to have to dig deeper to figure out what your folks did to piss them off."

She worried the plastic straw some more.

"Were your folks dopers in college? They still smoke a little weed every so often?"

Her eyes flashed. "They went to school in the '60s. Didn't everyone smoke pot back then? What's your point?"

"They could be running drugs. Help a little with their retirement."

Her ponytail whipped side to side, the same expression, same vigorous denial her brother had displayed.

"What makes you so sure?"

She froze, listened to some inaudible voice. "I'm not totally naïve. I used to hear them giggling sometimes late at night. And Connie's vanilla sand candles never quite masked the smell of something else, like incense at church."

"Church? Your folks don't strike me as holy rollers."

"God forbid. Secularists to the bone. Agnostic, I guess they'd say. No, church was my idea. A phase I went through in middle school. Weekly masses at Christ the King. Just to see why kids I knew couldn't eat meat on Fridays. I liked the rituals. Found them comforting at the time."

The hair streaming down her back switched again, brushing unseen flies away. She chewed on her nail, inspected it. Absently twirled the straw again.

"What about some developer?" she said. "The organization Mom works with is always making someone mad. If not developers, enviro-friendly types who say they aren't doing enough to save habitat? Or politicians who don't want to pay to keep the environment clean?"

"Developers who carry assault rifles?"

She bent the straw in half, fingers curling into a fist around it. "I don't know! I just ... It doesn't make sense. They're not violent. They're not criminals. They're ..." Her mouth worked. Nothing came out. She closed it.

"So, let's try this," I said gently. "Tell me everything you can think of about them. Maybe it'll shake something loose. Give you an idea of what sort of trouble they're in. Let's start with where they're from."

"Canada, some place."

"Some place?"

She looked away. Turned rosy under the light coating of make-up. "They didn't talk about it much."

"Grandparents?"

"Never met them. Clayt's are deceased. Died when he was younger. His mom a cancer victim when he was in his teens. His dad a few years later from a heart attack. Broken heart, he says. Connie says she didn't get along with her parents. Left home as soon as she was old enough and never spoke to them again. Doesn't know if they're alive or dead."

"Sad. Normal childhood?"

She rolled her eyes and made a show of looking around her chair. "Where's the couch?"

I smiled. "Joke all you want. Doesn't sound too normal so far."

"There's no 'dis' in your functional family? Give me a break."

"I didn't mean anything by it. Come on, Sarah. Help me out here. You want to find your parents, you gotta give me something to work with."

"You knew them." Her stare was churlish.

"A few holiday dinners. Get-togethers when everyone tries to put a good face forward. I didn't live with them."

She sighed. "Great childhood. Fun. Crazy. Spontaneous. Informative. Clayt and Connie—well, you know them—they were probably pretty lousy parents. We didn't have a lot of rules growing up. But they were incredible teachers, good mentors, the best friends you could hope to have. I just wish ..."

"What?"

"Nothing."

She stared into her cup for a moment. Chuckled at some recollection.

I interrupted her reverie. "I still can't believe you don't know where they're from. When did they move here?"

"Right before I was born."

"Charlie would have been about three?"

A nod and a smile.

"So Charlie was Canadian? When did he become a U.S. citizen? Eighteen?"

The smile turned upside down. "As far as I know Charlie's always been a U.S. citizen."

"Then he was born here, too."

"I think so. Clayt and Connie fell in love when they were students. The story I remember is that Mom was here in the States on a student visa when she had Charlie."

"That must have been a relief. Can you imagine him having to take a citizenship test before joining the service?"

"He wouldn't have taken it well." The smile reappeared.

"You think this might have something to do with Connie's job? Has she ever been threatened before?"

"No, not that I remember."

"And she's been there how long?"

"A long time. Twelve, fifteen years."

"Never had a problem? Any trouble like this?"

Slow headshake.

"And before that?"

"A bunch of different jobs."

I waited her out.

She laced her fingers around her cup, studied it for a moment. "When I was little she went back to school. Dropped me off at daycare—pre-school later—and took classes half the day. Worked part time as a waitress. Clayt was a teacher, so he was home early enough to keep an eye on Charlie and me while he graded papers, worked on lesson plans. As soon as she could, Mom got a job as a paralegal. Worked for several lawyers who shared space. Earned enough money to take night classes and get her law degree."

"Then what?"

"Same thing. Worked for more small firms."

"Nothing that stands out? No cases that might have made her an enemy or two?"

Her head wagged. "I don't remember her being all that enthusiastic about legal work until she took the job with the environmental group. Her dream job. It's what she always talked about, what she always wanted. She never talked about the cases she worked on before that. It was just about a decent paycheck." She raised her eyes. "She and Clayt worked hard to provide for us. Made sacrifices. They're good people."

I weighed that. "Has she said anything recently that makes you think someone's got a grudge? Against her or the organization?"

She shifted in her chair. "Well, no. But I'm not around anymore, Blake. We don't talk all that much. I'm busy with the kids, and she and Clayt have their life. You know, retirement and all. Well, Clayt anyway. I don't know when Mom's going to retire."

"And Clayt?"

"Enemies? I doubt it. He's opinionated; you know that. Probably rubs some people the wrong way. A lot of people, maybe. But he's a teddy bear."

"No causes that went sour? I thought I remembered him being as vocal about environmental causes as your mom."

"Well, yeah. But not like he forced his viewpoint on anyone. He's passionate about things he believes in. Enough that he volunteers for stuff. Writes letters to legislators in Olympia and the other Washington. Joins a protest or walks a picket line now and then, and marches around carrying a sign."

"Charlie told me he came close to arresting Clayt at the 'Battle of Seattle.'"

"The WTO protests? Sure, he was there. In the wrong place at the wrong time, that's all. He didn't break the law or get violent. He just got caught up in the crowd."

"Anything else he got caught up in that might've put someone's nose out of joint? Teachers union? One of the environmental groups Connie's organization worked with?"

She pressed her lips together tightly and swung the ponytail again.

"Nothing? You've got to admit, Sarah, your parents are a little out there compared to most of middle America. Maybe not radicals, but pretty left-wing."

She leaned forward. "But they didn't push it on anyone. Not even Charlie and me. Sure, they believe in environmental causes. They recycled long before Seattle put a program in place. And they wrote a lot of letters to encourage city council to start one. But they didn't wag their fingers in your face and make you feel guilty if you threw out a soup can by mistake. They both became vegetarians to show solidarity with the animal rights folks. But also because their cholesterol was so high their doctors told them to give up red meat. And they're not strict about it. They let us eat whatever we felt like growing up—burgers and fries if we wanted—and they both still eat seafood, cheese, even eggs now and then. They aren't tree-huggers."

"Not militants, you mean."

"Well, yeah. No, I mean." She heaved a sigh. "I don't know what I mean. I just can't imagine them mixed up in anything like this. Bad enough Charlie got shot. You get kind of resigned to the possibility with a cop in the family. But people with guns coming after Clayt and Connie? I just don't get it."

"Then we're right back where we started."

Worry creased her forehead. "Drugs?"

"It's the only explanation that makes sense."

She looked for another one at the bottom of her empty cup.

"What if those men had the wrong place? What if they were looking for someone else?" Her brown eyes pleaded.

"Then why did your parents run? I'm sorry, Sarah, the shooters came for them. They pulled back as soon as they realized your folks had bolted. I heard them. They said, 'They're not here.'"

Her shoulders sagged. She slumped in her seat. "Now what?"

I leaned back and crossed my ankles, stroked my chin. "I can ask questions, look around some, but the cops are all over this, Sarah. This is one of their own we're talking about. SPD will ride herd on the sheriff's office over on the peninsula. They'll turn over every rock they can find. See what crawls out. Not much else we can do except wait. Be patient."

"They're not your parents." She pushed away from the table and stood, hands pressed so hard on the laminate top her fingertips turned red. The chair wobbled and nearly tipped over. "Charlie's upstairs with a bullet hole in his chest. Clayt and Connie are on the run from some commando squad, and you tell me to be patient? How can you just sit there? Do something!"

"I saved Charlie's ass out there! Nearly got killed. I'll do what I can here, Sarah, but you're not helping. What the hell do you want from me?"

She raised her hands, took a step away, faced me again, cheeks aflame. "I don't know. *Some*thing. I ..."

Tears flowed instead of words. She bit her lip and hurried away.

Michael W. Sherer

CHAPTER 13

A familiar-looking blond cornered me in my favorite morning coffee shop. The only one in the neighborhood open for business that early. Fresh makeup, a light coat of pale pink lip gloss that matched her nail polish, and a well-rested air put her out of place. The restaurant was half-filled with hollowed-eyed night ghouls and adrenalized early risers. All-night revelers quiescent as they came down off whatever high they'd been on. Homeless kids who'd managed to panhandle enough change the day before to buy food, look for a little warmth and a glimmer of hope. Coffee-fueled construction workers and Seattle University students girding themselves for the day ahead.

Blondie leaned over the table. Nail tips lightly resting on the shiny surface. Waiting for an invitation. Or guarding against an attempted escape.

"We need to talk," she said.

"An overrated concept this time of day."

"Mind if I sit?" She slid into the opposite chair without waiting for a response.

Odors of pyrolized bread, bacon and burnt coffee permeated the worn industrial carpet and cracked vinyl seat covers. The barest whiff of floral perfume wafted across the table. The exotic scent a sharp contrast to the smell of grease that coated windows and other hard surfaces with a light haze. Reminding me how much I wanted a hot shower. And sleep.

"How did you find me?"

"It wasn't hard."

"Kiley, I don't—"

"It's Keely. Keely Radcliffe."

"Keely, then. I don't know what you hope to accomplish following me around."

"I want you to help me."

"I'm not interested."

Blue eyes drilled several holes in my resolve.

"I just turned twenty-one when my sister Jill died," she said in a low voice. "She was twenty-six. A grad student. In engineering. Unusual for a girl. At the time, anyway. But she really liked it. And she had something to prove. Or thought she did, I guess. She was the oldest."

A heavyset waitress ambled toward our table, a pot of coffee in one hand, pitcher of water in the other. Keely noted her approach and shook her blond locks. The woman's gaze shifted to me. I moved a hand over my cup and she veered away, another table already in her sights.

Keely glanced down, then leveled those blue headlamps at me again. "We weren't what you'd call close. She was too much older. Didn't want me hanging with her and her friends at any age. But she never treated me like a baby. I never felt like she resented me, or thought I was a pain. When our parents went out and she had to watch me and my brother, she usually took an interest in me. In what I wanted to do. She played games with me. Read stories to me. Helped me with homework. I looked up to her. Admired her. Loved her, in my own way."

My fingers drummed the edge of the table.

Her eyes slid toward the sound and back to my face. "The point is she was loyal. She treated me with respect and kindness. None of that sibling rivalry crap. No petty jealousies. And because of that I would have done anything for her, Mr. Sanders."

I ran my fingers through my hair. "Are you going somewhere with all this?"

"Do you know where my sister did her graduate work?"

"Enlighten me."

"Southern Illinois."

The words illuminated her route like a GPS device. But I still didn't know her destination.

"She was killed in the lab explosion," I said.

She tipped her head. "You remember."

"Hard to forget." I'd spent twenty years trying. "It was big news in my hometown, up the road from there."

"She didn't die in that explosion. She was murdered. Two shots. One to the heart. One to the head."

The dam she'd blown a hole in earlier burst, memories flooding my head with images, a torrent that drowned out her face, her voice.

Late one hot summer night, in the ruins of a lab on the top floor of the engineering building at SIU, campus security found the battered, bloodied body of a young woman, crushed from the waist down by the weight of a chunk of collapsed ceiling. Dead from gunshot wounds. Shots I'd heard.

"She was your sister?" A chunk of hot lead threatened to burn a hole through my gut.

She nodded, brushing aside a sheaf of hair that fell over her eyes.

"And now you want to find Perry Langford. Twenty years ... Don't you think he's paid up?"

"I told you. I don't think he—"

"They found him standing over her body, holding a gun."

Without realizing it, my fingers tattooed a tabletop drumbeat again. She reached across the table and covered them firmly, containing their energy.

"Do you really think your friend was capable of that?"

Capable? Wink had been more than capable of constructing and detonating a bomb. He'd been collecting—stealing— materials to make a contact explosive that same night. With my help. But the stuff he'd planned to make would have been a firecracker compared to the bomb that had ripped apart the engineering building. And murder? I hadn't thought him capable of that until his arrest. And because I'd never had the guts to face Wink after that night, the question had nagged at me ever since.

"Pretty strong evidence when you're holding a smoking gun," I said.

She shook her head. "Langford always maintained he saw a man in the hallway outside the lab before the explosion."

I leaned back and took a deep breath. "It's ancient history. And even if it's true, what good does it do? It didn't make any difference at his trial."

"I don't remember ever seeing you there."

"I was here. At U.W."

"Of course." She eyed me curiously for a moment. "You don't seem to have much faith in your friend."

I fingered the rim of my cup. "Wink liked to live on the edge. Always pushing the envelope. A challenge, any challenge, Wink was first in line to take it on. He had no fear. Willing to mix it up with guys twice his size. Tried things for the hell of it just to see what would happen. I saw him jump out of a hayloft holding a patio umbrella to see if it would slow his fall. On a dare, he rode a unicycle around the entire school building once—on the edge of the parapet, three stories up. Kid was a genius. Brilliant. Built a gyrocopter out of spare parts. A computer, too, back when a Commodore 64 was an expensive novelty. I wouldn't put anything past him."

"But that's my point. He was too smart to have done what they say he did." She propped her elbows on the table and uncurled a manicured finger. "First, he would have given himself enough time to get out of the building. Second, he would have checked to make sure the lab was empty. Third, he wouldn't have let himself get caught."

"How do you know? How do you know what Wink Langford might've done? Spend a lot of time with him?" I leaned forward. She didn't shrink from the heat radiating from my face. "I grew up with the guy. Called him my best friend once. We practically lived at each other's houses as kids. And even *I* couldn't tell you what happened that night."

What I'd seen that night might—*might*—have kept Wink out of jail. But the one thing I hadn't seen was what actually happened to that girl. Keely Radcliffe's sister. So I couldn't say for sure whether Wink was guilty or innocent.

She clasped her hands and rested her forearms on the table. "I don't know if I can adequately describe how I felt when my sister died. There's no way you can understand it. The pain. The anguish. Grief. And anger. I think I quite literally went out of my head for a time."

"I think I can picture it."

My tone brought her head up. She studied me. Decided not to press. I pushed away thoughts that circled in the depths below the surface of my consciousness, thoughts of— *No! Don't go there.*

"They had him dead to rights" she said. "Smoking gun and all like you said. I wanted nothing more than to see him put on Death Row. You understand what I'm saying?"

I nodded. "An eye for an eye." I understood perfectly.

She turned her palms up. Flipped them back over and clasped her hands once more. "I wasn't good for much during that period. Couldn't concentrate on school. Wasn't much interested in anything else. Even simple things—eating, sleeping... So I did the only thing I could. I took a semester off. Went down to Benton for the trial. Visited Centralia and found out everything there was to know about Perry Langford. You have no idea how much I hated him, how much I wanted to hate him. But the more I learned, and the more I sat and watched him in that courtroom, the more convinced I became that he didn't murder my sister."

"It could have been an accident."

The pale, unblemished skin between those Bahamas-blue eyes puckered.

I rushed on. "Not the shooting part. I meant maybe she wasn't supposed to be there, and when she got hurt in the explosion he put her out of her misery. I heard she was so badly injured she wouldn't have made it anyway."

She dipped her chin, eyes brimming.

"Sorry."

She fanned the air in front of her face. "It's the only reason he didn't get the death penalty."

My hand beat the table, the trembling completely involuntary this time. I snatched it away and clamped it between my knees, trying to still the tremors.

"Are you all right?"

"Sure." I blinked away visions of 124-grain bullets smacking into a human target. For a moment the ground dropped away in front of me, dark clouds roiling over an angry black sea far below, salt foam spiraling up to kiss my cheeks.

I stepped back from the edge. "I'm fine."

"Are you sure? You don't look well."

I took a sip of water, pressed the cool glass to my cheek. "Why do you want to find him anyway? Guilty, innocent, it doesn't matter. He did his time. Leave the poor guy alone."

"I think he wants the people responsible. I think he's looking for them."

"And you want him to lead you to them. That dish is seriously cold by now."

"Justice, Mr. Sanders. That's what I want."

"Blake."

"If you wish."

"What I wish for is twelve hours—eight, even—of uninterrupted, dreamless sleep in a warm bed. I wish my friend wasn't in the hospital. I wish I could talk to my son, Cole, one more time. I wish you'd go away and leave me alone."

She pressed her lips together and held her gaze on my face. I blinked and looked away.

If there was any truth to what she suggested, it could explain the FBI's interest in finding Wink. He wasn't just a skip-trace to them. And if he was innocent, he'd had a lot of time to think about who might have blown up that lab.

"You think Wink is out here somewhere. In Seattle. Why?"

She shrugged. "I don't know where he is, actually. I thought you might be able to help."

"How? How would I know where he's gone?"

"I took a chance. I thought he might try to find you first."

"Why on earth would he do that? I left him hanging. My best friend, and I didn't even say goodbye. If I were him, I'm the last guy I'd try to find. Unless he really is trying to kill me."

"Everyone in that damn town of yours said you two were connected at the hip when you were kids. You must know how he thinks, what he might do." Her eyes were pleading now.

"I *never* knew what he'd do. That was part of the thrill of hanging around with Wink. You never knew what was coming next. Twenty years later...?" I wagged my head. "No clue."

"But you might know where to start?"

I considered the question. Drucker had said Wink might be in the area. If Wink was on the trail of whoever had bombed the lab, then they might be here somewhere, too. Find the bombers, and we'd find Wink. Find Wink, find the bombers. All the same to Keely, no doubt. I wasn't so sure. To pick up Wink's scent meant going back to the trailhead, the place where it all started.

"You'll help me, right?" she said.

I stretched and got to my feet. "I'll sleep on it."

I'd made up my mind to look for Wink long before Keely walked in. For self-preservation, if nothing else. I owed it to him for that one act of cowardice long ago. I owed it to myself for not standing up for him at his trial. But I wasn't giving Keely the satisfaction of being the one to convince me.

She grabbed my wrist on my way past. "Wait! At least let me tell you how to get in touch."

I glanced down. She let go, pawed through her purse for a pen, scribbled something on a napkin and handed it to me. I put it in my pocket without looking at it and walked out.

* * * * *

The couple stepped through the darkened motel doorway quietly. She hesitated, pressing herself against the wall while he pulled the door shut, her eyes scanning the parking lot nervously. He turned now, face partially illuminated by the dim light from a fixture over the door. He, too, wagged his head to and fro as if looking for something, then the pair headed furtively for the stairs down to the lot.

Langford watched them from his car across the street, taking a sip of coffee from a large take-out cup he'd purchased at an all-night gas station less than an hour earlier. At the bottom of the stairs, the man raised his arm toward the SUV. The interior lights popped on as he thumbed the remote, the illumination barely visible through tinted glass covered with heavy dew. While the woman opened the passenger door and got in, the man opened the lift gate and deposited the small overnight case he'd carried from the room, then climbed behind the wheel.

The day before, Langford had followed the green SUV south from Washington all afternoon and evening. Long after dark, the couple had pulled off the interstate somewhere just north of Sacramento and had checked into the motel. Langford had waited until he was sure they were settled, then had parked in the back of a Wal-Mart lot next to an RV, where store security likely wouldn't bother him. He'd climbed into the back of the Scout, set the alarm on his watch and fell into a light sleep.

Only a few hours later, he'd topped off the gas tank and gotten coffee and a semblance of breakfast from the mini-mart inside. Figuring the fugitives would want an early start to minimize drawing attention to themselves, he'd set himself up in a good vantage point across the street from the motel well before dawn. The sky was just now beginning to turn gray as the couple in the SUV turned out of the motel lot and headed back toward the freeway. Langford waited until they were a few blocks away before starting the Scout and pulling onto the street behind them.

As soon as they turned onto the freeway entrance ramp heading south, Langford knew they were headed for Mexico. They were running. He'd known it the day before, but wanted to be sure. Now he was worried. They could easily make the border before dinner. He needed to come up with a plan long before then. In fact, the sooner the better, before day broke and the road filled with the normal flow of north-south interstate traffic.

Reaching behind the seat, he patted the stock of the old Remington 760 .30-.06 hunting rifle through the canvas and leather case, as if assuring himself that it hadn't walked off in the middle of the night. Then he leaned over, opened the glove compartment, removed the M1911A1 Remington .45 automatic pistol his father had been issued during the Korean War and laid it on the seat next to him. Putting both hands back on the wheel, he accelerated down the ramp onto the freeway, pulled into the passing lane and slowly began to overtake the green SUV down the road ahead.

CHAPTER 14

Frank Shriver nursed a shot of what looked like bourbon and chased it with a big gulp of beer. He wiped foam off his upper lip with the back of his hand, his sharp facial features softened by the brume hanging in the air as if smoking in restaurants hadn't been outlawed years earlier. The thin, dispirited lunch crowd barely raised the restaurant's volume above a library hush. A sudden clatter from the direction of the kitchen stirred barely enough interest to lift one or two heads. I eased into the chair across from him.

"Blake, buddy." Frank raised a hand in greeting and spewed questions before I opened my mouth. "How's the hero? Racking up points against future troubles with SPD? Your friend the cop okay? Heard his wife hasn't shown yet. What's with that?"

"Nice to see you again, Frank. Still have a job, I see."

"Touch and go."

"There'd been rumblings about selling the paper for a long time."

"Would have been better than shutting it down altogether and trying this online-only crap. Not many other websites out there looking for a metro editor, and I'm too old to start over. Won't be long before they dump me for some high school computer geek. What about you? You seeing your route get smaller?"

"Subscriptions are down, sure. Gee, must give me an extra five minutes of sleep a night."

He laughed until his eyes watered. Nicotine-stained fingers long and thin as a pianist's stripped wire-framed glasses off his face. With his other hand he pinched the bridge of a nose webbed with spidery red capillaries. Replacing his glasses, he raised his beer in salute and took another swallow.

"The shit you went through, I guess that's a good attitude," he said. "Just shows we might as well make the best of what we've got, right?"

I grimaced. "Breakfast of champions, Frank?"

He glanced at a blocky stainless watch too heavy for his thin hairy wrist. "Breakfast time for you, maybe. It's after noon; good enough for me."

"Things that bad?"

He glowered. "Your nickel, is all." He tipped his glass toward me again. "Let's see what it buys you besides halfway decent whiskey."

A short woman in jeans and a black sport shirt ambled over to the table to take our order. Body art decorated both arms, starting at her wrists and disappearing into the sleeves just above the bulge of biceps that had spent time in a weight room. Blond hair, dark at the roots, was pulled back tight. She wet the tip of a pencil with her tongue and waited, eyes on Frank. In keeping with the nooner, he ordered a patty melt and a double order of fries.

I handed the menu to the waitress without opening it. The Belltown neighborhood joint's nod to healthful food was a house salad consisting of a wedge of iceberg lettuce accompanied by a tasteless slice of indestructible tomato.

I smiled at her. "Half a Reuben and a cup of soup. Please."

"Navy bean, chicken noodle or cream of broccoli?"

"Surprise me."

"Anything to drink?" Her gaze flicked to the glasses in front of Frank.

"Water's fine."

She shrugged and walked away.

Frank watched her. "She reminds me of someone…" He shook his head and turned back to me. "What can I do you out of?"

"Other way around, Frank. I want to test your memory. What can you tell me about the bombing at Southern Illinois University back in the '80s?"

"You can find all this crap online now. Why come to me?"

"The Internet can't provide personal insight."

He sat motionless for a moment and blinked a few times. Idly, he swirled the ice cubes in his bourbon, and finally took a sip.

"You have any idea what I'm talking about?" I said.

"Yeah, yeah, I'm with you. Took me a moment, but I got it. Engineering lab. Girl got killed. Graduate student. What about it?"

"What do you remember about it?"

"Not much. The only reason I remember it at all—I mean, Christ, we're talking about some Podunk town in the Midwest, right—is that there was a local connection."

"Go on."

"Day after the bombing, E.L.F.—the original, not that Earth Liberation Front bunch, but the Environmental Life Force, I think it was—took credit."

"Why? What was the point?"

He rubbed his chin. "Something about protesting a research project. Coal, maybe? I think that was it. Coal gasification. Something they said would cause acid rain all over again. Wire services all said local cops caught a student at the scene. Lab that got destroyed didn't have anything to do with coal research. Two, three days later, E.L.F. issued a retraction. Said its people weren't responsible after all."

"And the student had no connection with the environmental group?"

"Hell, there *was* no group. Guy who founded the original E.L.F. went to prison down in Lompoc for some mischief and mayhem, and the group disbanded. That was, let me see,'78 maybe. Until the early '90s when the Earth Liberation Front started firebombing and burning shit, there was no E.L.F."

"Why'd somebody want people to think E.L.F. did it?"

He shrugged and drained his beer. "Why'd that kid set off a bomb? Crazies. All of 'em."

"You followed the investigation pretty close?"

"The part out here, yeah. My job, you know." He waved to get the attention of the waitress, held up his empty glass and pointed to it. "Okay, so there wasn't much of an investigation, when it comes down to it. Cops checked in with the guy who founded E.L.F. Said he didn't know what the hell they were talking about. He got religion or some such. Said he'd renounced violence. Had an alibi. Kept his nose clean after he got out of prison."

He waggled a finger. "Oh, yeah, that was another thing. Back in the '70s, before he got caught, the head elf was all about pesticides in food. Not acid rain or coal. Why pick a target in the Midwest so far from home when he had so many to environmental beefs to choose from here on the West Coast? And why would the guy wait ten years? So, that was that. Cops figured some nut job just wanted attention. Especially since the FBI, ATF and local cops back in Illinois had this kid at the scene. Along with a ton of evidence."

"And that was the end of it?"

His eyes narrowed. "What's this all about? Why the interest?"

"I knew the guy they put in jail for it."

"What, and now you want to prove he's innocent?" He snorted.

"Not me. He's out. Looking for the people behind it, I heard."

His ears perked. "Who from?"

"Reliable sources."

That made him smile. He sat back. "What's your part in this?"

"I don't know yet. Self-preservation, maybe."

He waited, attentive now, but I didn't elaborate. He looked up as the waitress came over with our food balanced on one forearm and a beer for Frank in her other hand. Frank dug into his patty melt with gusto, mouth full after two bites, a snail of melted cheese sliding toward his chin, leaving a trail of grease. Small and thin as an ascetic monk, there didn't appear to be room anywhere in his body for all the food on his plate.

He worked some food into his cheek and swallowed, making space in his mouth for words. "How well did you know this guy?"

"We grew up together."

"Close, then. You been in touch?"

"No."

"There a story here?"

"There's always a story."

He nodded. "You know where he is?"

I shook my head.

"But you're looking for him?"

"Unless he finds me first."

His eyebrows went up, and he stopped chewing. "So what do you want from me?"

"Root around. See what else you remember from back then. Anything that might tell me what or who he's looking for."

A glint reflected off his glasses like the one in his eye. "Like somebody responsible for a bomb twenty years ago? Sure, that'd play with readers. I'll dig up the file, see what I can find."

Michael W. Sherer

CHAPTER 15

A full-size dark gray government-issue sedan pulled alongside as I walked back to the lot where I left my car. Mr. Clean—*Taylor, rhymes with sailor*—jumped out while the sedan rolled slowly, keeping pace. He wore a friendly smile. Behind the wheel, Drucker's face carried no such affability. Taylor stepped in front of me, impeding my progress. The sedan stopped with a little jerk.

Taylor motioned to the car. "Get in."

I glanced at my watch and sighed, prospects of the short nap I'd envisioned before work quickly dimming.

"Why?"

Drucker leaned across the seat and growled through the open door. "Just get in the car."

I hesitated. Taylor took a step and clapped a friendly hand on my shoulder, steely fingers giving it a quick squeeze. I shook him off. He tipped his head and gave me a wink his partner couldn't see.

"Please," he said.

Ignoring the flare of heat coursing through my limbs, I stepped off the curb, opened the back door, folded myself in half and squeezed in. Taylor shut the door behind me and climbed in front. Drucker checked his mirror and stepped on the gas. The car spurted ahead with a chirp of tires on pavement, rocking me back against the seat.

"What do you guys want?" I said.

Drucker's eyes met mine in the rearview mirror, but neither one answered.

I looked out the window. "This is a waste of time. I already told you what I know."

A waste of breath, too, apparently. Five minutes later, Drucker pulled into the parking garage beneath the federal building downtown, wound down several subterranean levels and parked. They escorted me to the elevators and whisked me to a small conference room on an upper floor. Taylor offered me coffee. Drucker offered nothing but sour expressions that gave the impression he suffered from constipation.

I sprawled in a chair. Drucker paced on the other side of the small table. Taylor leaned against a far wall, arms folded, ankles crossed.

"You're in some serious trouble, Mr. Sanders," Drucker said.

"Why? What have I done?"

"Interfered with a federal investigation, for starters."

"That is such bullshit. How? You guys came and pounded on my door, woke me up, asked some questions. I gave you answers, and you left."

Careful. I took a deep, cleansing breath—*dirgha pranayama.*

"You need to tell us a little more about your relationship with Perry Langford," he said, jaw jutting beneath a downturned mouth.

"We went through this. What's to tell?"

"Oh, maybe the fact that on at least one occasion back in high school, you helped Langford rig locker doors with nitrogen tri-iodine, blowing several half off their hinges. Or the fact that you helped him build or set off explosive devices on dozens of other occasions. Homemade cannons, fireworks, guns, contact explosives—a regular arms depot for a couple of juvenile terrorists."

"We were kids. Sure, we set off some firecrackers, shot up some tin cans with BB guns. Terrorists? Give me a break. The Bush years made all you guys paranoid."

Drucker put his hands on the table and leaned toward me. "When I was a kid, Mr. Sanders, 'kids' blew up buildings on college campuses across the country. 'Kids' *killed* people blowing up shit. Now, half a dozen or more kids around the world blow themselves up every day, taking dozens of people with them. It's our *job* to take terrorism seriously."

I shook my head. "Practical jokes, sure. We pulled our share. We never hurt anyone."

Drucker straightened. "Where were you the night Langford blew up the SIUC lab?"

I blinked, and clamped my jaw shut to keep from answering, fishing through a school of thoughts like a greedy shark, watching them all dart just out of reach before I could sink my teeth into one.

"It's an easy question, Mr. Sanders. We know you weren't here at U.W. at the time."

I snapped at a passing tuna. "I never said I was."

He looked as if he was about to contradict me, and thought better of it.

I rubbed my jaw. "Been a long time. If I remember correctly, I was at home. Asleep."

"In Centralia. Witnesses who can vouch for you, of course."

I shrugged. "My mom, I suppose." Back then she'd had ways of knowing if I'd sneaked out of the house. She wouldn't be of any help to Drucker now, though. Alzheimer's had robbed her of most of her memories.

"What is that," he said, "an hour or so from Southern Illinois?"

"I suppose. About eighty miles, I think."

"You think?"

"I didn't have much reason to go to Carbondale."

"You never visited Langford down there? Your childhood buddy?"

"I may have."

He clenched his jaw and tugged at the corner of his mustache. Taylor stood attentively now, less relaxed, muscles bunched under the fabric of his suit, smile gone.

"What do you really want?" I said.

"We want to know where Langford is," Drucker said.

"This is getting really boring."

His eyes sparked. A muscle along his jaw twitched. A watch ticked loudly, and a pirr softly hissed from an overhead vent.

"We don't think your buddy pulled off that bombing alone," he said finally. "He had a partner, or partners."

My thoughts flashed back to nighttime images of four men in black.

Taylor threw in his two cents from the side. "Now he wants revenge."

"Or the truth, maybe," I said, heat rising into my face. "He always said he was innocent."

"Based on what we know, he's out for blood," Drucker went on. "If it wasn't you, then we want to know who, before Langford starts killing people. For all we know that still may be you. Now are you going to tell us where he is? Or do you want to be an accomplice to murder?"

I gritted my teeth. "How do I make it any plainer than 'I don't know'?"

He considered me. "You were involved in a shooting two days ago," he said.

The sudden change of subject threw me. Sweat dripped down my sides, and blood thrummed in my veins.

"If you don't cooperate with us, Mr. Sanders, we'll charge you with gun violations, take you down to FDC and lock you up."

I looked from one to the other. Taylor glanced at his partner and nodded. The Federal Detention Center in SeaTac just south of the airport might be moderately more comfortable than King County lockup, but jail was jail. I didn't relish another stay.

"Are you nuts?" I said. "I *am* cooperating. I already got a pass on the shooting. It was self-defense."

Drucker hardened his stare. "Unlawful discharge of a weapon. Using a concealed pistol without a license. Hell, we might even throw in assault." He turned to Taylor. "He assaulted you back there on the street, right? I saw it."

I folded my arms tight, holding everything in, and searched for a *drishti*. "Are you charging me, or am I free to go?"

Drucker's dark skin turned a mottled purple. "I can get the paperwork started if you want."

Taylor patted the air. "Let's not rush it." To me he said, "You're not under arrest."

I stood.

"Sit!" Drucker said, the command a pistol shot in the small room.

"I'd like to call an attorney now," I said, lowering myself back into the seat.

Taylor pushed away from the wall and put his hand on Drucker's shoulder. "That's it, Fred. We're done for the time being."

He rounded the table, lifted a black extension phone from a side table and set it down in front of me. Drucker didn't take his eyes off my face the whole time. When I lifted the handset he rose and turned for the door.

Molly wasn't happy to hear about my circumstances, but since she was a partner at one of the city's biggest law firms, I knew she could hook me up with someone who'd get me out of this jam. And since we were still on pretty good speaking terms, even after our divorce, I figured she'd at least be sympathetic.

She showed up in person fifteen minutes later, two spots high on her freckled cheeks glowing red against her pale skin, whether from a brisk five-block walk or anger hard to tell. She frowned at me when Taylor showed her into the conference room, but saved her most annihilative gaze for the two agents. They shuffled out reluctantly.

"I thought you'd send Cabot," I said. "I didn't mean to pull you away."

Annoyance flashed across her features. "Really, Blake, it's bad enough you get yourself into these situations. The senior partners would have fits if I asked Jeffrey to bail you out every time you got into trouble. This is easier."

I bit back the impulse to respond with some clever dig of my own, and quickly brought Molly up to date without prompting.

"You can't tell them anything?" she asked when I finished. "Or won't?"

"I can't. I have no clue where Wink is. Hadn't even thought of the guy in years until the other day. How can I give these guys what they want if I don't know anything?"

She nibbled the end of the pen she used to take notes.

"I told you about Wink," I said, as if that would explain everything.

She looked up. "Not much. I remember a few stories you shared when we first met, about when you were kids. You never talked about him after he went to jail. I always wondered why you never tried to get in touch."

I raised my hands. "What was the point?"

"I don't know. Show some sympathy, a little support for someone you said used to be a pretty important part of your life."

I didn't have a response.

She reached across the table and put a hand on my arm. "I'm sorry, by the way, about what happened to Charlie. And to you. Are you okay?"

I looked across Puget Sound at the snow-capped Olympic Mountains in the distance.

"Yeah, I guess." I left it there.

She nodded. "Let me go see what it is they want to hold you on."

While she was gone, I studied the spare room—round table with faux wood finish, swivel chairs upholstered with a nubby fabric a color that could only be called puce, small glass-topped table against a wall topped with the phone I'd used, beige vertical blinds on the window, white walls, gray industrial carpet. My mind focused on none of these things, flitting instead to a hundred other unrelated thoughts, a hummingbird moving from flower to flower, hovering only long enough to fuel up for the flight to the next beckoning blossom. I needed sleep, or another dose of meds.

Molly reappeared alone, and gathered up her purse and briefcase.

"You can go," she said.

I looked at her blankly. "The charges…?"

"All a bunch of crap. The gun violations they cited are state law, not federal. And they're so flimsy, given the circumstances they'd never stand up. I'm assuming you didn't assault or resist Special Agent Taylor—you didn't, did you? Anyway, they didn't bring it up, so you're clear there. And, as you pointed out, you came here on your own volition, so you're not obstructing their investigation."

She turned for the door.

"Thanks, Molly."

She looked back over her shoulder, a storm raging across her face. "I don't know what this is about, but the FBI isn't after your friend just because he violated parole. They'd let the locals worry about him. If I were you, I'd stay away from this. Don't go looking for him, Blake. Stay as far away from him as you can."

I didn't make any promises. She finally broke eye contact. When she met my gaze again, her eyes filled with sadness.

"I can't do this anymore, Blake," she said, her voice barely above a whisper. "I'm trying to move on. I don't want to rescue you anymore. Stop calling me."

Michael W. Sherer

CHAPTER 16

Worrisome as her last words were, I took Molly's advice, and went to visit Charlie. His pallor hadn't improved much, and he didn't seem as happy to see me. Eyes dull like before, the grimace on his face now said pain, not drugs, leached them of their luster. He shifted position, wincing with the effort, and fell back against the pillows. His groping fingers found the control unit, tethered by its cord to the bed rail. He pushed a button and the head of the bed raised him into a sitting position with a loud hum.

"This sucks," he said, his voice scratchy.

"No visitors?"

"Bunch of guys were here earlier, after the end of first shift."

I looked around the empty room. "Where's Sarah?"

"Taking a break. My orders. Told her to go get some sleep."

"Good advice."

"She probably went for a walk to get more coffee."

"Stubborn. Like her brother."

He glared at me. "You better watch yourself around her."

"What do you mean?"

"I know you're newly single again and all, but she's not. She's got a life. Tim's a good man. Bit of a nerd, but steady. Good father. Don't screw that up."

My shoulders rose up around my ears, my hands turned palms up. "Why would I do that?"

His eyebrows dove into each other. "Bullet hole or no, I'll kick your ass, so help me. I saw the way you looked at her."

"She's an attractive woman. I'd be a fool not to notice. Doesn't mean I'm fool enough to make a play, married or not. What do you take me for, Charlie?" I felt my fingers curl of their own accord, as if one of the buttons on Charlie's remote was linked to their circuitry.

He turned his hands over in his lap and inspected them. "She still carries a torch for you."

"After all these years? I doubt it. A case of the 'what-ifs,' maybe. We all do it. Hell, I was spoken for even back then, Charlie, and you know it."

"Yeah, and look how well that turned out."

My jaw clenched, and I took a step toward the bed before I saw him smile weakly and wave me off.

"Get a grip," he said. "I'm just giving you a hard time. You know I wish you and Molly would get back together."

"You hear from Babs yet?" It came out before I could squelch the impulse.

He grunted as if he'd been punched, a wince turning to something more morose. The tension drained out of my muscles, making me look for a chair. I stood my ground.

"You want to talk about it?" I said.

"Nope." He twisted the blanket in his hands.

I looked away. Walked over to the window and read the cards sticking out of the bouquets of flowers lining the ledge.

"You given any more thought to what happened to your folks?" I said.

His reflection looked at me. "Not much else to do in here but think. Not that these painkillers make it easy."

"And?"

"I don't have a clue."

"Maybe you should rethink taking that detective's exam."

His eyes bored into my back for a long time before he spoke. "Maybe I should." His reflection said something else.

"It's just as well Sarah's not here. She'd just be bugging me to find them."

"You? That's a laugh. Stay out of it."

"I intend to," I lied.

I stayed a while longer and tried to shake off the grumpiness that settled into my bones like a bad cold. But whatever Charlie had was contagious, and I left feeling frustrated and mean.

* * * * *

Frank called me late. Late for him, anyway. Early for me, since I was getting ready to head for the warehouse in Ballard to start work. He said he wanted to meet.

He'd moved twenty feet from where we'd eaten lunch, his wiry frame now settled on a stool. He hunched over the dark oak of the bar, a small paunch resting in his lap, elbows pointed bulwarks against encroachments on the half-empty pint glass centered under his nose. His arms circled it tightly when I slid onto the stool next to his. He glanced over, and his shoulders relaxed.

"Where's the patter?" I said. "The twenty questions?" His silence was uncharacteristic, but I'd never run across him after an all-day bender before.

He grunted. "You ever serve?" He went on before I could figure out what he meant. "I did. Army. Arty METRO, over in 'Nam. 'Sixty-eight, 'sixty-nine'69."

"You got drafted?

"Enlisted. There was no draft until 'seventy.'70. Screwed around too much my first year of college and flunked out. Didn't know what else to do." He shrugged and picked up the beer. "Figured they'd send me to Fort Lewis and train me as a grunt. Wound up in artillery at Fort Sill in Oklahoma instead. Ended up at a fire support base outside Tay Ninh, maybe sixty, seventy miles from Saigon. Sent up weather balloons during the day. At night, we went on patrol. Did that for the first month, twenty-four/seven. Slept in one-hour rotations. We finally got enough reinforcements we could work a normal shift. Do our work in the day, get drunk or stoned at night, sitting in our bunkers watching the fireworks—mortars and rockets the VC lobbed at us. We'd crank up some music—Joplin, Hendrix, Stones—and watch the show. Mortars, blue; rockets, red. A couple of times, the VC got through the fence, overran the camp and we had to fight them off."

He turned his head, his eyes taking a half second to focus on me. "I spent about two, maybe three months out of a thirteen-month tour over there unofficially AWOL. We'd tell our CO we were going to the beach at Cam Ranh Bay, spend a long weekend there. He didn't give a shit. Not too many did."

My knee bounced up and down under the bar. I ran a hand down the top of my thigh and pressed hard.

He stared into his glass. "When I joined up, there was still honor in serving. Barely. The shit hit the fan that year. King and Kennedy assassinated; the riots in Chicago. By the time I got back to the States, the whole fucking world had gone topsy-turvy. Demonstrators were everywhere. I went back to U.W., got interested in journalism. Covered the protests here in town, and the Seattle Seven trial down in Tacoma for a campus rag."

"This is a fascinating walk down memory lane, Frank, but I've gotta go to work."

His lip curled. "You probably weren't even born yet. Got no idea what I'm talking about."

"Yeah, I get it. Hippies versus 'The Man.' I'm not that young."

He leaned back to get a better look, eyes slowly focusing.

"Bet you were in diapers, then. The history lesson is important, smart guy. I'll tell you why. You got me thinking about the past this afternoon. Crazy times. A whole different world."

"What's your point?"

He waved and shook his head. "A while after that bombing you asked about—I don't know, maybe a year later—a guy got killed in a road accident. Guy named Fitch, Sebastian Fitch. I don't remember all the details. What I do remember is that the cops thought Fitch could be linked to the bombing. Fitch ran with a wild crowd way back in the day."

"Meaning?"

"He was a card-carrying member of the SLF—Seattle Liberation Front, the protest group."

"They protested the war, right? What's that got to do with what happened at SIU? Twenty years later, I might add."

His head bobbed on his shoulders, and his face tightened as he held himself together. "I'm just saying, leopards don't change their spots, you know? People complain about the weather when they don't have anything else to complain about. Some activists just gotta have a cause."

I absorbed what he was telling me. "You think if I find the people this guy Fitch ran with back in the '60s, I'll find whoever's responsible for the Southern Illinois bombing."

He nodded and took a long draft from his glass, Adam's apple bobbing rhythmically. He motioned to the bartender for another.

"It's a possibility," he said.

He was probably over the legal limit, and Frank had never known a conspiracy theory he hadn't liked. But he'd always been a good journalist, digging up the facts before writing a story.

"Are you still plugged in, Frank? Got some names for me?"

"I've been thinking about that. Some are dead. A few got religion. Most got respectable." He paused. "A lot of kids got mixed up in the protests. Like sheep. First time away from home for most of them. First taste of freedom. First chance to 'express' themselves. The real activists came from outside. Teachers, grad students, transfers. Even guys like Fitch who just liked the action. Lot of people at the time who'd tell you they were members of SDS that never went to a meeting or demonstration. A few hardcore activists who'd never let on now that they were with Weathermen or some other group back then."

"Names, Frank."

He shrugged. "Too many possibilities, and too much water under the bridge."

I gritted my teeth and sighed. "Thanks for nothing." I stood. "See you around."

He put a bony hand on my arm. "Lot of memories better off staying buried."

"I don't like surprises. I'd rather know what's coming at me."

"Cop who investigated the accident that killed Fitch is a guy named Ned Collins. Retired now. Lives up in Shoreline, I think." He took his hand away.

Michael W. Sherer

CHAPTER 17

The idling engine of the black coupe rumbled softly as the car rolled slowly down an incline toward the water. The driver stopped at the edge of the pavement, shut it off and stared into the inky darkness. His eyes slowly adjusted, allowing him to see the end of the breakwater against the water of the sound. Beyond, the lights of a freighter danced their way north across the water out to sea. In the distance, lights twinkled in houses on the far shore, the dark outline of the Olympics looming on the horizon above them.

The ghostly outline of a small sport cruiser materialized off the end of the breakwater, running lights appearing to float in mid-air. The driver flashed his headlights once and waited. Less than five seconds later, the boat's lights blinked off and on and turned toward a dock that jutted out from the headland twenty yards away. The driver climbed out of the coupe and made a slow turn, taking in his surroundings. The park to the north was quiet and deserted, even the late-night revelers gone, beach bonfires long since burned out, their embers now cold. Music that earlier had drifted over from the marina had gone silent, the last of the partygoers having gone home. An occasional car drifted past on the road behind him, but the only people out at this time of night would be locals getting home or early risers going to work. Confident he wasn't being watched, he strode down the embankment to the dock.

The cruiser had silently drifted alongside the end of the dock, and while one man snugged a line over a cleat on the dock, mooring the boat, another black-clad figure lithely leaped onto the dock and walked toward the approaching driver. His jet-black hair shone in the starlight, pale face beneath it wraithlike in the night. The two men met in the middle of the dock and turned to face north. They stood shoulder-to-shoulder looking out over the water as if admiring the view on a late evening stroll.

"You're late," the driver said.

He glanced at his companion, saw the flat planes of his face in profile, a hardness in his expression that suggested authority. Up close, he realized the man was much older than he'd thought from the way he moved.

"You know the risk I'm taking." The man from the boat spoke impeccable English, but couldn't completely hide an accent that placed him from somewhere in Asia.

"You think I'm not?" the driver said, amused and annoyed at the same time. He knew exactly where the Asian was from—Beijing—and how much trouble he'd be in if caught for entering the country illegally. But he had his own problems. Lately, he'd begun to think his partner suspected him of something. He was sure he'd been circumspect enough not to let on what he'd been up to, but his partner had seemed more curious recently about the few times he'd been late to work and the time he'd been spending on-line researching this project instead of the cases the two were working. They weren't that dissimilar, actually. He smiled to himself.

The Asian interrupted his thoughts. "So, do you have what we want?"

The driver shook his head. "Not yet."

"Have you made *any* progress?"

He felt anger flare up inside at the imperious tone in the man's voice, but he remained motionless, stonily looking out at the sound.

"Yes, we've made progress. We located the people we think may have the information. Unfortunately, they gave us the slip."

"Then what am I doing here? We could have covered all this safely at a distance using the usual communication channels."

"You're here," the driver said coldly, "because I wanted to see how serious you are. I'm not about to betray my country on a whim. If you want the technology badly enough, you'll meet my price, on my terms."

"*If* it actually exists," the Asian said. "And *if* it works. The information you seek to sell us is more than twenty years old. What makes you think someone else hasn't already come up with it, whatever this breakthrough was supposed to be?"

"Trust me. Someone else wants it, too, and judging from the interest they've shown, this is the real deal all right."

"Then next time we meet, have it with you."

"Or what?"

The Asian shrugged and walked away before he had a chance to react.

Michael W. Sherer

CHAPTER 18

Collins lived in a bungalow just east of the freeway. Gray concrete rose into an uncertain sky at the end of the block like the Berlin Wall, shutting off the cul-de-sac from the rest of the world. Traffic droned, too loud to be confused with the sound of the ocean despite the sound barrier. The incessant roar of a two-stroke engine nearby almost drowned it out. A cinder block on legs pushed a lawnmower across the grass in front of the house at the address written on the piece of paper in my hand. The only curve on his body was a tonsured scalp fringed with white hair, the rest all flat planes and chiseled angles.

I contorted my long limbs out of the car, stepped onto the walk and waved to get his attention. He pulled up short and cut the engine, curious.

"Mr. Collins?"

A pleasant smile crossed his face, but it didn't reach his eyes. "Depends on who's asking."

"Blake Sanders. Frank Shriver suggested I look you up."

"The man's not dead yet? What can I do for you?"

"Wondered if you might be willing to talk about an old case. Sebastian Fitch."

He maintained a poker face, but something other than surprise flickered in his eyes. Wariness, maybe, like a lounging cat that's gone on alert. He shifted his weight.

"There's a name I haven't heard in a while. Tell you what. I've got a couple more passes here. Let me finish up and I'll get us some iced tea. We'll take it out back."

I nodded. He bent and pulled the starter cord with a clean jerk. The mower roared to life. I stifled a yawn and rubbed the corner of an eye with my finger. The day was as bright as it had promised when I'd gone to bed that morning, the sky a patchwork quilt of blue and white.

Five minutes later, he walked me through the house into the kitchen, fetched two tall glasses from a cupboard and a pitcher from the refrigerator, and led me out the back onto a deck overlooking a small yard. A hemlock towered over one corner, branches shading the grass beneath. A cloud passed overhead, sprinkling us with a few drops even though the sun shone brightly. Collins tipped his face up.

"Not quite the weather for iced tea yet," he said, "but I keep thinking summer will get here faster if I drink it."

I took a sip. It had a hint of lemon and was sweetened with just enough sugar to take the bitter edge off the tea. "It's good. Thanks."

"How do you know Frank?" he said as we got settled around a patio table.

"I met him when I worked at UW. Later, I tried to get him to write stories about my clients."

"Past tense?"

"I don't work in that business anymore." I waved. "Old news."

He emitted something close to a grunt and waggled a finger, fat as a sausage. "I've got it now. I couldn't place it at first, but I recognized your name. You're the guy—"

"Yeah, I'm the guy." I sighed, hoping he wouldn't make me relive the events that had made me infamous six months earlier. "Is that good or bad?"

He shrugged, and didn't bother to pursue it. "Too bad what happened to the paper."

"The newspaper? At least they kept Frank on staff."

He cocked his head. "Sort of like me working security. It's not the same as being a cop."

"Is that what you do now?"

He laughed. "No, I'm retired. Every once in a while I'll work a private party or a fundraiser as a favor if people ask real nice. Otherwise, I've got plenty to do around the house. When I get caught up, I go fishing. Read. Talk to strangers about old cases..." His smile faded. "What's your interest in Fitch?"

I launched into the story. Without too many details, I gave him reason to think I might be in danger, hoping he'd be sympathetic enough to help. When I finished, he looked skeptical.

"So, you're trying to find this guy?" he said. "Your friend?"

I shook my head. "I'm just trying to avoid trouble if I can. If Langford does come looking for me, it'd be nice to know what or who he's after. Ditto the feds. I don't like being the center of attention, not when people are carrying guns." An image of black-clad commandos flashed through my head.

He wrapped his fingers around his glass and leaned back in his chair, his gaze settled on a squirrel foraging for food under the hemlock.

"Couldn't hurt, I guess." He took a sip of tea and wiped the corners of his mouth with his thumb and forefinger. "Seattle was a backwater in the '60s. Still is in a lot of ways, but Boeing put us on the map back then. Microsoft, too, later on. The point is, nothing happens here. We had that little world's fair that gave us the Space Needle. That was it. I was a rookie in the late '60s. Worked a beat around 'The Ave.' The U District was quiet, peaceful. Politically, the anti-war movement gained steam elsewhere—Berkeley, Madison, Columbia. We practically had to import it here."

I stilled a restless foot, and reminded myself that some people from that generation apparently liked reliving the flashbacks.

"The movement here started out peaceful," he said. "We didn't have a lot of militants. Not at first. SDS was pretty small on the U.W. campus, almost nonexistent. And even the group Seattle was known for in the '60s—SLF—started out as a nonviolent alternative to SDS and Weatherman. You know about any of this?"

The question brought me back, my attention already drifting off. "Some. All before my time, but I read about it."

He nodded. "What I'm getting at is that more radical arms of organizations like SDS thought violence was the only way to make their point. Since they weren't big in numbers, sometimes they hired professional agitators. Gave them cash if they had it.

Paid them with drugs, sex, favors sometimes if not. Fitch was one."

"Someone to stir up the crowd?"

"Organizers did a pretty good job of that. Guys like Fitch took things even further. Riled up the crowd around them, then provoked a response from security or cops. Maybe 'accidentally' shove a student into a barricade or a cop. Cops would react, and it would escalate. Like lighting a bunch of little fires around the edges. Pretty soon the whole thing goes up in flames."

"Where'd he come from?"

"He grew up around Chicago. Dropped out of high school and ended up in a biker gang. The Outlaws, I think it was. Decided it wasn't for him and left the gang on a road trip up to Wisconsin. Ended up in Madison. Kicked around and did odd jobs. Couple of minor scrapes with the law. Nothing too serious. Hung around the Wisconsin campus and got recruited by some radicals to provide protection and security for their meetings."

"How did he end up out here?"

"Fitch got to be friends with some of them. They sort of adopted him. One of them got into grad school at U.W. Half of a married couple, if I remember right. The wife came too, of course, and Fitch drifted out here after them."

"You remember all your cases this well?"

"No." He stared into the middle distance for a moment. "Fitch was different. A born troublemaker, but for all he went through—the biker gang, the protest groups—he never got busted for anything more than a misdemeanor. Big guy. Loved to fight. Go out of his way to mix it up in a bar. Deep down, though, kind of a teddy bear. Far as anyone knows, he never got involved in the really hardcore stuff—bombings, bank heists, that sort of thing."

His gaze didn't leave my face.

"I don't understand. How'd he get linked to what happened in Illinois?"

"Fitch didn't care about politics. It was more about belonging. He was a little slow. I guess they'd call him learning disabled or something now. He hooked up with the students

110

because they had a use for him, a job. He felt needed." Collins' gaze walked up and down my face. "Probably why he followed the ones who treated him well out here."

He drained a third of his tea, smacked his lips. "Fitch got killed in a motorcycle accident. Went off the road into a ravine. No helmet. Had no ID on him when he died. We ran his prints and registration. Bike came up registered to Fitch. We matched his prints with what we had on file from a couple of arrests back around the time of the antiwar demonstrations. Only reason I took any notice is because I ran into him a couple of times back when I was a beat cop."

He motioned toward my glass. "You want a refill?"

I looked at my empty glass, unaware that I'd finished the tea. "No, I'm good, thanks."

He reached for the pitcher, filled his own glass and took a sip. "I get dehydrated easy when I'm working outside. Where was I? Oh, yeah, the connection. Funny thing. When we were trying to ID Fitch's body after the accident, we sent a set of prints to the FBI. This was before AFIS. You familiar with it?"

I nodded. "Fingerprint identification."

"Right. I don't think the feds had their automated system up and running until the late '90s. Well, wouldn't you know, about ten years after Fitch got killed, we get a call from CJIS in Virginia. Some techie had been running the backlog of old prints against the database. Fitch's prints were close enough to match the partial print of an UNSUB found at the scene of the SIU bombing."

"Then it's possible that Fitch might have been involved in the bombing."

"Or not. It was only a partial print. Seems like a long way to go to do a job, and Fitch wasn't part of that crowd, remember."

"So that was the end of it?"

"Not quite. The FBI let us know about the prints as a courtesy. The SIU thing was their case. But we investigated Fitch anyway. I got the case. Asked for it, actually. Thought it curious that his name kept popping up, even after he was long gone."

"You find anything?"

He leaned back and rubbed the smooth skin on the top of his head. "First thought I had was that couple he followed out here. The Wilsons. Odd pair, those two. Got caught up in SDS, and worked behind the scenes in Madison. Made flyers, organized meetings. Stayed out of the limelight. Never arrested. Never even took part in a demonstration that we know. They didn't show up in any news photos, at least. Apparently got really disillusioned with the random violence during the Days of Rage in Chicago. When they came out here, they got involved with SLF because the group said it didn't condone that kind of crap. Hard to control mob mentality, though. When the demonstrations here turned ugly, the Wilsons split. Next thing you know, they showed up in Canada supporting a new cause—Greenpeace."

"But you thought they might be involved somehow?"

"They dropped out of sight after a couple of years. This was back in the early '70s. But I always wondered if they kept in touch with Fitch for old times' sake. Not much I could do about it anyway with them up in Canada. But around the time of the bombing out in Illinois, some rumors floated around that the Wilsons had affiliated themselves with the environmental group that claimed responsibility."

I pondered a moment. "In Canada? I thought ELF was based in Oregon or Northern California. Any way to track them down? The rumors, I mean."

He shook his head. "Happened a long time ago. Rumors cool pretty fast. We questioned the members of the environmental group at the time. They said they didn't know any Wilsons. I talked to Fitch's known associates. Never came up with anything solid."

"Sounds like a lot of maybes. Could be Fitch's fingerprint the FBI found down in Carbondale. But Fitch never bombed anything before, you say. Could be Fitch's friends, the Wilsons, were involved, but they went north and disappeared. Could be Langford is out here looking for Fitch or the Wilsons. Or both. Then again, maybe not."

Collins grinned. "I think you got the gist of it."

What bothered me more than the unknowns was that the Wilsons' story sounded familiar in some ways to another I'd heard recently.

Michael W. Sherer

CHAPTER 19

Late-afternoon traffic snaked slowly into town, a python heavy from a freshly swallowed meal. I barely made it to the restaurant in time for my shift.

Javier directed the symphony in the kitchen, using a large stainless steel spoon to conduct the chamber group of chefs and line cooks prepping for dinner.

"*¡Hola, mi amigo!*" he called when he saw me come in the back door. "*¿Cómo estás?*"

I waved. He glanced at his watch, held it out and tapped the crystal.

"Right on time," I said over the din.

White teeth flashed under the thin black mustache, an editor's penciled em-dash that split his face in two. He pointed his finger toward me, slashed a Z in the air and turned away. I headed straight for the dishroom, changed into a white work shirt, donned a clean apron and pair of latex gloves, and waded into the pile of pots and pans that already waited for me. Scrubbing away the cooked-on food required elbow grease in addition to hot, soapy water. The tropical confines of the dishroom coated me with a good sweat by the time the stack diminished.

The stream of soiled cookware slowed to a trickle. The flow would strengthen again later when orders flew out of the kitchen. With a moment for a short break, I helped myself to some of the food that had been prepared for the employees before the shift started. I took a plate to the dishroom and leaned against a worktable to eat. Soon, bus tubs full of dishes began to filter through the kitchen, waitstaff twirling and skipping around cooks and obstacles with their heavy loads. Stuffing a last forkful of *enchiladas suizas* in my mouth, I rinsed the plate and placed it in an empty rack. The kitchen filled with the boisterous music of clanging metal, bubbling sauces and pans of sizzling food on the stove accompanied by laughter and lyrics in rapid Spanglish. Faint strains of Spanish guitar music floated in from the dining room.

I found a rhythm to match the music—scrap, rack, load, empty, stack, and start over. Every time I caught up with a flood of dishes as the tables turned, the growing pile of sauté pans, hotel pans and sheet pans in the sink clamored for attention. Time passed quickly, which meant the restaurant was busy. Good for Javier and his wife, Maria, and for all of us who depended on paychecks.

The kitchen quieted after eleven as the pace slowed. The crew put away unused food and cleaned their stations, keeping the dishroom filled. Waitstaff bussed in dinner dishes from the last turn while the remaining guests still enjoyed desserts and coffee. At eleven-thirty Javier closed the kitchen, causing a rush on the pot sink. Cooks finished up, changed into their street clothes and left one by one. Waitstaff, too, as the dining room emptied.

Carlos, the chef, checked inventory for the next day's order and said goodnight. That left two of us in the kitchen, José the prep cook and me. José flipped on a small, dented boom box that sat on a shelf alongside tins of spices. Brassy mariachi music blared off the tile walls and stainless steel worktables. José sang along in a loud voice as he worked. He carried in the metal baffles from the ventilation hood and racked them to run through the dishwasher. As I finished washing the last of the pots and pans and ran the last few racks, José pulled the floor mats from behind the cooking line and took them outside to hose them off. When he returned, he filled a mop bucket and salsaed across the tiles to the music with the mop, crooning into the handle.

Javier entered from the dining room. Smiling, he clapped José on the shoulder. "*Buenas noches*," he said loudly over the radio. "I'm going home."

"Any dishes out front?" I said.

"All cleaned and locked up."

"Good night? Seemed busy."

116

He nodded, holding up a zippered pouch. "Very good, *ese*. Money's as good as in the bank."

He turned, hesitated, and walked back to the dishroom. For a moment he watched me silently. I stopped scrubbing and braced my hands on the edge of the sink.

"You've been with us a long time now," he said. "More than a year."

I nodded.

"Why are you still here, *ese*?" He waggled a hand. "Don't get me wrong. I'm grateful. You work hard. You're dependable. But you're a smart man. Too smart to be washing dishes, no?"

Heat crept up the back of my collar. "I like it here. You've been good to me, Javier."

"You have a little money now, no? The old lady, she left you a little something?"

Midge Babcock's wrinkled face flashed in my brain. "The estate paid me a fee, to be an executor, yes." I'd been arrested for her murder, too.

"So, you don't need this job, *ese*. Why do you stay?"

"Jobs aren't that easy to come by these days, in case you hadn't noticed."

"You don't have to remind me, *chico*. I'm tempted to close on Tuesdays to save money. Maria tells me to stand strong, but ..." He fell silent, waiting.

"This is good for me, Javier." I waved a soapy glove at the dishroom. "I can do this job because I don't have to think. I can let my mind go wherever it wants to. Don't have to try to keep it focused on anything. It keeps me grounded, connected."

"You could do better. You had an important job once, no?"

"This job is important. To you." I stared at him, wondering what he was getting at. "Baby steps, Javier. For now, this suits me. You thinking of letting me go?"

The corners of his mouth turned down at the idea. "No, of course not." His head swiveled for a glance at José. Turning back, he looked somber. "Everything else okay with you, *ese*?"

I smiled. "I'm good, Javier, thanks. Something wrong?"

"Two men came by earlier looking for you. I thought you should know."

The hairs on my arms stood up. "They say who they were?"

He shook his head. "Very hard men. *¿Entiendes?* I told them I had not seen you. You know them?"

I didn't answer. Javier would know if they were cops, which left a bunch of unknowns.

His eyes searched my face. "Lock up when you leave, okay? See you *mañana.*"

I wiped my brow on my sleeve and waved a gloved hand.

José and I pulled the garbage cans out to the alley on our way out the door, set the alarm and locked up a little after twelve-thirty. I stood and stretched, working the kinks out from hunching over the sink and dish table most of the night.

"*Adiós, señor,*" José said, head bobbing.

"*Hasta mañana, José.*"

He disappeared down the alley. I strolled after him, tired but content from the evening's hard work. With the sun gone, the night air's caress had all the warmth of a jilted lover. I zipped my jacket and stuffed my hands in the pockets. Daylight this time of year stretched as late as ten o'clock, but nights wouldn't feel balmy until July.

I'd left my car a few blocks east. After losing it a few times due to inattention or preoccupation when parking, I now kept a note on my dashboard reminding me to look at landmarks before locking up. I set my feet on autopilot, but my mind took a walk in a different direction. I got lost in the twisting maze of random thoughts whirling through my head. Molly's pronouncement. *What was that all about?* Charlie's parents, gone. *Where?* Sarah. *Dissatisfied with her life? Looking?* Wink. *Friend? Enemy?* Sebastian Fitch. *One of the apparitions I'd seen melt into the darkness of a summer night long ago?* Drucker. *What did the FBI want with Wink? Just to keep tabs on him? Were they after the same thing Keely was?* Keely ...

Only in my world, that sort of orderly mental progression sounded and looked more like nightmares than daydreams. *Molly ... doing dishes—with Javier? ... Drucker, in black, outside the ...*

Wink, unicycling, in jail ... Sarah looks good, really fine, except that frown ... Clayt and Connie on hands and knees in a dirt tunnel, Connie's hips widening until they almost filled the ... blood bubbling out of Charlie's chest, dripping into ... a hail of bullets worming into metal, then flesh ... Keely, Cole, Keely, Cole ... Newspapers ...

Newspapers. I had another shift to get through. I dug in a pocket for a dose of meds.

Half a block from the car, something outside pounded to get in. A feeling, or a sound. Or Javier's warning. Cars hissed down Broadway two blocks behind me. The fainter rush of freeway traffic floated up from the base of the hill. A siren wailed somewhere in the distance. The low rumble and burble of a big engine sounded closer, worming its way into the forefront of my mental meandering. The sound had been constant for a while, just unnoticed. It changed as I turned, pitch and volume quickly rising in intensity. A black shadow trailed me, an SUV the size of a small house. The engine cleared its throat and growled.

Everything was all wrong.

The confusing maze in my head vanished like fog vaporizing under a hot sun, leaving me with a single focus—big black car, coming fast. No lights. Tinted windows open, the black snouts of ugly gun barrels protruding from both. Dark figures leaning out behind the barrels. I turned and sprinted down the sidewalk, the drumming in my chest drowning out the engine behind me. The moves were automatic, ingrained in muscle memory years before. *Drive the floor. Head fake, stutter step, spin, break for the paint.* I dove behind a parked car. A thunderous eruption of bullets shattered glass and beat a tattoo on metal as the SUV roared by.

Michael W. Sherer

CHAPTER 20

They'll be back.

I scrambled to my feet and took off in the opposite direction, running toward Broadway. Dimly aware of gravel embedded in the palm of one hand and something wet trickling down my leg, my focus shifted to other senses, sound and sight. The SUV's engine changed pitch again, accompanied by tires squealing on pavement. I risked a glance over my shoulder when I reached the corner and saw the SUV bumping over a curb and sideswiping a stop sign as it made a wide swing through an intersection and headed back toward me. Rounding the corner onto Broadway, I ran faster, heart pounding against my ribs, feet pounding the concrete sidewalk. I couldn't outrun them.

The restaurant.

In the middle of the block I shifted direction and darted across Broadway, dodging a city bus and a car on the way. The shriek of rubber skidding on pavement behind me let me know the SUV was at the intersection. A couple on the sidewalk looked up, startled, as I ran past and vaulted a low wrought iron fence shielding a few outdoor tables from passersby. The roar of the SUV grew louder as it gunned down the street. I lifted a table and heaved it through one of the front windows of the restaurant, setting off the clanging bell of the burglar alarm.

I clambered over the low sill and dove for the floor in the darkness of the restaurant. The deafening chatter of automatic weapons fire let loose a spray of lead into the restaurant's interior, showering me with splintered wood and shattered glass. I scrambled toward the kitchen in a low crouch, zigzagging between the tables, banging my left hip hard on the edge of one. *No matter, it's titanium.*

The clang of the alarm pushed out all other sounds from the street except the faint wail of sirens. I raced through the darkened kitchen, twisted the deadbolt on the back door and burst through into the alley. Running on instinct, I vaulted a low cyclone fence behind the dumpsters and dropped to an apartment building parking lot below, avoiding the street. The lot led around the side of the building to the middle of the next block. I slowed, listening intently for sounds of the SUV, the burglar alarm fainter now behind me, but wailing sirens growing louder. The blood roaring in my ears and pounding heart sounded like screaming voices urging me to run, flee faster. I sucked in a lungful of air and swallowed the urge, quickly crossing the street instead for the shelter of the shadows on the other side. I ran to the corner and worked my way down the hill toward the steel and glass canyons of downtown, changing direction often, sliding down alleyways, cutting through parking lots.

My parietal cortex, the part of my brain that responded to and focused on the sensory information of playing moving target, finally disengaged enough to allow signals from the prefrontal cortex in. Questions, logic, cognitive processing, all helped by the meds kicking in.

Focus!

I turned slowly, scanning the street for signs of pursuit, checking landmarks to figure out where I was. I kept moving, trying to make sense of it all. But the torrent of images, questions, half-baked theories proved too much to orchestrate into any clear picture. Someone had marked me, but why? All I knew was that someone had effectively cut me off from my car, and if they knew where I worked, they knew where I lived. I needed a safe place to think, regroup, come up with some sort of plan.

I shoved a hand in my pants pocket and pulled out a wad of bills, receipts, scraps of paper covered with lists and notes to myself. I quickly shuffled through them until I found what I wanted, and held it up under a streetlight to read it. I turned left at the next corner and picked up my pace. Two blocks up I came out on a busy street and hailed the first empty cab that came by. More than anything I wanted to direct the cabbie north to the familiar old house on Capitol Hill. Reluctantly, I gave him the address in my hand and let him drive east. I leaned back, thoughts streaking by in a blur like the lights passing by the window.

Maybe I'd imagined the whole thing. My mind was funny that way. All the times I'd related a "remember when?" story to Molly, my voice gradually slowed to a halt by the quizzical look on her face, the denial that she'd ever known of the scene I'd recollected as clearly as this morning's breakfast. The times she'd erupted into tears and recriminations when the memory had involved a woman that could not possibly have been her, despite my insistence. Sometimes, a plausible explanation came to light—I'd been with a client, or I'd mixed up two events into one remembrance. In other cases, the only answer to why our recall didn't match was that mine was faulty or I'd dreamed it up.

A nagging pain intruded. I turned my hand over and held my palm up to the light coming through the window. The road rash wasn't bad, the abraded area on the heel of my hand about the size of a fifty-cent piece. More bruised than scraped, the wound showed minimal bleeding. I worked a couple of tiny pebbles out from under the skin with a thumbnail and wiped my hand on my jeans. The left leg had a tear at the knee, but the bleeding there had stopped, too, leaving only a short snail's trail of cracked and sticky residue.

I sat up and ran my fingers through my hair. Something dribbled between them, bounced off my shoulders and fell to the seat. Bits of glass glinting in the stroboscopic light. The cabbie's gaze darted from the road to the mirror and back. I brushed the glass to the floor, returning the cabbie's glances with an expressionless mask, and turned my face to the window. Broken glass and bloodstained pants were real enough.

Ten minutes later, the cab dropped me in front of a modern tan concrete and glass building at the base of Queen Anne. Staggered balconies protruded from the upper floors like giant steps. A few lighted windows stood out like yellow teeth in a gap-toothed smile. A banner outside the front door proclaimed furnished and unfurnished apartments for rent, but the street number on the scrap of paper matched another entrance several yards away.

Bright light from the lobby spilled through double sets of glass doors. Inside, a man in a blazer sat in profile behind a curved reception desk, the marble counter in front high enough to obscure all but his head and shoulders. Light flickered across his face from an unseen television screen. I opened the outer door and stepped into the airlock. The motion brought the man's head up. He glanced in my direction, his face masked with boredom, and turned back to the screen.

A telephone handset hung on one tiled wall alongside a panel of numbered buttons. I picked it up and stabbed a button with my finger, then stood and listened to the phone ring, once, twice. ... After five rings, I started to hang up, knowing it was far too late to be making social calls, when the handset clicked.

"Hello?" I said.

No one answered. Instead, the inner door latch clicked open with a loud buzz. Overcoming surprise, I grabbed the handle and pulled before the buzzing stopped and leaned back to hang up. The night concierge again acknowledged me with only a glance before turning back to whatever show had captured his attention. I gave a short wave on my way past to the elevators.

The elevator let me off on the sixth floor. I skirted around an open-air atrium and found the apartment. I hesitated in the hallway outside, wondering if this was a smart move. I didn't seem to have a lot of options. I rapped softly on the door, wishing it was Molly's.

CHAPTER 21

Keely Radcliffe opened the door a few inches, held it to her chest and peered through the opening.

"I'm sorry," I said. "It's late. I didn't know where else to go."

She stood barefoot in a pair of long navy straight-legged flannel pajama bottoms and a nylon warm-up jacket over a plain white cotton tank top. Her short blond hair was mussed, tangled spikes sticking up randomly.

She looked me up and down, her brows mingling in concern. "Why? What's happened? Are you okay?"

"Yeah, sure. I don't know. I ... I shouldn't have woken you."

"I was still up. No big deal. Come in, please."

She swung the door open to a small apartment furnished in comfortable modern, the straight-lined couch and easy chairs overstuffed to soften their angular planes, a smoked-glass coffee table atop a wrought iron base less harsh and industrial-looking than a chrome and clear version. Sliding glass doors leading to the balcony overlooked the dark expanse of Puget Sound and the flickering lights of houses and communities on the far shore, the black outline of the Olympics visible against the night sky beyond.

Gas flames shimmered behind glass in a corner fireplace. The only other light came from a shaded table lamp by the couch and lambent images playing across a flat-panel television on the opposite wall. An open book lay face down on the coffee table, an indented throw pillow leaned against the arm of the couch. A pair of half-frame reading glasses sat next to the book, a truer indication of her age than her girlish appearance.

She followed my gaze. "I have a little trouble sleeping. Reading relaxes me."

I put my hand up. "I shouldn't be here."

She reached out and gently grasped my wrist, eyeing my palm. "You're hurt."

I pulled my hand away. "It's nothing."

"You need to clean it. I've got some peroxide. Go rinse it under the faucet in the kitchen and I'll be right back."

She spun on her heel and disappeared through a door before I could object. I draped my jacket over the back of a chair and did as I was told. She emerged a minute later with a bottle of peroxide, cotton balls and a box of bandages. Leaning over the sink, she held my hand between hers under the running water and gently washed it with soap. She stood so close I felt the warmth of her body, sensed the lithe strength of it under the soft curves half-hidden by the loose-fitting clothes. I watched her long slender fingers work the lather carefully around the abrasion. She held my hand steady under the warm stream of water, rinsing away the suds, then wrapped it in a paper towel and patted it dry.

"You ready?" She unscrewed the top of the brown bottle.

I clenched my teeth and nodded.

She poured the peroxide over my palm. It bubbled and fizzed, its bark worse than its bite, the sting no more unpleasant than the ache in the knee or the scrape itself.

"Aren't you the brave soldier? Doesn't even look like it needs a bandage."

"Wouldn't stay on anyway. And it's nothing a stiff drink won't fix. Got anything?"

"As a matter of fact..." She circled behind me, opened a cupboard and pulled down a bottle of *añejo* tequila. "Will this do?"

"Perfect."

I shook the excess peroxide off my hand and dried it with the paper towel, then used it to daub the blood off my knee while she retrieved two glasses and carried them into the living room. She handed me a glass with a healthy splash in it when I joined her a moment later, lifting hers in salute. I took a sip. My hand trembled as I raised the glass to my lips. I lowered myself onto the other end of the couch. The tequila glowed in my stomach like an ember, warming me from inside out.

"What happened?" she said.

"Somebody tried to kill me."

"Your friend Perry?"

I shook my head. "Unless he hired a paramilitary group to get the job done."

I still didn't know why I'd come, why I thought I could confide in a woman I didn't know. Maybe because Wink Langford had irrevocably linked us through our past. Maybe because I was miffed at Molly.

I told her everything, starting with the picnic out at Clayt and Connie's house—the home invasion, Charlie getting shot, the lack of ID on the dead man—and ending with the serpentine escape from Capitol Hill after evading a posse of heavily armed men by breaking into the restaurant I'd just locked up.

She listened silently, feet tucked up under her. No wide eyes or gasps of surprise or fear. As if pitched gun battles were an everyday occurrence. Her calm demeanor gradually leached the tension out of me.

"Sounds like a drive-by," she said. "Street punks."

An image of the street racer shooting at me on the freeway flashed through my head. I briefly considered the possibility.

I shook my head slowly. "I don't think so."

"Could have been some gang mistook you for someone else," she said.

I wrinkled my nose, a corner of my mouth curling. "Hard to mistake me in a crowd. They weren't players or drug dealers."

"How do you know?"

I thought back, recalled the details. "The SUV—it wasn't some pimped out gangbanger's ride. More like government - issue. Black, nondescript, like a hundred others. The shooters were dressed in black, faces masked. Just like the commando types at Charlie's parents' place."

She turned and stared at the flames in the fireplace. "You think they're the same men?"

"Could be." I raised a finger to my lips and waggled it in the air. "That's another thing. Their weapons—that was automatic fire. *Brrrt, brrrt*, in bursts. Not *pop-pop-pop-pop* like semi-automatics. That's military hardware. Very hard to get.

127

Gangbangers don't use assault rifles anyway. Too big. Too conspicuous."

"Say you're right; why would they want to kill you?"

"If they placed me at Charlie's, maybe they want to get rid of witnesses."

"But you said you didn't see anything. Men in masks."

I threw my hands up. "I don't know. Just being thorough?" A shiver ran through me. "If so, Charlie's in trouble. They could try to get to him in the hospital."

She frowned. "He's a cop. Aren't his buddies in and out of there at all times of day and night?"

Not the same as a guard on the door of his room, but I saw her point.

An unrelated thought found its way out of my mouth. "Javier's place got really trashed. I need to let him know. I don't have his home phone, don't even know where he lives." Ironic.

Her eyebrows rose. "The restaurant? The alarm company probably already called him. The police, too, maybe."

"I have to make it up to him, make it right. Pay for the damage."

She watched me think it through, then expressed what Cole used to call a purple thought of her own. "What did you say those men wanted with—Charlie, is it?—Charlie's parents?"

She gripped her drink in her lap with two hands. It wasn't an affectionate squeeze.

"We don't know." I shrugged. "Could have been drug-related. Hard to say."

She looked at her hands and set her glass on the table. "It must have been a frightening experience."

"Twice in one week? I'm having trouble with bladder control."

A smile flashed across her face like sun poking through an overcast sky. Her eyes met mine, then slid past, shiny corneas reflecting the fluttering orange and yellow flames in the fireplace.

"I'm not sure what to do," I said after a moment. "I can't go home, can't go to work."

Her silence offered little help in weighing my diminishing options. A steer eyeing the chute into the packing plant, I considered a radical alternative.

I stood. "I need to make some calls. Would you excuse me?"

She looked up and nodded.

Michael W. Sherer

CHAPTER 22

I stepped into the kitchen and pulled out my cell phone.

Chance Reno answered with a cheery, "Hi, doll," after the third ring. His voice almost got lost in a background babble of voices and loud music.

"You're at the club. Are you working?"

"We finished the second show a while ago. Now I'm just hanging out with the 'girls,' ogling all the pretty boys in here tonight."

"Good show?"

"Mah-velous, darling. I'm doing Carol Channing these days. You need to come see it."

"Sounds like fun. Chance, I need to ask a huge favor."

"You want me to take your route tonight?"

"A couple of nights, actually. Something came up, and I'm going out of town for the weekend. Would you mind?"

"For you, doll, anything. Hope you got a hot date."

"Something like that."

"Come by when you get back. Peter and I want to hear all the juicy details."

"You're a lifesaver, Chance." I meant it literally.

Next I called Jeri's office number at the support group and left a long, detailed message asking her if she'd help find someone to fill in for me at the restaurant for the remainder of the weekend. Some of the younger volunteers who manned the suicide hotline often were eager to pick up some extra cash, and they were dependable. As I spoke, Keely quietly rose from the couch and disappeared into the bedroom.

I called the restaurant and left a message for Javier to tell him the bad men had come back, that I would pay for the damages, that I was safe, but wouldn't be at work for the next few days given the circumstances. I let him know that I'd arranged for a sub to take my place, and to call Jeri if he had any concerns. My apologies for bringing destruction to his doorstep sounded hollow, but then I didn't know why I was being targeted. Throwing a table through Javier's front window was on me, but I hadn't invited anyone to redecorate the place with lead.

I made one last quick call before I returned to the sofa and poured another finger of tequila into my glass. Keely's voice filtered through the closed bedroom door, loud, angry, punctuated by pauses, the words indistinct save for a snippet here and there.

"... insane? What ... *hell* ... thinking? ... No! ... you better ... I won't ..."

I gave up trying to listen in and sank back, exhaustion rolling over me as the adrenaline rush faded like an old memory. A few minutes later Keely emerged, mouth set in a grim line.

"Bad news?" I inclined my head toward the door she'd just come through.

She sighed and flopped onto the couch. "A little problem with work."

I raised my wrist. "Kind of late to be calling work."

"It's afternoon in Shanghai."

"What exactly is it you do?"

"Consultant."

That could cover myriad ills. "Any particular field?"

She lifted one shoulder. "Several. It doesn't really matter. Boring stuff, mostly. What about you? Did you get everything squared away?"

"I think so. I bought a little breathing room, I hope, until I sort things out."

She reached for her glass and took a sip, musing. "You know, the first time I saw you, you looked as if you thought you knew me."

"You reminded me of someone."

Her eyebrows arched. "Wife? Lover?"

Her words had a sharper edge than a blunt poker of curiosity, suddenly chafing me like a paper cut.

"Nothing like that."

The blond hair had thrown me the first time I'd seen her, the shaggy cut that had reminded me. Her features looked nothing like Cole, but in the dim light she suddenly seemed familiar in a way I couldn't define. She did remind me of someone; I just couldn't think of who.

She tucked her chin in and leaned back. "Sorry."

Too late. Like ice cracking on a pond, the paper cut widened and rived inward, snaking its way toward the deep chasm already carved out by Cole's death. The reverberations set off an avalanche of cascading emotions left over from the storms of the past week's events. The temblor rattled me from the inside out, shaking me uncontrollably until my teeth chattered.

Keely frowned and tipped her head sideways. "What's wrong?"

"I c-can't s-stop shivering." I grabbed opposite shoulders and held on tight.

She pushed herself up onto her feet and hurried into the bedroom, returning with a big duvet. She wrapped it around my shoulders and kneeled next to me, untied my shoes and pulled them off. Then she grasped the duvet with both hands and tugged at me.

"Here, come sit by the fire," she said. "It'll help."

I slid onto the carpet and shuffled toward the flames on my knees. She guided me to a spot a few feet away from the hearth, plumped a cushion under my head and straightened the duvet so it covered me, barely. My limbs trembled and my body shook with a palsy that left me breathless. I rolled onto my side facing the warmth of the fire and drew my knees up, clutching the down comforter under my chin. Keely rubbed my shoulders through its thickness, trying to stimulate some circulation.

"Are you getting warmer?"

"J-just can't stop shaking."

"Are you on something? Are these some kind of withdrawal symptoms?"

"N-not on drugs, d-damn it."

"Okay. Just asking. I don't need you dying on me."

"I'll b-be all right. T-too much all at once. Don't l-l-like being shot at."

She stood over me, her reflection in the glass doors of the fireplace watching me quake on the floor. She shrugged out of the warm-up jacket and tossed it on the couch. I turned my head to look up at her over my shoulder. She grasped the tank top by the hem and pulled it over her head, exposing a flat stomach and small breasts with rosy nipples that hardened in the chill air.

"What are you d-doing?"

"Shut up."

She pulled the pajama bottoms down to her knees, let them fall around her ankles and kicked them off to the side, leaving her in only a pink cotton thong. Bending and lifting a corner of the duvet, she slid in behind me on the carpet, wrapping the comforter around both of us. She pressed herself into me and wrapped her arms around my chest. Her fingers worked at the buttons on my shirt, helping me shrug out of the sleeves, then fluttered down the skin on my abdomen until they reached the waistband of my jeans. She deftly unfastened the belt and unbuttoned them.

Straining with the effort, I concentrated on controlling the shakes long enough to raise my hips off the floor and help her push my pants down over my rump. It was as much as I could manage before the tremors shook me so badly I couldn't hold my arms and hands steady enough to grip the fabric. Keely worked the pants down my legs and pulled them free, then snuggled into me and held me so tightly it was hard to draw a breath.

Gradually, the trembling subsided, leaving me drained and limp. Keely lay still, silent, but I became increasingly aware of her, of the heat that came off her skin in waves, radiating with more intensity than the fire's glow on my face. Suddenly, her touch ignited my skin as if I was soaked in kerosene, and I turned wordlessly into her arms, into lips that pressed themselves hungrily against my mouth, the tip of her tongue flicking against mine like a foil. Her fingers slid down my body and grasped me, guiding me to her center, already hot and slippery with ripeness, the filmy patch of fabric pushed to one side.

We consumed each other. I sopped up her heat and passion, her touch, like desert sand. Driven by hunger unlike any I'd ever known, I became aware of every movement, every breath, every heartbeat. She filled my senses, the scent and taste and feel of her becoming part of me, her body and its responses indistinguishable from my own, until I heard her tiny staccato cries of *oh! oh! oh!* at the same time I went over a cliff into a freefall of pleasure.

I had not been with a woman since my divorce from Molly. As Keely and I lay there, spent and exhausted, the fire quickly drying the sheen of perspiration that covered us both, guilt poked its hooded head out of a basket and fastened beady eyes on me. But to my surprise, it wasn't Molly's face I saw playing the *pungi*, it was Reyna's. Reyna, the naval intelligence officer I never expected to see again. Reyna, who'd saved me and then gone back to her life in D.C. My mind raced in confusion.

Keely was fast asleep when I wriggled out of her loose embrace more than an hour later to find my clothes. Her naked body posed languidly half on and half under the tangled comforter, a fistful clasped to her breast. I dressed quietly in a corner of the living room, retrieved my jacket from the chair in the kitchen, and tiptoed out the apartment door, easing it shut behind me.

Gray light on the street in front of the building and the sound of birds signaled the approaching dawn. I zipped the jacket, hunched my shoulders against the early morning chill and waited.

Michael W. Sherer

CHAPTER 23

A cab glided quietly to the curb, one of the newer hybrids, tires softly crepitating on the sand and grit collected in the gutter. The driver rolled down the passenger window, leaned across the seat and asked the great existential question—was I Sanders? Nodding, I climbed in back and told him to take me to the airport. I craned my neck for a glance up at the dim glow coming from Keely's apartment window, then turned my face and thoughts firmly forward.

Ninety minutes later I waited at a gate for a 6:10 a.m. flight out of Sea-Tac, a new overnight bag on the floor next to me packed with shirt, slacks, socks, briefs and toiletries freshly purchased from airport stores at even bigger mark-ups than traditional retail. The thought of all the times a time a sales clerk had run my card, depleting my savings, made me wince, but this qualified as an emergency.

I'd simplified my life since Molly and I had split, discovering I could actually live on what I earned delivering papers and washing dishes as long as I bought clothes at Goodwill and augmented my food budget with meals at the restaurant. Some of my asceticism had been necessary; Molly'd gotten everything in the divorce, and in a scandal I'd lost my well-paid job as a public affairs consultant in a scandal. The rest was my choice, a conscious effort to make a smaller footprint and keep out of the world's way in general. Recently, I'd added a cushion of financial safety to my bank account, thanks to Midge Babcock's largesse and a grateful government. I still chose the relative anonymity and quiet of the graveyard shift. Trouble was, I could run, but it seemed I couldn't hide behind the black cloak of night.

Colorful flotsam ebbed and flowed through the terminal, swirling in eddies and currents as travelers made their way to and from flights. The kaleidoscopic scene melded individuals until they became faceless, indistinguishable, something more amorphous. That elderly overweight couple at the ticket counter appeared the same as the one sitting in front of the windows overlooking the tarmac —down to the Hawaiian shirts on the gentlemen and the poodle-cut blue hair on the ladies. The young brunette with the stroller by the trashcan resembled the one on the moving walkway, who looked eerily similar to another in line at the coffee shop across from the next gate down the terminal. A herd of businessmen in dark slacks and dress shirts stood around the waiting area in various poses, some with newspapers, a few with cups of coffee, several peering intently at smartphones. Others appeared to talk to themselves or imaginary friends. A turn of their heads revealed the earpieces that connected them electronically to the rest of the world. They sported the bright bits of metal and plastic like diamond stud earrings, a fashion statement that came and went in the '80s, reserved now to hip-hop and Hollywood stars on awards nights.

Memory seemed such a fickle construct. It should have been easy to blend in, to disappear. *Is that man at the counter the same one who stood two sinks over as I washed my face in the restroom earlier?* Change the way you dressed, dye your hair, grow a beard, adopt a limp and friends might pass by on a busy street without a glimmer of recognition. *Had Wink done that? Or Clayt and Connie?* Maybe people really couldn't be found if they didn't want to be. Or, more likely, maybe it was a matter of finding a place where people didn't pay attention.

* * * * *

Sleep was another capricious concept. Tired as I was, airplane seats weren't constructed for comfortable catnaps. Even if my knees hadn't dug into the seatback pouch in front of me as if searching for a safety card or barf bag, and even if beverage carts passing by in the aisle hadn't threatened to break my elbow, my brain wouldn't shut off. I tried not to think about Keely, about what our frantic and needy coupling meant, or why, if it had been a mistake, we'd repeated the performance. I tried not to think about the taste of her skin, the scent of her hair... Instead, I focused on who wanted me dead and why. Running down the list of possibilities took all of thirty seconds. I had no clue. I closed my eyes and let my brain do what it did best—wander.

The connecting flight out of Salt Lake got into St. Louis a little after one-thirty local time. By two in the afternoon, I sat wedged in a small rental car headed south from the airport, already sweating in the new clothes. Recent thunderstorms had done little to wash any humidity from the air. The wet road now steamed under a hot sun. I turned the air conditioning on high and aimed all the vents in my direction. Fifteen minutes later I turned the fan down a few notches and caught an interstate east toward a place I once called home.

Centralia, Illinois, hadn't changed much. More fast -food restaurants and newer strip malls on the outskirts of town, but time had stood still downtown. Century-old brick buildings dominated the main streets, the old carillon tower in the park rising high above the treetops. Substitute old jalopies or horse-drawn buggies for the late-model cars and recreating a bygone era would have been easy. Pressed for time, I drove straight to the library, navigating from memory, making only one wrong turn.

The Langford house turned up in an online search of property tax records under the name of a trust. Wink's parents, Harry and Mavis, had set it up so the place would still be there for Wink when he got out of prison. The named trustee was James Holden, of the firm Holden, Skaar and Apley, LLP. A phone book look-up placed the law firm's offices on Broadway only a few blocks away. I left the rental in the library lot and walked.

A breeze brought some relief from the warm day, snapping the flags flying out front and rustling leaves, some still tinted with the light green blush of spring. The air had the weight of a Midwestern summer day, a humid blanket that induced lethargy as effectively as a dose of lithium. As kids on such days we rode our bikes to one of the diners or drive-ins for sodas, to the pool to cool off or over to Raccoon Lake to fish and dangle our bare feet in the water. As teens we found relief from the heat in the air conditioning and dim interiors of the movie theater or the bowling alley up the road in Sandoval.

Sometimes Wink would hitch his dad's seventeen-foot runabout with the Evinrude 90 outboard motor to an old Willys Jeep and take it over to Lake Centralia, where we'd water-ski. Never content to impress the girls with just decent skiing, Wink had converted an old army-navy surplus parachute into a sort of paragliding wing he used to do aerial stunts behind the boat on a short slalom ski. Years ahead of the kiteboarders on the Hood and Columbia Rivers or kitesurfers in California and Hawaii.

My prowess on a slalom ski didn't match Wink's. I wasn't as keen on trying his jury-rigged contraption. But I could carve turns that threw up a fifteen-foot wall of water and laid me out with my shoulder only inches above the glassy surface, so close I could take one hand off the towrope and let my fingers trail in the water. Or catch enough air jumping the wake to make it over the wash before touching down in the curl outside the other wake. Showboating had landed me in trouble on more occasions than I cared to remember. Never Wink. Always me.

Once, with me in tow, he buzzed a group of guys in another boat—Chuck and Ray from the football team, who we didn't care for all that much, and two of their coterie I recognized but didn't know. They laughed and shouted at Wink as he passed, their words lost in the wind rush of the wind and roar of the outboard. Wink yelled something back, and Chuck flipped him the bird. Seeing a chance to promulgate the supremacy of roundball players over pigskin lovers, I quickly skied across the wake, and cut back just before I reached them, carving a rooster tail that drenched their boat. Glancing back over my shoulder to see their reaction, I caught an edge and went ass over teakettle. I came up seconds later sputtering and wiping water out of my eyes.

Chuck fired up the boat, a cloud of blue smoke billowing from the stern, and rammed it into gear. His cronies pinwheeled backward and nearly went overboard as the boat quickly planed and hurtled toward me. It grew steadily larger until Chuck and the guys were no longer visible over the looming hull. Frantically, I fumbled with the clips on my jacket, slipped out of it and went under feet first, using a powerful arm stroke to push me toward the bottom of the lake. With a churning buzz, the water above me boiled white as the boat zoomed over my head. I kicked to the surface gasping for breath, head wildly spinning to see where the boat had gone.

Chuck wheeled it around in a big circle, his crew lined up along the gunwale, eyes hungrily focused on me. Wink came around at a right angle, and now both boats rocketed toward me, playing a game of chicken. With me as the chicken. They bore down, neither willing to give way, closer, faster. I floated, frozen with fascination as much as fear as they rapidly closed the distance. *Fifty yards, now forty, thirty...* Wink laid on an air horn, the long blast startling Chuck and his passengers. The bow of Chuck's boat wobbled then turned hard starboard as Wink flashed by between us.

Wink throttled back, the runabout immediately slowing and settling in the water. He spun the wheel and gave it some gas, the little boat pirouetting on its stern. Chuck came around, too, and idled toward Wink.

"Are you out of your freaking mind?" Chuck shouted. "You nearly fucking got us killed!"

"You nearly killed Legs," Wink said.

"Not even close," Chuck said, shaking his head. "Just wanted to scare him."

"You ran right over him!" Wink said.

"Must've missed." Chuck jerked his head in my direction. "He's still got his head above water."

"C'mon, let's take him!" Ray said. "Kick his skinny ass."

The two goons standing in the stern crowded forward, nodding and salivating like pit bulls. Wink and I should have had a spotter in the boat for skiing. An ally would have evened the odds a little, maybe given Chuck and the boys pause, though I wouldn't have been much help from where I sat treading water. But we didn't have a third man. Wink rarely followed the rules. And I usually followed Wink.

Wink raised a flare gun and leveled it at Chuck's boat. "Don't even think about it."

"You wouldn't dare," Ray said.

"Try me," Wink said.

Chuck elbowed Ray in the ribs. "Shut the fuck up, asshole. He could blow us up with that."

"He's bullshitting you, man," Ray said, his voice now a whine.

"Langford's crazy enough to do it, you moron."

"He-e-re's Johnny," Wink said, face splitting into a grin.

He squeezed the trigger. With a loud pop, a streak of light flew over the other boat, causing all four to duck and cover. The flare streamed out over the lake leaving a trail of blue-white smoke and landed in the water with a hiss. Wink quickly snapped open the breech, loaded another shell, and raised the gun again. With his free hand, he spun the wheel and maneuvered closer to me, holding the gun steady.

"Get in," he said.

I didn't need to be told twice. Once in the boat I leaned over the gunwale and fished the orange jacket out of the lake as it bobbed by.

"I'd leave it alone, boys, if I were you," Wink said. "Wet's better than dead any day."

He goosed the throttle, spun the wheel, and got us out of there. I reeled in the towrope and joined him at the wheel.

"Thanks," I said loudly over the engine noise.

He shrugged.

"What about the ski?"

His grin widened. "We'll come back later and look for it. If they take it, no big deal—I'll get another."

Skiing done for the day, we motored back to the boat launch.

CHAPTER 24

I stood on the sidewalk in downtown Centralia, the weight of the afternoon sun shortening me by an inch or two. As the reverie faded, a big plate glass window loomed in front of me painted with the word "Antiques" in large, gilt-edged green letters. Next door a clothing boutique sported headless mannequins in the front window dressed in fashions designed to appeal to matronly Midwestern women. A glass door stood between the two storefronts, a row of buzzers on the wall next to it. The street number stenciled on the glass matched the address I'd written down. A nameplate next to one of the buzzers confirmed it was correct. I pushed the button. A moment later the door buzzed.

Stairs led to a second-floor hallway. I guessed and turned left. Halfway down the hall a solid wooden door with brass numbers beckoned. I turned the knob and pushed through it to find myself in a small vestibule dominated by a reception desk and two chairs flanking a small side table papered with magazines—*Field & Stream, Sports Illustrated, Illinois Game & Fish, Newsweek.*

A woman with a pinched face and jet-black hair in a shoulder-length flip eyed me over the top of half-frame cheaters from behind the desk. A colorful rope of beads dangled from the earpieces and looped around her neck. Fingers with brightly painted nails hovered over a keyboard on the desk. The pink cardigan draped over her shoulders made me conscious suddenly of the air-conditioned chill.

"Help you?" she said.

"Is James Holden in?"

A shuffle of papers sounded through an open door over her left shoulder.

She tucked in her chin and frowned. "No, he's not."

I shifted my weight. "Do you expect him?"

She pulled the glasses off her nose and let them dangle on her ample bosom. "May I ask what this is in reference to?"

A deep voice rumbled unseen from the office behind her. "I'll handle this, Margaret."

I smiled politely and trained my eyes on the open door. A small mountain hove into view. The man's girth was so large it pushed his arms out to the sides, making him resemble a pyramid on stout pins. A couple yards of red suspenders over a starched white shirt held up voluminous pleated gray suit pants creased sharply enough to cut paper. A large head capped with short-cropped salt-and-pepper hair sloped from little round ears down to the shoulders, sagging jowls giving him the sad visage of a bloodhound. The man twisted to one side and eased through the doorway.

"James Holden is my father," he said, extending a hand. "Been retired for some time. I'm Jeffrey Holden. And you are ...?" He peered up at me and his eyes widened. "I'll be damned. Blake? Blake Sanders."

His recognition stirred old memories. A familiar face slowly emerged through the corpulence. Jigglin' Jeff, butt of schoolyard jokes and the one guy who could lift your spirits if you ever got to feeling sorry for yourself. I expected a soft, doughy handshake, but his grip was steely, unyielding. I'm big enough to comfortably palm a basketball, but it felt like trying to wrap my fingers around a catcher' mitt.

"What's it been, twenty years?" Still firmly grasping my hand, he clapped me on the shoulder and pivoted a half-turn, pulling me toward his office. "Come on back."

He indicated a chair on the way in. "Have a seat. Tell me why you're here. No, wait. Let me guess. Wink Langford." He leaned over the open newspaper on his desk and cocked his head.

"How'd you know?" I said.

He lowered his bulk into a chair. "How's your mom? Oh, right, you haven't been to visit, and she wouldn't recognize you if you did. And how about what's-her-name? The cutie you had a crush on junior year. Ellen. Wait a minute. She married a college professor. Lives down in Carbondale now. Has three kids. Oldest just graduated. Going to Michigan State, I heard. Me? I'm doing fine, thanks for asking. Took over the firm—" He leaned to his left, looked past me and raised his voice. "How long ago did Dad retire, Margaret?"

Margaret's boredom floated in on her answer. "Six years next month."

"Six years ago," he said to me. "Business is booming. Bankruptcies, foreclosures, wills, DUIs ... Signs of the times, I suppose."

I looked around the dark wood-paneled office, two three-pound bass and a big trout mounted on the walls along with framed degrees from a couple different of universities, the big oak desk with a brass lamp, leaded glass-fronted bookshelf holding a leather-bound set of law books, an expensive putter leaning against the windowsill, a half-dozen shiny white golf balls on the thick Persian carpet next to it.

He sighed and peered at me. "You still with me? What did you use to call it? 'Daydream dues?'" His voice shifted to a falsetto. "'Pay attention, Sanders.'"

"You remember all that stuff? I can't remember what I had for breakfast yesterday."

He smiled. "The point is I can't think of one damn reason for you to come back here after all this time except Wink."

"Wink always managed to get me to do what he wanted."

"He told you to come?"

I shook my head. "I need to know where he is, Jeff."

His eyes narrowed. "Why should I tell you something I won't even tell agents of the federal government?"

"Because I'm *not* one of them."

"I could hide behind attorney-client privilege, but I don't need to resort to legalities. I don't know where he is."

"If you had to guess where he might be...?"

He picked up a pen with both hands and rolled it between his fingers, then lifted it to his nose and sniffed. "I'd kill for a good cigar. Doctor says a good cigar will kill me." He held the pen up. "This just isn't the same. Dad once told me an interesting story about that night. He said Langford told him someone else was with him, someone who might have been able to corroborate his story. Someone who might have seen the men responsible."

He spoke as if the bombing had happened the week before, his words stripping away the intervening years like some trick of quantum mechanics. Bend the fabric of the space-time continuum like *this*, and—*voila!*—you're nineteen again. Holden's face was impassive, but his eyes glinted, ice chips reflecting winter light.

"That someone must have had good reasons for not coming forward," I said, shrugging. "If someone really *was* with Wink that night, maybe he didn't actually see what happened."

"People drift apart after high school, lose touch. You surprised me."

"Why? Because I found it easier to stay away than come home once I was gone?"

"People here looked up to you."

"I was flavor of the month on the latest Orphans roundball team to go to state. How many teams have gone since? Remember any of the kids on those teams? I'm a name on a plaque on a wall at the high school, that's all. Don't make me out like I was some big hero, Jeff. People didn't look up to me; I was just lucky enough to be on a winning team."

He stared at me and tapped the pen on his desk blotter. "Why the sudden interest?"

"Why do you think?"

He turned to look out the window. "You remember the raven's egg Wink hatched? What was that, eighth grade? Freshman year?"

Early spring one year, Wink had found an egg on the ground in the woods. Could have been bird, reptile or alien, Wink didn't care. Took it home and tucked it in his sock drawer with a desk lamp and thermometer and hatched the darn thing. Ground up birdseed, mixed it with water and fed the hatchling through an eyedropper. When the bird was old enough to fly, Wink brought it to the park. Tossed it in the air, watched it flap its wings on the way down and land with a thump. Finally it grew stronger, so that as it neared the ground, it built up enough air pressure under those madly flapping wings to stay aloft. Zooming along in the ground effect one day, the poor raven wandered into the path of an impromptu ball game, and flew right over home plate. The bird made too tempting a target. The kid at bat took a swing at it. Killed it instantly.

Holden swiveled toward me. "Toby Schneider. Dumb schmuck. Langford waited three, four years to get even. Remember? And he was careful not to do anything that could cause him real trouble if he got caught. Didn't poison Schneider's dog, or set his house on fire. Didn't beat him up, or have him killed. That might have been my personal choice if I thought I could get away with it."

I frowned, wondered if my memory was that faulty, that full of holes. "What happened?"

Hairy black caterpillars over his eyes marched toward each other. "Maybe it was longer than I thought. You might not have been here." He tugged at an ear. "First hard freeze of the winter, Langford went over to Toby's late at night and hosed down his car."

I raised a finger. "I did hear about this. Not from Wink, though. He never said a word. Someone must have told me when I was back on break. Stick, maybe, or Bud."

Jeff nodded, chin disappearing into the roll of fat below it each time his head bobbed. "Froze the car solid. Encased it in a block of ice. Coated it with enough ice the first time to make it impossible to open the doors. Went back a few more times after that. Toby couldn't drive it until spring."

I rested my cheek on the back of my knuckles, stared at the carpet for a moment. "Wink's got a long memory is what you're saying."

Michael W. Sherer

CHAPTER 25

"Take it however you want," Holden said. "I'm just reliving some old times, chatting about a mutual acquaintance."

I knew better. Wink was eidetic, his recall nearly photographic.

"I really need to find him, Jeff."

"What for?"

"Just talk. See what he knows."

"About the bombing? He's had twenty years to think about it. Research it. File requests with the DOJ under the Freedom of Information Act. I'd say he's pretty much an authority on it by now. Probably knows more than anyone. Including the investigative team." He paused. "So what happened? You get a visit from the FBI?"

I nodded. "They think I know where he is."

His jowls rose as he smiled. "I'm surprised. You sort of slammed that door shut tight, didn't you? Don't suppose you ever looked back until now. But I guess they had to at least try, given the history between you two."

"Someone else is looking for him, too."

His eyes widened. I told him about Keely.

"Might be better if I got to him before the FBI," I said. "And maybe Keely can help him, since she was the girl's sister."

"I'm not sure what advantage that gives him." He frowned. "I might just advise him to lay low. If he called and asked, that is."

"I thought he violated parole."

He waved a mitt. "Minor. He did his time. They released him a month early for good behavior. Technically he's AWOL, but really... The feds are just pissed they don't know where he is."

"The two agents who paid me a visit thought he might be in my neck of the woods. Bearing a grudge."

"A grudge? Now why would Wink do that? Just 'cause you bailed on him?"

I shifted in the chair. "What do you mean?"

"Where've you been all this time? You were around that summer. I remember seeing the two of you. Never saw you again after the bombing—until now. I thought friends stood up for each other."

I breathed a little easier. "Like you said, things change after high school. We go our separate ways."

"You didn't even show at the trial. Hell, half the town was there at some point in the proceedings. Not you. Conspicuous by your absence. Bunch of other kids in our class took time off from school to show a little support. Or gawk, depending. But they were there."

Heat climbed into my face like mercury creeping up a thermometer. "I was two thousand miles away. In school, on a scholarship. And if you remember, my old man blew a gasket end of senior year. We weren't exactly rolling in dough. Even with help from the grandparents, my mom was just squeaking by. Not like I could afford to just breeze in for the weekend, Jeff."

He rubbed his cheek. "I suppose you're right. It's just ... you and Wink seemed so tight. Like you'd never not be friends."

"Kind of tough to hang out with someone in jail."

"I managed."

I blinked. "You stayed in touch?"

Those big shoulders rose and nearly covered his ears. "I went to visit now and then. Passed on the latest gossip, books, and homemade cookies from his mom. Brought him things he asked for. He got a degree in there. Was working toward a master's."

I shook my head. "I didn't know."

"He's a smart guy. Always was. Guess he figured he'd still have a life ahead of him when he got out, so he worked hard. Studied. Never gave up."

It dawned on me I'd never considered what Wink might or might not have done in prison. I'd bricked up that wing of my life, gone on to build elsewhere.

"You never presumed he did it?" I said.

"Speculated once or twice, I suppose."

"Hard not to, based on the evidence."

"Exiguous, at best, though compelling. But I never really believed he did it, no."

"Not even by accident?"

"You knew him. Think he'd make that big a mistake? Not likely."

"Why'd you help him? Go see him and all? He didn't exactly go easy on you when we were kids."

He tented his fingers over his huge belly and touched the tips to his lips. "A lot of our schoolmates said and did hurtful things, spiteful things."

"Kids were mean to you. Cruel, even."

"People still are." He turned his palms out. "I mean, look at me. Easy target. I'm—"

"Fat. Huge. Morbidly obese. An example of why our health care system is so expensive." It came out before I could filter it, a sign of how long I'd been off my meds. "Sorry, Jeff. You were chubby before. You've gotten big as a house."

He smiled. "Not quite what I was going to say, but close enough. But Wink was an equal opportunity joker. Sure, he teased the geeks and the fatties, but he punked the cool kids and made fun of himself, too. I never minded the grief I got from Langford. The Chuck Bannocks and Sarah Fosters of the world were the ones who got under my skin. They had it all—looks, talent, friends. They needed to dump on people like me? What was the point?"

"Looks like things turned out all right for you."

"Hunky-dory. Better than they did for Wink. A little time with him always reminded me of that fact. And it seemed such a small thing, a few hours out of a Saturday once in a while."

"So where is he?"

"I don't know."

"All that time you spent with him, he didn't confide in you? Tell you his plans when he got out? Say where he thought he might go?"

Again his ears almost disappeared as his shoulders rose and fell. "No."

"But you saw him when he got out."

His eyes flicked away, then back to my face.

"I thought so. He told you where he was going."

His head swung back and forth like an old bull's. "Not true, and whatever he may or may not have said is privileg—"

"Bullshit. You're not his lawyer, are you? You're the attorney for his parents' estate."

"And by extension, Wink."

"Nice try."

He pursed his lips. "Fine. He came by to claim his inheritance. That's it. I went over the estate with him, he signed the papers, and he left, reasonably better off than when he came in."

"What else?"

He stared at me, silent for a moment.

"You were among the few people who didn't tease me as a kid," he said.

"Guess I was one of those who figured there was no point."

"No, I like to think you had a little empathy, *Legs*. Or did you prefer 'Spaz'?"

My turn to shrug. "Whatever."

"I can't tell you where he went. I honestly don't know. But one of the things his parents left him was a piece of property up in Washington."

The words sank in slowly. "My Washington? Washington State?"

"His grandfather on his mom's side had a fishing camp on Hood Canal. Wink said he had good memories of the place from family vacations as a kid. Apparently, it was a little too rustic for Mavis, and they only went back once or twice more. But Wink said he remembered it being quiet, peaceful. A beautiful spot, near the water. Lots of trees. The Olympics practically in the back yard."

I thought I'd known Wink pretty well. Now I wasn't so sure. Either he never told me about his trips to Washington or my memory was playing tricks. Then again, maybe it was one of those things that never registered. Maybe he and his family had taken their vacations around the same time mine went camping in Wisconsin and we never got around to comparing notes.

"Why go out there?" I said. "Why not stay here?"

"He said it sounded like a good place to get acclimated to the world again. Slow and easy. He didn't actually say he was going there."

"You don't think he went after the people responsible for the bombing?"

"I imagine he's contemplating it. Wouldn't you?"

"I don't know what I'd do. I'd want to put it behind me."

"Tough when you don't think you should have been there in the first place."

"But he was there." I paused. "Did he ever suggest a different chain of events? An alternate ending?"

"He kept his theories to himself. But he seemed to be fixated on the group that briefly claimed responsibility before recanting."

"E.L.F.? I heard investigators went down that road and hit a dead-end."

"He always thought there was something more to it, but I don't know what he found out."

"Not likely there are too many people left with first-hand knowledge of what happened."

He didn't respond.

We tried some small talk after that, quickly relating our C.V.s to each other, comparing notes on how life had treated us so far. Even a few reminiscences about high school couldn't prevent the conversation from devolving into an uncomfortable pretense that we'd ever really been friends. I stifled a yawn, exhaustion creeping over me. I soon made excuses, thanked him for the information, and left.

With no burning sense of nostalgia, no maudlin desire to recreate the past, I skipped a tour through the old neighborhood and a look at the house where I grew up. Instead, I got back in the rental car and drove down to Carbondale, found a motel on Main Street less than ten minutes away from the SIU campus, and checked in for the night. Body clock totally thrown off by the time change and sudden switch to a daylight schedule, I walked to a nearby restaurant, ordered takeout and took it back to the room. I wolfed it down and tumbled into bed.

CHAPTER 26

"Well?" he said. "Have you gotten anything from him yet?"

Keely's hand shook as she raised the glass of wine to her lips and took a sip, thoughts scrambling for a way out of this. She came up empty.

"No," she said. "Not yet."

"Why not? I'd have thought he'd be no match for your feminine charms."

Her face burned. *Was he having her watched?* "Is that what you expect? You think I'll just fuck him and he'll tell me what I want to know?"

"No need for that kind of language. You should have a little more self-respect."

"Sounds like you're the one who doesn't respect me. I've got a brain."

"Then use it."

She heard the sharpness in his voice through the phone and blinked back—no, she wouldn't even consider it. She swiped at her eyes with the back of her hand. *Had it always been this way? Jill had gotten all the attention, all the praise growing up. And then she was gone. What about her? What was so wrong with her that no one gave her the credit she deserved?* She took a breath and calmed her nerves, fighting back the emotion that welled up in her chest. She was a grown woman, for heaven's sake. It was ancient history.

"I've done everything you asked. *I'm* the one who found the first one on the list."

"But you haven't yet found the ones really responsible," he said. "*I* did that."

"And look what happened; they got away. I'm telling you, Sanders can lead us to Langford, and Langford will tell us where they are."

"So, *do* it."

She swallowed hard. He'd find out anyway. He always seemed to know what was going on before even she did. "I don't know where Sanders is."

"I thought he was there with you."

"He was. Don't worry, I'll find him. He's around. I just have to track him down."

"See that you do." The sharp tone was back in his voice. "I still say he's a liability, a loose end we should deal with."

"Have you seen the news? Half the police in the city are looking for the crew that shot up the restaurant the other night. They think it's related to the cop who was shot."

"The police don't know anything, not even who the target was. Don't worry. They're good men. They won't get caught. And if any do, no one can connect them to us." He paused. "Find this man, Sanders. Quickly."

* * * * *

The next morning, after a complementary breakfast of a desiccated sweet roll and thin, insipid coffee, I made my way over to the campus and found the administration building. I didn't hold out a lot of hope of finding anyone at school on a Saturday, but a young woman with a short utilitarian haircut and a pleasant demeanor offered to help. When I explained what I wanted, she roped in a student tour guide who normally would have shown applicants around campus and assigned him to me. Clean-cut and Midwestern wholesome, he tackled his mission cheerfully.

Stepping into the June sauna triggered old memories. In the hazy sunshine of early summer, color brought the campus to life, a picture postcard of bucolic academe, nothing like the photo negative the last time I'd seen it. Ponderous, muggy air portended thunderstorms. The heat sapped my energy, but my guide Alex didn't seem to mind. He kept up a steady patter of factoids and tidbits garnered from university puff pieces, throwing in enough personal anecdotes and campus myths to give the spiel his individual spin without straying too far from an admissions office script. My brain tuned out.

"You play ball?" he said on a path between buildings. "You look like a ball player."

The question brought me back from somewhere far away.

"A long time ago."

"Tough season this year. You an alum?"

"No, just doing a little research."

He nodded. Sensing the tour was wasted on me, he limited his comments after that to highlights.

The engineering complex soon came into view across the main road that circled campus, just the way I remembered it. The building's scars, though, had faded as if that night had never happened. Holes rent elsewhere by the bomb's blast hadn't healed so quickly. Alex led me through the door and into another memory. The door hadn't opened to my will back then and disgorged my friend Wink instead of the skulking figures in black that still haunted me. The dim interior was cooler than the blast furnace outside, but marginally so, the still air humid and close. Alex wound his way through the hallways and up two flights of stairs, navigating with the confidence of someone who knew right where he was going. He stopped suddenly outside an open office door. The room was occupied, so after I assured him I could find my way back to my car he left me there.

A short, grizzled fireplug of a man stood with his back to the door in front of a wall-mounted white board. All rough-hewn facets, with square jaw, a brush of steely gray hair cut in a flattop and broad shoulders, he looked more engineer than engineering professor. Thick arms bristling with dark hair sprouted from a short-sleeved, button-down shirt tucked into cargo shorts. Stout matching legs were stuffed into hiking boots infuscate like freshly dug Russets. Consulting an open textbook on a nearby desk, he jotted notes on the board with one hand, making corrections with an eraser in the other. I rapped on the doorframe, and his head whipped around at the sound.

"Yes?"

"Professor Waldron? I wondered if I could have a moment of your time."

"Does it have anything to do with coursework, grades or department meetings?" His jaw was set grimly.

"No. It's about—"

He erased the words with a wave. "Don't tell me. If it's not about school, by all means come in." The corners of his mouth turned up. Wiping his brow on a sleeve, he set the marker down and extended his hand. "Summer term starts in a week, which is why I'm cooped up in here outlining coursework, but it's bloody hell without the air conditioning."

I stepped into the office and introduced myself. "They said you're the department chair. I'm surprised you're here and not on vacation somewhere."

"I'm a teacher; I teach. Summer quarter actually is a lot of fun. More experiential. We get out and do more fieldwork."

"I'm glad I caught you. I understand you've been here quite a while."

He looked at me curiously and motioned to a desk. "What can I do for you?"

"I'm interested in the bombing here back in the '80s."

A cloud briefly darkened his face. "What's your interest? Doing a retrospective? You a journalist? I read they released the fellow who was convicted."

"You don't seem too eager to talk about it."

"It's history. It's not easy heading a department that's defined by a bomb blast twenty years ago instead of the work we do or the awards we win."

I shook my head. "I'm not a reporter, or a lawyer, either. I used to be friends with the guy." I explained why I was looking for Langford.

"He still says he's innocent?" Waldron ran stubby fingers through the short brush atop his head. "Figures."

"You think he did it?"

"No reason he couldn't have. And twelve of his peers said he was guilty."

"You were here back then. Can you tell me what you remember?"

He studied something on the desk, then turned his gaze back at me. "Shock, at first. We all were. No one could figure out why someone would want to blow up an engineering lab. It came without warning. We had no protests on campus, no burning issues. Not even any campus troublemakers beyond the usual fraternity high jinks. This is a pretty quiet place. We don't get the kind of radicals the bigger universities get, especially on the coasts. I hate to say it, but the small-town kids, the farm kids here are more naive. Besides, we're talking the '80s. What were people protesting then? Apartheid? Gay rights? Kids here didn't care all that much."

"Wasn't the bombing about the environment? Some group targeting coal research?"

"If I remember right, some eco-group—West Coast, I think—released a statement to the media listing a whole bunch of grievances. The group claimed they intended to destroy a coal liquefaction research project. Said it represented what was wrong with alternative energy policy in this country."

"They got the wrong lab."

"That's when shock turned to anger. At least mine did. They were so far off base, it's hard to believe they really meant to target coal research. The Coal Development Center where they run production-scale experiments is over in Carterville, and the research center itself is on another part of the campus. This is the engineering building. No way they could mistake the lab they destroyed for one experimenting with coal liquefaction."

"Do you remember what was going on in the lab that got blown up?"

His head bobbed. "Absolutely. That was Kwan Ji's lab. Korean guy. Brilliant. He was on the cusp of the nanotechnology revolution. The ground floor. Made some very promising discoveries while he was working with a defense contractor back in the mid-'80s, but apparently didn't like the people he was working for. We were lucky to get him."

"What was he working on at the time?"

"Battery technology. He was looking for ways to extend battery life. The Holy Grail these days. He was way ahead of his time."

I rubbed my cheek. "Here's what I don't get. Langford was a smart kid, at least when I knew him. He wouldn't have gotten the labs confused if he was working with the environmental group. And if he blew it up on his own, what was his motive?"

Waldron shrugged. "Did he need one? Maybe he just wanted to see if he could do it."

"I grew up with him, hung out with him. He loved a good prank. Blew up a lot of stuff, too. But not buildings."

He held up splayed fingers and ticked them off one by one. "He was found at the scene. Holding a gun. Carrying chemicals in his backpack. And traces of the type of explosive used were later found in his garage. Forensics said the blast was controlled. He used a calculated amount of explosive, probably in a shaped charge to limit the blast radius. Engineering-wise, a beauty of a job. Kid knew what he was doing. Or else he had help."

"Or he was in the wrong place at the wrong time. Didn't he say at the trial he saw other people running from the scene?"

"You're saying someone else set the bomb, and Langford just happened to be in the building. What about the dead girl?"

That was the part I'd tried to forget for twenty years. Hard to reconcile the Wink I knew with the image of him standing over a dead girl's body. But now I knew what had happened. One of the men who'd planted the bomb had heard the girl's screams, run back in the building and put her out of her misery, making sure, using two bullets, not one. I could picture it, Wink dazed and in shock from the blast, drawn to the sound of her cries of pain and then the *pop-pop* that silenced them, picking up the gun in disbelief after the assailant had run off. I'd known all along, but as a scared nineteen -year-old I'd been more willing to believe the evidence than in my friend.

"Say someone got the right lab after all," I said, changing the subject. "Why go to the trouble of blowing it up? What was so important?"

"The right...?" Waldron blinked. "Good question."

"I should probably talk to ... Ji?"

"Jim. We all called him Jim."

"Is he still around? Can you tell me where he lives?"

He shook his head, corners of his eyes turning down with his mouth. "He's dead. House caught fire about a week after the bombing. Middle of the night. Really tragic."

Michael W. Sherer

CHAPTER 27

The dead-end presented by Kwan Ji's untimely death sparked an internal debate that raged so intensely that it threatened to paralyze me with indecision. Another sure sign I'd been off my meds. The dissonance in my head offered one benefit—a surfeit of random notions, some crazier than others. A few of which germinated, took root, grew.

The campus library offered a distraction, a safe refuge from the pressure to decide a course of action, a valid excuse to procrastinate. A decision in itself. Wink looked more and more like he'd been a convenient scapegoat for someone. The question was who and why. I penciled some notes on a piece of scratch paper before they were trampled by the stampede of purple notions thundering through my head. For the next hour I cruised the Web, searching for anything I could find on the bombing, Kwan Ji, Sebastian Fitch, and the enigmatic Wilsons.

Kwan Ji got a mention in an encyclopedic entry on the history of nanotechnology, referencing pioneering work at West Coast defense contractor Ross Industries before his sudden departure to Southern Illinois. The Wilsons, Colin and Corinne, showed up in a monograph on nonviolent civil disobedience as a form of protest against the war in Vietnam. An example, to some, of the effectiveness of peaceful demonstration; the epitome of gutless cowardice to others. The hunt turned up no references to Fitch at all. Logic—the ADD kind, anyway—suggested a connection among them all, but I couldn't find one.

Eyes bleary from staring at the computer screen, I took a break and shoved back from the terminal. A reference librarian steered me to some books on the '60s. Those yielded a couple more notations on the minor roles the Wilsons had played at the two UWs—Wisconsin in 1968 and 1969 before radicals bombed Sterling Hall on the Madison campus, and Washington in 1970 during the riots in Seattle the day after the Chicago Seven verdict. Disillusioned, whether by the violent turn of antiwar protests or their own ineffectiveness, they skipped to Canada in 1971, joined Greenpeace and soon faded into obscurity. Again, nothing on Fitch.

I did, however, come across a photo in one of the books that stopped me dead in my tracks. Taken at Columbia University during the demonstrations in the spring of 1968, it framed black activists Stokely Carmichael and H. Rap Brown speaking to reporters in front of Hamilton Hall, site of the original student occupation. Clearly visible through the windows and doors behind them were black students who'd kicked SDS head Mark Rudd and the other white kids out of the building.

Vietnam hadn't been my fight, as a grunt or a protester. Frank Shriver was right; I'd been in diapers then. The war hadn't been my parents' fight, either, being older than demonstrators or soldiers heading overseas. I'd been a surprise baby, coming nearly ten years after my sister. My father might have been called up for duty in Korea except for the fact he'd been injured in the 1947 Centralia mine disaster that had claimed several of his relatives' lives. But the Vietnam era hadn't been such ancient history growing up in those turbulent times that the Black Panthers, Weathermen and Symbionese Liberation Army weren't familiar names.

What caught my eye, though, was the face of one of the students staring through the glass in the background. Most of them focused on the two black power leaders addressing the sea of microphones thrust at them. But one kid's attention was directed elsewhere in the crowd around Carmichael and Brown. As if looking for someone. I knew that face. I wracked my brain trying to remember where I'd seen it. Wondering why a forty year-old photo of a black kid in New York would seem remotely familiar. The connection, when I finally made it, elicited a laugh that drew a glare from the librarian and stares from the few patrons in the area. Mentally adding a mustache, a few wrinkles, and some gray hair turned the image of the kid into a dead ringer for FBI Special Agent Fred Drucker.

I gave up thumbing through tales of the excesses of youthful Boomers and traded the printed page for microfiche. With the librarian's help, I found boxes of film from the end of August, beginning of September, the year the bomb was set. The bombing remained front page news for a week after it happened, relegating the story of the house fire that killed Kwan Ji to an inside page. Sketchy details enumerated basic facts. A neighbor reported the fire shortly before dawn. By the time the first engine company responded, the house was fully engulfed. Two more trucks arrived, but all they could do was keep the fire from spreading. Two firemen were treated for minor smoke inhalation. The house was a total loss, and when the last hot spot cooled, two bodies were discovered in the ruins—Kwan Ji and his wife, Eun Joo.

I scrolled through another few weeks of issues before finding a follow-up article. Fire investigators from the city and the state fire marshal's office had determined a short circuit in the garage had caused the blaze, which had been accelerated by a can of gas and painting supplies nearby. They'd chalked it up to carelessness and called it an accident. I found it odd that an engineering professor, absent-minded or not, would leave a container of gasoline next to an electrical outlet, let alone overload the outlet.

I glanced at my watch, discovering I'd spent the better part of three hours in the library. I gathered the scraps of notepaper and shoved them into a pocket, then hurried across campus. I caught Waldron just as he left the engineering building. He acknowledged me with a nod, but didn't stop. I fell in step.

"You're back," he said.

"I thought of a couple more questions for you."

He grunted.

"What happened to Kwan's research project?"

"Nothing. It died."

"Why didn't someone take it over? Surely he left notes, protocols for experiments ..."

Waldron shook his head, gaze on the sidewalk in front of him. "Nope. Kept most of it up here." He tapped his temple with a forefinger. "The rest he carried around in a notebook. We never found it. It must have been destroyed in the blast."

Or the fire.

"No one else knew enough about what he was working on?"

"On a general basis, yes. But without his notes? Results of experiments? No way. The only person who might have been able to recreate what he'd done was his research assistant, the grad student who was killed in the explosion." He stopped abruptly and faced me. "Anything else?"

"Yeah, you said something about a shaped charge. Do you remember what kind of explosive was used?"

"C-Four."

"Military stuff."

"Looked like."

I started to think about that, but filed it away for later. "Thanks. Appreciate your help."

"Good luck." He turned and strode away.

The sun hammered down relentlessly on my head and shoulders, slowly beating me into submission, tenderizing exposed flesh, turning it pink. The cloying humidity plastered clothing to my body and left a damp sheen on my skin. I'd forgotten how oppressive summers could be in southern Illinois, had grown accustomed to the drier, cooler air of Seattle summers, a secret we kept from the outside world.

I thought of the potential risks that awaited me back home—trigger-happy commandos; a pissed-off former friend; a woman, not scorned exactly, but temporarily abandoned; a pair of unhappy federal agents; a disgruntled ex-wife; a wounded friend and his anxious sister. I considered staying, returning to the land of my youth, starting over. Plenty of people lived in one town all their lives. Many who traveled the world returned to their roots, settled down, contributed to the community, made their hometowns better places to live.

I climbed into the cramped oven of a rental car and turned over the ignition. A couple of passing students glanced through the glass, checking my degree of doneness. As soon as the air conditioning kicked in, rational thought returned. Whoever had tried to kill me wouldn't give up simply because I inconveniently changed locales. The clincher was the damn heat. It was bad enough to drive anyone loony. Carbondale, Centralia—there was nothing for me in those places anymore. I backed out of my parking slot, put the car in gear, and headed for the interstate.

CHAPTER 28

He swung the eight-pound maul high over his head and brought it down hard, hitting the log exactly where he'd aimed. With a satisfying *thunk* and a loud crack, he drove the head of the maul all the way through to the stump below, splitting the log cleanly. Turning the length that was left, he swung the maul again and split that, too. Though the sun hadn't yet burned through the overcast, he was shirtless, sweat running in rivulets down the center of his sternum and the hollow between his abs, tickling as it descended into the thin stripe of hair below his navel. Lean and wiry, Langford had never been in better physical condition. He smiled wryly. He'd had too much time on his hands in prison.

The work was mindless, physically satisfying, but he couldn't stop thinking about his quandary for long. He'd reached an impasse. He wasn't sure he could get anything else from the two people restrained in the cabin. They were wily, a little desperate, and both had lied through their teeth at various points in their confinement. He'd done his best to keep them separated ever since he'd abducted them, and the strain of being taken captive had taken a psychological toll. He hadn't given them a clue to his identity or a reason for kidnapping them. Short of physical torture, he didn't think he could chivvy anything more that might be useful. The question was whether he was willing to take that step, or, if not, what the hell to do with them.

He set another log on the stump and split it into thirds with three well-placed blows, feeling his muscles ripple from his calves up through his back, shoulders and out to his fingertips as he swung the maul. He carried the split logs to a neat pile between two trees and stacked them. As he walked back for more he felt his cell phone vibrate in the pocket of his jeans. Frowning, he pulled it out and looked at the display. The number was blocked. He'd shared the number with only one person. He opened the connection and held the phone to his ear without speaking.

"Perry, Jeff Holden here."

Langford silently breathed a sigh of relief. "Yes?"

"I'll keep it short in case anyone's listening. Legs was here. Looking for you."

"Sanders? What'd he want?"

"Said the Fibbies came and talked to him about you. I don't know where you are, and I don't want to, but thought you should know I told him about the old family vacation place."

Langford thought it through. He didn't have much time. If Legs came looking for him, God knows who might come waltzing in on his tail. It might be time to do something about that.

"You good?" Holden asked.

"Yeah, I'm okay."

"Don't hesitate to call if there's trouble."

"Thanks, Jeff, for the heads-up." Langford shoved the phone in his pocket, grabbed his shirt and strode purposefully back to the cabin.

* * * * *

A nonstop flight out of St. Louis put me in Seattle at around ten that night. I hadn't left the heat behind. A low-pressure trough had moved through the state and now hovered over Kalispell, Montana. High pressure had taken its place over western Washington, the combination sucking warm air up over the Pacific from the southwest. In the winter, it's called the Pineapple Express, bringing exceptionally wet, windy weather. In the summer, it brings humid heat. Uncharacteristic for June in Seattle, the temperature had topped out in the high 80s, according to the pilot's announcement when we landed. Records close to triple digits were predicted for Monday and Tuesday.

I took a cab into the city and directed the driver up Capitol Hill and down the street where I'd parked my car two nights before. It seemed like a week. I told the cabbie to drive slowly up the block, and checked the car for signs of a ticket or tampering as we passed. A few blocks up, I had him circle around and come down the street the opposite direction, this time looking for any signs someone was watching the car.

The cabbie dropped me off two blocks away, and I went back on foot. I passed the car without stopping, walking casually, but alert to the surroundings. Behind me, Broadway hummed with traffic, the sidewalks crowded with the usual mix of gays, Goths, gawkers and gourmands patronizing the restaurants and shops or just checking out the scene. The excess spilled over onto side streets, giving me plenty of company.

The warm weather had brought out more people than usual. Even in the dog days of summer, temperatures in Seattle rarely exceeded eighty-five degrees, and nights cooled down to comfortable levels quickly. Few people had air-conditioning, at least those in older houses and apartment buildings. Now many ventured out to avoid oven-like apartments. My gaze swung from parked cars to upper windows of buildings lining the street, open to catch any faint breeze. Seeing nothing unusual, I backtracked, unlocked the car, swung my overnight bag in the back seat and got in.

Saturday night. All dressed up with no place to go. And no date. My jaw shuddered in an attempt to stifle a yawn as a rising tide of exhaustion filled me. I leaned over and retrieved a spare bottle of meds from the glove compartment, popped a pill in my mouth and swallowed it dry. I turned over the engine and drove down to the warehouse in Ballard, stopping once to pick up a sandwich and coffee.

The trucks hadn't arrived from the printing plant yet, so I sat in the car and ate slowly. The lot gradually filled with cars. A couple of them were SUVs, but carrying only a driver, and none painted shiny black. Not long after, trucks pulled into the lot and jockeyed into position. Forklifts converged on the dock and off-loaded the papers, and men drifted from their vehicles toward the brightly lit building. I joined them and checked in with the shift supervisor for my route list, got a cart, and went to work.

My papers were almost assembled and ready to load when Chance showed up. Eyeliner still darkened his eyes, but he'd scrubbed the pancake off his face, revealing dark stubble along his jaw. Vinous polish covered his nails. A slender Vietnamese boy at another table eyed him from behind with a fey smile as Chance approached me.

"What are you doing here?" Chance said. "I thought you were out of town."

"Got in after ten. Thought I might as well work. Sorry I didn't call."

"Why didn't you?"

"I didn't want to bug you at the club, and wanted to see you anyway. Hope you don't mind."

He tilted his head. "You all right, doll?"

I sighed. "Been a long couple of days. I don't like spending that much time with an airplane strapped to my ass."

"Where'd you go?"

"Home."

He shook his head. "Oh, Blake, honey, don't you know Dorothy had it all wrong? There's no going back."

"I wasn't trying to relive my glory days. I was just trying to get a line on a guy."

"Switching teams?" The corners of his mouth turned up.

"You'll be the first person I call if I do. No, an old friend."

He glanced at the stacks of assembled papers. "So, you don't need me, then?"

"I do, actually. I'm running on fumes. I could use the help, if only to keep me awake."

Chance stepped up to the table, grabbed an armful of papers and laid them on the cart. I followed suit, and moments later we wheeled the cart out of the warehouse into the parking lot.

"My car or yours?" Chance said.

"Yours, if you don't mind." I didn't tell him why.

Still buzzed from working the club, he kept up a lively patter about the show. He'd changed it some, adding more stand-up, a couple of new songs, and it seemed to be working. Weekend crowds were bigger, Toji was selling more drinks, and everyone was happy.

"I'm surprised anyone in the club knows who Carol Channing is," I said. "Aren't they all a little young?"

"You've got to be kidding, doll. A: she was born here in Seattle. And two: she's one of the biggest gay rights supporters out there. You really did come from a turnip patch, didn't you?"

"Sorry. I didn't know. Cole was never into show tunes. Just sports."

It didn't make any difference whether Cole had been a fan of Barbra or Beckham. He was gone. The memory clawed at the inside of my chest. Chance threw a quick glance my way and motored on, chatting about nothing, yet everything that was important—friends, small triumphs, compassionate gestures, the business of everyday living. I was glad of the company. Chance drove, animatedly gesturing with alternate hands as the words tumbled out of his mouth. In the passenger seat, I folded and stuffed newspapers into plastic sleeves, read recipients' street addresses off to Chance, and tossed papers out the window.

The work went quickly with two people. I ticked off the addresses on the list until soon the end of the route was in sight. I couldn't avoid it any longer.

"You and Peter okay?" I said during a lull in Chance's monologue.

"Good. Why?"

I saw him shrug. "No excitement while I was gone?"

"The usual." He glanced at me. "What do you mean?"

"No one came looking for me?"

His head tipped and his eyes rolled. "Oh, that."

My shoulders tensed.

He put a fist in his mouth to stifle a yawn. "I'm sure you find it exciting—about time you got laid—but it's T.M.I. as far as we're concerned, Blake. I'm happy for you, but don't need the details of your love life, thanks."

"A woman named Keely?"

"That's the one. Wanted us to be sure to tell you she stopped by. Said she was worried about you. Something about not telling her where you were? I didn't tell her you were out of town."

"She gave you details?"

He shook his head. "Didn't have to. If she hadn't seemed so put out, she would have positively glowed. Morning-after regret, honey?"

I shook my head then stopped. "I'm not sure. She seems nice enough."

"But?"

I could have offered up one of half a dozen answers, but didn't know if any were right. Molly's face popped into my head, and again Reyna Chase's crowded it out, large dark eyes challenging me, full lips mouthing a soundless question. I said nothing.

"Maybe you're not ready yet," Chance said. "Or maybe you call this woman, apologize like a gentleman and see where it goes."

"Maybe."

We finished the route in silence. Chance idled at the curb after I tossed the last paper into a subscriber's yard. He sat hunched over the wheel.

"Where to?" he said. "Want me to take you back to get your car?"

I gazed out the window for a moment. "Nah, I'll cab over in the morning. Let's go home."

"Sounds good." He leaned back and gave the car some gas.

After a moment I said, "You haven't noticed anything else going on around the house?"

"Like what?"

"Strange cars hanging around out front. People lurking. Folks asking about me. Besides the woman. Anything out of the ordinary."

"Oh, my god, Blake, you're creeping me out. You're not in trouble again are you?"

"Just answer the question. Have you or Peter noticed anything weird? Anyone watching the house?"

"No. Not a thing. Other than your new girlfriend, it's been quiet. No weirdos pounding on your door or anything like that. No one skulking in the bushes late at night."

"You're sure? I just don't want anything to happen to you guys because of me."

"I'm sure. What's going on, Blake?"

"I don't know."

"What have you gotten yourself into?"

"It's complicated. It may have something to do with the cop who got shot last week."

"Your friend Charlie?" He glanced at me.

I nodded. "And she's not my girlfriend."

He rolled his eyes. "Whatever you say, doll."

I sat up straighter as we pulled onto the street leading to the house, senses on alert, watching for hulking black SUVs, silhouettes in car windows, early-morning pedestrians. The street was quiet, too late for clubbers and too early for the nine-to-five crowd. A pale blue sky tinged pink on the eastern horizon reflected pre-dawn light. Almost daybreak. Chance found an empty spot at the curb half a block from the house and parked. I got out and stretched while he retrieved costumes and a make-up kit from the back seat.

"Thanks for taking the route the past couple nights." I yawned hugely and followed him up the street.

"Glad to help. You know me; I can't sleep after a show anyway. Might as well put all that energy to good use making a little extra instead of partying all night."

"Well, money or not, you're a good friend to fill in."

Even in the pale light, I saw him blush. In the shadows ahead, sudden movement caught my eye and made me suck in a breath. I turned to look. *There!* A dark form slipped out of sight around the far corner of the house. Headed toward my apartment on the lower level.

I put a hand on Chance's arm. "Stay here," I said quietly.

Without waiting for a reply, I broke into a trot toward the house and pulled up at the corner.

I poked my head out for a quick glance down the slope toward the back. Nothing there. Cautiously, I slipped around the corner and down the hill. A dead broken tree limb lay on the grass by the fence. I picked it up and held it over my shoulder like a tomahawk. Hugging the side of the house, I peaked around the end toward my door. No one there. But a rustle and clatter came from the other side of the detached garage thirty feet away.

Pulling back out of sight, I opened my mouth wide and drew in a slow, silent breath. Chance tiptoed down the slope. Peeved, I waved him toward the side of the house and put a finger to my lips. The soft sound of footsteps shuffling on grass floated on the still morning air. Grasping the branch in both hands, I tensed. Now the sound breathing accompanied the footsteps as the figure labored up the slope. I sensed him, smelled him before the dark figure rounded the corner, and swung the heavy limb.

CHAPTER 29

A shriek rent the stillness and pierced my ears as Chance hit me from behind like a charging rhino. The collision felled me like a Douglas fir. I crashed to the ground, tangled in yards of hand-me-down high-fashion fabric and the slender limbs of my cross-dressing landlord. We rolled once down the slope and came to rest at the feet of someone in flip-flops and sweat pants. I spit out a mouthful of grass and dirt and looked up at the startled face of my other landlord, Peter.

"What are you two doing?" Peter hissed. "You'll wake up the whole neighborhood."

Chance sat up and unwound the dress wrapped around his torso.

"Are you okay?" I asked him.

He nodded. "You?"

"No harm, no foul." I got to my feet and gave him a hand, feeling a flush rise up my neck into my cheeks. "Thanks."

"For what?" Peter said, gaze turning from one of us to the other, nose wrinkling.

"Nothing," Chance said airily. His eyes narrowed. "What are you doing up so early?"

Peter sighed. "Damn heat. House never cooled off last night. I couldn't sleep."

"Time to spring for air conditioning, honey. What are you doing out here?"

"It's a lot cooler out than in. I've been sitting on the porch waiting for you. Figured I might as well do something useful. I was just taking out the garbage." He turned to me. "You're home."

"Got in last night—too wired to sleep and too tired to work the route by myself. Thanks for loaning me Chance for the weekend."

"I'm sure he was happy to help."

Chance pursed his lips and threw him a look. "*We* were happy to help."

"Yes, well, *we* have to go to work in a couple of hours."

"You're going to be a wreck today, aren't you, poor baby?"

"I'll manage."

Chance opened his mouth. I stepped on whatever he was about to say. "Thank you again, both of you. I'm turning in."

Their heads turned in unison, the same pleasant smile on both faces.

"Good night," Chance said sweetly.

"Good morning," Peter said, his smile souring.

I rounded the corner of the house down to my door wondering when I'd grown so paranoid I could nearly take Peter's head off with a length of dead wood.

* * * * *

Even with a fan doing its best to evaporate the glaze of perspiration coating me, the heat caused sleep to come in fits and starts, mottled by unsettling dreams. The sun's attempts to beat its way through the curtains an hour after I lay down pushed up the mercury in the thermometer like someone sucking it up through a straw. Shortly after midday, I gave up, rinsed off in the shower and threw on cargo shorts and a T-shirt. I cabbed over to Ballard, retrieved my car and headed north, careful to check for a tail. I threw in a few extra turns on the way just to be sure.

The front door of the small house in Shoreline was open, car in the drive. I walked up the steps to the porch, peered through the screen door into the dim interior and knocked loudly. Voices drifted faintly from the back of the house.

"Anyone home?" I called.

No answer. I knocked again and waited a few moments. When no one responded I opened the screen and stepped inside.

"Hello?" I walked toward the sound of voices. "Anybody here?"

The back door off the kitchen was open, too. The voices, louder now, came from the deck. I pushed the screen door open and leaned through the doorway. A small portable TV sat on the patio table in the shade, images of a baseball game flickering across its screen, announcer calling the play. A glass pitcher of lemonade beaded with moisture rested across from the TV, half-empty glass beside it.

"Don't move!" a voice said behind me. "Unless you're itching to get shot you'll want to raise your hands easy and place them on top of your head."

I did as I was told.

"Now turn around slow."

I did the turn. The cinder block on legs decocked the hammer of a semiautomatic handgun dwarfed like a toy popgun in his ham hock of a hand.

"Thought it was you from the size of you," Ned Collins said, tucking the gun in his waistband at the small of his back. "You shouldn't walk through a man's house unannounced. Especially an ex-cop's house. Could get yourself killed."

"I knocked. And announced myself."

"Guess I didn't hear you. I was kind of busy. Put your hands down."

I lowered them and self-consciously stuck them in my pockets.

"Sorry to barge in. I wondered if you might have a few minutes to talk."

He motioned toward the window. "You can see how frickin' busy I am." He sighed. "I suppose I could spare a minute or two."

He walked to the counter next to the sink, opened a cupboard and pulled down a clean glass, then pushed past me out onto the deck. I followed him to the table and sat, gratefully accepting the glass of lemonade he handed me.

He picked up a napkin and ran it over his bald head, then held his glass to the side of his face. "Can't remember the last time it was this hot in June," he muttered. "Everyone knows summer don't start here until after the Fourth of July."

"Lemonade hits the spot. Thanks."

He lowered his glass and peered at me. "Didn't expect to see you again. At least not so soon."

"Had some more questions, if you don't mind."

He tipped his head. "I'll help if I can."

I told him about my trip back to Illinois. About my conversation with Waldron and the information I'd gleaned from the library on campus.

"Something bothers you," he said when I finished.

"Fitch bothers me. From what you told me, he didn't have the smarts to pull off that bombing. Where'd he get C-4? Where'd he learn how to use it? And he's got no motive that I can figure. Why'd he do it?"

He leaned back and scratched a spot over his right ear, then combed the fringe of hair back in place with his fingers.

"I can't answer any of those questions," he said. "Maybe that puts your buddy back in the hot seat. What about him? Could he get his hands on military explosives?"

Harold Langford, Wink's dad, had been a tinkerer, a MacGyver type who loved putting things together out of nothing. An inventor, with a couple of patents, one of which had made him fairly wealthy. Before that, though, he'd worked for an arms manufacturer outside St. Louis. His workshop had been full of stuff he'd worked on at the factory. Wink had been playing with black powder and other explosives since he could walk. Could he have put his hands on stuff restricted to the military? Wink had never been one to let little things like rules get in the way of science or a good practical joke.

"Yeah, it's possible," I said. "Probable, even. But I still don't think he did it. What about the gang Fitch used to ride with? Not exactly peaceable folk, I imagine. Could they have helped him put his hands on explosives? Did he keep in contact?"

"Now there's a thought." He paused and looked out into the yard. After a moment he pushed back from table. "Come with me."

Collins led me back into the kitchen and through a side door into the garage. He stopped just inside the door, and I almost bumped into him before my eyes adjusted to the dimness. He snapped on an overhead fluorescent fixture from a wall switch. A workbench on one wall was littered with fishing reels, line, lures, fly tying equipment, several pairs of needle nose pliers and assorted flotsam and jetsam. Fishing poles, creels, nets and other gear were arrayed in stands next to the bench. A row of mismatched file cabinets lined the opposite wall. Stacked boxes obscured the wall at the end of the garage. A small runabout on a trailer took up the remaining floor space in the middle of the garage.

Collins made his way over to the bank of file cabinets and pawed through a drawer until he found what he wanted. He pulled it out and motioned me over.

"Grab us a couple of beers out of that fridge on your way over," he said, pointing.

A refrigerator stood to my left not far from the door. I opened it, took out two cold bottles and walked them over to the boat. Collins legged it up over the side and spread the file out on one of the bench seats.

"Climb aboard," he said. "A little cooler here than on the patio."

I swung a leg over the gunwale, handed him the beer and climbed all the way in. I scanned the file drawers, taking a sip.

"These all your old cases?"

He nodded. "I'm a pack rat. What can I say? Let's see what we've got here."

As he flipped through copies of arrest reports and notes, a photo print slipped halfway out of the file. A sheet of Fitch's mug shots.

I leaned over a pinched the edge between thumb and forefinger. "May I?"

"Go ahead."

I slid the photo out from under the pages he was reading and held the photos at an angle to eliminate the reflective glare from the fluorescent bulbs. Fitch had a broad face with small eyes set close to a nose made crooked in a fight. A scruffy beard nearly hid thin lips pulled tight in a menacing grimace. Something in his eyes, though, suggested he didn't take himself too seriously. The same look on fellows who didn't give a shit would have made me leery enough to steer clear if I ever saw them in person. Fitch's eyes had life in them, almost a St. Nick twinkle, not the empty blackness of your average psychopath.

And he looked nothing like the face in my memory from that night twenty-some years ago.

Though cooler, the air in the garage was still and heavy. The roof absorbed the sun's heat and radiated downward. I felt its weight on my head, beads of sweat breaking out on my forehead. The sound of shuffling papers was loud in the stillness.

"Got nothing in here that suggests Fitch stayed in touch with anyone in his old gang," Collins said. "Doesn't surprise me. He pretty much left that life behind back in Madison."

"But he could have reached out."

He shrugged. "Sure. Don't know why he would have, though. Most of his arrests were D-and-Ds, and after the riots in the early '70s, he pretty much kept his nose clean. Got busted in a couple of drunken bar fights in the mid-'70s and slept it off in the tank. Nothing after that until the accident."

"A year after his prints were maybe found at the scene of the SIU bombing."

He frowned and looked down at the file, thumbing through the pages.

"That was when? August, 'Eighty-nine?'89? Fitch was killed in October. Six weeks after the bombing, not a year."

The skin between my eyebrows wrinkled and my pulse pounded a spike behind my left eyeball. I pinched the bridge of my nose between thumb and forefinger and rubbed. Maybe Frank got the timeframe mixed up. Did it matter?

"You're thinking if Fitch was involved in the bombing, maybe somebody cleaned up a loose end," Collins said slowly.

"I don't know what I'm thinking." Trying to pin down a single thought was like shooting a fly out of a swarm with a blow dart. I took a few slow breaths and silently recited a mantra. "So this guy Fitch was clean for, what, fifteen years?"

"Looks like."

"A born troublemaker. Hell's Angel type. With a history of arrests. He get religion?"

"Maybe just grew up. Like a lot of kids back then. How many angry anti-war demonstrators ended up with a wife and kids in the suburbs a few years later? Sure, the hardcore, the radicals, kept at it for a while. Some were caught and went to jail. Others went underground. But most of those eventually ended up fat, happy and middle-class. Hypocritical assholes, most of them."

"So, what? He grew up and became a doctor? A fireman?"

Collins glanced down briefly but didn't consult the file. "Nah, nothing like that. Just got a steady job and stayed out of trouble. Your average working Joe. He worked as a janitor for the school district. That much time in, probably partially vested in a pension, too, before he died."

"In Seattle?"

This time he did check a page in the folder. "Yeah, mostly at Ingraham High School."

One of the blow darts pinned a fly to the inside of my skull right behind my forehead. Messy. Now I just had to learn to read entrails to figure out what it meant.

"Care to share with the rest of the class?" he said.

"What?" I looked at him and shook my head. "It's nothing. A wild notion. Random."

He looked doubtful, but left it alone.

"Why aren't you out fishing?" I said.

"Too damn hot."

"Golfing with your buddies?"

The look on his face told me that wasn't likely.

"Right," I said. "Too damn hot."

"Most of the guys on the force with me married young, had families, raised their kids together. The ones still married see each other occasionally, socialize, travel together even. The ones that aren't pretend they're twenty-five and looking to get married. I've always been a fifth wheel, either way."

It struck me he wasn't so much interested in helping me as he was in having a little company, someone to share his memories with. I asked him about his other cases, and his face grew animated as he related some war stories from North Precinct, the house where he spent most of his career. When both our bottles were empty, I clambered out of the boat.

"You fish?" he said.

"Some."

"You should come along sometime."

I reached in my pockets and pulled out a scrap of paper and a pencil stub, and wrote down my number.

"I'll bring the beer," I said. "Thanks for the help."

CHAPTER 30

He knew he was taking a big chance. Too many things could go wrong. For one, the couple could get away, though he didn't know how. He'd left them comfortable enough, for prisoners, one in each of the two small bedrooms upstairs in the cabin. He'd removed all the furniture in both rooms excepts the beds, but he'd provided both of them with plenty of reading material—books, magazines—bottles of water and a chamber pot. And he'd left each shackled by a chain to a heavy iron ring bolted into the log wall.

They might talk to each other through the wall, and even yell their heads off trying to attract attention. But his nearest neighbor was more than half a mile away where the road surface changed from pavement to dirt, and his was the last property on the road. The road did curve in front of the cabin back up into the woods another quarter mile where there was an old shed his father had converted into a workshop with a tiny bedroom loft. When Harold had gotten into one of his tinkering moods, he'd often slept at odd hours, sometimes not for days at a time. Langford's mother, Mavis, had been just as happy to see him out of the cabin when he'd been like that. "We're supposed to be on vacation," she'd say.

The road ended in a large field a hundred yards farther, where Langford remembered his dad happily blowing things up or testing a new invention. No one ever made it as far as the cabin, let alone the end of the road. He was pretty sure he'd taken enough precautions that he needn't worry about the couple.

But exposing himself in public probably wasn't wise, either. The thought made him grin. He'd done that, too, junior year. Streaked bare-assed naked through a school assembly in the gym on a dare. He'd made a hundred bucks off Chuck Hanson on that one. *Get serious.* This was worth it, too, he decided. Good thing, since he was already in the city heading south on I-5.

Holden's call had worried him. If the FBI had gone to Blake Sanders for information on his whereabouts they were desperate. They had to know from his prison correspondence that he and Sanders hadn't been in touch since the night he'd been arrested. That meant they already knew he was in the area, or had reason to come out here from Illinois. He didn't know how they could have found out he was already here. After his parents had died, he'd asked Holden to sell the cabin. Only he'd set up a trust with cash from the estate, and had the trust buy the property so it didn't appear on public records in his name.

That left the other option, the one he'd considered when they let him out: The FBI believed someone else had been involved in the bombing Langford had gone to prison for. Too bad they hadn't believed him twenty years ago. They knew about his research, all the requests for information from the DOJ and the FBI under the Freedom of Information Act. He'd made no secret of the fact that he intended to find the people who'd planned the bombing. They knew that the first thing he'd do when he got out was track down the people who'd set him up to take the fall. And he'd spotted the tail almost as soon as he walked out the prison gates in Marion. But he was pretty sure they hadn't followed him. He'd taken a very circuitous route, booking and buying tickets to several destinations at once, renting cars between destinations, driving to another nearby city and doing it all over again. His first stop after leaving Centralia, in fact, had been Milwaukee, where he'd rented a car and driven to a small town outside Madison, Wisconsin.

So, that meant the FBI had some intel that the people he'd spent so long trying to find were here in the Northwest. And they had sucked Legs into the whole thing, using him as bait to get to Langford. He'd hoped he wouldn't have to deal with Legs yet. He'd wanted to save him for later. But Legs had found a way to step in it, forcing his hand. And something else was in play now. He frowned. The gun battle he'd heard out at the couple's house was no FBI raid. Someone else wanted them, too. And he was confident he knew who it was. He shook off the thoughts, letting his brow ease, checking the traffic around him. Finding answers is why he'd decided to brave a trip into the city, and now he needed to be alert and aware.

The only address he had for Sanders had come out of from an old UW alumni directory, listing a house in the Ravenna neighborhood. When he turned off the freeway and found the house five minutes later, he reconnoitered the neighborhood carefully before parking a block away and walking back. As he drew closer, a casually dressed man in his thirties walked out the front door and got into a car in the driveway. Langford watched him back into the street and drive off. When the car was out of sight, he walked up to the front door of the house and rang the bell. The woman who answered the door said she didn't know a Blake Sanders. She and her husband had bought the house about a year earlier from a woman named McHugh. Langford thanked her and turned to leave. He was halfway down the walk when he heard her voice call out behind him.

"Mary McHugh, actually," she said.

Langford stopped and looked back.

"The name she signed on the documents was Mary Catherine McHugh," the woman said.

"Thanks." Langford smiled.

Michael W. Sherer

CHAPTER 31

Charlie was reaming a nurse for some minor infraction of his notion of the rules when I walked into his hospital room. She didn't cut him any slack, responding in a calm but firm voice. Her fingertips on his sternum fueled rather than suppressed his anger, spreading a claret stain up his neck and cheeks. Pale spindly legs poked out beneath the hem of his pastel blue hospital gown. Dark circles rimmed his eyes. Whiskers, as many gray as brown, sprouted from his cheeks like plants in weak soil deprived of sunlight. He stooped, mouth contorted and jaw clenched with pain, aging in front of me, turning into the fusty, crotchety geezer he'd likely become in thirty or forty years.

He glared at me. "What?"

"How do you ever expect to get out of here if you don't do what they tell you?"

"I need a shower," he growled. "She says it's against the rules."

"Sponge bath's as good as it gets, mister," the nurse said.

"For chrissakes, at least let me do that myself," he told her. "My luck, you'll send in some old crone, or worse some huge hairy guy named Bruno."

The nurse turned away to hide a nascent smile. "I'll make sure you get a basin and a sponge."

"Could you maybe get me a razor, too?"

"I'll see what I can do." She walked to the door, glancing at me on the way past, and jerked a thumb over her shoulder. "Good luck with that."

Charlie flopped onto the bed, wincing as he bounced, jarring the arm in a sling at his side.

"God, I hate hospitals." He sighed.

"The sooner you heal up, the sooner you're out of here."

His eyes narrowed. "I should be out of here already. It's been almost a week. You sound like everyone else in this fucking place. Pass out pom-poms and put together a cheer squad."

"What the hell's eating you?"

"Trade places and tell me you wouldn't bitch about being here." He snatched at the thin blanket bunched at the foot of the bed and pulled it over his bare legs.

"You're right, I'd hate it," I said.

He picked at a thread, eyes downcast. "Babs is home," he said quietly.

"That's great! When?"

He didn't share my enthusiasm. "Friday night. She came by yesterday." He raised his eyes slowly, the pain on his face from something other than his shoulder. "She wants a divorce."

My stomach clenched, and I searched for something to say. "Charlie, I'm sorry. Any chance she—"

"She served me papers. Delivered them in person. Told me she would've waited until I was out of the hospital, but the boys had already missed too much school. She said if I need some time to find a place when I get out, I can stay with a buddy. She doesn't want me in the house."

"Ouch."

"Yeah, ouch. I worked my ass off for that house. I can't afford my own place, too. Shit, I'll have to pick up extra shifts, get a second job just to make ends meet."

"I'm sorry," I said again. Then more hesitantly, "You can bunk at my place."

His laugh was short and derisive. "You're the last person I'd stay with, Sanders. But thanks for the offer."

My ears burned. "Why? Not good enough for you?"

"Think about it. Your place is a shoebox. One of us farts the other'll asphyxiate. God, what a nightmare."

"Suit yourself."

He looked at me sharply. "Get over it."

I walked to the window and stared out at Smith Tower and a ferry plying the bright blue waters of Elliott Bay beyond.

"They find out anything more about the guy I shot?" I said.

"Yeah. Fingerprints came back to a former Army Ranger. Served in Iraq when I was there. Got drummed out of the service for brawling and dropped off the radar. Sources say he went mercenary, fought in Kosovo and maybe Chechnya. No one knows when he got back to the States."

I faced him. "They don't know who he worked for?"

"We'd know who to look for then, wouldn't we?" He plumped the pillow with his good arm and lay back. "PMCs aren't going to just give us lists of their personnel. Where were you, anyway? You haven't been around for a few days. Sarah was worried about you."

"Sarah."

"Well, yeah. So?"

"I was trying to keep from getting my ass shot off."

His face went blank, like I'd spoken Mandarin. I told him everything that had happened, about the drive-by with the automatic weapons, the narrow escape after trashing the front window of Javier's restaurant. He listened without interruption, stifling a yawn once or twice and pushing away the exhaustion on his face. I told him about the flight to St. Louis and the trip back to the place I grew up.

He blinked. "Wait a minute. You went back to Illinois? What for? Laying low? If you think someone's after you why come back? Why are you here?"

"To find Wink."

"Wink?" He frowned, then his eyes slowly widened. "The kid you grew up with?"

I nodded and told him that Wink was out of jail, but missing. That the FBI was looking for him and thought Wink might have been in touch. I told him what I'd learned on my trip from Holden and at SIU from Waldron and the library search. The only things I didn't tell him about were Keely and the theories bouncing around my head.

"You've been busy," he said quietly. "Who else've you pissed off lately?"

I frowned at him, decided he couldn't be that slow. Asked him a question instead. "You know Ned Collins? Retired cop?"

He scratched the crown of his head. "I've heard the name. Don't know him."

"Collins worked 'The Ave' when he was a beat cop. Forty years ago."

Charlie looked puzzled. "What, the '60s? What's that got to do with anything?"

"Try to follow me, here. You remember me telling you why Wink went to jail?"

"He set a bomb on some campus. Back when we were maybe sophomores, juniors."

I nodded. "Okay, so ten years later when AFIS comes on line, FBI flags a fingerprint found at the scene, and ties it to a guy Collins knew here back in the '60s who was an agitator for student radical groups. The guy followed a couple of protestors out from the University of Wisconsin in Madison, a married couple he got to be friends with. Collins busted him a few times back then."

"Okay," he said slowly. "I still don't know where you're going."

"The guy's name was Sebastian Fitch. Ever hear of him?"

He stiffened, then shifted on the bed with a grimace as though in pain.

"Nah, doesn't ring a bell." His eyes slowly met mine. "So, what, Collins thinks this guy might be good for that bombing? Maybe your friend gets a pardon?"

"Maybe." I waved impatiently. "Guess I'm not explaining this right. I forget who I've talked to about what." I took a breath and put my thoughts in order. "Like I said, Fitch was tight with a married couple back in the '60s. They supposedly split for Canada when things got too hot here after the riots in '70. Twenty years later, Fitch leaves a fingerprint at the scene of a bombing at SIU, for which my childhood buddy Wink goes to jail. Fitch, of course, is long dead."

He started, eyebrows arching.

"Right, sorry," I said. "Something else maybe you didn't know. He died in a motorcycle accident not long after the bombing. But here it is twenty years later, Wink gets out of jail, disappears, and all hell breaks loose around here. You don't think that's a little strange?"

Confusion played across his face, and he looked away, brows knitting in concentration.

"I'm still not tracking. What are you talking about?"

"Your parents are gone, Charlie. The men who shot you and tried to kidnap them tried to blow my head off a few nights ago. They didn't come after you?"

The thought hadn't occurred to him. "Why would they?"

"Hell, I don't know. Eliminate witnesses, maybe? I can't think of why else they'd come after me. You've got so many cops in and out of here maybe they're just playing it safe. I'd watch your back when you get out. Anyway, the FBI and the bombing victim's sister are after Wink and think I know where he is. It's all gotta be tied together somehow. Don't you see?"

"Wait ..." He frowned, sucked in a breath and started again. "You think Clayt and Connie had something to do with this? With a twenty-year-old bombing?"

"You're the one who keeps telling me they weren't into drugs. So what else could it be? I went to see Collins this morning. He kept copies of old cold case files. He showed me what he had on Fitch." I paused.

Charlie's mouth tightened, but he said nothing.

"Fitch worked as a janitor at Ingraham," I said. "Where Clayt taught."

Muscles at the corners of Charlie's jaw worked and his face colored.

"'Cause this guy worked the same place where my dad taught school makes my parents bombers? Terrorists? Are you out of your freakin' mind?"

"He had to have known him."

"I'm sure he did. Clayt's a friendly guy. And he was always nice to the staff. Just 'cause he might've known who this guy Fitch was doesn't mean he *knew* him. And you think they hung out with him in the '60s? Organized antiwar protests?"

"Like they didn't? Get real, Charlie. They've admitted they hated the war."

"Big difference between holding up a sign and bombing buildings. Besides, the time you're talking about they were living in Canada. I was a baby."

"What, you remember that? Or is that what Clayt and Connie always told you. You couldn't have been even two years old."

His face darkened to a blotchy purple, and his hand balled into a fist on top of the blanket.

"Fuck you. You don't know shit about them."

"That's the problem; neither do you. Fact is, that's another thing that bugs me. Clayt and Connie told you they're from Canada, and that's where the Wilsons disappeared to after things got too hot here in Seattle. Coincidence?"

"Damn straight."

"Really? Where were you born, Charlie? Here in the States, right? Where?"

His jaw worked, and I know he wanted to hit me. Instead, he said, "What does the bombing have to do with it? The war in Vietnam was long over. Maybe Fitch *was* involved. And sure, Clayt probably knew him. That doesn't mean he and Connie had anything to do with it."

"They *ran*! They knew those assholes were coming. They had high-tech security and an escape route all planned out. A tunnel, for God's sake! They're guilty of something, Charlie."

"You keep trashing them," he growled, "and so help me I'll take you with one good arm."

His head turned at the sound of the door, and I followed his gaze. Sarah walked in, the smile on her face fading as she looked at each of us in turn.

"What's going on?"

Charlie looked away quickly, and Sarah swung her gaze back to me, hands on her hips.

"Ask him," I said.

"It's no big deal," Charlie said.

I rounded on him. "You're in serious denial if you can't see it," I said.

"See what?" Sarah said.

"I think your parents were into something. Something bad."

Sarah's eyes widened. "What?"

"You two figure it out." I headed for the door.

"Where are *you* going?" Charlie flung the question at my back.

I stopped and turned. "Your place."

"What for?"

"To get your other back-up piece. I'm sure Babs doesn't want it in the house, and where I'm going I might need it."

I walked out before he could say no.

Michael W. Sherer

CHAPTER 32

Langford found the big house on Capitol Hill where Molly lived, and whistled. Someone was doing well. He sat in the old Scout and thought about what approach to take. Straight in was probably best. Maybe fudge the truth a little, depending. Sweat broke out on his upper lip, and he wiped his mouth on his sleeve. The day had turned into a scorcher, which might hide his nervousness; he hadn't had much practice at social graces for a while. He checked his appearance in the mirror and climbed out of the car.

A copper blond woman with a thin, attractive Irish face answered the door. Tall and willowy, she stood nearly eye-to-eye, and looked at him curiously.

"Can I help you?" she said.

"Ms. McHugh, I'm sorry to bother you on a Sunday, but I'm looking for Blake Sanders."

She started to say something, but he rushed on before she got a word in.

"We were classmates back in high school. I'm out here on vacation and thought I'd look him up, but the only information I have is from an old UW alumni directory."

He saw her expression change, a note of suspicion flashing in her eyes. He kept going without any hesitation, giving her no indication he'd noticed.

"I assume you two are no longer married, and I wouldn't have thought of disturbing you except that Blake's not listed in the phone book. I wondered if you could tell me where I might find him."

"I'm sorry, who did you say you are?" she said.

He stuck his hand out and smiled broadly. "Where are my manners? Chuck Hanson."

"How, exactly, did you find me, Chuck?" Her tone was cool, but she kept a pleasant half-smile on her face.

"I went to the house you two must have owned on Ravenna before you divorced. That was the address I had. The woman there said she and her husband bought the house from you, so I looked you up. I hope you don't mind."

She relaxed her weight onto one leg, but she still guarded the doorway uncertainly.

"No, that's quite all right. I'd certainly be happy to get in touch with Blake and give him a number where you can be reached."

He let his face fall. "I really was hoping to see him. See, we're only in town for the day, and then we're off on a cruise to Alaska. I'd love to drop in on him. Does he live nearby?"

"Not far," she said. She looked at him and nodded. "Tell you what, I suppose it wouldn't hurt to give you his number. You could give him a ring and see if he's up for a visit."

He forced himself not to push it, to keep his expression genial, his voice enthusiastic. "That would be great. I can't wait to catch up. You wouldn't believe some of the stories I could tell you about what Legs and I did in high school."

Her throaty laugh took him by surprise. "I haven't heard anyone call him by that name in years. I think the only one who dares is a cop, and one of Blake's friends put him up to it." She looked at him in amusement. "Wait here while I get a piece of paper and a pen."

Excitement pulsed through him, pushing aside his nervousness. Blake Sanders, after all these years...

She reappeared in the doorway, opened the screen and stepped onto the porch to hand him a slip of paper.

"Here you go—Chuck, is it?" she said. "He may not be up yet. He works nights and tends to sleep in, so he should be home. But I'd call first to give him a little warning."

Langford looked at the paper in his fingers. "Thanks, I really appreciate this."

She shrugged. "Wish I could be there to see the look on his face."

Langford gave a little wave, turned and headed down the steps, suddenly aware that she hadn't looked all that enthusiastic when she made that last comment. He glanced over his shoulder. She swung the door shut with one hand, eyes on the cell phone in her other hand. He quickened his pace.

* * * * *

Babs wasn't happy to see me. More like surprised.

"Charlie's still in the hospital," she said when she opened the door.

"I know. I just came from there. He told me. I'm sorry."

Sadness rippled off her like curls of mist wafting from a block of dry ice, her frown of resentment and disapproval cold.

"It's not like I wanted this," she said. "He should have seen this coming."

"I had no idea how bad it was between you two, Babs."

"I'm not taking him back." Her voice rose in pitch. "You can't talk me out of it. He shouldn't have sent you."

"He didn't. I'm not here for Charlie."

"Oh." Her shoulders fell, and the emotion drained from her face.

"May I come in?"

She looked at me blankly and stepped back. The interior of the boxy split-level was dim and cool as a morgue. Shrunken, her face lined with fatigue, Babs couldn't fill the quiet and empty house. Without the boys home, she would rattle around the space like a pea in a tin pot. And their presence, for a long while at least, would likely be a reminder of the hole in all of their lives. Divorce does that, much as people think they want it. Molly popped into mind unbidden.

"Why are you looking at me like that?" Babs said.

Molly's visage slowly dissolved, replaced by the more careworn lines of Babs' puzzled face. She was a year or two younger than Molly, but the creases and dark circles etched by worry and sleepless nights made her look a decade older. An inch of gray showed at the roots of her dark hair, and she hadn't taken the time to put on makeup.

"Sorry," I said. "I was just wondering if this is really what you want."

"Of course this isn't what I want." Her voice was shrill. She held her arms rigid at her sides, holding herself together. "I want a husband who talks to me about his day, who buys me flowers for no reason, who takes me to dinner someplace special on my birthday, not some stranger I see at odd times of the day and night between shifts. A husband who's home at night, safe with me and the boys, not someone in the hospital with a bullet wound in his chest. God damn it, Blake, what do you think I want?"

Tears rolled silently down her cheeks. She sniffed. "I'm sorry, you didn't need to hear all that. It's not like me to just fall apart."

Heat crept into my face, and I shifted my weight. "It's okay."

"What are you doing here? What do you want?"

"I need Charlie's spare gun," I said quietly.

She tipped her head slightly with narrowed eyes and sighed, swiping away the tears with her fingers. "You, too? You're mixed up in this? Of course you are. What am I thinking?"

I started to object. She waved the words away before they formed on my lips.

"Wait here, I'll get it," she said. "The key's on the rack under the wall phone in the kitchen."

I made my way to the kitchen, nearly unnerved by the quiet. Charlie's presence was everywhere, from the spit-polished black brogans by the front door to the sporting magazines strewn in the den. An open suitcase stood on a folding luggage rack next to the couch in the family room, a reminder that Sarah was still in residence. I wondered if she was taking sides. I knew better. She'd do everything she could to negotiate a truce between them.

I found the key to Charlie's gun case where Babs said it would be and waited.

Babs returned and held out the gun safe. "Charlie knows about this?" She quickly waved a hand. "Never mind. I don't want to know. Take it."

I tucked the box under my arm. "Where are the boys?"

She shrugged. "Steve's at a baseball game, and Chuck went over to a friend's house." She paused. "I'm trying to keep things as normal as possible."

"It must be hard. I'm sure it'll all work out somehow."

She blinked back more tears and reached for a tissue from a box on the counter.

"Is there anything I can do?" I said.

She blew her nose noisily and shook her head.

I held up the gun box. "Thanks for this. I—"

She straightened her arm, palm toward me, and turned her head to the side. "Don't. I used to be proud, you know, married to a cop. Now..." She glanced at the box and shivered. "Good riddance."

I turned to go and stopped. "Babs, where was Charlie born?"

She frowned. "I don't know. Somewhere in the Midwest. Does it matter?"

"It could be important."

"I think his birth certificate's in the lockbox in the den. He doesn't trust banks. You need to know now?"

"If it's not too much trouble."

She hesitated. "What's going on, Blake?"

"Charlie and Sarah asked me to help them find their parents. This could help."

"They just disappeared? It's not like them."

I hesitated, but she had the boys to think about. "I think Clayt and Connie are in trouble, Babs. I think they're on the run from something in their past."

She put her hand to her mouth, her eyes widening.

I shook my head. "I don't think you and the boys have anything to worry about. Charlie and I were in the way of whoever's after them, that's all. They won't bother you."

She didn't need to know the rest of it.

"Are you sure?" She pulled on an earlobe. "Okay, then, wait here."

Gone for only a minute or so, she returned with a piece of paper in her hands. She held it out. I took it and unfolded it on the counter. Charlie had been born in May, 1968, in a little town in Wisconsin. Not Madison, but close I'd have bet. Mother's name was listed as C. Constance Jones. No father. I frowned. Maybe I was wrong. Maybe it was a coincidence that Clayt and Connie Jones from Canada really had gone to school in Madison at the same time as the Wilsons. And maybe Colin and Corinne Wilson had just happened to end up in Canada when things got too portentous for them here back in the early '70s.

And maybe I could sprout wings and fly.

.

CHAPTER 33

My phone rang on the way out to the car. I tucked the gun case under an arm and flipped the phone open.

"We need to talk." Sarah's voice.

"About what?"

"You can't just walk out like that, Blake."

"Sure I can. I did."

"Please, Blake. He needs you."

"Like a sharp stick in the eye."

"*We* need you, then."

I didn't have a reply to that. My phone beeped, signaling another incoming call. I ignored it and let it go to voicemail.

"What's going on with you two?" Sarah said.

"He didn't tell you?"

"Clammed up after you left. Said he didn't want to talk about it. But I do. Meet me. Please? A cup of coffee somewhere. Five minutes, ten, max. You can spare that much."

"You're not going to like hearing it anymore than he does."

"What? Not like hearing what?"

"Are you still at the hospital?"

"Where else would I be?"

I gave her the name of a coffee place across from Seattle University, a short walk away.

"I'll be there in twenty minutes," I said.

She was there when I arrived, sitting at a table in back, chin resting on her palm, staring at the baristas behind the counter, worry etching her face. She'd let her long, straight hair down out of her usual ponytail, and now she tucked one side behind her ear with her fingers. The familiar gesture reversed time for an instant, revealing a glimpse of the past. She gave a little wave when she saw me, the sunshine of a smile hesitantly breaking through fast-moving clouds and disappearing again.

I skirted a table of students, books and papers spread across their table. Two girls and a guy leaned in over their open books in an animated discussion. A fourth leaned back, chair tipped on its back legs, his sandaled feet propped on the edge of the table, an open textbook resting on the fleece vest that covered his belly. He scratched his chin, fingers lost in a tangle of scruffy beard. Blue eyes peered out of a face as pale as a Finn in winter. Thick, matted dreadlocks spilled out of a colorful Rasta cap over his collar. The itinerants standing outside the day labor office down the street looked cleaner.

"Thanks for coming," she said as I eased into the chair across from her.

"Not like I seem to have much choice with you two."

"What's that supposed to mean?"

I shook my head. "Nothing. Look, Sarah, you asked me to help find out what happened to your parents. I thought Charlie was on board with that, but he doesn't want to hear anything bad about them."

"What do you mean 'bad'? You alluded to that before. What's this about? What'd they do?"

"I think they organized a raid on a research lab back when we were kids."

Her eyes widened, but she didn't flip out. "You really are nuts."

"Maybe."

For a moment I considered leaving, walking away from everything. Dumping the mess in her lap. She was right. Charlie was the cop. It was his job to figure this out, not mine. But someone wanted me dead, too. If anything, a sense of self-preservation should keep me going. The impulse to quit should have warned me it was time for a dose of meds.

"Sebastian Fitch." The words popped out of my mouth.

She started. "What about him?"

I stared at her. "That name means something to you?"

"Sure. Uncle Sebastian. You remember him." She frowned.

"*Uncle* Sebastian?" I shook my head. "I don't think so."

Her brow furrowed. "Maybe you never met him. He died when we were in college. My sophomore year, I think. I was sure you must have met him at some family dinner."

"Nope. Never heard of him before a week ago."

"Why? Where'd you hear his name?"

"Long story." I chased thoughts around my head like a flea-bit dog after his tail. "He wasn't your real uncle, was he?"

The corners of her mouth turned up. "God, no. Just one of mom and dad's good friends. I knew him ever since I was tiny. He'd come around once in a while, roughhouse with us kids when were little, talk with Clayt, stay for dinner. Clayt always called him 'Uncle' Sebastian around us."

"You know what he and your dad talked about?"

Her head wagged. "Their private talks were just that—private. Around us he didn't talk about anything in particular. The usual stuff—sports, weather, school, whatever."

"Nothing unusual around the time you started college?"

Her mouth formed the word 'no,' but no sound came out. She cocked her head. "Now that you mention it, I saw him around the house a lot the summer before my freshman year. Never gave it much thought. Just figured he was bored. Brought over a friend of his a couple of times, too. I don't remember his name, though. No, wait, it was Phil."

She paused and focused on thoughts that hovered somewhere over my left shoulder.

"The strange thing? That fall? He got religion, I swear. Born again. Always talking about 'the Word' and 'what would Jesus do?' I thought it had something to do with, you know, what happened to me freshman year. But now I see that's pretty silly. Something happened—to him, not me." She stared at me, gaze flicking across my face. "What's this about?"

"He helped blow up a building on a college campus back in Illinois. Looks like your parents were involved. Maybe planned the job."

Her hand went to her mouth, and her eyes grew wide. "Clayt and Connie? They wouldn't hurt a fly. And Uncle Sebastian? He was a big teddy bear."

"The FBI found Fitch's fingerprint at the scene. Never connected him with the case, though, until long after he was killed."

She was shaking her head. "They couldn't have done it. They never left town that year. Didn't even take a vacation. You know, because of what happened to me. They wanted to stay close, just in case."

"I never said they were there. But they were involved, Sarah."

A grim storm clouded her expression. "I don't believe it."

"Believe what you want." It came out more harshly than I intended. I had an impulse to shake her until she started making sense. "Didn't you ever think your parents were weird?"

She blinked. "Not really. A little eccentric, I suppose."

"Come on, Sarah. You can't believe all that hippie-dippie shit is normal."

"Just because they love nature and have eclectic taste?"

"I'm not just talking Connie's earth-mother act or Clayt's lectures on how all of today's political problems wouldn't exist if the Boomers hadn't capitulated and bought into the Establishment instead of continuing '60s-style activism. They're strange people, Sarah."

The heat lightning of a summer storm of anger flashed in her eyes. "It's all relative. Weren't your parents weird in their own way? We had a lot of reminders around the house of those days. Books, record albums, artwork... So what?"

"Your parents also read stuff like Che's diary, Mao's 'Little Red Book,' Eldridge Cleaver, *Civil Disobedience*, *Guerilla Warfare*, all those Yippie manifestos ..."

"For God's sake, Blake. They also read Ken Kesey, Tom Wolfe, Timothy Leary, Hunter S. Thompson and a bunch of other drug culture books, but they weren't druggies. And tell me you didn't read Kurt Vonnegut, or *Catch-22*, or *Trout Fishing in America* when you were in school. Does that make you a counterculture revolutionary? Are they left-leaning liberals? Sure. Do they believe passionately in causes like clean water and clean air? Absolutely. We all should. Do they vote, and write letters and advocate for alternative energy, better schools and healthcare coverage for people in minimum wage jobs who can't afford it? You betcha.

"But did they ever tell us the way to achieve energy independence, or equal rights for women and minorities, or more public transportation was to bomb buildings or foment revolution? No way. They never suggested that freedom of speech, or fighting for what you believe in, involved use of your fists or physical confrontation of any kind that might harm another living being. Or property, for that matter. They don't resolve disputes with violence. They're good people, Blake. What's the matter with you?"

"You never heard them talk about a campus bombing? Or Southern Illinois? Or a research lab? Coal gasification experiments? Nothing like that?"

"No, damn it! The only times I heard them talk about things like that were in reference to the antiwar demonstrations during Vietnam. Like history lessons. They were in Canada then, anyway. They didn't get mixed up in all that."

"They never told you about Uncle Sebastian? About his SDS activities back in the day? The fact that he was an agitator at demonstrations here? And back at the University of Wisconsin?"

"No, never. He was just a guy Clayt knew at work. A friend, that's all."

"Charlie *lied*, Sarah. I asked him about Fitch. He said he never heard of the guy. Why would he lie? He knows something. Trying to protect your parents maybe. Whatever. Clayt and Connie are in this thing up to their necks, and whoever shot Charlie wants them dead."

"Why? That's crazy!" Her eyes darted back and forth, reflecting panic. She swallowed hard, calming herself. "I'm not saying I believe it, but even if they did something stupid back then, why would someone want to kill them after all these years? It doesn't make sense. You must be mistaken."

"I don't think so. If you and Charlie want to live in denial, okay by me. Just don't expect me to be much help if you're not willing to admit the truth."

"The truth?" Her eyes glistened. "Calling my parents terrorists, that's your idea of the truth?"

She stood so quickly her chair fell over onto the floor. She glared at me across the table, shaking with anger.

"Forget it, Blake."

"What, you ask for my help, but don't want it because you don't like what you're hearing?"

"Just forget the whole thing!"

"Sarah!"

"Stay the hell away from me! From us!"

She stormed out, leaving me fuming, insides roiling and building up pressure like a volcano about to explode through a rotten lava dome.

CHAPTER 34

Langford watched his old friend Legs climb out of the car. There was no mistaking his size—as he unfolded his long limbs and stood upright, the vehicle appeared to shrink to the size of a circus clown car. His features had changed little over the years, face maybe a little fuller and more mature.

A memory of Sanders flashed in his head, two feet shorter, standing stupidly in the hall at school as Langford had rounded the corner at a dead run, two jerks hot on his heels trying to catch him and pay him back for a practical joke he'd pulled. Sanders, his usual spastic self, had unintentionally gotten in the way, taking them both down in a tangle of arms and legs, allowing Langford to get away.

What had bonded them? Sanders had been like a big puppy, offering unconditional adoration and near constant companionship. Sanders had admired him, liked him for who he was. That was it. Langford had always been able to talk Sanders into going along with whatever crazy scheme he came up with. Never as a participant, but Sanders hadn't hesitated to be an observer. Almost like an official witness or attester, someone who could chronicle his derring-do. For a while—years in fact—they *had* made a pretty good team.

Now he wondered if Legs was still a friend. He extended his arm, pointed his index finger, sighted over his raised thumb and quietly said, "Bang." It would be that easy to take him out. He watched Legs stomp toward the house and disappear around the side down an incline to the back.

Movement down the street caught his eye. A gray sedan pulled into an open space at the curb half a block down from the house Sanders had just entered. Langford waited, but no one got out. Curious, he pulled a pair of binoculars from under the seat and trained them on the windshield of the sedan. Two men sat in the front seat, one white, younger than Langford, broad-shouldered, one black, older, neatly trimmed graying mustache, slight stature. Both wore suit coats and ties over white shirts, bored expressions on their faces. They may as well have stenciled "Property of U.S. Government" on the car doors and the breast pockets of their suits.

Langford sucked in a breath. He recognized the older man, a memory immediately coming to mind that placed him in an interrogation room in the federal building in Benton, Illinois, where the trial had taken place. A pair of sheriff's deputies had driven him up from the Jackson County jail in Murphysboro, had led him into the federal building shackled as if he posed a threat the likes of King Kong. The black guy had been one of four FBI special agents asking questions about the night of the bombing, the night that had changed his world. *Drucker, Fred Drucker*, the name as easily accessible in his memory banks as the pattern of the blue tie the FBI agent had worn that day.

Langford didn't know the younger agent behind the wheel, but realized the man probably would have been in high school, maybe even grade school, when Langford had gone to prison. He settled back in his seat to wait. Things were beginning to get interesting.

* * * * *

I made one stop on the way home to buy several boxes of ammunition and a few spare magazines for the gun I'd gotten from Babs. Not a good idea given the mood Sarah and Charlie had left me in. I didn't like where the past week had taken me. I never thought I'd have a gun in the house. Then again, I never thought I'd need one.

Still sour and vengeful when I got home, I stripped down to shorts and eased into a series of yoga sun salutations, gradually pushing myself until my muscles were warm and loose. Then I switched to a taekwondo *pumsae* and moved through a half-dozen forms I still remembered until sweat dripped off my nose and my muscles burned. It was still too bloody hot to exert that much effort, but some of the anger and frustration evaporated with the sweat. I drained two glasses of ice water and stepped into the shower to rinse off. With the water on cold, the spray felt like little icicles needling my skin.

When I started to shiver, I twisted the valve closed and toweled off. I padded out and sat on the bed, both energy and reason sapped. Exhausted, I tried napping, but I couldn't sleep. Snippets of conversations kept running through my head, reminding me of all the times I'd let my mouth flap before I'd had a chance to think about what was coming out of it. Instead, I got dressed, went into the kitchen and made myself a sandwich. I put it on a plate, uncapped a beer from the fridge and took them to the table in my small living area. While I ate I took the supplies I purchased out of the bag, spread them out on the table and loaded the magazines.

I carried the empty plate back to the kitchen, washed my hands and sat back down in front of the table. I took Charlie's gun out of its case and spent the next thirty minutes practicing, loading and unloading magazines until I could do it with my eyes closed in just a few seconds with my eyes closed.

Satisfied, I packed up the gun and magazines in the gun case and put it in a small sports duffel along with an extra box of ammunition. I looked around the apartment to see if I'd forgotten anything, picked up the bag and left, locking the door behind me.

* * * * *

Sanders had been inside the house for more than an hour when Langford noticed a car pull up alongside the gray sedan. The younger agent opened the driver's -side window, and Drucker leaned over to say something to the new arrivals. After a moment, the car backed up several feet, giving the gray sedan room to jockey in the tight space and pull away from the curb. Langford ducked down until Drucker and his partner had passed. When he raised his head, the other car was parking in the spot the gray sedan had just left. *Changing of the guard.*

Less than fifteen minutes later, Sanders rounded the corner of the house and walked to his car, a blue bag slung over his shoulder. Sanders stopped to open the trunk and slung the bag inside. He slammed the lid shut and folded himself behind the wheel, started up and pulled away. A moment later, Drucker's replacements pulled out and followed. Langford smiled and waited a moment or two before starting up the Scout and making it a parade.

Langford was careful to keep a several cars between him and the tail on Sanders. The Scout was too recognizable, and he chided himself for using it. But he doubted they'd think to check for someone following them. Sanders led them aimlessly, up the hill, taking random turns. Not as if he suspected he was being followed, but as if preoccupied and unaware of his surroundings. At one point, he swung into the curb and stopped, engine running. His tail cruised on by to the end of the block and turned the corner. Langford took a right a block behind where Legs had stopped. He pulled up in front of hydrant, got out and ran back to the corner to see what Sanders was up to. The block looked familiar. He scanned the houses and realized that he'd been there earlier to talk to Sanders's ex.

Langford shook his head. How Legs had let that one get away he'd never know. He guessed it hadn't been without regret—Sanders sat parked across the street from her house, but he made no move to get out of his car. After five minutes or so, Langford saw the car's back-up lights flash on. He hustled back to the Scout and slowly drove around the block, giving the tail time to fall in behind Sanders before he brought up the rear.

From there, Sanders led them up into a park on top of Capitol Hill. The sedan that followed him slowed and nosed into the entrance. Langford drove on past, and accelerated up to the corner of the park, casting glances to his left, trying to get a glimpse of the two cars in the park. He took a left and followed the perimeter of the park for another block or two, but he could see little from the street through the trees. He caught a glimpse of the back of a low building in the park, but couldn't see the road that Sanders had taken into the park. He cursed under his breath.

At the next corner, he noticed a pedestrian entrance into the park on the other side of the street and made a quick decision. Swinging into the curb, he parked, darted across the street and jogged deeper into the park. The building he'd seen was ahead to his left, and as he drew closer, he figured it for some sort of museum. He slowed to a walk—he saw plenty of joggers in the park, but he wasn't exactly dressed for the part. The last thing he needed was someone to think he was a mugger or rapist running from the scene of a crime.

Numerous parking spaces had been striped on the pavement in front of the museum. He scanned the cars quickly and spotted Sanders's tucked in between an SUV and an old Volvo wagon. He stooped to one knee and yanked a shoelace loose, and took his time retying it, alert for signs of the two men tailing Sanders. He finally located their car, parked in the farthest space away from him, facing the museum. The driver had remained in the car. Langford caught sight of his partner on the sidewalk in front of the museum, feigning interest in a sign, but turning for occasional glimpses across the road behind him. Langford followed his gaze and saw a small reflecting pool across the road and down a short slope beyond that a larger reservoir.

Park benches lined the sidewalk overlooking the reservoir. Sanders occupied one almost directly across the road from the man in front of the sign. He sat facing west, arm draped over the back of the bench, not moving. Langford stood and casually sauntered a few yards toward the museum entrance, pretending to admire the flowerbed set back from the sidewalk, turning every so often to keep tabs on the others. He sidled closer and suddenly realized Sanders wasn't waiting for anyone. He was simply taking in a breathtaking view of the Space Needle backdropped by snow-capped peaks of the Olympic Mountains across the sound in the distance.. Bright and hot, the sun dropped toward the horizon, its position so far north surprising Langford. He checked his watch—nearly nine in the evening and still a half-hour of light left.

Langford wandered off, conscious of drawing attention if he loitered in one place too long. A few hundred yards down the road a park bench perched at the end of a grassy field, set back in an alcove of shrubbery. He crossed the street and walked across the grass toward the bench, the day's heat sapping his energy and lulling him to lethargy. He sagged onto the bench, abruptly aware of how tired he was from the strain of the past several days—the long drive on the trail of the Jones couple and the longer drive back with them as his prisoners. Constantly keeping watch. He put a hand to his mouth and stifled a yawn. *Not now.* He couldn't afford to sleep yet.

Even at this distance, he still had a view of the road in front of the museum. If Sanders walked back to his car or the agents tailing him moved their positions, Langford would know. Earlier, he'd considered knocking on Sanders's door and confronting him face-to-face. The FBI's presence had quickly changed his mind. They probably hoped Sanders would lead them to him. He should have left already for the cabin. But Sanders didn't seem gung-ho about finding him, despite the fact that Holden had told Sanders where he was. It made him curious enough to blow off a little time relaxing in the park.

Sanders was on the move. Langford's senses went on alert, but his body showed no outward stress. He slouched casually on the bench as Langford walked in his direction, glanced over his shoulder to check for traffic and crossed the road to the opposite side. Even as he drew abreast, Sanders was a good sixty yards away, his gaze on the ground in front of him as if in thought. A minute later, the suit who'd been standing in front of the museum sauntered along behind, his attention strictly on Sanders. Langford waited until they were well past before he got up and stretched. He stepped out of the alcove and crossed the grass to the sidewalk. He looked for Sanders and the suit near a building that looked like a greenhouse at the edge of the park. Instead, they followed the curve in the road that led to a park exit.

Langford headed for the botanic gardens and watched from there as Sanders continued on toward the park exit. Discreetly, Langford followed, but when Sanders crossed over to his side of the road, Langford hung back. He sprinted to a copse of trees on the opposite side of the street, and stayed out of sight until he got a fix on where Sanders and his tail were headed. A hundred yards down the road, Sanders stopped and stood on the outskirts of a large playground.

The shouts and laughter of high voices drifting toward him froze Langford where he stood. He hadn't heard those sounds since he was a kid himself. They churned memories of carefree days and all the time that had been taken away from him. Sanders just stood there, watching the children play. *Was he some sort of perv? A pedophile? Did he have kids of his own? The house the ex-wife lived in was large enough to handle a whole passel of them.* Langford frowned, wondered if he'd ever have children of his own, or if that possibility was yet another thing that he'd been denied. He didn't even know if he wanted children, hadn't ever considered it. Those weren't the sorts of thoughts one fostered in prison.

Dusk shrouded the park in growing darkness. Mothers and fathers had already been rounding up their offspring, trickling out in small groups for some time. The cheerful noises slowly died along with the light as the park emptied. Langford sat comfortably on the grass, half-hidden by a flowering shrub at the edge of the path.

The streetlamps luminesced, glowing orbs atop ten-foot iron posts slowly growing brighter. The playground was long empty and night had fully taken hold when Sanders walked back the way he'd come, head down, hands thrust deeply into his pockets, shoulders hunched. The lights cast shadows that advanced and retreated as he moved. Langford stood and eased away from the sidewalk deeper into the copse of trees. Sanders passed by without looking up.

Melting into the darkness, Langford watched until he was sure Sanders was headed back to his car, his government-paid escort close behind. Then he found his way back to the street where he'd parked, unlocked the Scout and climbed in to wait. It wasn't long before Sanders's car pulled out of the park exit under the streetlight at the next corner. The dark sedan wasn't far behind. Staying well back, Langford pulled onto the street and followed.

Sanders led them randomly through town for another hour, stopping only once more, this time to buy a cup of coffee at an espresso stand. Twice, Langford was sure that Sanders had spotted the cars tailing him, but his erratic, haphazard turns never materialized into attempts to shake pursuers. Langford was beginning to rue his decision to dog his old friend when Sanders pulled into a large parking lot down near Ballard locks that linked Lake Union with Puget Sound.

The sedan pulled into the lot entrance of a waterfront restaurant next door, already closed for the night. Langford craned his neck to see Sanders park behind him. He passed the restaurant entrance and halfway down the next block swung the wheel into a tight U-turn. Stepping on the accelerator, he drove past the restaurant and the lot where Sanders had parked. He saw Sanders climb out of the car and walk toward a large warehouse. Speeding up, he drove to the end of the building and found another entrance on the far side. He wheeled into the lot in the back and followed the perimeter of the building down to the side facing the water.

Far ahead he saw Sanders and a few men headed toward the light spilling out of the open door of a loading dock in the warehouse. Sanders towered over the others. He drove slowly now, getting a little closer to the lighted warehouse door. An open space with a good vantage point beckoned, and he quickly braked and backed into the slot, giving him a full view of the loading dock. Above the door on the side of the building large letters spelled out "Seattle Times."

His eyes widened. *Sanders, a newspaper boy?* The information he had must be outdated. Sanders was supposed to be high up in some consulting firm, dealing with public affairs for clients like sports teams and local companies. As he absorbed this new development, a figure stepped out of the shadows of a small shed on the quay and intercepted Sanders. A woman. Sanders stopped dead, obviously taken aback by her presence. She turned slightly, giving Langford a glimpse of her face as she accosted Sanders. Langford was just as surprised.

He knew that face. Back row, closest to the door of the courtroom in Benton. She'd been there every time he'd turned for a glimpse of the gallery that had rooted for his conviction. Had asked his attorneys who she was. And now had no trouble remembering that her sister Jill Baines had been the one who'd died, the one he'd been accused of shooting at point-blank range. The one whose body they'd found him standing over. A chill ran through him and for a brief instant, panic. He squelched it, cleared his head and thought about what it meant.

Pieces of the puzzle he'd labored for years to solve suddenly dropped into place, rendering a more complete picture. It made sense. He was closer now. But so were they. He didn't have much time. Especially since now he knew he'd have to make an additional stop on the way back, one that would take him the long way around the Sound. He put the Scout in gear and slowly pulled out of the space, turning away from Sanders and the woman and quickly leaving them behind.

Michael W. Sherer

CHAPTER 35

I drove in a daze for a while trying to put it all together, not really sure where I was going. I know I spent time up in the park where Molly and I used to play for long hours with Cole when he was little. The gaping hole his suicide had left ached like a heavy weight pressing on my chest. The abscess had almost turned gangrenous by the time Molly and I split, but it had slowly closed over. Volunteering with Jeri's suicide prevention group had helped, but every so often I went a round with the what-ifs and the twin harbingers of depression, regret and remorse, that ripped the wound open again. If I wasn't careful, my mind would walk into an ADD trap of negativity, a ruminative cycle on everything I'd ever done wrong.

Thoughts of Cole and Molly weren't all that distracted me. Too much had happened in a week for me to process, filling my head with bits and pieces of information that darted around like microbes on a slide, none of which I could quite manage to bring into focus. My usual dose of meds hadn't helped, either, unable to counteract the exhaustion that pulled at me. Every movement, every thought felt like swimming in molasses.

Work beckoned, an oasis to a thirsty man, a place where I could let myself get swallowed up in routine and push the thoughts aside. I drove down to the warehouse in Ballard early enough to find plentiful parking. A few other route drivers pulled in as I got out and walked toward the steps next to the *Times* loading dock. The open doorway yawned widely, spilling bright white light from the metal halides lamps inside. Halfway there, someone stepped out of the shadows at the edge of the wharf overlooking the marina, bringing me up short. Keely.

"Where have you been?" she said.

Shadows made it hard to read her expression.

"Around." My face grew warm.

"Around? Around where?"

I shrugged. "You're mad at me."

"More like worried. I didn't know where you were."

"What difference does it make?"

"What diff—?" For a moment her mouth hung open. "I stopped by your apartment, checked with your landlord, waited to see if you'd show up for work." She ticked the points off on her fingers. "No sign of you."

"Now you're stalking me?" I smiled, tried to make light of it.

She wasn't buying. "For god's sake, you come by in the middle of the night and tell me someone tried to kill you. When I wake up, you're gone, nowhere to be found. What the hell am I supposed to think? I thought you were dead, damn it!"

"'Fraid not." I held my arms out and looked at them. "Sorry to disappoint you. Still here."

She slapped me. Hard. I didn't see it coming, and it landed with a loud crack like the snap of a wet locker room towel on bare ass, attracting the attention of two Vietnamese co-workers passing by. They may not have understood what we were saying, but they didn't mistake the hand-delivered message.

I rubbed my cheek, eyes widening. "What the hell was that for?"

She turned away quickly, but not before I saw tears glistening on the edge of her eyelids.

Confusion running through me, I hesitantly put a hand on her shoulder. "Hey, don't do that. I'm sorry. Whatever I did, I didn't mean it."

She whirled to face me again, incredulity painting her features. "Are you kidding? I said I thought you were dead. I didn't say I *wanted* you dead. What's the matter with you?"

Anger trumped confusion. "What's wrong with *me*? What are you doing here? Accosting me at work? In the middle of the night? If you're not stalking me, it's a damn good imitation."

"I'm not supposed to care about you?"

"And I don't, I suppose. You were right. Someone tried to kill me. I've been trying to figure out why. Who. I *left* because I didn't want to involve you any more than I already had. I was afraid I might have put you in danger."

Her abrupt laugh stopped me. "*You* were looking out for *me*? That's pretty funny coming from someone who wouldn't even offer his best friend a little support when he needed it."

The confusion was back. "Wait. What? Are you talking about Wink? Langford?"

Her silence signaled affirmation.

"You want to know where I was?" I said. "It just so happens I flew back to Illinois to see if I could figure out where Wink might have gone. I've been pretty busy the past few days."

She widened her stance and put her hands on her hips. "And you didn't think you could tell me? You couldn't even spare a few minutes to call me and tell me you were okay?"

The tears were back in her eyes. She sniffed and blinked them away.

"Whoa! I told you, I was trying to protect you. And then I got so caught up in following in what I was doing I kind of forgot."

"You forgot?"

"I do that!" I snapped. "I get involved in what I'm doing and I forget things sometimes."

"You just left! No note or anything!"

"Is that what this is about? You're pissed I didn't call you?"

"We made love! Or don't you remember that part?"

"We had sex. Great sex, Keely, but I don't know you well enough to make love to you. Don't give yourself so much credit."

"You bastard!"

She came at me with both hands raised high. I got my arms up in time, elbows out, hands protecting my face as she pounded me with her fists. The rain of blows bounced mostly harmlessly off my shoulders and arms, but a few caromed off the side of my head making me glad she wasn't any bigger. I finally clapped both hands around her wrists and held them tight. She wriggled and aimed a pointed toe at my shin.

"Stop! Stop it! Shit, Keely, I'm sorry. I shouldn't have said that. I didn't mean I didn't enjoy it. You. Or that I'm not grateful for what you did for me."

She sagged, fight gone out of her, and I let go. She stepped back, looking at me from under her eyelashes, nostrils flaring.

"No, you're just the 'fuck-'em-and-forget-'em type I hated so much in high school." Her voice held more bitterness than a double shot of espresso.

"I—" My ears rang and my heart pounded. "We shouldn't have done that, Keely. *I* shouldn't have done that."

"Why not?" She sniffled.

"I'm not ready," I said. It wasn't that simple, but I couldn't articulate why. "I made a mistake."

She looked at me thoughtfully, but didn't reply.

"I should have left you a note," I said. "Or called. I'm sorry."

My hand moved to touch her cheek. I thought better of it and willed it back down. It hung awkwardly at my side. I shoved it into a pocket and shifted my weight onto one leg.

"Look, I have to go to work. Are we okay here?"

She inhaled sharply and let it out slowly, shaking her head. "No, we're not fucking okay here."

"I said I was sorry. What else do you want me to say?"

"It's not okay. Not until you tell me about Langford."

I blinked. "Not much to tell," I said slowly. "I have a lead on where he might be. Figured I'd follow up on it when I finish my route."

"I'm coming with you." She set her mouth in a determined line.

"I don't think that's such a—"

"I'm not asking."

I put my hands up in surrender. "Don't blame me if something goes wrong."

"Like what? What do you think he'll do?"

"Oh, I don't know. Kill us?"

"Don't be melodramatic."

I lifted a shoulder and let it fall. "I really don't know what to expect."

"I thought you had to go to work," she said.

"I do."

"So?" She nodded toward the loading dock. "Lead on."

CHAPTER 36

We missed the first Edmonds-Kingston ferry by five or ten minutes, which put us close to the head of the line for the next one, leaving at 6:25. As soon as we parked aboard, I got out and made my way straight up to the passenger deck, leaving Keely to fend for herself. I hadn't been able to figure her out. She'd expressed concern at the warehouse, but her sudden shift in attention to our game of "Where's Wink?" had thrown me. And her rebuke still stung—I wasn't sure what I'd done wrong. Well, I knew, but I couldn't admit it.

I bought a large coffee and took it outside to the forward observation deck. Blue water slid by the steel hull as the ferry got underway, the breeze picking up as we gained speed and moved away from shore. The salt air filled my nose with the briny scent of decaying seaweed and denizens of the deep. A gull floated on air currents ten feet overhead, effortlessly keeping pace with the ferry, sharp eyes watching for errant crumbs from some passenger's breakfast.

Already well above the horizon, the sun blasted radiation through the back of my shirt as if the material didn't exist. My shadow danced on the rippling water, staying just ahead of the racing bow. I was grateful for the cool air standing my short hair up on end. The nighttime temperature hadn't fallen much below a balmy sixty-five degrees, and another cloudless sky augured a carbon copy of the prior day's heat. I hoped the coffee and cool air would revive me and clear the fog out of my head.

Keely came up beside me and rested her forearms on the rail, staring at the water below. I tensed involuntarily. I hadn't exchanged more than a dozen words with her during the night other than to ask her to hand me alternate newspapers for certain customers on the route. She'd worked tirelessly, hadn't complained, and I knew she had to be as tired as I was. She gave no indication.

She raised her head and scanned the far shore. "What's the plan?"

"No plan."

"Is that a good idea?"

"Hell, I don't know. I figured go in quiet, see what's what. If we don't get shot, knock on the front door."

"That might work."

I glanced at her. "I still don't know why you're so gung-ho on finding him."

She turned her head, one blue eye peering up at me visible under a sheaf of blonde hair. She looked relaxed, a vacationer or tourist headed for a week of rest and recreation. A painted nail fluttering in the sun drew my eye. A forefinger softly tapped the rail in triple time, revealing how tightly wound she was.

"Like I told you," she said, "he didn't do it. He didn't deserve to have twenty years of his life taken away from him."

"So this is out of the goodness of your heart? Might make you feel better, but it won't give him his life back." No more than I could by telling him I was sorry for leaving him in the lurch. But I had to try.

"No, I'm not that altruistic." She looked down at the water for a moment. "The question is, if he didn't do it, who did?"

"Been asking myself the same thing."

"I want the people who killed my sister."

I considered her, the tone sending a shiver up my spine.

"Guess we're all convinced Wink knows more than the rest of us," I said. "A neat trick if it's true. Since he's been locked up all this time."

"He knows something. I'm sure of it."

I wasn't sure of anything, particularly the reception we'd get from a guy who'd had more than twenty years to grow a chip on his shoulder.

"Why'd you change your mind, anyway?" she said.

"I didn't. Not really. I owe him. It's bugged me over the years. You know, one of those things you did or said you wish you could take back? Get a do-over? I just figured it was too late. Until you showed up, that is, and let me know he was out."

I stood there and let the breeze caress my face, emptying my head of everything but the images surrounding me. Dark blue water dappled with silver flashes of light and dotted with white triangles of fabric taut and pregnant with wind. A cyaneous sky deepened by degrees to ultramarine overhead, reflecting the deep water below. Shoreline bluffs and receding hills lush and verdant with dark shades of emerald and virid conifers. Sage mountains in the distance topped with dollops of frozen whipped cream.

For a moment, a fleeting desire to turn around and go home and spend the day in bed with the woman beside me nearly intoxicated me. But the rift I'd caused seemed unbridgeable. Tension still radiated from her, a low hum that vibrated through the soles of my feet, tenor harmony to the bass of the engine below decks. I couldn't tell if it was anger, hurt, disappointment, and didn't have the courage to find out. But something else drove the fantasy out of my head. A feeling I still couldn't articulate. *This just won't work between us, darling. But believe me, it's not me, it's you.*

And there was still the question of why I kept thinking about someone else. Someone who had displaced Molly in my thoughts. But someone who wasn't even in the picture any longer.

The Kingston ferry dock hove into view. Wordlessly, I turned and walked back inside to the companionway down to the car deck. I climbed in and watched the well-rehearsed dance of the deck crew as the ferry glided in toward the dock, deck suddenly rumbling loudly as the captain threw the engines into reverse, churning the water alongside a foamy green. The boat slid slowly into its berth. A lone cormorant perched atop one of the massive pilings, wings pinned to the sky by its alulae, a pterodactylean crucifix. It remained motionless as we slid past.

The ferry settled against the dock with a gentle bump. Deck hands made it fast with thick hawsers thrown over heavy cleats bolted to the hydraulic gangplank already being lowered onto the deck. Car engines fired up, and a deckhand waved the middle lane off the boat. I fastened my seat belt and started the car. Brake lights flashed in the line ahead as drivers put their cars in

225

gear. The passenger door opened and Keely climbed in with a smile on her face, a little breathless. Easing my foot off the brake, I let the car roll, following the line ahead.

"Cutting it a little close?"

She shrugged. "I've never been on a ferry. I wanted to see it come into the dock." She strapped herself in and looked out the windshield. "Where we headed?"

"Other side of Hood Canal. Why?"

"Are we in any special hurry?"

"I guess not."

"Buy a girl breakfast? I'm hungry."

As soon as she said it, the coffee churned the acid in my stomach, and I realized I was famished, too.

"Sure, why not?"

I passed up the few restaurants along the highway close to the ferry terminal—a couple of pubs, a pizza joint and a family restaurant that wasn't open yet. On the other side of town, I started to pull into a fast -food restaurant where the food at least was cheap when I spotted a little place behind it that looked like it served decent coffee and baked goods. It was nearly empty— either too early still or a bad sign regarding the food—so we had our pick of tables. Strong scents of cinnamon, butter and yeast suggested we'd get a far better breakfast here than at the fast food joint next door.

Keely led the way to a table in the back, away from the windows. She eased her purse off her shoulder and hung it on the back of her chair. A waitress stopped at the table with menus and a pot of coffee. We accepted both gratefully. After a minute or two of perusing the choices, I set the menu to the side and took a sip of coffee. Keely did the same a moment later, gaze drifting around the room, avoiding me.

"Well, this is awkward," I said.

A smile bloomed and faded quickly. She toyed with her coffee cup, twisting it one way then the other. I waited her out.

"I'm sorry about last night," she said.

I rubbed my cheek, still feeling the imprint of her fingers. "I think I'll live. Anyway, I probably deserved it."

"You did. But I ... well, I guess I didn't have to hit you so hard." She paused. "You said you weren't ready. For what?"

"For what we did. I mean—"

"Look, I don't have any claim on you. I'm not so delusional I thought we'd fall madly in love based on a one-night stand."

Relief flooded through me. I tried not to show it. "I didn't think you were."

"Oh, you mean you're not ready to have sex? Why?" Her eyes widened. "There's someone else."

"There was. We're divorced."

"It was recent, I take it."

"It's been a while. I just haven't gotten used to the idea. It's hard to talk about it."

"You still love her?"

I cocked my head, found myself listening to the pounding in my chest as if it would give me the answer to that question. And felt confused over who it pounded for, Molly or... Talking about Molly was easier.

"Yes and no. I guess I love what we had. I can't figure out why we aren't trying to get back to that place. But we're not the same people we were then." I searched her face to see if that made any kind of sense. "What about you?"

She looked up. "I was married once. It didn't take. Lasted only a few years. I don't think about it much."

She fell silent, absently looking out the windows across the room.

"So, you're taking the day off work?" I said. "Don't you have to call in sick or something?"

"I've been taking some time off."

"So that call the other night...?"

"I stay in touch."

"What is it you do, again?"

"I told you, consulting." She waved a hand. "I don't want to talk about work. It's boring."

She seemed eager to avoid the subject. I was about to press when the waitress showed up to take our order. As soon as the woman left, Keely turned the conversation to another topic.

When we finished eating, Keely excused herself to go to the restroom. I told her I needed to gas up the Toyota and suggested she meet me at the station across the street. She hadn't shown by the time I topped off the tank. I pulled away from the pump and parked by the side of the service bay. I was about to go look for her when I spotted her crossing the street. She circled around the back of the car and got in.

"Problems?" I said.

"No, everything's fine. Sorry it took so long." She offered a hesitant smile, but no explanation.

The road out of town meandered north up through the little town of Port Gamble, then west to the floating bridge over Hood Canal. From there we turned south down a little finger of land between the canal and Dabob Bay. From Kingston, we had less than thirty miles to drive, but the rural two-lane roads slowed our travel time to nearly an hour. The air conditioning, already set on cold storage, struggled to keep up. I cracked a window to create a little more air circulation, but the heat slowly won out, turning the car into more bread warmer than a fridge.

I drew Keely into conversation a few times, trying to elicit more details about her—where she lived, her family and friends. She deflected direct questions with the skill of a fencing champ, with little parries that left us still engaged but pointed a few degrees off center. She was evasive, but I didn't quite understand how she was doing it or whether it was even deliberate. We drove the last twenty minutes in silence.

I turned off the main highway onto a side road that quickly ran out of pavement, changing to gravel. I slowed, carefully steering around potholes washed out by spring rains. A half-mile farther, it narrowed to one lane through dense trees, slowing us to a pace a jogger could match. When end of the road appeared to turn into the driveway of a small bungalow, I pulled over and stopped. We'd passed only one other house, and the only noise filtering through the woods was the chirping of birds. Dust kicked up by the car slowly caught up and enveloped us in a brown haze, coating our sticky, exposed skin with a fine layer of mud. The tall trees gave us some shade, but blocked any breeze, letting the heat settle on the forest floor like a hot iron.

"Is that it?" Keely pointed at the house up ahead.

I consulted the maps I'd printed out the day before and shook my head. "No, we're going in the back way."

Throwing the car in reverse, I backed up until I found a spot wide enough to turn around and maneuvered the car facing the way we'd come. The house at the end of the road was out of sight. I drove onto the shoulder, and parked the car as close in to the trees as I could, nosing it the car in between a couple of big firs.

"We walk from here," I said, getting out.

I shoved the maps in my back pocket and walked around to open the trunk. I retrieved Charlie's gun and tucked it into my waistband, pulled my shirt down over it, and pocketed four of the extra clips. *This is Wink we're talking about here. He used to be your best friend.* I took two clips out of my pockets and started to put them back in the sports duffel. Then I changed my mind and slammed the trunk lid. Keely stood in the road waiting. I joined her, and we walked back toward the end of the road.

When we reached the driveway, I led the way into the woods, skirted the house by a wide margin and turned east. The first three hundred yards were slow going. We picked our way through the undergrowth beneath the thick canopy of conifers, oaks and sumacs that blocked out the sun. The terrain sloped gently downhill, but we battled dense thickets of blackberry brambles and brush, waded through seas of ferns and went over or around fallen tree trunks lush with moss. But we soon broke into a clearing the size of a football field covered with bear grass and stubby pines. Beyond it was another dirt road.

The road descended toward a point of land that poked an elbow into the canal. Through the trees I caught occasional glimpses of blue water both ahead and to our right. The sun beat us mercilessly. Keely swiped the back of her neck and wiped her hand on her slacks as she shuffled along, kicking up puffs of dust with her beige leather flats. She'd abandoned a light cotton sweater in the car. Her sleeveless blouse was smudged with dirt, and a diagonal slash of green stained one leg of her slacks. Her tousled hair hung in damp strands, and thin red streaks crisscrossed a forearm raked by thorns. She hadn't uttered a peep.

Exhaustion pounded me as relentlessly as winter surf breaking on the Nā Pali Coast of Kauai. Shadows flitted past the corners of my vision, but when I turned my head they vanished in the bright sun. Hallucinations, brought on by lack of sleep. Or maybe the light was playing tricks. Keely's profile again reminded me of someone I knew, but I couldn't dredge it up from memory. Wired on adrenaline, caffeine and the remains of the amphetamine-like stimulant in my last dose of meds, my muscles were taught, nerves tightly wound. But my insides felt queasy and unsettled. Sort of like a toasted marshmallow—crispy on the outside, gooey on the inside.

When I glimpsed a structure of some sort through the trees I stopped and motioned to Keely, putting a finger to my lips. She nodded and joined me at the side of the road.

"No sense announcing ourselves," I murmured.

We walked along the edge of the road, sheltered from view. More peeks of the structure revealed its shape—a large log cabin. Honest Abe's boyhood home on steroids. Dark blue water sparkled in the sunlight behind it. To the right of the cabin, in a cleared sandy area fronting a small beach, stood a boxy building almost as large as the cabin. A lack of windows suggested a garage or storage shed of some sort, big enough for several cars, maybe a boat. An old utility vehicle sat parked in the drive between the two buildings, but the cabin showed no sign of life.

Over the hum in my ears from lack of sleep, a man-made sound intruded. The growl of a large engine in low gear drifted down from somewhere above us. The road in front of the cabin took a sharp left out of sight up the hill to the entrance from the main road. *Someone coming.* Keely stopped and tipped her head. I pointed into the woods. She followed as I stealthily picked my way between the trees. The engine grew louder until a black SUV burst into the clearing with a roar and skidded to a stop in a cloud of dust. The doors flew open and all hell broke loose.

CHAPTER 37

Five men emerged from the vehicle, all in black, all carrying assault rifles. They fanned out in front of the cabin, moving with purpose, unaffected by the heat. Two headed for the corners of the building. Two went straight in for a direct attack. One stood guard a few yards from the SUV. I quietly bobbed and weaved to get a better view through the trees as the men disappeared and reappeared.

Motion beyond the cabin caught my attention, and I darted to the next tree for a better angle. Two, no, three people hurried away from the other side of the cabin toward the water, a man roughly shepherding an older couple. Hard to tell at this distance, but the graying heads looked like Charlie's parents. But even after twenty-plus years, I could have easily picked Wink out of a crowd. The cabin blocked them from view of the assault team, but they'd soon be visible to the man circling around to the left.

Decision time.

I knew what the men in black would do. They were a recurring nightmare that bathed me in sweat and glued my tongue to the roof of a mouth so dry it put the Mojave to shame. On the other hand, I didn't know how Wink would react to seeing me after all this time. My guilt had festered a long time, turning it fetid and rancid. I'd buried it deep, but now it bubbled up, toxic waste leaking from an old, rusty steel drum. On top of it all were confused thoughts about Keely—concern, gratitude, aversion, attraction—compounding my distraction. I wished I could flip a switch and turn it all off, a surge protector that would shut everything down, even the vampire power that lit all the standby indicators.

"What are you doing?" Keely screamed.

My subconscious had already made the decision for me. Instinct and impulsivity had kicked in like the old days on the basketball court, making me move without thinking. I crashed through the underbrush, gun already in hand, oblivious to the branches that whipped at my arms and face and tore at my clothing. The lookout near the black SUV turned at the sound of Keely's voice and the left flanker spotted Wink and the Joneses and shouted a warning. Wink appeared to shove Clayt forward into Connie and shouted, "Run!" He whirled, firing a blast from a shotgun. The flanker returned fire, but Wink had already bolted for the trees and disappeared from sight. The lookout let loose a burst in our direction that ripped into tree limbs around me with the hum of angry bees, showering me with bits of bark and leaves.

I ducked behind the trunk of a large fir, poked my head out and got a fix on the shooter, then pivoted the opposite direction clear of the tree. I raised the gun with both hands and fired off half a clip through a gap in the greenery, lowering the sights a smidge after each recoil before pulling the trigger again. The man clutched at his arm and dove behind the SUV. The pair advancing on the front door spun around and hit the dirt, blasting away indiscriminately into the trees. I bent down, and bulled my way five yards closer through the underbrush, pausing for breath behind another thick tree trunk.

The gunfire stopped for a moment, the reverberations still rattling my eardrums like a church bell clapper. I slowly stood, back to the tree, and risked a glance toward the cabin. On the far side, Clayt stood motionless, bent over something on the ground. Connie was nowhere to be seen. I wondered if she'd been hit. Two men slowly approached him, their rifles at the ready. A shotgun blast from the woods sent one diving for the ground and the other racing toward Clayt, keeping Clayt between him and another blast from Wink's gun.

Black hats poked up on the other side of the SUV, bringing my attention back to more immediate matters, like survival. Two pairs of sunglasses searched the woods for a sign of me. Like I wasn't a big enough target that I didn't stand out. I straightened, took a bead and squeezed off the rest of the clip. Before they could return fire, I ran for cover, ejected the clip and fished in my pocket for a new one. Diving behind a fallen log, I rammed the clip home and reminded myself to breathe. The explosive clatter of their weapons reverberated through the woods. More debris rained down on my head. I heard the chatter of more automatic weapons from farther away, and the answering boom of the shotgun.

I crawled a couple of yards to a spot behind a bushy sumac before they could pinpoint my position. They shouted to each other now, relaying information and instructions back and forth, only some of which I could make out over the din of gunfire. I rolled over into the tall grass at the edge of the road and cautiously raised my head. I had a clear view of the cabin and SUV parked in front, but still no shot at the men prone in the dirt behind the vehicle.

The two commandos behind the cabin marched Clayt toward the SUV. One of them had slung Connie over his shoulder like a sack of cement. Her arms dangled limply, swinging with every step. She was either dead or unconscious. A third marauder joined them, covering their rear, crabbing sideways and scanning the woods, rifle at the ready. Wink's gun was silent. I wondered if he was already gone. As often as he'd played practical jokes, he'd always known when to cut and run—except that once.

A shout drew my attention back to the SUV. The sight of an outstretched arm and pointed finger sent me rolling back into the woods. Bullets mowed the grass and chewed up the ground where I'd lain with a percussive song of death. Heart pounding, I scrambled onto all fours and scuttled deeper into the trees, feet slipping and limbs flailing in a desperate attempt to get away. I heard the snorting of a pig rooting for truffles, and realized the sound was coming from me.

Pulling up short behind a tree, chest heaving, I stretched a two-handed grip around the trunk, closed one eye and fired until the slide locked open. Dropping low, I scrabbled behind another nearby tree, thumbed the magazine catch and fished in my pocket for a loaded clip.

Breathe!

"They're in!" someone yelled.

"Go! Go! Go!"

An engine came to life with a roar. I stood and stepped around the tree to fire again, but flinched and ducked as bits of bark exploded in front of my face, gunfire deafening me. *Shit! Shit! Shit!* I dove to the ground and pressed my face into the dirt, wishing I had some of Alice's "DRINK ME" potion. Two or three guns fired at once now, pinning me in place. A swarm of bullets tore into the brush around me, filling the air with debris and certain death, the dizzying cascade of objects and sounds swelling my brain with sensory overload. I even thought I heard the boom of another gun join the cacophony. Slower, spaced shots. Not the shotgun, but not the chatter of an assault rifle either.

A raw bellow of frustration ripped from my throat. I couldn't stop them now. I had no last-second cut-through or pick-and-roll to get clear for a winning shot. Nothing left in the playbook. Suddenly the firing stopped. I lay motionless, afraid of another onslaught. But the only sound over the ringing in my ears came from the SUV's straining engine, slowly receding as it climbed the hill into the woods. I slowly got to my feet and looked around.

Keely.

The prefrontal cortex is largely responsible for keeping us focused, handling short-term memory and wrestling with abstract problems. It's also in charge of self-control. The problem with this chunk of brain tissue is that it's easily overloaded. Focus hard on one thing, add a couple of distractions, and self-control goes out the window. Concentrate on exercising restraint, using willpower to resist an extra slice of a favorite cake, say, and tough problems are more difficult to solve. Since the ADD I struggled with meant I probably had less gray matter in that area of the brain than the average human, I tended to tune out more external stimuli in order to focus. Could be the average Joe would have forgotten Keely under the circumstances. That didn't make me feel any better for having done it.

"Keely?" I called. "You okay?"

No answer.

I swallowed hard, and my heart hammered my ribs. I pushed through some brush to the road and got my bearings, then backtracked to where we'd been when the assault team had pulled into the front yard. No sign of her.

"Keely? Not funny. Where the hell are you?"

I turned slowly, straining to hear some signal—breathing, moaning, something—to let me know she was alive. A ship's horn sounded far out on the water. A nearby raven cawed, answered a moment later by another up the hill somewhere. The gentle lapping of little waves licking the shoreline drifted up from the water's edge. Something rustled faintly in the woods. My breath caught as I tried to determine the direction of the sound. Across the road, and gone now. A small animal, maybe. Squirrel or chipmunk.

I shoved the gun in my waistband, picked up a big stick and frantically beat the brush aside, wildly turning in circles in search of more places she might be hidden. My arms quickly tired and my breath came in ragged gasps as I thrashed aimlessly through the woods.

Get a grip and think!

I stood still for a moment and listened again, letting my breathing return to normal. I closed my eyes, thought of a mantra, and let it tumble and burble through my head to help find a *drishti*. Calmer now, I went back to the spot where I'd left her, and worked my way out in concentric circles, covering the ground slowly, fixating on every movement and change in color in the brush. Sweat trickled into my eyes and dripped off my nose, and salt stung the myriad cuts and scratches on my arms and face. Thirty feet out, cold, hard metal pressed against the back of my neck, stopping me dead.

Michael W. Sherer

CHAPTER 38

"Easy, Legs." Wink's voice, still familiar after all these years. "Put the stick down. No sudden moves."

I let the stick drop, raised my hands and slowly turned to face him. He took a half-step back, lifting the barrel of the shotgun until it seemed I could almost see straight down to the crimped end of the shell in the breech, waiting to be fired.

"Okay," he said quietly, "now ease that gun out—two fingers, that's it—and toss it in the dirt here. Gently!"

Still lean and wiry, he was bigger than I remembered, broader across the shoulders, biceps bulging below the short sleeves of his T-shirt. His face was lined, but youthful, a more grown-up version of the one I'd seen last.

I wet my lips. "You don't seem surprised to see me."

He cocked his head. "I heard you were looking for me."

"Holden." I saw acknowledgement in his eyes. I glanced down at the shotgun. "Is that necessary?"

"Let's see, here you are in the middle of nowhere, on my property, no car. Armed, no less. I haven't heard word one from you since my ass got sent to prison. And when you do show up, so do a bunch of heavily armed assholes intent on starting a small war."

"I had nothing to do with that." I lowered my arms halfway.

"You brought them here."

"No, I didn't. I swear it. Christ, Wink, I tried to stop them. What the hell you think they were shooting at over here? Raccoons?"

"Tell me why I shouldn't kill you where you stand. You *led* them here."

I shook my head violently. "No way! They want me dead. I don't want them near me. And nobody followed me, either." I thought back to the ferry and the drive from Kingston. No black SUV that I could recall.

"A blind man could follow you. Hell, I was on your tail for hours yesterday."

I blinked and tried to wrap my mind around what he was saying. "You followed me? Why?"

"Why the sudden interest in a reunion, Legs? For twenty years I don't hear jack, and all of a sudden you're looking for me?"

I put my hands out, palms up. "I was just trying to help."

"Help? Now you want to help? Where the hell were you? You skipped out on me. After all those times I had your back, you left me hanging."

I flushed, and felt my fingers close into tight knobs.

"You never had my back. *Ever.*" I thought the words, once spoken, would taste bitter. But the truth tasted as clean as new-fallen snow.

"What the hell are you talking about?"

"Every scrape you got me *out* of," I hooked two fingers on each hand around a two-foot stretch of air, "I wouldn't have been in if I hadn't been hanging out with you. If anything, I'm the one who had *your* back. Who else was crazy enough—or a big enough chump—to go along with your schemes?"

"That's bullshit. Nobody forced you."

"That's right. You never twisted my arm. So don't go telling me I left you hanging."

"Yeah, well, the one time you decided to bail ended up costing me my freedom."

"So you're going to kill me for it?"

He shrugged. "It's an option."

A soft voice from over Wink's shoulder froze us both in position. "Put the weapon down!"

A woman's voice. Familiar, but not Keely's. I frowned. Wink tensed, eyes flicking from my face to his sides, trying to get a glimpse of the speaker.

"I'm training an HK Forty-Five Compact with ten rounds of plus-P ammunition at the back of your head, Mr. Langford," the voice said. "And at this distance I won't miss. Please rethink what you're considering and lay down the weapon."

238

Wink stooped slowly and set the shotgun down next to him on the bed of pine needles covering the ground under his feet.

"Thank you," said the voice.

A slight figure stepped out from behind a tree, arms extended, black semi-automatic gripped in one hand. She wore a green T-shirt and woodland pattern camo pants held up by a nylon web belt, pant legs tucked into lightweight black combat boots. The sides of her dark hair, normally worn in a chin-length bob, were tied up in a short ponytail on top of her head. Her face was smeared with dirt. She'd blended into the foliage so well that had she not moved I wouldn't have known where to look for her. Now I couldn't look anywhere else, the stark contrast between her looks and toughness mesmerizing. Her symmetrically sculpted face, with its delicate nose, full lips and doe eyes, sent my heart up into my mouth.

"Reyna?" My mind was reluctant to believe my eyes.

A small smile passed over her lips as she gave me a quick glance.

"How've you been, civvy? Looks like you really stepped in it this time. Might want to close your mouth now before you start catching flies." She returned her attention to Wink.

My head reeled with confusion, and my chest felt too tight to take a full breath. Reyna walked up behind Wink, crouched and pulled the shotgun away. Still aiming the pistol at him, she lifted the shotgun with the other hand and stepped back to lean it against the trunk of a fir.

"What are you doing here?" I said.

"Saving your butt, maybe. Again."

She circled to Wink's left, forming a triangle where Wink could see her and she could cover both of us.

Wink took her in, eyes taking a casual walk from her head to her toes and back.

"Someone want to clue me in?" he said.

"Wink, meet Reyna Chase, lieutenant commander, U.S. Naval Intelligence." I looked at Reyna for confirmation. "It is still lieutenant commander. They haven't promoted you to admiral or something, have they?"

She looked amused. "Nope. You got it right."

"Hasn't been that long." A little more than five months. And she'd made an impression.

"Excuse me," Wink said. "Am I interrupting? You two want to go somewhere and reminisce? Get a room, maybe?"

The day suddenly seemed warmer by degrees, but Reyna took no notice.

"The only reminiscing I want to hear, Mr. Langford, is an account of how you've spent the last few weeks."

"Perry," he said. "And why am I going to tell you what I did on my summer vacation?"

She shrugged. "You're a fugitive, a convicted felon. I could call the local cops. Parole violation, possession of a firearm... Want me to keep going?"

He shook his head.

"Besides," she said, "I'm holding a gun."

"Point taken." Wink swung his arm in an arc toward the cabin. "Might as well be more comfortable. Iced tea, anyone?"

"Sure," Reyna said. She motioned with her gun hand.

Wink nodded and turned. Tension drained out of me, and I took a step, falling in behind him. He stopped abruptly, bent at the waist and lashed out with a back kick that I barely saw coming. Instinctively, I shrank from the motion and caught his foot high on the hip. He followed with a roundhouse kick aimed at my head, but I anticipated him this time and warded it off with a forearm block, stepped inside the arc of his foot and punched him in the chest with an open palm. He staggered back, quickly regained his balance and bounced into fighting stance. I dropped back and did the same, watching him warily.

"Hey, you two!" Reyna said. "Cut it out!"

The menace on Wink's face dissolved in laughter. He straightened.

I scowled at him and rubbed my hip. It would bruise. "What the hell was that for?"

"For being such a chickenshit, candy-assed pansy back then. Looks like you learned a few tricks."

"We're not in fourth grade anymore, Wink. I can fight my own battles."

"Jesus, boys, there's so much testosterone floating around here it's making my eyes water," Reyna said. "Let's say we dial it back a bit and go have that iced tea. It's too damn hot to fight."

Wink and I locked eyes. He relented first, averting his gaze with a small shrug. Reyna retrieved the shotgun and tucked it in the crook of her arm. I found Charlie's pistol under a sword fern, brushed off the dirt and stuck it back in my waistband. This time, Wink led the way without a word. Halfway to the cabin I remembered why I'd been tramping the woods in the first place and stopped.

"Keely," I muttered. I did a slow three-sixty. The others turned to look at me curiously.

"Your girlfriend?" Wink said. "She's gone."

"She's not my girlfriend," I said, sounding more defensive than I'd intended. "And what do you mean gone?"

He put his hands on his hips. "I mean in all the ruckus I saw her running up the road. My guess is those guys grabbed her on the way out. Or else she made it up to the main road to hitch a ride somewhere."

Reyna's eyebrows reached for the sky and she mouthed the word "girlfriend?" I scowled at her and caught up to them. I wasn't sure what to make of either scenario Wink had suggested.

Inside, the cabin was as rustic as the log exterior promised, consisting of little more than a great room with a big fireplace on one wall, a small galley kitchen tucked in a corner, and an oak dining table large enough to seat ten in another. A small hallway led to two bedrooms, and a narrow staircase on the wall just inside the front door climbed to a balcony overlooking the main room and doors to two more bedrooms.

The log walls were dotted here and there with mounted fish, a creel and net, and framed photos of people in mostly outdoor poses—on the water in boats, on shore holding up large salmon, in group shots with mountains as a backdrop. Picturing family and guests, probably. Cedar paneling weathered a dark brown sheathed the interior walls. Large, overstuffed couches and chairs formed comfortable seating areas around the room without entirely dominating or filling the space. Braided rugs and animal skins covered a dark hardwood floor worn smooth by years of traffic. Tall bookshelves lined the walls on either side of the entry to the hall, the shelves bowed with the weight of hundreds of old hardbound volumes.

Picture windows on the side facing the water opened onto a view of Hood Canal and let in lots of light. Yet the cabin was dim compared with the nuclear incandescence outside, and cooler for it, insulated by the thick log walls. A ceiling fan slowly stirred the heated air, circulating musty scents of old leather, mildew, wicker, and dusty chintz.

True to his word, Wink fetched a pitcher of iced tea from an ancient round-shouldered refrigerator and grabbed three tall glasses from a cupboard. He brought them to the dining table and gestured at the empty chairs. Reyna acknowledged him with a nod, walked over to the fireplace first and leaned the shotgun against the stone hearth.

"Nice place," she said. "Family vacation home?"

She gazed around the room, eyes finally lighting on Wink. I stared at her, mind racing with dozens of questions I wanted to ask. She refused to look at me, as if she wanted to prolong my confusion and discomfort. My forearm rested on the table. Unbidden, my fingers quietly drummed the wood.

"It was in my mother's family," Wink said. "I came here a few times as a kid. It—"

"What are you doing here?" I blurted.

Reyna gave Wink an apologetic look before she slowly turned her gaze on me.

"If he hadn't asked, I would've," Wink said.

I pressed my lips together and nodded.

"I mean, why is the Navy interested in me?" Wink went on.

"We're not," Reyna said. She didn't say more.

She'd lost me, but Wink's face cleared as if she'd explained everything.

"Care to tell us why *you're* here?" Reyna's jaw tightened, steel evident in her voice.

"Where else...?" Wink closed his mouth and reconsidered. "They let me out early. For good behavior, they said. Commuted my sentence."

"Why? Why now?"

Wink pulled his brows down in annoyance. "Why not? I did enough time."

"The Feebs must have been pretty pissed," she said. "They just let you go without a fight?"

"You'd have to ask them."

Something in the way Wink said it made me think he was holding back, but Reyna didn't pursue it.

"You had houseguests when all this started," she said.

Wink pulled his shoulders up around his ears and wrinkled his nose. "You might say that."

"You think they're somehow responsible for you going to prison?"

"I think they're involved, yes."

"You think there's more to it than that."

Wink rubbed his mouth. "I 'invited' them here to talk about it. They denied knowing much more than the fact that it wasn't their idea, but they bought into it and set it up."

"You're talking about Clayt and Connie Jones," I said, to make sure I was on the same page.

Wink looked at me. "I'm talking about Colin and Corinne Wilson. Student radicals back in the '60s. Jones is the name they use now."

"Her maiden name," I said.

His eyes widened briefly. "You figured it out."

"I didn't know for sure." I paused. "Fitch seemed to be the connection."

He nodded. "I thought so, too." He stared at his hands clasped on the table.

"What happened back then, Wink?" I had to know.

He glanced at me sharply, then stared into the distance, collecting his thoughts.

"I told all this at the trial."

"I wasn't there."

"No, duh." His peeved expression turned thoughtful. "Maybe you really don't know."

The way he notched that arrow I thought he'd let it fly straight at the target labeled guilt pinned on my chest, but he simply stated it as a fact.

He went on, playing back the details on a holographic screen in the middle of the large room only he could see. "I went in the building and up to the lab like I said I was going to. I got the tubing, stuffed it in my backpack and was on my way out when I heard noises in the hall. Guys in black sneaking through the door to the stairwell. Two of them. I got worried, and hunkered down for a few minutes until I was sure the coast was clear. I'd just made up my mind to leave when, *boom*, the sky fell. I didn't know what to do. I froze, I guess. I don't know how long, but I eventually realized I heard someone screaming. It sounded far away until I figured out that I could barely hear over the ringing in my ears.

"I knew someone was hurt, so I went out in the hall to figure out where the screaming was coming from. Then I heard two gunshots, *bam, bam!* I ducked back into the lab where I'd been hiding and waited a few more minutes. I finally got up the courage to go look in the lab they bombed. Christ, what a mess! I found the girl in the office next door. The gun lay on the floor next to her. I don't know why I picked it up. To look at it up close, maybe. Doesn't matter. You know the rest."

"So, you didn't kill her," I said.

His eyes narrowed. "You really think I could have done that?"

I shifted in my chair and looked away. "I thought about how much pain that girl must have been in. So, yeah, I wondered."

Wink looked at Reyna and waved a hand. "There's loyalty for you. Some friend."

I clamped my jaw shut to dam up the flood that threatened to spew. Reyna saved me.

"The Wilsons are pretty popular folks," she said. "Someone else wanted their company, too—badly. Why?"

Wink rubbed his chin. "Same reason I did, I suppose. To find out what they knew."

"You didn't want to kill them for what they did to you?" I said.

His blue eyes reminded me of pools of water in arctic ice.

"They say Fitch approached them with the job." His tone was as cool as his gaze. "Sold it to them as one last hurrah, a last chance to relive their old days as radicals. Convinced them that no one would get hurt, and that he had a crew all lined up. Wilson said Fitch even brought another member of the crew around a couple of times to help sell the idea."

Reyna tipped her head sideways. "You don't buy it?"

"Fitch wasn't smart enough to put a job like that together," I interjected.

Wink nodded. "The explosives were military. And the lab they bombed wasn't the one Fitch told the Wilsons about."

"You don't think he made a mistake?"

"Fitch? He made a huge mistake. He trusted whoever really set up the job. And it wasn't the Wilsons."

"They got played." Reyna sighed. "They have no idea who set them up?"

Wink looked at the floor and wagged his head slowly. "Look, I'm not proud of what I did, but I sweated them for days. They don't know."

Reyna considered him. "But you have an idea."

He pulled at an earlobe, not meeting her gaze. Something he said finally registered.

"Wait, you said Clayt—Wilson, whatever—met someone else on the crew?"

Wink looked at me curiously. "Yeah, a guy named Phil."

Sarah had mentioned that "Uncle Sebastian" had brought Phil around the house that summer. It got me thinking about how even when people like the Wilsons changed identities they used new names close to their old ones so they wouldn't easily forget them. Some people didn't even bother changing their first names. It made me wonder if old man Donato had been on the hit list along with Fitch and the Wilsons and it had just taken twenty years to find him.

Reyna cocked her head. "We've got company."

I frowned, then heard tires crackle softly in the dirt out front.

CHAPTER 39

Reyna was on her feet, halfway to the door, gun in hand, before the sounds ceased.

She glanced over her shoulder and murmured, "You expecting anyone?"

Wink shook his head, slid out of his chair and padded toward the fireplace to retrieve the shotgun. An amplified voice filled the room, stopping him cold.

"Perry Langford! This is the FBI. Come out with your hands in the air!"

Reyna cursed under her breath. "Stay here."

She holstered her gun, opened the door, letting in a flood of sunshine, and stepped onto the porch. Wink and I followed partway to a vantage point where we could watch her from the shadows of the interior.

She held her ID aloft. "Morning, boys. Name's Chase. Lieutenant Commander with ONI. Something I can do for you?"

A small black man in a suit approached and stopped ten feet from the bottom step. *Drucker.* He peered up at her, face pinched with suspicion.

"Naval intelligence? What's your interest here?"

"Perry Langford has information concerning a case we're working."

"Is Langford inside, Lieutenant Commander? If so, you'd best send him out."

"Has he done something wrong?" Her voice was all innocence.

"Violated parole, ma'am."

"Well, we were just having a conversation. And when we're finished, Mr. Langford is accompanying me to Naval Base Kitsap. A little matter of national security."

Drucker frowned and his hand trembled. "Like hell he is. I don't care who you are or what bullshit you invoke, you don't have jurisdiction here. Langford's ours."

Taylor showed up at Drucker's side in shirtsleeves, cuffs rolled halfway up his forearms, tie loosened and collar unbuttoned. Glossy shoes were already coated with dust. His shaved head, wet with perspiration, sparkled in the sunlight. He held a gun with both hands.

"Shall we let our bosses decide?" Reyna reached for the phone in her hip pocket.

Taylor sighted on Reyna. "Hold it right there!"

She took her hand away slowly.

Drucker pulled his suit coat aside revealing a shoulder holster and slid his hand into his pocket. His shirt was crisp and unwrinkled despite the heat. He waved his other hand airily.

"Got anybody else in there? No? Didn't think so. Me and three of my agents. One of you. Your odds aren't too good. Let's try this again. Send Langford out here."

Reyna shrugged. "You want him. Come get him."

She folded her arms and leaned against the rail, lips pressed together in a grim expression as Drucker marched up the steps with Taylor right behind him. Drucker breezed on past without looking at her and through the open door. He stopped just inside, letting his eyes adjust to the dim light. Taylor stepped in and stood at his shoulder.

"You!" Drucker said when his gaze settled on me. "What the hell are you doing here?"

He turned to Taylor without waiting for an answer. "Get Andrews in here, have him cuff this sorry bastard and put him in your car."

Taylor spun on his heel and walked out, twisting a shoulder to avoid running into Reyna. She stood in the doorway, framed by the bright light. Drucker noted her presence with a grunt and faced me again.

"Sanders, you're under arrest. If I were you I wouldn't open my mouth until I had the best lawyer I could afford. Langford, quit thinking about making a move for that shotgun and sit your ass back down at that table. We need to have a little chat. We had a deal."

I jerked my head around and stared at Wink. "Deal? What deal?"

He raised his shoulders and offered a rueful smile.

Drucker grimaced. "We offered him early release in exchange for his cooperation. Which has been lacking."

I stared at Wink. "Cooperation for what?"

"They want the Wilsons," he said.

Drucker jutted his jaw. "I've been chasing those two for forty years. Langford said he knew where to find them. Based on what he told us, I was willing to give him a chance. But he gave us the slip after he was released." He scowled at Wink. "Where are they?"

"Not here." Wink settled wearily into a chair at the table.

"What the fuck did you do with them?"

"An assault team came in, I don't know, maybe twenty, thirty minutes ago and took them."

Drucker looked as if Wink had just told him the dog ate his homework. "Assault team."

"Same team that shot my friend the cop," I said, reminding him he knew damn well what Wink was talking about.

He brushed me off with a wave, glare still focused on Wink. "Guess you're screwed then. Deal's off."

A beefy man with a round head and no neck quietly excused himself as he squeezed past Reyna in the doorway. A roll of flesh crept over the too-tight collar of his starched shirt. Perspiration covered his florid features. He gestured toward me while looking at Drucker for confirmation. The furrow between Drucker's eyes deepened as he nodded impatiently.

A flash flood of anger coursed through me, its currents twitching muscles that rippled the skin on my arms and face. Unanswered questions swirled through my head, stirring up frustration and confusion that clouded an already overtaxed and spent brain. I could feel the flood rise to the point of spilling over. I never knew what form that might take—usually just an inappropriate comment, but sometimes I lashed out physically.

The meds helped me control it, but my system was so fried from exhaustion they probably wouldn't have done any good even if I'd remembered to take another dose.

Just when I thought I might explode, I saw Reyna pat the air, pushing her palm toward the floor. I heaved a sigh and held my arms out, wrists pressed together. Andrews lifted the flap of his coat and reached behind his waist for a pair of cuffs. He stood in front of me and snapped them on, looked up at my face and said, "Let's go."

Before we reached the door, Reyna put a hand on my chest and said, "Hold it!"

All eyes turned to look at her. She wrapped an arm around my waist, tugged the pistol loose and held it up. Then she fished in my pocket and pulled out one of the extra magazines and held that up, too. A tic jerked at my eyelid, and my fingers balled into a fist. I glared at her. She stared back, her face impassive, then swung her gaze away and looked pointedly at Andrews. Andrews spread his hands and glanced at Drucker with a sheepish expression.

"Christ, get him out of here," Drucker growled.

Andrews led me past another agent standing at attention on the porch to one of the sedans parked out front. He walked around to the far side, opened the back door and gestured me in. I ducked to fold myself inside, and he pushed my head down to keep me from banging it on the frame. He straightened and put a hand on the door.

"Hey, hold on!" Reyna lightly skipped down the steps and hustled over to the car.

I hunched over and peered sideways at her out the opening.

"I need to talk to him a minute," she told Andrews.

"Suit yourself." He took his hand off the door and stepped back.

She crouched by the opening and looked over her shoulder at him. "It's okay. I got this."

He stared at her for a second, shrugged and walked back to the cabin.

Reyna turned to me, leaned into the car and spoke in low tones. "Don't talk, just listen. I've got a friend, a commander over at the sub base, who's got a cottage over here, a couple hours away, maybe less."

As she talked her hands were busy slipping a thin piece of metal into the keyhole on one of the cuff bracelets. She popped it open within seconds.

"I'll figure out a way to get Andrews and his buddy to come in with me," she said. "As soon as they're inside, get the hell away from here. I'll meet you at the cottage as soon as I can."

"That was an act in there? Reyna, why—"

"Shut the hell up. We don't have time. We can talk later."

She fumbled with the second cuff and finally released it. Quickly reaching into a pocket, she pulled out a card and handed it to me. An address was written on the back. Her hand went behind her back and reappeared holding Charlie's gun. She slid it across the seat to me.

"Take this. You might need it."

Before I could reply, she rocked back on her heels and stood up. She slammed the door and stalked toward the cabin, even from the back looking like a woman rebuffed. Andrews stood facing the other agent, arms crossed, leaning against the railing. Their heads turned to watch her curiously as she walked up the steps. She said something I couldn't hear, and their expressions smoothed into friendly grins. She engaged them in conversation for a moment, then headed for the door. Pausing in the opening, she turned. Her mouth moved again, and her eyebrows arched. She waited a moment, twitched a shoulder and went in the cabin. The agents looked at each other. Andrews pushed away from the rail and followed her in. The younger man trailed behind.

Heart pounding so loud it drowned out other sounds, I sucked in a deep breath and levered open the car door with both hands. With an eye on the cabin, I slid out and crouched next to the car. Hunching over, I ran up the road, keeping the car between me and the cabin as long as possible. After a couple hundred yards the road curved up the hill. Once around it the cabin was out of sight. I slowed to a jog, chest heaving from the uphill climb, intent on increasing my distance before they discovered the empty car.

When I left the road and headed through the woods the way Keely and I had come, my breathing came a little easier. But my mind chivvied a hundred different thoughts and questions like a dog gnawing a bone.

* * * * *

The drive took closer to three nerve-wracking hours. It traced the shore of the Hood Canal south to its elbow, east to its tip and south again along one of the many inlets of Puget Sound. I kept my speed below the limit and a twitchy eye out for cops. By the time I found the place, I'd gone beyond exhaustion to something approaching a fugue state that had me wondering who and where I was. Sort of like a dream from which I couldn't wake up.

The clapboard cottage was weathered a rusty gray, and looked ramshackle, dilapidated. Nestled in a stand of trees, it fronted a wide beach on a rounded point of shoreline. A low tide exposed sand flats that stretched a hundred feet out before dropping steeply into deep water. With the nearest neighbor at least a nine-iron over the trees, the small house was private and semi-secluded. Some of the tightness in my neck and shoulders eased for the first time in hours.

I walked out to the water's edge, working out kinks in places cramped for hours in a car built for the average Japanese office lady. My limbs still vibrated at the same high-pitched hum of the little four-cylinder engine. A couple of small boats plied the dark blue water offshore, leaving white froth behind that quickly disappeared. The fishy smell of decayed seaweed was stronger with the tide out. I picked a flat stone out of the sand, turned it sideways and threw it hard, skipping it across the water's surface. I tried to remember the last time I'd done that.

I found the key to the cottage where Reyna said it would be. It turned smoothly in the lock. I swung the door open and replaced the key before going inside. The air in the cottage was close and musty, ripe with mold, suggesting water damage somewhere. A stain on the ceiling in the kitchen indicated a leaky roof could be the source of the problem. The weather service forecasted showers once the heat wave ended, but they wouldn't arrive for a few days, so leaks wouldn't be a problem. I opened all the windows, despite the heat, to air the place out.

The cottage was simple, but reasonably comfortable. The main room took up nearly three-quarters of the space, and contained a couch, two easy chairs, a low coffee table and a secretary's desk on one side. On the other were a small round dining table and four chairs. In lieu of a kitchen was a refrigerator in one corner next to a sink and a butcher -block-topped worktable on which sat a propane camp stove and a coffee maker. Off the main room were a single bedroom and a bathroom. A combination bookshelf and cabinet in the living area held a stereo and collection of CDs, mostly classical. Otherwise, the place appeared devoid of modern conveniences, somewhere to go to get away from the bustle of the real world. I saw no television, computer, or phone, even. A telescope standing in the corner, binoculars on the table and small collection of bird books in the bookshelf gave me a pretty good idea of how the owner occupied his time there.

A door on the other side of the refrigerator opened to reveal a small walk-in pantry, its shelves stocked with a few dishes, dry and canned goods, cleaning supplies and other sundries like paper towels, light blubs, toilet paper and plastic garbage bags. I found a box of coffee filters and, after more searching, a sealed bag of whole bean coffee in the freezer. The pantry offered up sugar, but there was no milk in the refrigerator. An open box of powdered milk stood on a shelf in the pantry wrapped in a plastic bag. I took it out, sniffed it warily and set it next to the brewer while the coffee dripped into the pot.

Cell reception sucked, but I managed to find a spot outside clear enough to call Chance, and I asked him to take over my route again. I told him I didn't know when I'd be back and not to worry if a bunch of suits came knocking on my door. When I told him not to mention any of our conversation to Molly, he knew I was in real trouble, but he didn't press. A true friend.

I finished a mug of coffee and was pouring a second when the sound of an approaching car stopped me. I traded the mug in my hand for my gun, sidled over next to a window and peered out. A muscle in my thigh bunched, and my palms grew sweaty.

CHAPTER 40

Too late!

Anger coursed through his veins, a river of molten steel hardening his resolve as it cooled in his extremities. He wanted to pull his weapon and start blasting at everyone and everything in the cabin, but while that might make him feel better it wouldn't solve anything. They'd really screwed the pooch this time. The couple was gone, and probably any chance at the intel he knew they possessed gone, too. Not only were they too late, but everybody and his brother had gotten here before them. He vowed to have someone's head on a pike for that. *To get beaten by a rank amateur... Christ!*

It rankled him that Sanders had figured out Langford's location before him. More concerning, however, were the mercenaries who'd grabbed up the couple. They'd conjectured that Langford had hired some guns to help him go after the pair who'd planned the bombing that put him in jail most of his adult life. That cop getting shot had been their first break, their first inkling that the Wilsons had been hiding in plain sight all this time, not up in Canada like some people thought. But Langford was sitting here swearing up and down that someone else had suckered the couple into the job. That he'd been trying to sweat it out of them when the kidnap team had blown in and snatched them.

He had a pretty good idea of who might be behind it even though Langford wasn't saying. No way was he about to share that hunch, though. For now, he might be able to use it to his advantage, maybe jump a step ahead of everyone else for a change. He'd better, or he wouldn't be able to deliver squat to his "clients." And he was determined to deliver. What they were willing to pay meant early retirement. No more worries. He was damned if he was going to end up his career broke and bitter with nothing to show for years of service to the agency—to his country, for fuck's sake—save a lousy pension.

The other wrench in the works was this ONI gash. Where the hell had she come from? She was obviously clued in. The question was how much she knew, and what she wanted. Jesus, he hated surprises, hated it when someone else knew as much or more than he did. Her mere presence meant his own intel had fallen short. It made him look stupid. The one thing he decidedly was not was stupid. Not like the dumb fucks in this room. He wasn't ending up like them. There was a way to salvage this situation. There was always a way.

He turned to another agent, pulled him aside and murmured some instructions, keeping his voice low enough to prevent others from hearing. The agent nodded and walked out the front door. He felt instantly better. He could still save this play. Langford was still his ace. He knew he could convince his partner to let Langford go. They'd just have to keep him on a tighter leash this time. He could definitely save this play. The thought of all those millions in an offshore account even started to make him smile.

Until his agent ran back inside shouting, "He's gone! Sanders is gone!"

His head whipped around, sharp eyes taking in every expression in the room, until he focused on the woman, his lip curling, nostrils flaring.

* * * * *

A small dark sedan pulled up out front, the little cloud of dust in its wake slowly catching up and coating the rear bumper and trunk before the door opened. My index finger lifted off the barrel of the pistol and twitched toward the trigger. I pressed it firmly back in place. *Breathe.* Reyna got out and stood next to the open door and did a slow pirouette, scanning the surroundings before turning to the cottage. She'd traded the boots for a pair of sandals.

I lowered the pistol and set it on the table with shaking hands.

Reyna marched up to the door, mouth set in a determined line. I waited for her knock before opening it. Relief flashed across her face when she looked up at me, but it vanished quickly, replaced by a small frown and brows that threatened to do battle. She put two fingers on my sternum and pushed.

"That was the *dumb*est, most *am*ateur move you could *poss*ibly *make* back there." With each stressed syllable, she pushed again, forcing me back into the room. "Are you *try*ing to get yourself *killed*? *Damn* it, civvy!"

Her final shove was hard enough to knock me off balance, and I fell backwards onto the couch. She was on top of me in a flash, straddling my hips, fingers fumbling with my belt, mouth hot on mine, lips devouring me, tongue darting into my mouth. She broke the kiss with a moan and pressed her cheek against my face.

"Reyna, I—"

"Shut up," she whispered. "God, I've been thinking about you for the past two hours. Wanting you. Don't say a word. Just kiss me, damn it."

I took her face in my hands and kissed her, gently at first, then with increasing hunger as she pressed her breasts against my chest and ground her hips on me. We tore at each other's clothes, she yanking my trousers down over my raised hips as I pulled her T-shirt over her breasts. She relinquished her arms long enough to let me strip off the shirt, then resumed her efforts on my pants. I kicked off my shoes to help, stroking her face, her hair, her soft rounded shoulders. She stood and pulled my cargo pants all the way off. I sat up, stripped off my shirt, and wrapped my arms around her waist, drawing her close and pressing the side of my face to her breast. Her heart *ka-thumped* loudly in my ear, strong and fast. She bent and I turned my mouth up to meet hers, my fingers now frantic to unfasten her fatigues. I pulled them down to her ankles, and she stepped out of them, dressed now in only black bra and panties.

I leaned back for a moment to savor the sight of her, the curves of breasts and hips and ass, hard lean muscles under soft smooth, flawless skin, long slender fingers resting casually on my shoulder, wings of dark hair framing her face. My breath caught. I reached out and touched her, letting my fingertips trail down her belly, tracing the line of her panties down between her thighs. The fabric was damp with anticipation. With a single motion, I hooked my fingers into the waistband and pulled them down to the floor. Putting my hands on her hips, I turned her around and traded places, gently pushing her down on the couch, kneeling on the floor next to her.

I kissed her hard, felt her hands roaming over my shoulders, arms, back, and moved my lips to her earlobe, her throat, kissing my way down to her pert breast until I sucked the nipple into my mouth. She gasped as I rolled it gently in my mouth. I planted little kisses down her belly, stopping to tease her navel and trace the outline of her pubis with the tip of my tongue. My face hovered over her center, my breath hot on her sex. She cried out when my lips closed over her and I parted her with my tongue.

A fever raged through me, setting my face, my flesh, on fire. I wanted her as much as she said she wanted me, with a surge of lust and desire that made me grow almost painfully hard and cleared my mind of anything that didn't have to do with her, the scent and taste of her, the texture of her skin and her hair, the heat coming off her body, the sound of her rasping breath and tiny moans of pleasure. I focused on that, on bringing her to the brink, pleasing her with hands and lips and tongue until she twined her fingers in my hair, threw her legs over my shoulders and shuddered in a series of gasping cries of delight.

She pulled my face up to hers and kissed me, arms around my neck, pulling me close, and inexorably my hardness was drawn into her wet center until I was deep inside her. We rocked together slowly, until the tension in both of us built to the point of explosion. With each touch, each kiss, we anticipated each other's needs, desires, finding a natural rhythm with no awkwardness, no hesitation. As if we'd been lovers for years. Yet her hands, her mouth, her body took me places I'd never been before.

Our tempo slowly increased until all that energy, the pent-up desire turned combustible. One final touch sparked a searing flash of heat and light, a crackling bolt of lightning followed moments later by the slow rolling rumble of thunder that went on and on, shaking us to our very core. The sheer power of it rendered me senseless, turning my vision black, shutting out all outside noise, but creating an explosion of colors inside my head and the roar of some gigantic waterfall in my ears.

I lost track of time and space. When Reyna's face finally materialized in front of me, her eyes shimmered in the light and a shiny trail of wetness followed the line of her nose and disappeared at the corner of her mouth.

"What's wrong?" I said.

She leaned forward and kissed me lightly on the lips. "Everything's right for once, you big dope. Can't you tell when a girl is happy?"

I shifted my weight onto one elbow, chin in my hand. "So, that wasn't just a reaction to getting shot at?"

"You mean like last time?" She smiled and touched my face. "You really are clueless, aren't you? I wanted you even then."

My eyebrows wrinkled my forehead in an effort to climb up to my hairline. "You're kidding. Then why...?"

"I didn't know you. And the timing wasn't good for me. For either of us, it turned out." One corner of her mouth turned down. "Are you okay with this?"

I checked in with my feelings. Surprisingly, no alarms went off, no voices implored me to reconsider, no gremlins tweaked my sense of guilt.

"I am very okay with this, Reyna."

Her eyes filled with concern. "I'm not making any promises, you know."

I put my finger on her lips. "Shh. I'm okay with whatever happens with us. I don't have any expectations. But just so you know, that meant a lot more to me than simple sex."

She grinned. "Yeah, but that part was pretty good, too."

I laughed for the first time in what felt like weeks.

Michael W. Sherer

CHAPTER 41

Reyna scooted down until she snuggled into me, head on my chest, my arm curled around her shoulders. We lay like that until our breathing slowed. Our bodies cooled, and the sheen of perspiration that coated us dried, leaving a salty residue.

Her eyelashes fluttered, the slow beats of butterfly wings. She peered up at me.

"Are you all right?"

She wasn't asking about us this time.

I nodded. "Maybe I'm not supposed to be. I don't know. A shrink would probably have a field day with me. I'm supposed to feel bad about shooting people, but I don't. I wanted to kill those bastards."

Her fingers touched my face and her palm rested on my cheek. She finally swung her legs over the edge of the couch and stood.

"We need to compare notes," she said. "I don't know how much time we have."

"Probably a good idea."

"I'm going to rinse off first. Is there any coffee left?"

"I'll make a fresh pot."

She leaned over and kissed me. I watched her walk into the bathroom, my heart racing. Drawing a deep breath, I got up to make more coffee. The sound of water running in the shower stirred my imagination, and more, I realized. Quietly, I slipped into the bathroom and stepped into the tub with Reyna. I wrapped my arms around her and cupped her soapy breasts in my big hands. She sighed and leaned against me. I bent and kissed her neck, one hand sliding down her belly between her legs.

"Mmm, we won't get very far if you keep that up," she said.

She turned in my arms with eyes closed and a dreamy smile, and tilted her face up for a kiss. Her eyes opened and looked up at me.

"Damn, you're big," she said.

Her hand brushed me and she blinked.

"Oh!" Fingers grasped me. "*Really* big."

Another laugh bubbled up from deep inside, and I kissed her playfully. We lathered each other with soap and stood under the spray locked in a kiss until the suds rinsed down the drain. After toweling off, we retrieved our clothes from the other room, dressed and brought coffee to the dining table.

I smiled at her. "I'm dreaming, right? How did you find me?"

She covered my hand with hers. "I'm sorry. I should have told you sooner. I've been keeping tabs on you."

I stared at her. "For how long?"

"Weeks." She dropped her eyes and pulled her hands away.

"You've been following me? Why?"

She shifted in her seat. "Not following you, exactly. Keeping tabs on you. Just checking up to see if you were all right after what happened last winter."

"But you're supposed to be back in D.C." I'd been so happy to see her it hadn't really occurred to me to wonder about the how and why. "Why *are* you here?"

"You're right, I'm not a field agent. But I'm good at this. The DDNI thinks so, too. When your name came up in connection with Langford..."

She tucked a stand of hair behind her ear and gazed out the window. "I wasn't kidding when I told Langford this is a matter of national security. I'm not sure how much I can tell you."

I pulled back. "You don't trust me?"

She spread her hands. "No, no, it's not that. Yes, I trust you. I'm worried the more you know, the more danger you'll be in."

"Jesus, Reyna, I've been shot at more times in the past week than most soldiers in Afghanistan during their entire tour. Like you said, I'm already in this. Up to my neck. Throw me a life ring here. Give me something to work with."

"Okay, okay." She flicked imaginary crumbs off the table. "DOD, DARPA, the Navy, they've all got a ton of research projects running on new stuff all the time, right? New weapons systems, flight systems, navigation, engines, controls, you name it, we're working on something bigger, better, faster, more lethal."

She waved a hand in the air, erasing her notes, and started over. "Sorry. I almost got up on my soapbox. Not important. Here's the deal. For years—decades—we've been working on new technology for submarines. Back in the mid-'80s, a defense contractor working on Navy projects seemed on the brink of breakthroughs in a couple areas of interest. A scientist on the contractor's research team thought problems they were encountering in both areas might be solved by nanotechnology. Really cutting-edge stuff at the time."

I felt a sense of déjà vu. "What were the projects?"

"Aluminum seawater combustion systems, and—"

"Aluminum what?"

She pulled her earlobe. "Aluminum burns at high temperatures. Raise the temperature to a certain point, bring it in contact with seawater and you get a controlled burn and instant steam, which you can use for propulsion or to drive a turbine. The smaller the particles of aluminum, the easier they burn, giving you more control over the whole combustion process."

"I don't get it. I thought the navy switched to nuclear subs because you can't burn things on board without using up too much air."

"That's the potential advantage of the system. Burn the aluminum in the presence of water, and it actually uses the oxygen in the water to keep burning."

"You're kidding."

She shook her head. "It works, but no one's developed it on a large enough scale yet to be practical on board a sub. We've been looking at it primarily as a propulsion system for torpedoes."

Sitting up straight, she shifted gears. "Okay, so the other area these people thought they might lick with nanotechnology was battery storage. When you think of rechargeable batteries, what comes to mind?"

I looked at her blankly for a moment. "What type? You mean, like, lithium ion?"

She gave an enthusiastic nod. "Exactly. Remember NiCads? Nickel-cadmium batteries. Not many around anymore. Nickel-metal hydride rechargeables replaced them. And now lithium ion batteries are the big thing.

"Batteries are basically containers for chemical reactions. Reactions that are reversible. Apply an electric current to the container and you get one reaction that stores that energy. Release that energy—power a device with the battery—and you cause the reverse reaction. You know how that works, right?"

I spread the fingers on one hand, trying to remember high school chemistry. "More or less. A positive pole, a negative pole and an electrolyte that carries electrons from one to the other."

"Close enough. The point is that the more surface area you have on the cathode and anode—the two poles—the more electricity you can store. The research scientist back then theorized a way of creating thousands of tiny nanowires sprouting out of the anode, multiplying the amount of surface area in the same amount of space."

"More power per battery," I said.

"Right. Well, longer-lasting power, anyway. Batteries that last ten times as long as existing lithium-ion batteries, for example."

I thought about what she was telling me. "But you've got all the power you need on a nuclear sub. It's like having your own nuclear power plant."

"True." She fell silent for a moment. "Did you know all our nuclear subs have diesel generators for back-up power in case a reactor fails?"

I saw where she was going. Longer battery life meant a sub could operate for longer periods of time before surfacing to recharge. Fuel savings would add up, too.

"There's more," she said. "Nuclear subs generate noise from pumps and turbo-machinery needed to operate the reactor, even at low power levels. As silent as they are, they're not as quiet as a sub operating on electric power. That's why both projects were, and still are, so important."

"What happened?"

"The defense contractor said the lead researcher working on the projects had gotten ahead of himself, that he wasn't able to replicate what he'd claimed. The company fired him."

"Let me guess," I said. "Kwan Ji. The guy whose lab blew up at Southern Illinois."

Her face was somber as she slowly nodded.

"How did you get involved?"

She swallowed some coffee. "Several months ago, we started getting back-chatter that the Chinese were onto some new technology to extend battery life. No big deal, since there are research teams all over the world working on the problem. I mean, think about it. A battery with ten times the storage life of what's out there now instantly makes plug-in electric cars a viable alternative to gas-powered vehicles. And the Chinese are rapidly becoming big players in the auto industry. A battery like that? It'd be worth billions."

"But...?"

"The chatter was coming through military, not industrial, channels. That piqued our interest. We looked into it and learned whatever the technology is the Chinese don't have it yet. They're trying to buy it. From someone here in the States."

"That still doesn't explain what you're doing out here."

She punched me on the arm. "I'm getting there. Be patient. We got wind that the FBI planned to intercede on Langford's behalf and push for clemency. The timing seemed odd."

"I don't get it. Why would you even care?"

Her eyebrows arched. "About Langford? ONI kept track of Kwan. Southern Illinois didn't have a defense contract, but Kwan's research had been promising. When his lab was bombed, we paid attention. And when he was killed soon after, it looked suspicious. Langford was the only one implicated in the bombing even though some environmental group initially took credit.

"So, now we hear rumors that the Chinese are trying to get their hands on some new technology about the same time the FBI is negotiating for Langford's early release. It makes us wonder if maybe Kwan wasn't further ahead than we thought at the time, and maybe Langford is trying to broker a deal with whatever he found in Kwan's lab before he blew it up."

"You think Langford set that bomb? He was just a kid at the time."

She just looked at me.

"Look," I said, "I thought Kwan's death was a little convenient, too, when I heard about it. But Wink couldn't have killed him. Wasn't he in jail at the time?"

"He could have had accomplices." She paused. "Why'd he come out here? Don't tell me just to visit the family vacation home."

"You heard him. He came to find the people he took the rap for."

"They also could be accomplices who left him twisting in the wind."

"I just can't see Clayt and Connie Jones masterminding a plot like this." I shook my head, feeling like a dog chasing its tail.

"But Colin and Corinne Wilson would have been perfectly capable," she said softly. "And you know as well as I do that there isn't much doubt anymore that they're one and the same."

She rose and walked to the window, standing there a moment with her hands in her back pockets.

She faced me. "There's something off about this whole thing. Your friend Langford—what did you call him? Wink? He gave everyone the slip. He's been a ghost for the past two months. And now all of a sudden everyone knows where he's hiding out?"

"How did *you* find him?"

"Followed you, of course." She grinned. "I told you, civvy, I've been keeping tabs on you."

"You tagged my car again. Like last time." Heat crept up my neck, sparked by anger or embarrassment, I wasn't sure. Maybe both.

She nodded. "But that doesn't explain how the FBI caught on."

Exhaustion tugged at me again, fragmenting my focus and filling my head with half-formed purple thoughts.

"They got him out so they could follow him," I said. "But he outsmarted them somehow."

She frowned. "What do you mean?"

"I think Drucker is convinced Langford's innocent. But Wink knows something. He learned something while he was in prison. All that time to think about what really happened back then. Something changed. Now Drucker wants the people responsible—the Wilsons—and he thinks Wink can lead him right to them. So he arranges early release. But whoever was assigned to keep an eye on Wink after he got out lost him."

Reyna's eyes brightened. "Sure. Drucker's wanted to get his hands on the Wilsons all this time, but he didn't know where they were. So he let Langford sniff them out."

"Why does Drucker have such a hard-on for these people? You know anything about him?"

She nodded. "I looked him up. Drucker's old-school. The agency recruited him as an undercover informant to spy on student radicals at Columbia University when he was a kid. I think he was barely eighteen."

I recalled the photo I'd seen of students barricaded in a building on the Columbia campus, a younger likeness of Drucker clearly visible.

"The agency moved him out west as part of COINTELPRO," she went on. "He infiltrated Black Panther meetings here in Seattle around the time of the race riots the summer of 'sixty-eight.'68. Later, he signed on with the agency permanently."

"So he would have been here in Seattle when the Wilsons arrived from Madison and did behind-the-scenes work for SDS at UW."

"That sounds right. But I wonder why he waited till now. What changed? And how did he get wind of Langford's place over here?"

"The technology the Chinese are after—maybe the Wilsons had it all this time. Maybe they decided whatever Kwan was working on was valuable enough to try to sell."

"And that's what those goons are after." Her voice held a note of excitement.

"The shooters? Maybe. Where the hell did they come from, anyway? Seems like every time I turn around they show up."

"You've seen them before?"

I squinted. "I thought you said you've been keeping tabs on me."

Reyna looked quizzical. I filled her in on my run-ins with the commando team—the assault on Charlie's parents place and the attack outside the restaurant. Her eyes widened.

"I'm sorry," she said. "I had no idea. I knew you were Langford's friend once. I thought that's how you got mixed up in all this."

"I didn't know they were connected at the time. But it looks like they are."

A freight train of thoughts rumbled by, too fast to catch a glimpse of more than a couple of words written across the side of each car. Soon, the jumble was nothing but a mesmerizing blur. One stood out.

"Keely," I said.

"The woman?"

I thought it through out loud. "She was the only one who knew where we were going. She had plenty of time. I left the maps in the car on the ferry. And we stopped for breakfast, giving them time to come after us. She was slow coming out of the restaurant after. Probably checking in to see where they were."

"So, you *were* followed."

"They didn't have to. She could have given them the exact location."

Reyna wrinkled her nose. "Who is she?"

"Keely Radcliffe. Her sister was killed in the lab explosion. She said she wanted to find the people who did it. She said she didn't believe Wink was responsible."

She peered at me. "Her sister? Are you sure?"

"Pretty sure. Why?"

"Radcliffe's not the name from the file."

"Maybe her sister's name was different."

"I'll get my laptop and see if we can find out."

She walked out to her car and returned a moment later with a small notebook computer. She set it on the table, plugged a cellular modem into a USB port and booted it up. When her browser opened she typed Keely's name into a search box.

The search engine returned several hundred thousand hits. A few scattered near the top came from short news pieces in the entertainment sections of both San Francisco papers. The most recent, from nearly ten years earlier, documented an apparently messy divorce from James Radcliffe, a San Francisco investment banker. Messy, the papers said, due to Radcliffe's alleged penchant for younger men. Keely, according to the rumored settlement, was pretty much set for life. Financially, anyway.

Reyna scrolled through a couple of pages and found earlier stories on social events Keely and James Radcliffe had attended. Lots of philanthropic events—charitable auctions for non-profits groups, openings at new hospital wings and museum galleries— and the usual social gatherings— at symphonies, art galleries, theaters. Recent photos had them in groups of mostly same-sex couples, standing slightly apart, wearing forced smiles and dead eyes. Earlier shots showed them hanging onto each other's arms, or holding each other around the waist, their smiles genuine, expressions animated.

"There." Reyna pointed at the screen.

An older photo showed a bright-faced, younger Keely hugging an adorably cute mongrel puppy at a function for San Francisco Bay Humane Friends. I couldn't make out what had caught Reyna's attention until I scanned the caption a second time. The reporter had listed Keely's name formally as Keely Baines Radcliffe.

"Baines was the sister's name?" It rang a distant bell. I hadn't followed Wink's trial back then, hoping to hold the guilt I felt at bay. Avoiding the newspaper clippings my mother sent had been harder.

"I thought that was right," Reyna said. She looked at me over her shoulder. "Jill Baines. Part of the reason her death was such a big deal was that she was Tucker Baines's daughter."

I pinched the bridge of my nose. "I don't follow."

She gave me a look that begged to know what rock I'd been living under.

"Baines is head of Ross Industries," she said. "Well, he is now. Back then he was in charge of marketing or sales or something. Ross is a big defense contractor based in California. You never heard of him?"

"Should I? I mean I know about the company, but—"

"Maybe not. Company got started way back in the 'Thirties'30s by a guy named Thomas Wainwright Ross. He picked up a lot of contract work during WW II and the business took off. One of those genius types who helped create Silicon Valley. Tucker Baines married the boss's daughter. Worked his way up through the ranks. Took over from Ross a while back, maybe fifteen years ago. The company's big push recently has been remote warfare."

It slowly sank in. "The contractor working on your submarine projects. The one Kwan worked for before he went to SIU."

She nodded slowly.

"No wonder Keely wants revenge," I said. "Baines must be bankrolling her. Not that she needs the money. But, damn, he must have been doubly pissed. His other daughter was working with a former researcher on his staff. And then she's killed?"

Reyna stared out the window, preoccupied.

"What?"

She gave her head a little shake. "Nothing. It might explain the commando team is all. They're all pros, using military equipment. Hard for anyone to get that stuff even on the black market. Easy enough, though, if you're in that business."

"So, maybe this doesn't have anything to do with the Chinese after all. Sounds like straight-up revenge to me.

Langford, Keely, Baines—they all want the same thing. The Wilsons."

"Maybe." She didn't sound convinced.

I stared at the photo on the screen. Keely's hair had been long then, swept back into a ponytail with the sides left hanging straight. Her gamin features were set in a serious expression, The total trust and unconditional affection of the little dog she held softened it slightly. She looked less careworn, less hardened by life than I remembered her just hours before across the table at breakfast. The longer I stared, the more the individual pieces of her face stood out, until I realized what my subconscious had been niggling all this time. The most ianthine notion I'd ever had filled my overtaxed brain.

Michael W. Sherer

CHAPTER 42

Langford waited twenty minutes after they finally left before he moved from the table. The one thing he'd learned in prison was patience. Finally, he picked up his empty glass, collected the rest of the glasses at the table and washed them in the sink. He dried them carefully and put them away. He'd already cleaned up most of the cabin when he'd returned the night before, even taken the garbage out in anticipation of a quick exit. He hadn't been quick enough. But all was not lost. He knew more now than he had twenty-four hours earlier. Enough, perhaps, to guess where they'd taken the Wilson couple. He had to figure out what to do about Sanders, too. But for now, the Wilsons were his number-one priority. Legs could wait.

He worked quickly and methodically, closing up the cabin as if leaving for the season, even though summer hadn't even officially arrived yet. He didn't know when he would return, or if. He hadn't really given thought to what he would do with the rest of his life, only what he had to do now. He thought only about finishing what he'd set out to accomplish when they let him out of prison. The rest, if he was still alive, would take care of itself, somehow.

He still heard the screams in his head as if it had happened yesterday. Still remembered the heft of the gun in his hand, the sight of her blood mingling with the chalky dust that covered her face and clothing, the smell of gunpowder even more prevalent than all those released by the explosion that pulverized wood and concrete, that bent and fractured steel. He shook off the memories and kept moving.

They hadn't arrested him, or taken him in after questioning him, for the same reason they'd found a way to commute his sentence. They wanted to follow him. They wanted him to do their work for them. He wasn't sure how they planned to keep him in their sights—a homing device on his SUV, maybe, or a tail when he left the property—but he wasn't going to give them the chance. They'd pushed him to keep his end of the bargain, freedom in exchange for whatever he knew about the SIU bombers. He'd balked long enough to be convincing and told them what they wanted to hear. But he was damned if he'd let them put a choke chain on him. He'd do this on *his* terms, no one else's.

He'd already packed most of the things he thought he'd need. As he closed up the cabin, he picked up a few other items that might be useful and stuffed them in a backpack. When he finished, he collected the pack on his way out. Stopping in the doorway, he turned and surveyed the interior, going through a mental checklist one more time. Satisfied, he pulled the door shut, locked the deadbolt and descended the steps.

With a growing sense of urgency he turned away from the Scout and strode around the side of the cabin toward the woods where he'd hidden from the assault team. An overgrown trail led along the forest's edge parallel to the water. He followed it for a hundred yards and came to a fork that led a few short steps down to the water. Half hidden by the low-hanging branches of sumac growing at water's edge floated an old Zodiac. Until recently it had been in storage. Now it was packed and ready and sported a 40-hpforty-horsepower outboard motor he'd purchased new.

He untied it and stepped aboard, shoving off from shore as he climbed on. After donning a lifejacket, he adjusted the choke and throttle and gave the engine a couple of quick pulls. It caught and growled loudly until he throttled down and pushed in the choke. It burbled merrily as he took his seat and put it in gear. He turned its nose to the south and let it idle out into deep water, anxious now.

He wasn't sure how much time he had. If he was right, they wouldn't kill the Wilsons right away. They wanted information, information he knew now they didn't have. When their captors figured that out, the couple was as good as dead. He couldn't let that happen. He wanted them all. He wanted to make them pay. And now he had a bargaining chip. His hunch had paid off, the stop he'd made on his way back early in the morning well worth the extra time it had taken.

When he rounded the point, putting the cabin out of sight, he opened the throttle so the little craft planed and skimmed the surface of the water. It wouldn't take long. The end of the peninsula was only about five miles away. His parents had stored the family boat there, an old forty-two-foot trawler, in a small marina. Dry-docked until he'd shown up a month before, the boat now was afloat in tip-top shape. It was just what he needed. But he was running out of time.

He opened the throttle as far as it would go.

* * * * *

Reyna looked at me curiously.

"She's not Baines's daughter," I said, the purple notion expanding and popping like a sticky sphere of grape bubblegum.

Reyna stiffened as if zapped with a stun gun. "What?"

"Keely's not Baines's."

She chewed her bottom lip. "Have you ever met Baines? Seen a picture of him, even?"

I shook my head. "Doesn't matter. You were the one who said there's something odd about this whole thing. I'm telling you I don't think Baines is her biological father."

After considering me for a moment she finally said, "So what?"

"I don't know what. It just changes things, that's all. It might explain her obsession with finding out who was really responsible for killing her sister. If Daddy favored Jill, then maybe Keely's motive is a little different. Maybe she's doing this to win her father's love, respect, whatever."

Her face pinched with worry. "You're losing your focus here. Why the psychoanalysis?"

"I'm not trying to 'shrink' her. I'm just trying to figure out what the hell's going on."

"I'm not sure it's important."

I spread my hands. "Look, I don't know how, but I think it is. I need to find out."

Reyna's eyes flashed. "How the hell are you going to do that?"

I shrugged. "Talk to the mother."

Her mouth hung open. "Are you always this impulsive?"

I shifted, feeling her gaze.

"You're crazy, you know that?" she said. "You think this woman will even speak with you, let alone suddenly confess to an illegitimate daughter from a forty -year-old affair?"

"Why not? Probably been eating at her for years. Thought she'd managed to keep it secret, but has been looking over her shoulder all this time, wondering, worrying. I'd think she'd be glad to get it off her chest."

"You're serious." She stared at me, wide-eyed.

"What else am I going to do? Keely's in the wind. The FBI has Wink. And somebody—maybe Keely, maybe even Baines—has Clayt and Connie. You got any better ideas?"

She inspected a pale pink fingernail, brought it up to her mouth and nibbled it. She dropped the hand into her lap and sighed.

"Okay, you do what you have to. I'll work it from this end and see if there's any buzz about the nanotechnology now that the Wilsons have been grabbed up."

"Only one problem," I said. "Drucker and Taylor must have cops out looking for me."

Reyna sighed again. "Me, too. They're not very happy."

"Because you let me go?"

"They couldn't prove it, so they let me out of there. But they threatened me with aiding and abetting. Drucker put in a call to NMIC. My boss trusts me, but if they find out I'm helping you, I'm out in the cold. I'm on my own."

"What do we do?"

She pushed back from the table and paced the length of the small living room, eyes downcast, raven wings of hair curving over her cheeks. She stopped and looked up.

"I know a guy may be able to help," she said. "I'll see if I can reach him. Why don't you see what you can find out about Baines's wife?"

276

I nodded and slid into the chair she'd vacated. She pulled a phone from her pocket and stepped outside. A twinge of something—jealousy, anger or fear—set off facial tics that jerked at my eyelid and upper lip. She still didn't trust me. I shrugged it off and turned to the screen.

By the time Reyna returned, I'd pulled up most of what I needed. Petronella "Pepper" Baines, née Ross, lived with her husband up in the hills overlooking Los Altos, a few miles from Stanford University and Ross Industries headquarters. A satellite view of the property showed it was gated from the road. Along with a sprawling main house, there was a tennis court, pool and cabana, and a guesthouse next to the tennis court on the big lot. Parallel rows of plantings stretched south down the hillside away from the property, running into a large building with a dormered roof and what looked like a cupola on one end.

Keely may have gotten her high society do-goodism from her mother. Pepper sat on the boards of a handful of charitable organizations in the area, and was active in several more. She, in turn, had probably inherited the gene from her mother, Elizabeth, a member of an upper-crust San Francisco family before marrying Ross and moving south. After pages of searches, an item on an obscure link a caught my eye. Pepper served as deacon at a small Evangelical Christian church not far from her home. It could be helpful.

I also learned that the middle sibling, Tucker, Jr., was the black sheep of the family. Shunning the family business, he spent his time making, and drinking, wine at a small local winery. The rows of green visible in the satellite photo must be grape vines. He'd invested large sums of money in the little vineyard, mostly his mother's since he had none of his own, and Daddy apparently thought Junior and his dreams of being a vintner were several ounces shy of a full glass. The spat was public enough to make the gossip pages.

"Any luck?" Reyna said, jutting her chin toward the laptop.

"Enough to go on."

"You're sure about this?"

"I'm not sure of anything. I don't know the good guys from the bad guys."

"The bad guys are the ones who aim *at* you instead of away from you."

I shook my head. "I wish it were that simple."

She cocked her head and studied me for a long moment. "You slept with her."

I started to deny it. My mouth worked like that of a fish out of water while I tried to come up with some version of the truth. I knew that anything less and Reyna would walk.

The best I could come up with was, "Not in any way that means anything."

"You don't inspire a lot of confidence in a girl." She smiled, but it didn't look like her heart was in it. Her stance was coiled, shoulders bunched.

"Reyna, look, I didn't mean to. It just happened."

She shrugged. "You don't owe me anything, civvy. You and I, we're good."

I frowned, unable to find words that might be adequate. I wanted more than just good.

"You're conflicted," she said. "About her."

"Not in the way you think. It's just... Something's not right about Keely. That's why I have to find out, you know, about who her father really is. I've got a hunch, but I don't know what it means yet."

The tension drained out of her, her face smoothing into a neutral expression. "Well, you're all set. I've arranged transportation down to the Bay area for you."

"A guy you know..."

"I trust him."

"That's it?"

"What else is there? Look, he's willing to drop everything to help me. Us. Do you really need to know anything else?" She came over and put a hand on my shoulder. "You look beat. You should catch a short nap if you can. He'll be here in a few hours."

I'd managed only a couple of hours of sleep in the past three days, none in the last forty-eight hours. A nap sounded appealing. I nodded and went into the bedroom.

Michael W. Sherer

CHAPTER 43

The roar of a loud engine brought me out of fitful dream. I didn't remember falling asleep. I struggled for a moment to remember where I was. The window in the small bedroom was indigo. As it slowly came into focus, a spattering of white dots filled the upper third. Night had fallen. I padded out to the living room in bare feet. The front door stood open, and Reyna was gone. The engine's reverberation settled into a steady growl, punctuated occasionally by a brief increase in pitch. I pulled on shoes and stepped outside, searching for the source of the sound.

White and red lights moved across the water off shore, then turned and headed toward the beach, a green light visible now. Running lights, but too wide-spaced to be a boat. The beam of a flashlight led from the beach out over the water and quickly played across it twice, giving me a glimpse of wings and spinning propeller. The light source silhouetted a dark figure on shore. Reyna. The pilot snapped on a bright landing light in the left wing, illuminating the beach, then throttled down, and the engine burbled to a stop. I hustled down the slope and joined Reyna as the floatplane silently drifted in. She kept her eyes directed out on the water, not bothering to acknowledge me.

The pilot clambered out of the cockpit onto one of the floats and bent down to attach a line. He straightened and stood motionless as the plane glided toward shore. Twenty feet out, he heaved the coil of rope at us. It snaked through the darkness. I caught it as it descended and pulled steadily, walking backward up the gentle slope until the floats slid onto the sand jerking me to a stop. The pilot waved an arm up the beach, pointing.

"Maybe just loop it over that driftwood over there and tie it off," he called. "Won't be here long enough to worry about the tide taking her out."

A short, powerfully built man with unkempt black hair and scraggly beard, he stepped off the float and wrapped Reyna up in a bear hug.

"How you been, girl? I hear you're gonna make admiral soon."

"Jesus, Toby, let me go. You're going to squish my guts out like toothpaste."

He dropped her gently on her feet in the sand and stepped back to look at her in the bright light from the plane.

"You look good, kiddo."

"You, too, Toby. Civilian life agrees with you." The wide smile on her face shone as brightly as the landing light.

"Can't complain," he said. "Life's good."

I strolled up to them slowly, reluctant to intrude. Reyna dropped her gaze to her feet, her smile falling with it, and looked at me coolly.

"Toby, this is Blake Sanders. Blake, Toby Russell. Toby's an old buddy from the Navy. We served in the Persian Gulf together."

Though shadowed, even in the dark the flat planes and chiseled bones of his cheeks and nose suggested he was Eskimo, maybe Inuit or Inupiat. He stuck out a paw and gripped my big hand with such force I was sure I heard something crack.

His face split into a smile. "Big fella, huh? May have to shove you through the cargo door, but we'll make you fit." He turned to Reyna. "Got any grub? And a cold beer would be nice."

She laughed. "We'll find something."

"Give me a minute to shut her down."

With a nimbleness that belied his size, Toby danced down the float, threading his way around the struts, and leaned into the cockpit. The landing light and running lights blinked off, leaving us in sudden darkness. I was blind for a moment until my eyes adjusted to the light of the stars. Toby hopped down on the sand, draped an arm around Reyna's shoulders and turned her toward the cottage. I followed along behind like an obedient mutt.

* * * * *

We took off a little after midnight, pontoons slicing through the calm water with hardly a splash. The wide, square-tipped wings quickly found lift, and Toby pulled back the stick after a short run, lifting the nose into the air. With the floats free of the water, the plane gained speed and altitude fast, and within seconds, the scattered lights below glittered like tiny jewels on black velvet. My ears popped as the plane climbed skyward, its propeller clawing a path toward inky blackness and bright stars overhead. The little plane's power, combined with the short take-off, surprised me.

I yelled over the engine noise. "What is this?"

He scrunched his broad face into a question mark.

I twirled a finger in the air. "What kind of plane?"

He handed me a pair of headphones, with a microphone boom attached, and plugged the other end into a jack.

His voice came through the earpieces. "Maule M-seven-four-twenty. Turboprop."

"Big wings," I said. "STOL?"

He nodded. "I can take off and land on a pond a little larger than a football field."

"You a bush pilot?"

He grinned. "Smarter than you look. What gave it away? My WASP-ish good looks?"

My face lit up the cabin in red. "Something like that. Figured you must be from Alaska."

He nodded. "My mom's Inuit. She married a white guy, a wildcatter from Texas. He split when I was a kid."

"Explains your name."

"Real name is Taqukaq, but no one can pronounce it, let alone spell it. I settled on Toby."

"What's it mean?"

"Grizzly bear."

It fit. I laughed.

"You flew down from Alaska for this?"

"Yeah, Ketchikan."

"To ferry a complete stranger all the way down to California?"

"Wasn't doing anything else." He flashed a quick smile.

I stared at him, setting his beard on fire and boring a hole in his head.

He finally glanced at me. "How well do you know Reyna?"

"Not as well as I'd like, but I hope to change that."

Now his gaze cut into me like a laser. He tipped his head once, as if making up his mind.

"She saved my butt a couple of times in the service." He didn't offer an explanation. "It wouldn't make any difference if she hadn't. If you knew her, you'd know why I came."

We fell into silence save the occasional crackle of the radio and Toby's responses to air traffic controllers. At altitude, the sky was awash in stars, so many that it hardly seemed possible one among them wasn't like our own sun, shining on a blue-marble planet like ours. A black curtain covered the stars in the lower quarter of the western sky, a sharp line demarcating the front that hung out over the Pacific. The thick, wide band of clouds waited patiently for a ridge of high pressure over us to weaken, biding its time until it unleashed rain and likely some brisk winds. Relief after the few days of heat.

A waning crescent moon rose over the eastern horizon some time after two in the morning, casting a blue glow over the land far below and lighting up bodies of water in flashes of silver as we glided by. We droned on through the night, and though pushed all the way back, my seat grew teeth after another hour. I was glad when Toby started a descent, but confused when nothing below us glowed with the expanse and brightness of a major city.

I thumbed my mic. "What's up?"

He glanced over. "Pit stop."

Soon the lights of a small city on the coast came in view, and Toby nosed the plane down ever closer until the black expanse of a large bay rushed up to meet us. The plane lightly kissed the surface and scudded across the water toward a long dock.

"Eureka," Toby said.

"Yeah, nice landing."

"No, this is Eureka. California."

Night Tide

We skirted the big industrial dock, and I saw he was aiming for a marina just beyond it. He busied himself with controls as we came in, jockeyed the plane in close and cut the engine to glide in the last thirty yards without power. He quickly climbed out on the pontoon, fastened a line, hopped onto the dock and tied the other end to a cleat. But for pools of light under evenly spaced light poles the dock was deserted and dark. The air was still and almost deathly quiet after the loud drone of the engine for so long. Through the ringing in my ears I heard the soft lapping of water, the creak of boat hulls against the dock, the muffled ding of a line hitting a metal mast.

I unfolded myself and climbed out while Toby went to rouse a night manager to unlock the gas pumps. I stretched and paced the dock in the cool salt air as the plane was gassed up. When Toby returned I held out some plastic and offered to pay for the fuel. He waved it away and said he'd just bill it to the government. He looked serious. I put the card back in my wallet. Toby disappeared with the manager, showing up five minutes later with two huge cups of steaming coffee. Five minutes after that we were back out on the bay, accelerating across the smooth onyx surface until we were airborne once again.

Soon, the eastern horizon gradually lightened, black turning to indigo and then a dusky Union blue before rapidly paling to the fragile color of a robin's egg. Soon the nuclear blast furnace of the sun rose above the Earth's rim, changing from rosy pink to flaming orange on the way. Not too much later we touched down again on the south end of San Francisco Bay.

Michael W. Sherer

CHAPTER 44

She called the familiar number. He answered on the first ring, as she knew he would. The last few times they'd spoken he'd been more brusque than usual, on edge. If she didn't know him better, she might even have thought he seemed anxious. She'd never seen him as anything but cold, calculating. She couldn't imagine him panicking in any situation, not even one in which he faced death. But she definitely heard the strain in his voice. Something made him nervous.

"We have them," she said.

"They're secure?"

The sarcasm she detected in his voice hinted at how irascible he'd become.

"Yes. We're at the compound. They're in restraints, locked up, with guards pulling four-hour shifts."

"Good. Any casualties this time?"

"Jensen. Flesh wound. Not serious."

"Glad to hear it."

She seethed with anger, the sudden attack leaving her quaking almost uncontrollably.

"It was my fault. It never should have happened. The pigeon got his hands on another gun. I should have anticipated that."

"He's an amateur. They're unpredictable. The important thing is you found them."

"I suppose."

She hesitated, wondering whether to tell him. She knew it might displease him, incense him even. But she worried now that he hadn't told her everything. For the first time since he'd convinced her to help him catch her sister's killers she wondered what he wanted. What he really wanted. They'd stolen something from him, he'd said. That much may have been true, and for a long time it had been enough for her. If she helped him they'd both get what they wanted. But now she was no longer sure. Something felt wrong.

"I'm concerned," she said.

"About what? Everything is under control now."

"They don't know where it is." She blurted it out and bit her tongue with instant regret.

"You are *not* to question them! Under any circumstances."

The sharpness of his tone made her wince. "All right!"

"Wait until I get there," he said, calmer now. "I leave first thing in the morning."

She didn't want him to come, she realized, actually dreaded the thought of seeing him in person after all this time. She wished he could see that he could accomplish nothing by questioning the couple further. She wished for once that he trusted her. But only big girls, it seemed, not baby sisters, earned that from him.

She made a last half-hearted attempt. "But what if they really don't know anything?"

"Not to worry. Let them imagine what's coming. By tomorrow, I'm sure they'll be so unnerved I'll get them to talk."

The certainty in his voice sent a shiver through her.

* * * * *

The plane glided around a point toward a wide estuary before touching down with a spray of water. Toby cruised inland past a large dock and into the shallower water of a marsh, moving at a fast clip. At the far end, over the top of a low embankment, rows of light planes sat parked on tarmac under the hot sun.

"Where are we?"

Toby motioned out the windscreen. "That's the Palo Alto Airport. Get ready to bail. I shouldn't be in here. Get as close to the front of the pontoon as you can. When we get near that embankment, hop off, but stay ready. I may need your help to shove off." He fiddled with the controls. "Down the road a little ways is a rental car agency."

"What are you going to do?"

"Find a place to gas up. Nearest place is probably up in Redwood City. When you're ready, call me on my cell and I'll meet you back here."

He rattled off the number, and brought the plane around in a sharp arc.

"Out you go," he said.

I clambered out the cockpit door and sidestepped toward the front of the float. Toby cut the engine as the plane glided toward the embankment and the spinning prop slowed to a stop. With the tide in, the plane rode high enough for the wing to easily clear the top of the embankment. As the plane curved in close, I stepped onto the embankment and crouched until the wing swept over me. I turned to see if Toby needed help, but the little plane's engine caught with a throaty growl, and it continued its turn back out toward the bay.

I figured the rental car agency wasn't open yet, so I stopped in a café across from the airport's main office. I couldn't really call it a terminal. More like a place for pilots to file flight plans, pay the rental fees for their hanger space and buy aviation supplies. I ordered coffee and breakfast, found a place to sit and discovered that as hungry as I thought I was I couldn't choke down any food. A combination of nerves and lack of sleep left me with an unsettled stomach and a case of jitters. I killed some time drinking coffee and reading a paper.

At eight, I hoofed down to the rental agency. They gave me a nondescript compact that looked barely large enough for me if I sat in the back seat. I managed to wedge myself in the front, knees sticking up on either side of the steering wheel.

The cross-town drive took me past some of the giants of Silicon Valley, their parking lots already half-filled with commuters. I stopped at a mall and window-shopped until a clothing store manager took pity on me when I flashed a credit card up against the glass door and opened early. I picked out a few things I thought might come close to being long enough to fit my frame and took them to a dressing room. The slacks I found passed muster though a little big in the waist to get the length I needed. A roomy tropical shirt in pale blue concealed the fault nicely. I looked around the store for a travel bag, and picked up some toiletries while I was at it, took everything up to the register, paid for it and went back to the dressing room to put on the clothes. I stuffed the old clothes in the travel bag with the toiletries. Out in the mall, I cleaned up and shaved in a men's room, studying the results in the mirror. Satisfied, I walked out to the car, threw the bag in the back seat and headed west toward the foothills.

The road climbed into the rolling hills past the developed city streets, terrain changing to open grassland dotted with trees, mostly oaks. Despite heavy winter rains, years of drought and a spate of dry spring weather had already turned the hills brown. Higher up, the open space gave way to large lots on winding, hilly streets with big houses protected from view by both natural growth and landscaped yards. Geography that was at once familiar and as foreign as the moon.

Ten minutes later, the road opened up to a view of an orchard climbing the hillside to the right and grapevines on the rise ahead. The road forked, and I steered to the right, slowing now to look for house numbers. The hill rose steeply to my left, trees and vegetation screening any view of the property. I passed a gated drive I remembered from the satellite view that led to the building I assumed was a winery. It wasn't visible from the road, nor was the house above it. Matching pairs of brick pillars and old-fashioned lampposts marked the next drive.

I turned in and rolled slowly past tall, evenly spaced arbor vitae on one side and a low box elder hedge on the other. A hundred feet farther, a low iron gate stretched across the lane. A black steel box with a keycard slot and a speaker hung on a stanchion by the side of the road at window height. Nervously, I checked my watch and gave a quick glance at my appearance in the mirror. I rolled down the window and stabbed an intercom button with a finger. A tinny voice asked me to identify myself and state my business.

"Blake Sanders, here to see Mrs. Baines."

"Is she expecting you?"

"I doubt it, but I think she'll want to see me. Please tell her I need to speak with her about her daughters."

"You must be mistaken, sir. Mrs. Baines has only one daughter."

"The older one was killed. This concerns both of them."

The speaker went silent. If I couldn't get past the gate, I wasn't sure what I'd do next. I banged the heel of my hand on the steering wheel. *Stupid, not to have a plan. At least a backup.*

The speaker crackled. "Just one moment. I'll see if Mrs. Baines is accepting visitors." Even the poor audio quality couldn't disguise the voice's displeasure.

The speaker went dead again. I shut off the engine and leaned back in the seat, sunshine streaming through the open window, the glare making me squint, heat slowly roasting bare flesh. Flies buzzed lazily, their drone lulling me half asleep. *California dreamin'.*

A rattling sound startled me alert. The gate slid into the bushes to one side, pulled by a motorized chain. I started the car, nosed ahead until the opening grew large enough and drove through.

The asphalt lane merged into a cobblestone circle enclosing a grass donut with a small fountain in the center. At the top of the circle sat a two-story, multi-gabled house that stretched eighty feet from the front door in each direction. Mature trees flanked the two corners, with gardens of low shrubs and flowers bordering the middle section of the house. The tarmac lane resumed on the far side of the circle, branching off in two directions. There were no cars in the drive. I parked at the top of the circle and walked to the front door.

A push of the doorbell yielded a low, resonant bong from somewhere deep in the house. After a decent interval, a short middle-age man with gray, receding hair opened the door. I'd heard no footsteps, suggesting he had a very light tread or he'd been waiting. He wore black trousers, starched white shirt, black tie and a vest. His sleeves were turned up once at the cuffs, a nod to informality that suggested he'd been working, cleaning something, perhaps, or polishing silver. Critical eyes took quick measure of my size, clothes, general appearance. Though the neutral expression gave nothing away, one eyebrow rose.

"Mr. Sanders?" He shifted slightly to one side to admit me.

I nodded, stepped inside and stopped in the middle of a black cherry parquet floor inlaid with black walnut and merbau. Curved staircases on either side of the foyer rose to the second floor. Hallways led right and left to each wing of the house. Directly ahead, partially open, tall, paneled pocket doors revealed a large airy living room with two-story glass doors and windows on the far end that looked out on a tiled patio, strip of grass and pool deck beyond that.

The door closed behind me, and the manservant stepped into my sight and beckoned with a hand as he set off down a hall.

"Mrs. Baines is in the solarium," he said. "This way."

His crepe-soled black shoes made no sound on the hardwood floor. Voices drifted from an open door down the hallway, and grew more distinct as we drew closer. My guide turned into the room and stopped a few feet in. I followed as far as the doorway.

I was expecting wicker or rattan furniture hiding in the midst of a jungle of ferns and fuchsias. The room was open and decorated with modern furniture in clean lines, most of it leather. A bright patterned rug covered most of the bamboo floor, and tall windows in the far wall let in tons of light. The two people in the room turned their heads as we entered.

A handsome woman in her fifties sat in the corner of a cream-colored couch, one arm resting on the back support, the other elbow propped on the armrest, a finger idly toying with a strand of hair. She wore a navy skirt, white silk blouse and teal cashmere cardigan, feet tucked under her, covered knees primly clasped and angled to the side. At the window facing her stood a dark-haired man about my age dressed in jeans and a white oxford button-down shirt, the sleeves rolled up onto his forearms.

The resemblance between them was startling, and as my gaze passed back and forth, I realized I had to up my estimate of her age by twenty years or more. She'd either had some work done or she'd aged extremely well. That Keely looked so little like either of them steeled my resolve to see this through.

"Excuse me," the butler said, "Mr. Sanders to see you, ma'am."

"Thank you, Stephen." Throaty and rich, her voice was like cognac and honey.

She gave him a brief nod of acknowledgement and turned curious eyes back on me. He slipped past me without a glance. I heard the door shut softly behind me. The room was quiet save for the ringing in my ears and thumping in my chest.

"Well, Mr. Sanders," she said, "you've piqued my interest. Who are you and what do you want?"

"Straight to the point." I wet my lips. "All right then. Your daughter Keely came to me recently and asked for my help to find someone. A man named Perry Langford. You may recognize the name. He went to prison for killing your other daughter, Jill."

Just before her face hardened into a mask, sadness, fear and finally distaste played across her features, as if she didn't want to revisit painful memories.

"Are you a private investigator?"

"Perry Langford and I grew up together. Keely thought I might know where he'd be. That's not the point." I glanced at the man by the window. "You're Tucker? Keely's brother?"

He nodded, a small smile playing at his lips, as if enjoying the intrusion. I turned to his mother.

"I'm not sure you want him to hear what I have to say, Mrs. Baines."

Now she looked amused. "What could you possibly say to me that might offend my son? We don't even know you."

I shrugged and steeled myself. "Keely isn't really a Baines. Not biologically anyway."

"Don't be absurd," she said. "Of course she is."

Her smile was grim, as if running out of patience, but her eyes were guarded now.

Tucker looked confused, but hadn't completely lost the grin. "What are you saying?"

"Keely's your half-sister," I told him. "Your mother had an affair when you were very young."

"That's enough!" she said. "I think it's time you left."

"Whoa!" Tucker said. "Wait a minute, Mother, this is just getting interesting."

"Tucker, you don't for one moment believe him, a complete stranger."

Tucker tipped his head slightly, eyeing me critically. "He hasn't told us what he wants, Mother. So, what is it? A shakedown? You want money? You think we'll just bow under the pressure if you threaten to spread a few lies about the family?"

I shook my head. "No. Nothing like that."

Turning to her again, I spread my hands. "I don't care what you did, and I have no interest in telling anyone else about this. It's your business. What I need is the truth."

"The truth?" Her nostrils flared and she sat up on the edge of the couch. "About what? Exactly what part of my private life, my family's life, do you wish to pry into? What purpose would it serve? Who are you trying to help here, Mr. Sanders? Keely? Your friend, what was his name? Or yourself?"

I let her questions bounce around in my head for a moment before answering. "All of the above. And if I'm right, maybe it helps her real father most of all. Isn't it time, Mrs. Baines?"

"Her *real* father? My husband is her real father."

I shrugged.

"How do I know you're even acquainted with my daughter?"

"Get her on the phone," I said.

She called my bluff, getting up and walking to a phone sitting on an end table in the corner between two easy chairs. She picked up the receiver and dialed.

"Keely, dear... Yes, it's me. I'm surprised I reached you... No, I'm fine. There's a man here by the name of Sanders who says he knows you. Blake Sanders... You do... Yes, he's standing right in front of me... No, of course not. I'm fine... Other than say a few things I found upsetting, no... No, there's no need. I just wanted to be sure you knew him... No, really, dear, that's not necessary. I'll talk with you soon... Yes, goodbye."

She hung up and appraised me, then returned to the couch and sat primly with her hands on her knees.

"My daughter seems to think you're dangerous, Mr. Sanders. Are you?"

I shook my head. "I'm no danger to you, Mrs. Baines. I wish I didn't have to bother you at all. Fact is, I think Keely's the one in trouble. I think she's in over her head."

"You may be, too," Tucker said softly. He glanced at his watch. "I'd say you have about twenty minutes before the cavalry gets here."

I blinked at him, uncomprehending for a moment. The problem with an ADD mind was that I sometimes focused on one thing to the exclusion of everything else. It hadn't occurred to me until then how truly well Keely had played me. She had the vast resources of her father's company available to her. Of course she'd call in the troops. Just like she had at Wink's.

"Colin Wilson," I said, the sudden sense of urgency sending adrenaline racing through me.

The blood drained from Pepper Baines's face, painted lips against her pale cheeks temporarily giving her the appearance of a very old geisha.

Michael W. Sherer

CHAPTER 45

Tucker looked from his mother to me and back again, smile gone. "You two have things to talk about. If you'll excuse me, Mother, I've got work to do."

She stared blankly until he was halfway to the door before she realized he was leaving.

"Tucker?"

He turned and saw the expression on her face, at once forlorn, fearful and defiant.

"As far as I'm concerned, this is none of my business, Mother. I didn't hear a thing. You can tell me later, or not. Your choice. Otherwise, it's forgotten."

He spun on his heel before she could reply. As he passed me, in a low voice he said, "Careful. I don't care what she did. But hurt her and you're a dead man."

His words still hung in the air when the door closed softly behind me. I crossed to a chair opposite the couch and sat leaning forward, elbows on my knees.

"I'm sorry—"

"Tell me what you think you know, Mr. Sanders." Her mouth was a grim line, white at the corners.

"I think you and Colin Wilson met somehow. Had an affair of some kind. Keely's the result. I really don't know anything, and can't surmise much beyond what I've just told you."

"Why do you want to dig up the past? What's the point?"

I considered the most convincing way to tell her. "You knew what Wilson was. He and his wife and baby fled to Canada when things got too hot for them here in the '70s. After that, they dropped out of sight until they were linked to a campus bombing in the '80s. The one that killed your daughter Jill."

"How? How were they linked? The man who did it was caught and convicted."

Michael W. Sherer

I was asking her to give up too much. It was time for me to 'fess up, not her. Caprice sent words tumbling out of my mouth.

"He didn't do it. I've never told anyone this, but I was there. Four men came out of the building right before the explosion. Wink—my friend—was still inside when the bomb went off. When the girl ... when Jill..." Tucker's words echoed in my head, and I struggled to rein in the thought. I wondered how long it had been since my last dose of meds. "One of the men went back inside just before the gunshots."

"I don't understand. Why didn't you say anything? Why didn't you go to the police?"

The shame I'd felt, had carried with me all those years, came rushing back. "I was afraid. Afraid of losing my college scholarship. Afraid of going to jail. I was a kid. I couldn't be sure that my friend hadn't done it. But I should have known better. He didn't deserve to go to prison, and it's my fault. I have to live with that."

She looked at me with sadness. Pity, too, which made it worse.

I remembered her question. "The Wilsons were associated with the people who initially took credit for the bombing. An environmental group. The group retracted the claim a few days later."

She thought for a moment. "And Keely? What does she have to do with this?"

"She wants to avenge Jill's death. She wants the people responsible."

"After all this time? I thought sure she'd gotten over it. Though you never really do, do you? Have you ever lost someone close, Mr. Sanders?"

An image of Cole flashed through my head, and how the first time I'd seen Keely's blond mop had reminded me of him. Before her face had reminded me of someone else, that is.

I nodded slowly and swallowed the lump rising in my throat. "She doesn't think Perry Langford had anything to do with the bombing. She says she didn't believe it at his trial, and it's been weighing on her."

"And you? You believe your friend."

"I always did. I just didn't want to admit it."

She nodded knowingly. "Trust is a fragile thing."

"I should have believed him. Doubt was the only way I could excuse my own cowardice."

Her silence confirmed my self-assessment.

"I think she may kill them," I said. "The Wilsons."

I expected shock, dismay. Instead, she frowned and seemed to think it through.

"Keely's no killer."

"Not yet, maybe. Grief does strange things to people. Especially when it's festered this long. The guilt, though, will be far worse if she kills her own father."

She stared at me for a moment, and sighed.

"I don't know what good this will do anyone, but since you've already guessed so much... This may be difficult for you to understand, given your age. Women had few opportunities in my day. I graduated *magna cum laude* from Stanford, Mr. Sanders. But I was expected to be a dutiful wife and mother. So, I married an ambitious man, had children, and played my part. Rather well, I might add. My husband went to work for my father's company. Now he runs it."

"Ross Industries."

She nodded. "I entertained my husband's clients, kept a tidy house and raised the children. Don't get me wrong. I loved my husband. I still do, I suppose, though it's much different now."

Her gaze wandered off, mind lost on a twisting branch of memory lane. With a little shake she came back to the present and focused on me.

"God help me, I was bored. A venial sin, but a sin nonetheless. I had two young children, a husband who was rarely home at the time, and too much time on my hands. We had household help, even then, so I had little to do when I wasn't with Jillian and Tucker. And the world was changing around us, first with the civil rights movement and then Vietnam and the student protests. It sounds clichéd, Mr. Sanders, but my world was in as much turmoil as that of the world around me.

"I was raised in a family of conservative ideals, in a society to which both values and appearances mattered. But for the first time, I saw people who actually lived according to their values, who had purpose, and passion for their ideals. It was literally breathtaking, dizzying, to contemplate doing something that mattered, standing for something besides a certain level of wealth and privilege."

She paused and looked out the window. Tucker's comment about the cavalry worried me, but I didn't dare push her. My breath caught and I held it. She faced me finally.

"We met in nineteen-sixty-seven1967, the 'summer of love.' I went to Haight-Ashbury that summer. My parents still lived in the city, and I visited often, stayed there sometimes for days when Tucker was gone. I walked the district just to drink in the sights and sounds of all the kids in their wild clothes and long hair, the smell of the hashish they smoked and the incense they burned. I went to Golden Gate Park and listened to the music, ate the food they handed out, and talked to people. And, yes, I met Colin Wilson, young, charming, charismatic, decent-looking, and seemingly fascinated by what *I* had to say. Colin Wilson was interested in *me*, my ideas, my thoughts. And, I have to admit, my body, too, even after two children.

"He wasn't dishonest with me. I knew he was married. Or involved, at least. Corinne, I believe her name was. I'm sure she was there somewhere. Maybe not. Perhaps they hadn't gotten married yet at that point. Maybe he left her behind in Wisconsin, or wherever it was they went to school. I do know they were together in some fashion. More important, I knew *I* was married.

"You had to have been there, though, to understand the atmosphere. Free love. Free everything. People were taking drugs and making love right out in the open, without fear or shame. None of them, myself included, realized at the time there's truth to that old adage about free lunches. There may not be an entry fee, but people sure as hell have to pay somewhere down the line. And I don't use that word lightly, Mr. Sanders. There is a hell. I hope I don't end up there, but if I do it's because I've done things to deserve it."

"I doubt that."

"It wasn't just that I committed adultery, Mr. Sanders. I think I might even have forgiven myself for that if I'd fallen in love, or if my husband had become gravely ill or incapacitated somehow. No, I deserve whatever comes to me because I didn't care. I didn't give two hoots about Colin Wilson. He was just my excuse to sow some wild oats." She paused. "Why do *you* care? If he did cause my other daughter's death, maybe Keely is quite justified in killing him."

I shook my head. "He wasn't there. I care because he's a parent, too. He and Connie—Corinne—have a son and a daughter. I've known them ever since I was in college. Charlie was my roommate, my fraternity brother. He's a cop now. He got shot trying to defend his parents from some mercenaries Keely seems to be working with."

"I'm sorry about your friend. This business seems to have touched you as much as me."

I started to brush her concern aside, but saw from her face how genuine it was.

"Thank you. Look, if the Wilsons ordered the bombing, then they certainly should pay for it, and for Jill's death. In a courtroom. It's not Keely's call, not her job."

"Keely was my payment for all that free love," she said. "I never once regretted the decision to carry her and give birth to her. I don't want anything to happen to her, Mr. Sanders. Can you stop her?"

"I don't know. I'll try."

I didn't know where I stood with Keely anymore. She seemed to have chosen sides in the shootout at Wink's. But then we'd probably never been on the same side.

Pepper thought about what I said. Then, "I truly believed I could easily keep her paternity a secret from my husband. I thought I had, until today. How did you know?"

I shrugged. "She looks more like her father than she does you. She kept reminding me of someone. It wasn't until I saw a photo of her as a young woman that I thought I knew for sure.

She looked just the way Charlie's sister Sarah looked in college. Being half-sisters explains it."

She lightly rested her chin on her thumb and a curled forefinger. "That's a lot of conjecture. You seemed quite sure of yourself."

"I get a little impulsive. Bad habit."

She opened her mouth, but craned her head at the sound of the door opening. The butler was back.

"Yes, Stephen?"

"Sorry to disturb you, ma'am, but Thomas Colby is at the gate with some of his men. He says that Ms. Radcliffe sent him. Apparently she's concerned for your safety."

"I'm perfectly fine, as you can see. Please tell Mr. Colby that Keely's concerns are admirable, but we don't need his services."

"Thank you, ma'am."

He gave a short nod and silently backed out, closing the door.

"Colby is one of my husband's security chiefs," she said.

"That would be my cue to leave."

She waved a thin, well-manicured hand. "They're supposed to do as I say when they're on personal detail. But they could barge in if they want to. They have security codes and keys to all our properties."

I stood. "Thank you for your honesty."

"Don't abuse my trust, Mr. Sanders. I'm sure you know what will happen if she's hurt."

"I'll do my best to see that Keely comes out of this as well as she can. But she may have dug herself in too deep already."

"I understand. You'd better go."

I briefly clasped her hand between mine, and hurried for the door. In the hallway, I nearly ran into Tucker.

"They're coming for you," he said.

"I know. Stephen announced them. Your mother told him to send them away, but they're likely to be persistent. I'm out of here."

He grasped my elbow. "Hang on."

Stepping back, he let his eyes climb from the tips of my shoes up to the top of my head.

"Look, I think I better—"

The low chime of the doorbell reverberated down the hallway.

"Yeah, you better," he said. He spun me around, pointing with his other hand. "Go down to the end. Last door on the right is the kitchen. Back door leads toward the tennis court. I live in the guesthouse next to it. Take the car in the drive. The black one."

He fished in his pocket and held out a set of keys.

"Why...?"

"I've never been much enamored with my father's little Gestapo. It pisses me off when they show up here."

"I couldn't—"

He pressed the keys into my hand. "Just go."

"Thanks." I swapped my keys for his and broke into a run.

A Hispanic woman in an apron standing at a kitchen counter glanced up, startled, as I flashed by, but said nothing. I smiled and waved to reassure her. She shook her head, giving me no reassurance whatsoever. I flew out the back door, squinting in the blazing sunlight until I made out a swatch of green and brick red tennis court through the trees. A heavyset man in blazer, slacks and tie rounded the corner of the garage off to my left. They'd sent someone to cover the rear. *Fight or flight?* I ignored him and kept going. Maybe he'd go away.

"Hey!"

From the corner of my eye I saw him change direction. *Flight.* I broke into a trot.

"Hey, you!" he yelled again.

I stopped and turned. "Who, me?" *Fight.*

"Yeah, you." He stabbed at me with a finger as he came up to me. "Who are you?"

My surprise was genuine. They hadn't been given a description. *Shit! Fight or flight?*

I put a look of annoyance on my face. "Friend of Tucker's. Why? Who the hell are *you*?"

"Security, sir. We were told there could be an intruder on the grounds. If you'll just wait here a moment, I'll check."

He pushed aside the flap of the blazer and reached for a walkie-talkie on his belt.

Fight! I whirled and landed a spin kick high on his shoulder, just missing the side of his head as he pulled away, reacting instinctively. He lost his balance and stumbled. I swarmed over his broad back, wrapped a forearm around his throat and grabbed hold of my wrist with the other hand, cutting off his windpipe. He went down hard, and I almost lost my grip. His hands clawed at my arm as he bucked and heaved, trying to throw me off. I pulled back harder. He flung an arm out and rolled us both over putting me beneath him. His weight squeezed the air out of my lungs, too.

Fear tightened my grip. He reached back and dug his fingers into my face trying to gouge my eyes. I buried my face in his neck, the smell of locker room and musky cologne nearly overpowering. He got hold of my ear and started to pull. I twisted my head violently to prevent him from getting a good grip, and yanked my forearm back against his throat. Finally, his fingers let go and he went slack.

I rolled his bulk off me, and got up unsteadily. The scuffle hadn't attracted attention, but I knew I didn't have much time. I left him where he lay and ran toward the guesthouse past a fence enclosing one end of the tennis court. Two cars sat parked in the drive, one black, one blue. I headed for the black one, a BMW, unlocking it with a button on the key fob. Quickly, I climbed in, started it and backed up. A ball cap lay on the passenger seat. I grabbed it and yanked the brim down low over my eyes, scrunched down into the seat and pulled out of the drive. The blue car, I noted with a degree of envy, was a Murcielago. Tucker must have made expensive wine.

A large black SUV and gray sedan boxed in the rental car in front of the house. I drove around the opposite side of the circle, exerting all my willpower to keep from tromping on the accelerator. The gate opened automatically, but I still had to stop and wait while it trundled across the drive. I pounded the top of the steering wheel with a fist. Nervously, I kept one eye on the rearview mirror, and nosed the car forward.

Just as the gate cleared the road, the front door of the house behind me opened and two men stepped out. As they came down the walk another man ran around the far corner of the house, looked at the BMW and gesticulated wildly. The other pair ran for the SUV. I gunned the BMW down the drive and hauled the wheel to the left, cornering onto the road with a shriek of protest from the tires. The car leaped ahead when I stepped on the gas, winding down the hill to another intersection. Ignoring the stop sign, I took another left and shot down the road like a rocket.

A quarter mile down, the car headed into a small curve at seventy-five. Lights turning onto the road behind me flashed in the mirror just before I left the straightaway. Pressing my foot down, I watched the speedometer needle crept up past eighty, eighty-five, ninety... Trees and bushes alongside the narrow road closed in like the walls of a tunnel, rushing by in a blur of green and brown.

An in-dash navigation screen glowed, a red arrow tracking along a line on a shifting map. A quick glance showed a freeway entrance a little more than half a mile south. A stop sign at a T-junction up ahead loomed in the corner of the windshield. I took my foot off the accelerator, but waited to apply brakes until the last minute. There was nothing in the mirror but pavement. Checking for cross-traffic, I swung into the intersection without stopping and powered through the corner. If I hadn't been so nervous I would have shouted with the sheer joy of what a hundred-thousand-dollar car will do. Especially compared to the beater I still drove.

Three minutes later, I headed north through the valley, traffic now diminished to independent contractors, yard service trucks full of immigrants and tools and soccer moms on the way to yoga or Pilates after dropping kids at school. Rush hour had ended, making it possible to hold my speed to five over the limit with some creative weaving in and out of the gaps. It never occurred to me that they'd anticipate where I'd end up after coming down from the foothills.

The sight in the rearview mirror of the black SUV weaving in and out of traffic behind me came as a shock.

CHAPTER 46

Traffic bunched as it slowed for a traffic light. I shot into an open space and weaved around a couple more cars, trying to put as many as possible between the Beemer and the pursuing SUV. The parade of red brake lights came to a stop. Stupidly, I followed the rules and waited my turn in line. A few car-lengths behind me a truck blocked my view and any sense of how far back the SUV was. I drummed the wheel with my fingers, checked the mirror again. Finally had the sense to check the side mirror, too, and saw the black SUV maneuver into the bike lane along the shoulder. I felt a jolt in my chest as if someone had pressed a jumper cable against my skin, and my hands got sweaty.

I cranked the wheel hard, and with a chirp of the tires swung into the bike lane and accelerated. The SUV did the same as soon as the driver saw me, bearing down as I slowed at the light. Barely glancing left for cross-traffic, I squealed around the corner, hugging the curb. A car swerved around me, horn blaring. I merged into the lane behind it, saw the SUV turn the corner in the side mirror, and quickly edged over another lane, squeezing into traffic. Vehicles headed the opposite direction were clearing the intersection behind me. A little more than half a block away, another phalanx of cars cruised toward us. But the gap was enough.

I swung into the oncoming lanes, did a U-turn across four lanes, and ended up in a right-hand turn lane that would put me back on the expressway. I glanced across the street. The SUV pulled into the lane I'd just left, forcing a car to slam on its brakes to avoid a collision. With horn blasting, it pulled into oncoming traffic. I turned away, too busy now accelerating into the merge lane back onto the expressway, but I heard no thumping crunch of metal. Gunning the engine, I leaped out ahead of the cars at the intersection just as they got a green light.

Michael W. Sherer

The next signal was less than a mile away, and I made the best use of the distance I could. The BMW hit close to a hundred when the sign for the next exit appeared. As the car drifted right onto the exit lane, I saw the SUV far behind me, coming fast. It could still pick me up unless I lost it for good on surface streets. I skirted around a huge medical center and cut across acres of parking lots, passing buildings that housed major software and computer hardware companies along with a defense contractor or two. After weaving through a residential neighborhood with no sign of pursuit, I figured I was safe.

Breathe!

For a moment, I focused on *pranayama*, slowing my heart rate. I pressed my right hand down hard on my leg, calming the shakes in both. The navigation screen indicated I was a block or so from a major thoroughfare that would take me back to the road that leading to the airport. They had to figure an airport is where I'd go, either San Jose to the south or San Francisco to the north. They probably couldn't call out the manpower to cover them all. They'd pick one. I'd been heading north, so I hoped they'd choose San Francisco International, far from where I was going.

Traffic was light now, and I made good time. It took only a couple of minutes to get to the same cross-town expressway that had taken me out to the Baines estate less than an hour earlier. Keeping an eye out for the SUV, I got out my phone and called Toby.

"You're still alive," he said.

I didn't laugh. "I'm five minutes away."

He heard something in my tone. "Problems?"

"I don't think so." Without realizing it I stretched the words like taffy.

"I'll stow my fishing gear."

"I thought you were going to catch some Zs."

"This was more fun. Remember that big dock when we came in? That's where I'll be. I better not come all the way in."

"Okay. See you there."

I pocketed the phone and concentrated on driving. The expressway quickly came to an end, traffic slowing to a sedate pace. The rental agency rolled by on the right. Behind a forty-foot-high screen on the left, golf balls plopped into the verdant green of a driving range. Past the end of the range came the golf course clubhouse, parking lot and entrance. The airport property started across the street, the main office tucked behind a small parking lot on the corner.

In the last space, twenty feet from the corner, a man stood next to the open door of a gray sedan, scanning the street over the roof of the car. The BMW caught his attention and he locked eyes with me through the windshield. Face lighting up with recognition, he stuck a foot in the car and ducked his head to get in. I noticed a heavy-set man in the passenger seat. My heart jump-started my heart with another jolt.

I jammed the gas pedal to the floor as the gray sedan backed up. The BMW's engine whined louder and higher as it redlined, the force of the sudden acceleration pressing me into the seat. I flew past the lot before the sedan even got out of its space. The car shifted gears and went even faster as it rounded a small curve and headed for the marsh. Ahead, the road ended in a T. *Right? Left?* I couldn't remember which way I'd come that morning. *There!* I spotted familiar landmarks. *Left!*

I curved around the top of the mud flats, ignoring the speed limit signs that screamed at me to slow down. A half-mile across the flats, Toby's yellow and white plane floated next to the big T-shaped dock jutting out onto the water's surface. *Pay attention!* I flashed by a rest area standing in a grove of trees. On the far side, a pedestrian stepped out of the shadows onto a crosswalk. I hit the horn and swerved to avoid him. I swallowed hard, trying to clear my heart out of my throat. Dead ahead lay nothing but salt marsh where the road took a sharp right turn down to the dock. An attractive wood building sat on pilings a hundred yards catty-corner across a pond. An interpretive center, according to signs. I slammed on the brakes when I got close, slid around the corner and opened the throttle again the last three hundred yards.

The road ended in a cleared area the size of a football field, a staging area for sailboat trailers. The dock extended from the far corner of the big lot. I angled for the dock, sped across and skidded to a stop. I scrambled out and raced to the dock, eyes searching the road across the mud flats for signs of pursuit. I craned my neck, twisting halfway around before spotting the gray sedan as it approached the turn at the interpretive center. The sight spurred me on faster. Eyes ahead, I raced down the dock to the T at the end where the floatplane sat, its propeller a lazy pinwheel spinning in the sun.

Toby had positioned the plane on one end of the T, leaving the passenger door open. I sprinted to the end, grabbed the line off the dock cleat and unclipped the carabiner that fastened the other end to the pontoon. The engine growled, changing pitch as I threw the rope in the back, grabbed hold of the strut and shoved with all my strength. I dove into the passenger seat as the plane quickly pulled away from the dock. Grabbing the door handle, I slammed it closed, and saw two men in suits step out of the gray sedan into the dust cloud swirling around its wheels. The one on the passenger side steadied a pistol on top of the doorframe. The muzzle spit flame. Half a second later I heard a distant crack, muffled by the roar of the plane's engine.

Instinctively, I cringed, pressing myself down in the seat. Toby swung the plane around and headed out to sea, putting our backs to the dock. Twisting in my seat, my last sight of the pair behind us showed the gunman holding his weapon muzzle down with an expression of disgust, his partner looking resigned. I swung around and stared out at the sparkling deep blue water of San Francisco Bay, heart pounding, mouth dry as a desert and drenched in sweat.

"Nice wheels," Toby shouted over the sound of the engine. "Is that a rental?"

He pulled back on the yoke and the plane leapt into the air.

* * * * *

Keely sat hunched over, arms clasping her knees, head resting on her forearms. Two men, faceless in the dark, stood on either side pointing carbines at her, small steel snouts snuffling at her short, shaggy hair. Guarding her. Not from harm. Preventing her from escape. She slowly raised her head, eyes baleful, accusatory, teeth bared vengefully. The gun barrels prodded her to her feet, her captors intending to lead her to her fate.

I watched with curious detachment, uncertain whether to feel concern or elation. That depended on the identity of the men in shadow. But as she stood, shadows played across her face, changing her features, filling them out, turning soft into hard, delicate to rugged, feminine to masculine. With growing horror, I realized that it was Cole, not Keely, and his expression beseeched instead of belittled. I couldn't let them take him. I knew the outcome if they did—he would die. I couldn't go through that again. I lurched toward him, but someone held me back. Someone put a hand on my shoulder, preventing me from running to his aid, and the two men led him away into the dark.

"Blake, time to go."

Reyna stood over me, a hand on my shoulder. I blinked and turned my head, trying to see where they'd taken my son. The hard edges of reality came into focus as the dream faded, the vaguely familiar furnishings and dimensions of the cottage replacing the shadows. I wet my lips and swallowed. My shirt clung to me in spots, the turquoise fabric stained navy.

"What time is it?"

Daylight filled the room, but no direct sunshine. I sat up, rubbed my eyes and looked out the window. The shadows in the yard had lengthened, but the sun still blasted the roof with heat, turning the cottage into an oven.

"It's getting late," she said. "Come on, we need to move."

"Why? What's happened?" I swiveled my head. "Where's Toby?"

"Already gone," she said. She handed me a mug of coffee.

I took a sip, nearly scalding my tongue, and got my bearings.

Toby had set the floatplane down in Puget Sound late afternoon. Needing sleep as badly as I did, he beached the plane and we both crashed in the empty cottage, me on the couch and Toby in the bedroom. I'd fallen into such a deep sleep I hadn't

311

heard the plane take off again. I stifled a yawn. A couple of hours of shut-eye were better than nothing.

Reyna moved to the table and closed her laptop. She was dressed in a service uniform of khaki blouse replete with Navy insignia and black trousers. Her bearing was stiff, martial. I'd never seen her in full regalia before. More awake now, I sensed a canyon between us far wider than the few feet from the couch to the table. Dregs of panic and fear brought on by the dream lingered.

"I thought this place was safe."

"Not any more." She glanced over. "What the hell did you do down there?"

"What did I...? I did what I said I'd do. I talked to Pepper Baines. Found out I was right. Colin Wilson is Keely's biological father."

She stared at me. "And?"

"And nothing. For my trouble, Keely apparently sicced a Ross Industries security team on me. They chased me. I got away. Why?"

"You ruffled somebody's feathers but good. I went up to the sub base at Bangor today to do my *job* and see if I could nail down what the Chinese are after. It wasn't even lunchtime before two masters-at-arms showed up looking for me. I overheard the MAs when they came in. Lucky for me, the NAVCOMTELSTA folks know me. The petty officer on duty stalled them so I could slip out."

"Damn!" The thought of Keely had brought back the memory of Cole's face in my dream.

Reyna's eyes widened. "What? What is it?"

"I forgot Cole's birthday!" I squeezed my eyes shut and rubbed my forehead. "I can't believe I did that."

"What the hell are you talking about? Have you heard anything I've said?"

"Cole—my son. His birthday was three months ago. I can't believe I fucking forgot."

"Blake! Three *months*?" She shook her head. "We've got more important issues here."

312

I promised myself I'd keep Cole's memory alive—one of the reasons I still volunteered for Jeri's suicide prevention organization and attended group support meetings on occasion. And I couldn't even remember his damn birthday. But Reyna was right; I was off-task, a signal that I'd been off meds for a while. Not without effort, I mentally backtracked and picked up the trail of her conversation.

"Why would base police want you?"

"That's what I wondered. I got the hell out of there first, then put in a call to my friend who owns this place. Near as he can tell, the master chief got word to have me brought to the CO's office because some big mucky-muck was raising holy hell about a civilian terrorizing his family. A civilian the Navy let loose, he said. He was talking about you, Blake."

"I swear I didn't. The woman agreed to see me. I didn't have to threaten her. But she did call Keely to check up on me. Keely's the one who called in security. Hell, the brother—Tucker?—loaned me his car so I could slip past the security folks. No love lost there, apparently, between Baines Junior and Senior."

"You didn't cause any trouble?"

I thought back to the morning's whirlwind of events. "Well, one of the security guys may have a few bruises."

Reyna looked grim. "You know what this means, don't you? My boss didn't even give me a heads-up first. This guy Baines has so much clout he can go all the way to the top. Or ONI is involved somehow in all this. Either way, I'm out in the cold."

"You're angry."

Reyna stood so abruptly she knocked the chair over backward. She paced two steps one way and reversed direction. "Damn straight, I'm angry. I knew I shouldn't let this get personal. I knew I shouldn't get involved."

I set the coffee cup down before my trembling hand spilled it. "Is that what this is all about? Now *you're* the one with morning-after regret?"

"Not you, damn it. That's not what I meant. I meant I never should have let you go off on a whim and chase down stories about who slept with who a lifetime ago. I never should have let you know I was here."

"You *do* regret it. Or is it because I slept with Keely?"

"Blake, stop it! This isn't about you and me. This is about my job, about my mission."

"Fine. Don't get pissed at me. I didn't call in the cavalry—sorry, the Marines or whatever. You stepped in all on your own. I'm just trying to keep from getting killed. And maybe help Charlie's parents out of a bind. If we ever find them again. Besides, that hunch paid off."

She stopped and put her fists on her hips. "How?"

I didn't answer right away, hoping we'd both cool down some.

"I'd say it's a safe bet that Keely's working with her father. Which puts Ross Industries behind the attempts to snatch Charlie's parents."

She pursed her lips. "Go on."

"Keely said she wanted the Wilsons because she thought they were behind the bombing. Baines might want them for the same reason. But why would Ross Industries want them?"

I watched her think it through.

"The battery technology." She frowned. "If the Wilsons have it. Langford said he didn't think they knew what they were getting into."

I barely heard her answer. My mind had already caught the scent of something else and was bounding down a different trail.

"Guy at SIU told me Kwan Ji kept a notebook for stuff that wasn't in his head," I said. "They never found it. Assumed it was destroyed in the explosion."

She waved impatiently. "We think it was stolen, either from the lab or from Kwan's home before he was killed in the fire."

"If it was stolen, why hasn't anyone capitalized on Kwan's research?"

"I don't know."

"Makes more sense that it was destroyed."

"Then what is everyone after now? If Ross Industries got wind that the notes still exist, it would explain why they're after the Wilsons. The interest from the Chinese, too."

I stiffened, a hound on point as my mind denned a critter of some sort. "Fitch. He was the link, the go-between. What if he figured out at the last minute he and the Wilsons had been set up? Sees the notebook and takes it for insurance."

"Or knows all along that Kwan is the target and sees an opportunity."

"Sure. Either way, it's possible."

I pawed at the idea, trying to get close enough to see it, not just smell it. *Something about Fitch, something Collins told me. No, Sarah. Sarah had told me that Uncle Sebastian had gotten religion.*

I swore softly. "I know where it is. The Wilsons had it all the time. Probably didn't even know it. I've gotta call Sarah."

I stood, fished my phone out of my pocket and retrieved her number from my contacts list. Reyna went into the bedroom and with no self-consciousness stripped down to utilitarian but flattering white cotton bra and thong. I dialed, pacing a short path in front of the doorway while watching Reyna pull on jeans. Sarah answered after the eighth ring.

"It's Blake."

"Blake, I—"

"Sarah, don't talk, just listen. I don't have a lot of time. I found your parents, but some people took them before I could get to them. They're okay. At least I think they are." I cringed at my own lie, remembering how Connie had gone down. "To get them back we need a couple of things from their house. Is there a way to get in?"

"I've got a spare key in my purse." She sounded subdued. "I'm at the hospital with Charlie now. You could stop by."

"No, I can't. I'm not anywhere near you. Is there a neighbor with a key, maybe?"

"Yes, yes there is." Her voice grew more animated. "The people next to them. The Reynolds. Down the road, on the corner. The ones with the horses. I'm sure they have a key."

"Okay, good. Thanks."

"What's going on, Blake? Who's 'we'? Where did you find them?"

Reyna walked in carrying a tote bag and rolled her hand in a circle, urging me to finish up.

"I can't talk now, Sarah. I'll explain later."

"Tell me where you are, at least."

"I can't."

"Look, if it's about what I said at the coffee shop, I'm sorry."

"It's not."

"I really didn't mean all those—"

"Forget it. Sarah, I need the alarm code."

"The alarm? I don't remember it. Hold on, I'll ask Charlie."

"Hurry, please!"

Muffled sounds came through the phone for what seemed an eternity. I tapped my foot. Finally she came back on and rattled off the number. I repeated it silently several times like a mantra, imprinting it in memory.

"Thanks, Sarah. Gotta go."

Reyna glanced at her watch and grabbed the laptop off the table. "We have to move. You know they have our cell numbers. They might be able to triangulate our position. We can't stay anyway. They find us here my friend gets implicated for aiding and abetting. Not going to happen."

I looked around. I'd already stowed my things in the car, so I checked the windows and put away the few things in the kitchen we'd taken from the cupboard or pantry. I preceded her out and waited while she locked up and put the key back in its hidey-hole.

"We need a new car," she said.

I rubbed my forehead. "Rental's not good enough for you?"

She wrinkled her perfect nose. "They'll be looking for ours."

"Oh."

Thoughts spread out in my head like an endless patch of lily pads on the virescent water of a pond. I leapfrogged from one to another, not settling long enough to get a real sense of any of them before getting distracted by the dragonfly on the next one, or the water lily on the one after that. My ability to concentrate was deteriorating. I closed my eyes and slowed my breathing, mentally chanted a real mantra, uprooting all the lily pads and picturing the flat, empty surface. I opened my eyes.

"We'll take your car as far as Clayt and Connie's house," I said. "*I'll* drive. They'll be looking for single passengers in both cars, a female driver in yours. Be right there."

She shrugged, walked around the rental and got in. I hurried over to the Toyota. From the trunk I retrieved the gun and extra magazines, filling my pockets. I got in and dug my extra pills out of the glove compartment, swallowed one dry and pocketed the rest. I started the engine and rolled down the window as I pulled up next to Reyna's car. She opened her window.

"Follow me out to the road," I said. "I'll find spot to dump this."

She nodded and climbed over the console as I pulled away.

Five minutes later we were on a loop road out to the main highway. Up ahead, flashing blue lights appeared around a curve.

Reyna put a hand on my arm and calmly said, "Easy does it."

I took a breath, checked my speed and watched the oncoming car. A county sheriff's car flashed past silently without slowing. Reyna craned her neck and watched it as it vanished behind us when we took the curve in the opposite direction.

"You think he's looking for us?" I said.

Reyna straightened and stared out the windshield.

"Oh, yeah."

Michael W. Sherer

CHAPTER 47

Sunlight slanted across the road, frosting the tips of the tallest Douglas firs with a golden glow, shadows darkening lower branches to hunter green. The road tunneled through the trees, occasionally breaking into a clearing of pastures or a lone house. We'd stayed on the highway for the first twenty minutes to quickly gain some distance from the cottage, but had veered onto back roads once Reyna mapped a route on a GPS device.

I broke the silence. "Do you have a plan?"

I glanced at her. She stared straight ahead, thicket of hair across her cheek hiding her expression.

"Plan?" she repeated softly. "No, no plan. We are so far from the plan we're flying blind."

For a moment she looked out the passenger window, then faced front again.

"How about you? You got any brilliant ideas?"

"Me?"

The mindlessness of driving and the meds had calmed the maelstrom in my head, letting me consider possibilities in a more rational manner. But I hadn't figured anything out.

"Look, I don't think I have much choice here," I said. "Charlie and Sarah asked me to look into what happened to their parents. I told them I'd try, but to let the police handle it. Charlie, of all people, knows that. But whoever snatched them keeps trying to kill me. That seems to be Ross Industries. Or people working for Tucker Baines.

"Keely Radcliffe shows up out of nowhere and asks me to help find my old pal Wink Langford because he might have spent twenty-plus years in jail for something he didn't do. Only I find out Wink's after Charlie's parents, and, oh-by-the-way, so is Keely. And Keely's probably doing it to help out her father, Tucker Baines. The guy who likely hired the men who've been trying to kill me. And who, it turns out, isn't Keely's father after all. That would be Clayt Jones, or Colin Wilson, or whoever he is, the guy who also happens to be Charlie's and Sarah's dad. Who I've known since I was in college. Plus, come to think of it, I'm wanted by the FBI."

I glanced at her. "I think I got all that right. I guess my point is I have to see this through or I'm likely to end up dead. And I'm not gonna wait for them to come to me."

She didn't speak, letting it marinate. Five miles farther, she seemed to come to some decision. Wresting the GPS unit off the dash, she fiddled with it a moment.

"When you get to the highway up ahead, go south," she said. "Take the first exit."

Curious, I followed her directions. She steered me to a shopping mall somewhere outside Gig Harbor, and we pulled into the parking lot outside a big-box discount store. I waited in the car while she went in. I flipped through some stations on the radio. Though out of touch for several days, the news sounded like the same old thing. Smooth jazz and soft rock had a soporific effect. Classical sounded too sad. Alternative rock set my teeth on edge. A minute or so of country started to drive me insane. I turned it off and drummed my own tune on the wheel.

Ten minutes later, Reyna slid in the passenger seat and told me to drive. I followed orders while she plugged in a disposable cell phone she'd bought and started making calls. Unable to grasp the one-sided conversation, I concentrated on following the route mapped out by the GPS unit. The house where all this had started a week earlier wasn't far now.

Reyna held the phone away from her ear. "Did Keely give you a contact number?"

I dug in my pocket, pulled out the wad of cash, receipts and scraps of paper, and handed it to her.

"Should be in there somewhere."

She shuffled through the stack, rattled off a number, and closed the phone a moment later.

"A friend of mine at ONI," she explained. "Apparently, not everyone's gotten the memo that I'm *persona non grata*. It's time we turned the tables. If Keely uses her phone, he'll get her location for me."

"You think they're okay?"

"The Wilsons? Depends on how badly she was wounded, but I think they're alive. Unless Baines has already found out where the notes are. Assuming you're right about all this, that is."

"I don't know if I'm right about anything. Keely played me pretty good. Could be I'm wrong about a lot of other things, too."

"Don't be so hard on yourself."

I blinked at the harshness in her voice.

More gently, she said, "For an amateur, I think you've surprised a lot of people."

"What? That I haven't gotten myself killed yet? Probably an office pool on that. You have any money on it?"

"For God's sake, stop trying to make a joke out of it! You think I jump into bed with every man I meet?"

"I was kidding. I'm not exactly used to people trying to kill me."

"I was trying to pay you a compliment. Christ, Blake, get a clue. I care about you."

Molly's face suddenly flashed in my head, the image seemingly so random my chest tightened as if pressed in a vise. Feeling a twinge of guilt for having been taken in by Keely's charms I could understand, but the sudden image of Molly triggered panic that I fought to quell with deep breaths. I felt Reyna's eyes on me and glanced at her. Her features registered disappointment, shame, embarrassment, even anger. With a sinking heart, I realized that how she must have interpreted my lack of response and sudden gasping like a fish out of water.

"Reyna, I'm sor—"

"Forget it!"

Silence ballooned inside the car, squeezing the air out. My face felt flushed and hot. One of these days I would have to figure out who the hell I really wanted to be with, Molly or Reyna. Unfortunately, now wasn't the time.

I clamped my jaw and drove.

* * * * *

Langford finished securing the boat and wheeled the electric scooter across a gangplank onto the dock. The only thing that saved the folding bike from being completely dorky was the fact that the tubular aluminum frame, flared fenders and raked seat post made it resemble a kid's BMX bike. No banana seat, but he'd substituted a short-rise BMX handlebar for the flat handlebar it came with—as a practical matter, of course, making it more suitable for taller adults—and that added to its curb appeal. It was no Pinarello, but the hub motor propelled it at a steady eighteen mph for up to twenty miles on a charge. He could pedal it faster in a short sprint, but it was an effortless way to get around. And it was deadly silent.

He'd paid for a week's dock rental in cash at the office, letting the manager know in casual conversation that he intended to do some sightseeing in the area. Now dressed in jeans, an old T-shirt with a line art drawing of an orca on the front, and a Mariners ball cap, he waved and smiled as he walked the scooter past the office.

Slipping on a pair of sunglasses, he adjusted the straps on his backpack, straddled the bike and pedaled up the street. He knew exactly where he was going. Mindful of both the vehicular and pedestrian traffic in the small seaside town, he carefully threaded his way through the business district. Tourist season had barely begun since many families still had kids in school, but the hot weather had brought out travelers earlier than usual.

In the backpack he carried a bottle of water, a couple of protein bars, thermos of coffee, flashlight, binoculars, light windbreaker and two of the pistols he'd taken from his father's collection, a J.P. Sauer 38H and a Beretta M1935. He wasn't expecting trouble, but one never knew. Made near the end of WW II, both were pristine, .32-caliber semi-automatics. He could have brought more firepower—like the beautiful, Belgian-made Browning Hi Power his father had gotten in 1970 to test some new 9mm parabellum ammunition. But the small-framed guns were easier to conceal. Getting caught with any of them, of course, was a parole violation with no chance of ever using a "Get Out Of Jail Free" card.

On the outskirts of town, he flipped on the electric motor and sat back, enjoying the ride. The terrain was flat prairie broken occasionally by stands of conifers or a tall Pacific madrone, easily recognized by its peculiar reddish, peeling bark. Rows of crops—potatoes, squash, lavender, strawberries—filled several fields he passed. About three miles out of town he saw the long, low buildings of the complex ahead. They stood several hundred feet from the road, looking like every other stable or poultry barn in the area.

The property wasn't fenced, and from all appearances had no security. Incongruous, really, considering what they made inside those buildings. The whole idea of a high-tech manufacturing facility plunked down in the middle of bucolic farmland in a remote location, in fact, seemed a bit ludicrous. But with a navy airfield ten miles north and an auxiliary airfield less than a mile east, the location made more sense. Take into account that the deepwater port of Anacortes lay only thirty miles north and Seattle about sixty miles south, and it became obvious the choice had been strategic. The only people in the area were navy personnel, farmers and local townsfolk, making strangers readily identifiable for the most part.

Three smaller buildings sat adjacent to the manufacturing shed closest to the long drive from the road. One actually resembled a Victorian farmhouse replete with octagonal turret, gabled roof and gingerbread trim. The others were nondescript two-story boxes: one windowless, the other more reflective of an office building.

As Langford glided past, he took note of the electric eye on low posts flanking the entrance to the drive and the camera mounted discreetly on the modest sign that announced the occupant simply as "Ross Industries." It gave no indication of what the company made or what might be inside the complex of buildings. Except for the unusual number of cars parked in the spaces around the three smaller buildings, the compound might have been a corporate-owned farm. Langford was confident that the cattle guard he saw stretched across the pavement at the entrance housed sensors and cameras to capture weight and scans of the bellies of vehicles passing over.

He nonchalantly swung his head the other direction, playing tourist for any cameras that might be watching. He looked instead for a possible vantage point that would give him a decent line of sight and provide some cover at the same time. From this side of the property he could see nothing but open fields. Half a mile farther, the road curved into a patch of thick forest. He switched off the motor and coasted to a stop on the shoulder. Setting his backpack on the ground, he took a long drink from his water bottle while he took a mental look at the map of the island he'd consulted the night before.

Though roundabout, he traced a route in his mind that would lead him to the back of the hundred-acre property. He pulled out some aerial photos he'd printed off the computer a few days earlier and compared them to memory. A small subdivision had been built near the auxiliary airfield, probably to provide housing for service personnel. The landing strip was little used these days, he knew, which meant that some of the houses were likely to be vacant due to because of the crappy real estate market of late. Satisfied, he hoisted the pack and mounted his bike.

Half an hour later he'd found the perfect spot. Just as he'd thought, real estate agents had staked "For Sale" signs in front of several of the houses in the neighborhood. In the far corner, separated from the boundary of the Ross Industries property by a copse of trees, stood a house "for sale or rent" with no car in the drive. He wandered up to the front door and knocked, and after a suitable interval knocked again. When no one came to the door, he took the bike around back, climbed the steps to the back porch and peered in the windows. The house was empty. He'd noticed a Realtor's key box on the front door. He jiggled the handle on the back door. Locked. For the hell of it, he stood on tiptoes and ran his fingers over the top of the frame. *Bingo!* His fingers touched cold metal. He slid the single key over the edge of the doorframe and let it drop into his other hand. If someone asked, he could always say he found the door open and wanted to take a look around. Agents sometimes got sloppy and didn't lock up properly.

He let himself in and headed for the facilities to relieve himself first. The house was staged with a bare minimum of furniture to give the rooms scale, and several were completely empty. The owner or previous tenant had left a patio table in the backyard, so Langford refilled his water bottle and went out to sit in the sun. He ate one of the protein bars slowly, knowing he might have to make the other one last quite some time before he had a decent meal again. Finished, he carefully stowed the wrapper in a side pocket of the backpack. Retrieving the field glasses, he wandered toward the trees and looked for an easy way through. Someone, kids probably, had trodden a path into the copse from a spot next to a large storage shed behind the house.

Wending his way cautiously, he followed the path less than a hundred feet to its end at the edge of a large pasture. The rear of the third manufacturing building in the Ross compound was five hundred yards away. From this angle, he couldn't see the entrance to the windowless building, but he figured that wouldn't be a problem. The building was dedicated to lab work, and he still had a relatively unobstructed view of the entrances to the other buildings. He backtracked to the yard, wheeled the bike behind the storage shed, hid it in some bushes, and returned to the path's end. Staying back in the trees, he trained the binoculars on the building, brought it in focus, and slowly scanned the property. Other than a car pulling into the parking area, nothing moved. The complex was quiet, but he imagined the interior of those buildings hummed with activity.

When he felt comfortable with the layout, he lowered the glasses and took in the countryside around the complex, watching, waiting. Occasionally, he lifted the binoculars again to get a closer look at a bird, a cloud formation, a distant tractor working a field, or some movement that attracted his attention. Mostly, he was content to let the day settle on his shoulders like a comfortable cardigan.

The space of the flat green prairie and endless blue sky beyond nearly overwhelmed his senses. After years of confinement, the limitlessness of the vistas he'd encountered since his release filled him with awe and appreciation. Every day he watched people myopically go about their business with heads down or eyes straight ahead, indifferent or inattentive to their surroundings. From the road out of town he'd been able to see the snow-capped peaks of three of Washington's tallest mountains—Baker, Rainier and Adams—and the entire Olympic range to the west. How anyone who lived in the area could fail to take time out each day to admire such beauty, such majesty, saddened him. So many people took too much for granted.

Movement in the compound again caught his eye, and he tensed, senses alert. A black Jeep wheeled out of a space in front of the office building and headed toward the first of the long buildings. Through the lenses, he saw it was manned by only the driver. He could make out a company logo on a side panel, but no other insignia. The driver stopped at the first building and disappeared inside. Langford noted the time on his watch, and when the driver reappeared about five minutes later, he noted that, too.

After getting back in the Jeep, the driver aimed it onto the grass and slowly encircled the entire building before bumping back onto the paved lane connecting the buildings. Langford watched as he repeated the process at the next two buildings, marking times on his watch. After the Jeep returned to the parking area, Langford stayed where he was, waiting patiently. Half an hour later, the Jeep's driver repeated the entire process, and Langford checked his watch frequently, comparing times to his mental notes.

When the security guard returned to the office, Langford relaxed, sitting cross-legged at the base of a tree. The sun arced high in the sky behind him, and soon people drifted out of the buildings in twos or threes and walked toward the complex of smaller buildings, some heading for cars, others disappearing into the office building. Lunchtime. He sipped his water and bided his time until the employees returned to work. All told, he counted fewer than three dozen, suggesting a high degree of automation in product assembly.

It didn't concern him. He was more interested in what went on in the Victorian building. Meetings with clients, probably, as well as serving as a guesthouse for out-of-towners. And something else, he suspected. His patience was soon rewarded. A woman appeared on the front stoop of the house. Short, blonde hair. He raised the glasses. The sister, Keely. She appeared to be waiting for something, or someone. He panned the lenses left. A black SUV headed down the drive from the road and pulled up in front of the house. The driver hurried around to the passenger side, but a silver-haired man had already opened the door and stepped out. Langford had done his homework. Though the photo he recalled showed a much younger man, the hooded eyes, a sharp nose and thin-lipped mouth were instantly recognizable. *Baines.*

Obviously more accustomed to boardrooms than farm country, Baines wore beige slacks, dress shirt with French cuffs, the cufflinks glinting in the sun, silk tie and expensive-looking cordovan loafers. A shark in Zegna accompanied by well-fed remoras. Baines' only concession to the heat was the blazer slung over his shoulder with a hooked finger. Keely's lips moved as she descended to the bottom step. Baines ignored her, making a slow pivot as he surveyed the grounds. Apparently satisfied, he rounded the hood of the SUV and approached his daughter. He offered a quick air-kiss as he passed her on his way up the steps. *Arrogant bastard.*

Langford felt a corner of his mouth turn up. He was pleased his hunch had played out so far. If Keely was here, he was fairly certain the Wilsons were here, too. Baines himself showing up meant they were important to him, even though Langford was convinced they didn't have what Baines wanted. None of it mattered now. He was so close he could taste sweet victory—vindication, and revenge, finally within his grasp. But he had to make sure. He needed verification, absolute certainty that the Wilsons were in the compound. Then he'd be able to put the wheels in motion.

Michael W. Sherer

CHAPTER 48

Marion Reynolds was a diminutive woman who had to crane her neck to peer up at me. Her wizened face, yellowed by the porch light, was a leathery map of a lifetime of joys and sorrows. She wore a red gingham shirt with an embroidered yoke, the top two buttons—plastic made to look like mother-of-pearl—undone to reveal a chicken neck tanned the same terracotta color as her face. The shirt was neatly tucked into worn, loose-fitting jeans held up by a wide rawhide belt cinched with a pewter buckle the size of my fist embossed in the shape of an eagle. The jeans ended in white athletic socks stuffed into open-toed scuffs. At my feet, two pairs of cowboy boots, one large, one small, stood next to the door. Both chafed and dusty, emanating a not unpleasant, earthy scent of loam, grass and dried horse manure in little whiffs.

The old woman narrowed her eyes. "A key, you say?"

"Yes, to the neighbors' house. The Jones's."

"I know who they are." She admonished me with a finger. "Haven't lost all my marbles, just a few. Nice enough couple, but odd. Tree-hugger odd, if you know what I mean. How do I know you're not some crook trying to rob the place?"

"You can call their daughter Sarah. She'll vouch for me."

To Reyna, she said, "He always got his guard up like that?" She didn't wait for the answer. "I was having a little fun with you, big fella. Shoot, I could have only half a sack of cats' eyes and pick a man your size out of a line-up. Not likely to forget that face, either. Don't think you'd be here if you intended to bust into the neighbors'. Don't need to call the girl, neither. I know her. And the brother—the cop. I'll take you at your word. You wait here, I'll get the key."

She retreated into the interior of the house, and returned a few moments later with a single key in her outstretched hand. When I reached for it, she pulled her hand away.

"Big gunfight over there last week. Made a hell of a ruckus. Surprised they don't still have the place wrapped in crime scene tape." She eyed me suspiciously. "You wouldn't be souvenir hunters, would you?"

"I know all about the shooting, Miz Reynolds. I was there."

She grinned slyly and looked at Reyna. "He really don't know when his leg's being pulled, does he? Son, you're hard to miss. I know you were there. I know who you are from the news."

She pressed the key into my palm. "When you're done with it, leave it in the mailbox out front. No need to disturb me or the husband."

"Thank you."

Before I could pull away, she clutched my wrist with strength I didn't expect.

"Might not have been so easy if not for this girl here," she said with a nod at Reyna. "You military, miss?"

"Navy, ma'am."

"Thought so. You got that look, even without the uniform. Well, you might be tough enough for this one. He's gonna be hard to pin down, though. Too fidgety. Short attention span. I can tell. Take one helluva woman to hold his interest. You might just be the one."

Heat rushed into my face, and I felt myself shrinking till I was a little under Marion's height. I squirmed under her gaze.

"Are you always this blunt?"

"At my age I can say whatever I damn well please. Most people take no notice. The ones that do just figure I'm a crotchety old so-and-so."

Reyna saved me, patting Marion's arm. "I think I can handle him. Thank you so much. We'll get the key back as soon as we can."

Marion gave her a crooked smile and released my wrist. Reyna took my elbow firmly, turned me around and led me down the steps, tractable and docile as an old Clydesdale. Angular shapes, black against a sky the color of a bruise, flitted and swooped after crepuscular insects.

In the car, Reyna let loose a chuckle. My ears burned, but it was better than stony silence.

"See? At least I have entertainment value."

Her chuckle escalated to throaty laughter. "I was worried about how we might get along while we muddle through this. But you may be worth keeping around for a while."

"Sure you can handle me?"

"No worries there, mister. Let's get going."

I put the car in gear and headed up the road. When we reached Clayt and Connie's, Reyna directed me inside to open an empty garage bay door so we could park the car out of sight. She climbed in the driver's seat while I let myself in the house and made my way to the garage. As soon as she pulled in I closed the door behind her and waited for her to join me.

Inside, the house felt cold despite the balmy weather, the empty silence a chill reminder that they were still out there somewhere, Connie likely wounded.

"What are you looking for, anyway?" Reyna said.

"A Bible." I led the way through the kitchen into the family room and flipped on the lights.

Reyna wore a small frown. "Why a Bible?"

"Because it doesn't belong. Clayt and Connie weren't religious."

She shrugged. "Lots of people who don't go to church have Bibles."

"As an intellectual curiosity they have books on religion. They might even have Bible study books. But the Bible itself? It looked out of place here."

I walked to the bookshelf and turned to the spot where I remembered seeing the worn copy. It wasn't there. Not even a space existed where it had been. I wracked my brain, leafing through the file card drawer for related memories, double-checking the accuracy of my recall. The Bible had lodged between *Das Kapital* and some philosophy books—Hegel, Kierkegaard, maybe Nietzsche. I was sure of it, the discord of the pairing inculcating the image in my head. Or had it been a red book?

"What's wrong?"

"It's gone. Someone took it."

"When did you see it last?"

"The day they disappeared. The day of the shooting. I noticed it when I came in."

"Okay, okay. Calm down." Reyna chewed her bottom lip. "I guess the good news is that you could be right about Kwan's notes."

"Yeah, well, too bad we don't know where they went."

"Is it possible the Wilsons took it with them?"

I opened my mouth, but closed it before anything came out. Gave it some thought.

"Possible. But they didn't have a lot of time. Even if Wink's wrong and they knew all about the notes, I'm not sure that would have been the first thing they thought of. They got out in a hurry, Reyna."

"We better check the rest of the house to be sure."

I heaved a sigh. "I'll start back in the bedrooms. You want to start in the kitchen and meet up in the middle?"

She shrugged and turned on her heel. I tromped back to the furthest bedroom and did a cursory inspection. It was a Bible. I figured they weren't likely to hide it after letting it sit out in plain sight all those years. I went through the second bedroom as quickly as the first. By the time I got to the master suite, I'd cooled down enough to do a more thorough search. As expected, I saw no sign of a Bible or a notebook.

As I headed down the hall, a bell chimed somewhere in the house. I detoured to the front door. Reyna intercepted me there, finger held to her lips. Before I stepped to the peephole, movement on the little video monitor on the wall caught my eye. I pointed to it and took a step closer. A white sedan near the entrance from the road crossed the small screen. Above a diagonal orange slash across the car door was the word "POLICE" in blue letters.

"Shit!" I said. "What do we do now?"

Words in smaller type across the bottom of the door were too hard to read on the moving vehicle. Reyna moved closer, peering at the monitor as the car drove into range of the next camera.

"That's Navy police out of Bremerton," she said. "How the hell did they find us?"

"The lights! Get the lights! Follow me!"

Reyna ran to the family room and hit the light switch, plunging us into relative darkness. The glow from a bathroom nightlight down the hall gave us enough light to navigate. Reyna raced down the hallway behind me as I ducked into the master bedroom and stopped in front of the linen closet next to the bathroom. I bent down and clawed at the carpet.

"What are you doing?" Reyna said. "We need to get out of here!"

"There's a tunnel down here."

I pulled back the flap of carpet and felt for a way to open the hatch with my fingers. "Got a flashlight?"

She tapped me on the shoulder with a tiny penlight a moment later. By then my fingers had hooked the ring of the recessed pull latch, and I yanked the hatch open.

"Come on," I said, scrambling down the ladder into the black hole below.

I slid down the last few rungs and stepped away in the tight space as Reyna swung her feet over the edge, holding the penlight in her teeth. The hole was so shallow that the top of my head was only a foot or so below the opening, and barely wide enough for the two of us. I pressed myself against the wall while Reyna secured the hatch door and descended the last few steps. She took the flashlight out of her mouth and shined it around the hole and down at the tunnel entrance. The light played across a packed dirt floor and rough cinderblock walls painted a ghostly gray and a packed dirt floor.

The mouth of the tunnel was about five feet tall. Reyna bent and pointed the beam inside. I squatted next to her as she poked her head into the opening. Pressure-treated six-by-six beams held sheets of marine plywood against the walls and ceiling. The floor was dirt. The passage narrowed to a black square in the distance where the light no longer penetrated. Damp earth, wood and mildew crowded out all other smells, disguising the edginess that dampened my shirt.

"This is how they got out?" she said in a low voice.

"Cops said it comes out about three hundred yards from here. Shall we?"

She put a hand on my arm. "Wait. Let me think."

Like faces around a campfire telling ghost stories, hers was lit from below. Instead of casting her features in creepy shadows, it accentuated the symmetry of her sculpted visage—*de Milo* in a darkened Louvre. I touched a fingertip to her lips, marveling at the sensation. Her brows curved into a question mark. I yanked my finger away like a kid touching a hot stove.

Dispassionate, she murmured, "The rental—it's got a GPS locator. ONI must have called Navy Region Northwest and dispatched a patrol car."

"Then they definitely know we're here," I whispered. "Let's go!"

"No, listen. The cop only knows what they told him, and I doubt they told him much. He's a scout. They want to verify our whereabouts first, then send in the troops. Like you said, there's no way they could know you're with me, so he's only looking for me. Let's hang tight. The car's out of sight. He'll do a walk around the perimeter, check the doors, find everything locked up tight and figure they must have given him the wrong location."

"You sure?"

"Bremerton doesn't even know about this place, about the shootout. HQ does, but all they gave this cop was an address. Trust me, big guy. You didn't see Navy personnel out here, right?"

I thought about the assemblage of emergency vehicles on scene the day Charlie was shot. "No. County, Seattle, Port Orchard, EMT vans... I think that's it."

She nodded and leaned into me. "We'll be okay. Give it a few minutes."

After one, a different bell from before chimed above us, followed by a distant pounding like the rumble of a woofer in a gangbanger's ride. After two, a faint voice called out something unintelligible, sounding first from one direction and a few moments later from another. After five, silence gnawed at me, amplifying the ringing in my ears to a roar and causing my muscles to twitch and my scalp to tingle. The wall sandpapered my arm in the tight space, its chill seeping into my back through the thin shirt fabric. Reyna put a hand on my shoulder and drew it slowly down my arm, her touch calming me.

"What if he stays?" I whispered. "He might call in and wait for reinforcements."

"Then we'll try your way. But we need wheels, Blake. Give this a little more time, first."

"Okay, okay."

She stood up on tiptoes and gently kissed the corner of my mouth. "Just so you know, I'm glad you're with me in this."

"Misery loves company?"

The corners of her mouth turned down. "No, because I... Damn it, Blake."

She turned away and shut off the light. I bit my lower lip hard, drawing blood, hoping it would take away the taste of my foot being where it didn't belong. I put my hand on her shoulder. She drew away from my touch. Extending my arm, I put my hand between her shoulder blades and pulled her close.

"I'm sorry. I'm nervous. Scared."

She tipped her head back. "It's okay. I get that. No reason you—"

I bent and kissed her. Her body stiffened momentarily, then melted into me as she returned the favor, hands gently caressing my cheeks.

"I'm glad I'm with you, too," I said when we broke the kiss.

"Oh, shut up." She laughed and punched me on the arm.

A sound stood me upright and accelerated my already racing pulse. For a long moment, all I heard was the syncopated rhythm of two hearts. Then came a low exhale of breath. I let mine out, too.

"It's nothing," Reyna whispered.

"Then why are you whispering?" I murmured.

She turned around and climbed the ladder, aiming the penlight at the hatch. Before I could object she cracked it a few inches until she could peer through the opening. She opened the hatch wide, and clambered through, leaving a gray rectangle in her place.

"Reyna!" I said softly. No answer.

I climbed out after her. The master bedroom was empty and still. I stood motionless outside the small closet until dark shapes revealed themselves against darker or lighter background—bed, bureau, nightstand, doorway. A muffled tread emanated from an unseen part of the house. I followed the sound, expecting to catch up quickly. But Reyna proved elusive as a ghost, vanishing from each room before I entered, leaving only a vague remnant of her scent in her wake. I steered clear of windows and ducked low past doorways, mindful of the possibility that someone was still out there, watching. The dark house closed in oppressively, shifting shadows threatening menace. I shook off the nervousness, chiding myself for allowing in childish fears.

New sounds led me to the garage. Reyna busily transferred gear from the rental car to the Prius I'd seen parked in the drive the week before. I bent over the open trunk of the rental and unzipped the bag containing the few clothes I had. I pulled out Charlie's gun, tucked it in my waistband and put two full clips of ammunition in my pocket. As I stashed the bag in the back seat of the Prius, I noticed that Reyna now wore her .45 holstered on her hip. I wondered if maybe my case of nerves wasn't unfounded. A muffled buzz stopped Reyna mid-stride, and she dug into her jeans for the throwaway cell.

"Yeah? ... Okay, that's good... How long ago? ... Hang on ..." She leaned into the car and pawed through a soft-sided computer case that doubled as purse, coming up with a pen and scrap of paper. She lifted a shoulder, pressing the phone against her ear, pen poised over paper. "Again? ... Got it, thanks."

Slipping the phone into her pocket, she held up the piece of paper. "We've got her."

"Where?"

"A couple hours' drive north."

She eased into the passenger seat and pulled her laptop out of her bag. In seconds the screen lit, coloring her face blue as her fingers flew over the keys. Moments later, she'd mapped the location her source had provided. Peering over her shoulder at the screen, I recognized the north end of Whidbey Island. She tabbed to a blank search screen and typed in something so fast I didn't have a chance to see it before the search engine served up a page of results. Reyna clicked a link and quickly scrolled through pages on a site before stopping on a contacts page. She scrolled down quickly toward the bottom before stopping. The cursor hovered near an address on Whidbey, giving me a chance to identify the website—Ross Industries.

"Bingo," she said softly.

"Baines? Keely's at a company facility?"

"Manufacturing plant. Guidance system components, according to this."

Toggling back to the map page, she pulled up a satellite view and zoomed in on the property. I moved in closer for a better view, almost brushing her cheek, the faint floral scent of her shampoo making my head spin. I slowly drew in a deep breath, hoping she didn't notice the effect she had on me, forcing myself to focus on the images onscreen.

Onscreen... The little wireless icon in the tool bar winked. I straightened, pulling my face away as if the screen had just hissed at me.

Reyna glanced over her shoulder. "What?"

"Can they trace your computer, too?"

Her hands hovered over the keyboard. "No, I don't think so. This is mine, not Navy issue."

"Even so..."

"I'll use it sparingly." Closing the laptop, she peered up at me. "You up for this?"

I shrugged. "Rock and roll."

"The notebook?"

I shook my head. "No sense looking anymore. It's not here. The Wilsons didn't know what they had. Someone else came and took it." I just hadn't decided who yet.

After keying in the alarm code, I pressed the button for the garage door. It opened with a rumble as I walked to the car and got in. Reyna handed me the keys. I backed out, put it in gear and glided silently down the drive. The first drops of rain splattered the windshield with loud plops, and the crowns of the big firs lining the narrow lane dipped and swayed in the intensifying breeze. An ominous black sky, darker than night, replaced the twilight from earlier.

Reyna pointed right when we reached the road. I cranked the wheel and headed that direction. We hadn't gone more than a few hundred yards when the car's interior lit up with alternating flashes of blue and red.

CHAPTER 49

The front moved in quickly, a high line of maleficent black clouds soaring in over the coast and blotting out the lowering sun, bringing night on early. A stiff wind barreled down the Strait of Juan de Fuca ahead of the rain, channeled by the Olympics on one side and the Vancouver Island Ranges on the other. The temperature had dropped twenty degrees in a matter of minutes, and the mercury was still falling slowly. Langford zipped the windbreaker tight up under his chin and wished he'd brought a rain slicker instead. The jacket would repel a light drizzle, but a hard rain would soak through quickly. Too late to worry about it now, he shrugged and raised the field glasses again.

A security guard had patrolled the complex every half-hour during the workday, but the patrols had come more infrequently since early evening, about once an hour. Guards on the later shift also seemed more lax, less punctual. After the parking lots had emptied at the end of the day, the campus had seen little activity. A few employees had straggled out of the windowless building after hours, likely working late on projects, and more had left the office building even later. The only sign of life in the house had been the illumination of a couple of ground floor windows when the sky had darkened with clouds.

Now nearly ten, his attention was drawn back to the house as floodlights blazed suddenly, bathing the parking area in light. Through the lenses he watched two men escort Baines out the front door. Langford recognized them, both dressed in black slacks and windbreakers, as the driver and bodyguard who had accompanied Baines earlier. The driver opened an umbrella and held it up, but Baines ignored him and walked straight to the waiting SUV. The driver hurried to catch up and open the passenger door. While he rounded the front of the vehicle, the other man stood by the open back door and turned a full circle, scanning the area before getting in.

Langford watched for several minutes after the SUV drove off, but no one else emerged. Lights brightened two more ground floor windows, and Langford saw shadows pass in front of them several times. Thirty minutes later, two different men emerged from the house, both in black fatigues. Hunching their shoulders and leaning into the wind, they jogged across the open space to the office building. The exterior lights on the house blinked off. One by one, the lights inside were extinguished, too, leaving it dark. Moments later, a lone upstairs window glowed.

Water trickled off Langford's hair down the back of his neck, sending a shiver down his spine. The light rain had even penetrated the shelter of the trees, soaking leaves, needles, and branches until they dripped as steadily as the gray clouds scudding across the night sky. He checked the rest of the compound for activity, slowly scanning the grounds, then returned his attention to the house.

Nearly an hour later, the upstairs window finally went dark. Langford cupped a hand around his watch and briefly illuminated the dial. About forty minutes until a patrol if the security team was on time. He still didn't know for sure if the Wilsons were being held in the house. Which meant he had to risk getting inside to find out. After all those years in prison and coming this close, he wasn't about to quit now. At least by the time another patrol made the rounds, whoever was still inside should be asleep. He considered returning to the empty rental behind him to dry out, but he couldn't chance being seen. Instead, he squatted and took the thermos out of the backpack, drank what was left of the coffee and leaned back against a tree trunk to wait.

Before the guard on the next patrol had even entered the office building after his rounds Langford was on his feet and running across the dark field, backpack snugged tight. The open space worried him, but he crouched low and hoped the rain and darkness would provide enough cover. He thought it through one more time even as his eyes darted from one side of the compound to the other searching for movement, ears alert to the sounds of alarm.

He'd seen no one else enter or leave the Victorian house, which made him believe Keely was the only person remaining, asleep upstairs. Since no lights had been on earlier, he had to assume the Wilsons, if they were on the premises, were confined in a basement or subfloor. Despite the firepower he'd brought, he didn't intend any heroics. All he had to do was confirm that the Wilsons were there. He didn't need to rescue them. Indeed, the idiots deserved whatever lay in store for them. He just needed to get in long enough to find them, then make the call.

He moved to his left, keeping the dark house between himself and the office building. He sprinted the last hundred yards, pulling up against the side of the house, breathing heavily. When he could hear over the pounding of his heartbeat, he listened carefully for sounds other than the steady patter of the rain or the wind's loud conversation with the few nearby trees. He heard nothing that wasn't imaginary, and ignored everything that was. Quickly, he made his way from window to window, applying pressure to each, looking for something unlocked, an easy way in.

He poked his head around the corner of the house, quickly taking stock before ducking back out of sight. The parking area and front porch remained dark and deserted. Retracing his steps, he followed the wall to the back of the house, and repeated the maneuver. It, too, was dark and devoid of life, but within sight of the office building. Steps led up to a screened porch. Pressing himself into the shadows, he slipped around the corner and up the stairs, crouching low. At the top, he eased the screen door open and silently stole through the narrow crack. The inner door was locked, no surprise. But the top half was mullioned glass.

Hastily, he removed his backpack and stripped off the wet windbreaker. He wrapped it around his arm, braced his padded elbow against the pane nearest the doorknob, and made a fist. With his other hand he delivered a swift open-handed blow to the back of his clenched fingers. His elbow shattered the glass with a muffled crack and a tinkle as shards hit the wood floor inside. Langford sucked in a breath and waited, listening intently. When no warnings sounded, he carefully reached in and turned the knob. Only when he stepped inside and turned to shut the door behind him did he notice the blinking red light above the screen door on the porch.

As soon as he saw it he realized he'd just made the second biggest mistake of his life.

CHAPTER 50

"Damn it! I *knew* it!" I slammed the steering wheel. "Son of a bitch was waiting for us!"

Reyna slumped in her seat as if shrinking from my anger. I glanced at the flashing lights in the mirror. For a moment, I considered pressing my foot to the floor.

As if reading my mind she said, "No way you can outrun him."

She twisted and peered between the seats out the back window. Facing front again, she drew her HK semi-automatic and checked the slide.

"Where's the rheostat?" she said.

"The what?"

"The dimmer for the dashboard lights! Come on, civvy, find it! Turn it off."

I scanned the dash again, found the little wheel and thumbed it down until it clicked.

"Good, now put on your blinker. Let him know you see him, but don't pull over yet. If he approaches this as a high-risk stop he'll draw his weapon and order you out of the car."

"A high-risk stop? What's—"

"Are you listening to me? If he treats it as a routine traffic stop just keep your hands on the wheel," she said. "Either way, do what he says, but when I tell you, drive like hell."

"What are you—?"

"Blake! Just do what I tell you, okay?"

The worry in her tone didn't mollify me, but I angled the hood of the car toward the shoulder, letting the car roll to a stop. The cop followed and stopped thirty feet behind me, aimed a hundred-sixty-thousand-candlepower searchlight into the back of the car, and sat there. Reyna slumped lower, making herself even smaller than the petite size she wore.

"He's running the plates," Reyna murmured. "Keep an eye on the rearview mirror. If he approaches the car, let me know when he steps into your blind spot."

I gripped the wheel to counteract an impulse to wipe my sweaty palms on my pants.

"Here he comes."

"Okay, don't look at me." Her voice was barely audible over the ratamacues of rain on the roof. "I don't want him to know someone's in the car with you. Whatever happens, keep watching him. Don't take your eyes off him. Where is he?"

"Fifteen feet, closing fast," I whispered. "In my blind spot in three, two, one, now!"

A muffled click accompanied a huff of cool air through the car and a momentary increase in volume of the sounds of the building storm. I shifted my gaze to the side view mirror and watched the cop's measured approach alongside the car. Just as he reached my door, three loud fast explosions—*blam! blam! blam!*—jerked the cop's head up and nearly jolted me out of my skin. My head automatically turned toward the sounds. *Watch him! Focus!*

I yanked my gaze back to the cop, saw his hand at eye-level grasp the butt of his pistol and draw it out of his holster in slow-motion. Instinct screamed at me to stop him, prevent his hand from drawing the weapon out any further. A barrier of glass and steel stood between us. Without thinking, I pulled the door handle and threw my weight at the door. It slammed into the cop, knocking him backward. He staggered and fell.

"Go!" Reyna screamed. "Drive!"

I pulled myself back up behind the wheel and yanked the gearshift into drive. Reyna dove into the passenger seat and slammed the door. Wheels spitting gravel, the little car spurted ahead. I steered it onto pavement, where the tires got a better purchase, launching us down the road as if flung out of a slingshot. The rear window suddenly crazed with a small pop, the louder crack of a gun registering an instant later. With a kneejerk reaction, I jogged the wheel savagely. Two more cracks sounded, more distant this time.

"Shit! Reyna?"

"I'm not shooting back," she yelled. "Just keep your head down and your foot to the floor."

"What the hell did you do?"

"Shot out his tires and put one in his radiator for good measure."

I groaned. "We are in *so* much trouble."

"We have to dump this car fast. He'll be on the air quick as he can. You can bet he's pissed enough to call out every law enforcement vehicle this side of the pond."

"Where are we going to get *another* car? We just got this one."

I glanced over and caught her demented grin in the reflection of the headlights.

"Steal one? Of course. Why not? We're already going to jail for life. What's another felony? Do you even know how to hotwire a car? I don't."

"Just drive, civvy. Fast!"

"Where?"

"Head for the ferry. Be quiet and let me think."

I drove in silence, pushing the car as fast as I dared on the rain-slicked road. Thoughts popped up in my head and vanished as quickly as telephone poles in the headlights.

"Isn't the ferry the first place they'll look?"

"Yes. Now shut up."

Her face was scrunched up in concentration. She felt me looking at her and glanced over.

"The ferry is so damned obvious that of course they'll post someone there. But it's too obvious. They'll figure we're smarter than that, so they'll direct the search the other way."

I turned my attention back to the black ribbon of asphalt unspooling in the headlights. The jumble in my head defied orderly filing, snippets and threads so tangled they'd become Gordian.

Eons of silence later, she said, "You did good back there."

Good seemed a relative term, but after weighing the cop's bruised hip and ego against the possibility of a bullet in the head, I acknowledged the comment with a grunt.

"How far now?"

"A couple of miles," I said.

Any second I expected to see a parade of flashing lights bearing down on us at high speed, the wail of sirens like banshees heralding our fate. But even if the cop had been able to mobilize the Navy police in Bremerton immediately, they were at least fifteen minutes out with lights and sirens. If he'd roused the locals in Port Orchard, we still had a few minutes head start.

A public school hulking in the dark signaled the outskirts of town. I let the car coast, slowing closer to the speed limit. Reyna sat up and peered ahead.

"There." She pointed toward a large structure coming up on the right. "Pull in there."

A church steeple loomed out of the rain. I nodded.

"No, no," she said. "Here!"

She indicated the entrance to a park-and-ride lot several hundred feet from the church.

"Stay with me, Blake."

I tapped the brakes hard, turned in and headed toward the back of the lot. Despite the late hour, cars filled a quarter of the spaces. I backed the Prius into a slot between two other cars to make the bullet hole in the rear window less noticeable.

Reyna unclipped her holster and put the gun in the bag with her laptop. Leaning over the back of the seat, she rummaged through her duffel bag, retrieved a spare clip and stowed that with the gun. Then she pulled out a brand new hooded sweatshirt imprinted with a UW Huskies logo, ripped the tags off and slipped it on over her head.

"Got it for my nephew," she said, "but I can buy him another."

She twisted and leaned over the seat once more, this time retrieving a plain black ball cap.

"It's wet out there," she said, twisting her hair up into a knot and tugging the cap over it. "You ought to find a jacket or something."

"Gee, guess I should plan my out-of-town trips better."

She didn't bite. I sighed and turned to look in the back seat, noticing for the first time that Clayt and Connie used the same housekeeping techniques in the car as they did in their house. The rear was littered with an assortment of trash and treasures that had probably accumulated daily since the car had been purchased. Books, papers, two boxes of tissues, an unfurled umbrella, a pair of rain boots, an old clock radio, a rumpled lady's trench coat, a bag of potting soil, a cardboard box on the floor marked "Donations," dry cleaning still in a plastic bag, and a paper fast-food bag overflowing with trash.

I popped the hatch, got out of the car and walked through the raindrops to the rear to see what the cargo compartment held, half-expecting to find a decomposing body. More mess, but nothing rotten. I pawed through the piles and found an old poncho that probably dated back to Clayt's hippie days. I threw it on, and leaned in to grab my bag off the back seat. The nice slacks I'd bought in Palo Alto that morning were trashed already. Turning around, I sat under the open hatch, stripped off the slacks and changed into the cargo pants I'd worn before. After transferring the contents of my pockets, I closed the hatch and met Reyna at the front of the car.

She looked me up and down with a hint of a smile. "Very stylish."

"All I could find."

She nodded, serious. "It hides the gun. Color's not too loud; your size attracts enough attention as it is." She rubbed the fabric with thumb and two fingers. "Wow, wool. The real thing, *vaquero*, not some cheap imitation."

"Means it'll smell when it's wet."

"Only if it's dirty. Tight weave, too. Might even keep you dry."

I lengthened my stride in the direction of a bus shelter, not interested in finding out. The route schedule posted in the small shelter indicated that shuttles ran from the lot to the ferry only during rush hours. I started walking.

Reyna called after me. "What?"

"No bus," I said loudly.

I heard running footsteps. She came abreast, breathing hard, and fast-walked to keep up.

"What's wrong?"

"I thought you were going to steal another car," I said.

"Come on, Blake. What's with you?"

"I'm tired, hungry—" I held out my arms "—and wet. You shot a cop car, Reyna."

She took several steps with downcast eyes. "It gets worse."

"What do you mean?"

"The cop didn't see me. Only you."

"He knows *someone* was with me. He knows *I* didn't shoot up his car."

"But he only saw you. You're the one they'll be looking for."

"Wait! He had to have heard your voice when you yelled at me. He must have realized he heard a woman's voice."

"Look, forget I said it. It probably doesn't even matter. They might not even have their act together yet."

But by the time we walked the mile down the sloped curve of the road to the ferry terminal the cops were holding dress rehearsal. The asphalt sprawl of the vehicle staging area stretched out to our right as we came down the hill. Two green county sheriff's cruisers flanked the ferry tollbooths, strobes flashing. A deputy made his way down a line of waiting cars swinging a long flashlight. The movement of a second flashlight beam in the long, narrow parking lot next to the ferry waiting lanes gave away the location of the other sheriff's deputy.

"Looks like we'll have to split up," Reyna murmured.

"They're checking cars."

"And when they don't find the one they're looking for?"

"They'll wait for it."

"How long before they check pedestrians, you think, Blake? Use your head."

My teeth clenched so hard my jaw ached.

"Fine. We split up. Then what?"

"Regroup on the other side if we both make it on. If not, well..."

"You mean if one of us gets caught."

"You know where you're going if I don't make it?"

"You'll make it," I muttered. I saw her nose wrinkle. "I'll figure it out."

She grabbed a fistful of poncho and yanked me off the road under some trees. "This isn't going exactly the way I planned, you know."

"I got that part."

Taking the front of the poncho in both hands, she pulled hard until she bent me over, and kissed me firmly. Before the heat rushing through me had time to register she let go and held out her hand.

"Give me your phone."

Still feeling the brand of her lips, I handed it to her. She turned it on and squinted at the small screen in the dark.

"Don't you ever check for messages?" she said.

"You said not to use my phone."

She held my cell next to hers, keyed a number into it and handed it back.

"I'll look for you on board. If I don't see you, text me if you make it so we can hook up."

I nodded. "You go first. You've got a better chance."

Hesitating, she put a hand on my arm. "Be careful."

She pulled the sweatshirt up over her cap, hiding most of her face and turned away. I watched her until she disappeared among the cars in the big lot next to the staging lanes. Following as far as the lot entrance, I stood behind a chain link fence, spotted her and marked her progress. She walked purposefully, but unhurriedly toward the little terminal building down near the water. It held a few vending machines and provided shelter from the rain, but little else. The deputy checking cars in the lot straightened as she walked past, turning to watch her for a moment. Uninterested, he swung back to his task.

349

Unaware that I'd been holding my breath, I expelled it with an explosive huff audible over the sound of the wind. I didn't want to take the same path down to the terminal while the cop was conducting his search. I leaned against the fence and waited instead. Intermittent drops of rain slowly plastered my hair to my skin.

Three staging lanes had filled with waiting vehicles, an odd assortment of late reverse commuters, retirees in pickup trucks with camper tops, tourists, a few empty delivery trucks, and kids out for a joyride to the big city. Wet metal and glass glistened under the streetlights, casting their cool glow over the scene. Almost smack dab in the middle of the pack of fifty or so, a late - model Caddy with blacked -out windows rocked and bounced on its suspension, unseen occupants moving in time to the loud bass beat of a gangsta rap song. They'd turned the volume up so far that about every fourth word of the foul, misogynistic lyrics were unambiguous despite normally incoherent hip-hop pronunciations few people understood.

Parked immediately in front of the Caddy was a well-used pickup. The driver's head appeared over the roof as he got out, walked back to the Caddy and knocked on the window. Burly, dressed in jeans and an unbuttoned plaid shirt over a T-shirt, he seemed calm until an arm appeared from the Caddy driver's window and extended the universal fuck-you gesture. The burly man yelled a few epithets of his own and stormed off toward the tollbooths. An orange-vested WSDOT employee soon headed for the Caddy while the pickup driver stomped up the hill toward the grocery store on the corner. The noise emanating from the Caddy went down a few notches as soon as the orange vest approached the car.

A school of iridescent thoughts swam by, as tempting as chum. My attention darted after a brightly colored one here, a shiny one there—*no sign of Reyna ... wonder if Tucker got his Beemer back ... what's that idiot in the ferry lane trying to do? ... damn, it got chilly in a hurry ... this thing with Reyna, is it ... hope Molly remembered Cole's birthday; still can't believe I ... there goes that rap music again ... I knew this ratty piece of cloth would smell when it got wet ... oh, shit, here come reinforcements...*

With effort, I reined in my attention as it gamboled after one last brightly hued denizen of the deep. Taking stock of the scene, I fished in a pocket for meds, found two pills and popped them like candy. Off to the left, an unmarked SUV with flashing lights pulled up next to one of the county cruisers by the tollbooth. Another vehicle quickly followed, this one a white sedan with the same markings as the Navy Region Northwest cop car that had pulled us over earlier. The uniform climbing out of the SUV donned a dark campaign hat and walked over to confer with the sheriff's deputy. State patrol. Two uniforms from the Navy cop car joined him.

The second county cop headed back from the parking lot to join the party. Lights out on the water drew my attention. A few hundred yards offshore, a ferry as brightly lit as a birthday cake steamed toward the dock, less than five minutes from landing. Now seemed as good a time as any to figure out how I was going to get aboard unnoticed. I walked around the end of the fence into the largely empty parking lot and surveyed the scene one last time.

Pedestrian passengers boarded first and last, no ticket needed on this side of the sound. Ferry workers wouldn't let anyone on foot board while vehicles were driving on. That left me with two choices: board with the first group of passengers, which might attract attention to Reyna; or hang back and board after all the vehicles were loaded, which would make me stand out like a sore thumb to all the law enforcement officers waiting on shore. Neither choice had the same appeal as the spicy Thai red curry I craved right about then.

The two Navy cops broke away from the confab around the tollbooths and walked alongside the far lane of waiting vehicles, their billed caps visible over the car roofs. They didn't bother looking at the cars, which meant only one thing. I glanced down the long lot at the small terminal building. Beyond it, the ferry was slowly gliding in the last few feet between the pilings at the end of the dock. No sign of Reyna. The staging area came alive as people returned to their parked vehicles after stretching their legs, walking dogs or getting coffee or something to eat.

The driver of the pickup truck lumbered down the hill from the store. I slipped between two parked cars, vaulted the low fence into the staging lanes and swam upstream toward him, an impulsive, half-formed thought taking charge. I stepped in front of him as he made his way down the narrow alley between two staging lanes. He stopped and looked up.

"Hey," I said, "that your truck in front of those kids in the Caddy?"

He frowned. "Yeah. So?"

"I'm pretty sure I saw one of them messing with your truck. I don't know if they did any damage, but I thought you ought to know."

A corner of his lip curled up briefly in a sneer of disgust, and his hands clenched into fists.

"Thanks, man."

"Any time," I said, stepping out of his way.

A line of headlights snaked up the dock and swept abreast of the staging lanes as the ferry disgorged its westbound load of vehicles. I slipped over a lane and weaved between several cars. Behind me, I heard a shouting voice and the sound of pounding.

"Get out of the car, motherfucker!" More pounding. "Get out of the fucking car!"

The commotion stopped the Navy cops in their tracks. They looked at each other and said a few words. One backtracked, waving his arm at the three officers standing up by the tollbooths. The other angled across the lanes, zigzagging between the cars. I glanced back and saw the burly man take a tire iron out of the bed of his truck. Both county deputies shifted over for a look down the alley between the lanes, saw the potential threat and broke into a run.

Burly man brandished the tire iron and screamed at the Caddy, "Did you mess with my truck, asshole! Get out here! I'll teach you to fuck with people!"

The state trooper sauntered after the deputies. Reluctantly, the other Navy cop cut across a lane, and all five officers converged on the man before he could smash the Caddy's windshield with the tire iron.

Looking around quickly, I spotted a landscape truck sitting at the back of an outside lane. Casually, I made my way over to the open lane closest to the fence and walked back to the end of the line. People's attention seemed to be on the cops talking the crazy man down from his rage.

"Calm down?" he shouted. "You want me to fucking calm down? When that asshole is the one causing trouble?"

The driver of the landscape truck climbed down from the cab and watched the ruckus. The cops spoke in low voices I couldn't hear. I sidled along the side of the landscape truck.

"Didn't you hear that shit?" burly-man shouted. "They play that crap so freakin' loud you can't hear yourself think!" He paused and turned toward one of the deputies. "Fine! You want me to put it down, it's down."

He turned around and threw the tire iron into the back of his pickup. It landed with a loud clang. Satisfied, he faced the cops again.

"Look, I didn't do anything wrong." His voice was loud enough to carry, but he stopped shouting. "That's the prick you ought to arrest. He messed with my truck!"

I eased closer to the back of the truck.

"How do I know? Somebody *saw* him do it! Guy right over there!"

The burly man pointed in the direction he'd last seen me. Heart running laps around my chest, I ducked around the back of the truck out of sight. Putting a foot up on the bumper, I slowly eased my weight onto it. The truck was big enough that the suspension didn't even feel me. I swung a leg over the tailgate, kept my head low, and squeezed in between two big push lawn mowers. With barely space to sit, I managed to crouch under the handle of one of the mowers and tugged a half full canvas bag of grass clippings close enough to hide me from view.

Minutes later, car engines all around us rumbled to life. The truck door slammed, and the bed beneath me shuddered and vibrated as the driver started it up. In a moment I felt the truck moving.

CHAPTER 51

The noise woke her from an uneasy slumber. She thought about the sound that had lifted her toward consciousness, wondering if it had been real or part of her dream. A small bell, perhaps. Or breaking glass. She came fully awake, shaking off the vestiges of shadowy images that had been part of her dreamscape. They retreated, wisps of fog confronted by an advancing sun. She rose on one elbow and listened intently.

She didn't like staying out in the middle of the countryside alone. She knew she wasn't; the compound had around-the-clock security. And, of course, the couple was still downstairs. But they didn't count. They weren't exactly guests. A couple of former radicals who'd never actually been all that insurrectionary or nihilistic. By now she fully believed them when they said they'd never blown up anything before the lab in the Midwest. And even that had been the work of others. They'd only been peripherally involved. That despite all their talk back in the day—of revolution, and "offing the pigs," about an egalitarian and just society—they never did anything except grow comfortable off the capitalistic society they'd railed against. She'd heard that story before—it. It was almost a running joke about Baby Boomers who'd been activists in the '60s.

She shuddered at the incredible naïveté and ignorance of the pair. The wife was in bad shape; she'd lost a lot of blood, and her wound was probably infected. And in the past thirty-six hours the husband had gone downhill fast. Of course, the interrogation techniques her father had ordered had a lot to do with it. Wilson's face was practically unrecognizable through the bruises and swelling. One eye had swollen completely shut, and the left side of his face was the size and color of a melon blackened with rot from, the result of a broken jaw and four missing teeth.

They didn't know anything. Of that she was sure, but her father wanted to be certain. He'd be back in the morning. She wondered if the Wilsons could hold out that long, wondered if they knew it didn't matter one way or the other. They were as good as dead. The knowledge didn't give her the sense of satisfaction she once imagined it would.

She was here because of them. Here, not home in California. Here, not warm and comfortable in a hotel like the self-important Tucker Prescott Baines. Here, because she'd wanted answers for more than twenty years, and because she'd become desperate for something from him, some small sign that she now realized would never come. A realization that had slowly soured the affection and admiration she'd once felt for her big sister until now all she felt was a soul-shriveling hate, black and acidic. For what? What had been the point? Neither she nor her father had gotten what they wanted beyond a small measure of revenge— no, justice—on some of those responsible for Jill's death. The real story, perhaps, lay buried too deep in the past to unearth. But it was too late to go back, and now she had blood on her hands.

She stiffened suddenly at the sound of a muffled creak from somewhere downstairs. Someone was in the house. *A security guard on rounds? Her father?* She shuddered. She recalled the sound that had roused her, swung her legs out from under the covers and pulled on a pair of jeans as quietly as she could. She didn't see how anyone could get past all the security, let alone break in, but the odd noises had set her on edge. She looked around the room for a weapon of some sort, then shook her head ruefully at her own foolishness.

She sat on the edge of the bed for a moment, unmoving. The only sounds now were the wind whistling through the eaves and the syncopated drip of rainwater in a nearby downspout. She stood and silently padded across the floor to the dresser, rummaged in a drawer for a sweatshirt in the dim light from the window and pulled it over her head. Resolved, she took a deep breath and stole out of her room.

* * * * *

The truck inched ahead. From the other side of the truck box came the voice of the man I'd goaded into a rage.

"I can't believe you pulled me over, not him."

"Sir, you need to calm down," a cop said.

"I swear, officer, them kids was messin' with my truck. Guy told me he *saw* 'em screwing around."

"What guy?"

"*Big* guy. Like ballplayer big. Tall. You know them kids, blasting that trash they call music..."

The voice faded as the truck passed by, picking up speed. For a moment I felt bad for the guy. The cops were likely to let him get on the next ferry with a warning, but if they believed his story and compared notes, they might put someone on board the ferry to look for me. I wasn't out of the woods yet.

Five minutes later, the vibration of the truck bed had changed from the buzz of the truck's three -hundred -fifty -horsepower diesel V-8 to the low rumble of the ferry's five thousand horses. Car doors opened and shut as drivers and passengers emerged and made their way to the passenger deck. After a minute or so, I heard the truck door open and close, too. I slowly counted to thirty before easing out of my hiding place and peering over the tailgate. The truck was next to last on the ferry, the car behind it empty.

I stripped off the poncho and stuffed it in the bag of clippings. I repositioned Charlie's gun from waistband to a deep pocket in the cargo pants, and checked once more to see if anyone was watching. I climbed over the tailgate and hopped down. The car deck was deserted. I walked a few yards to the stern, pulled out my phone and powered it on. Six missed calls and two messages. All but one from Chance. The other an old one from Molly. I frowned and dialed Chance's mobile.

"Where in God's name have you been, doll? You had us worried sick. Are you okay?"

"I'm all right, Chance. I'm sorry I forgot to call. I've been distracted. You okay with taking the route again?"

"Yeah, sure, it's fine. I've got it covered. Where are you?"

"Southworth ferry. Chance, I need a favor."

"Whatever you want, honey."

"We need a car. Can you borrow Peter's or Toji's for me?"

"'We?' What's going on, Blake?"

"I'll tell you when I see you. Can you do it? We have to get up to Whidbey tonight. Fast. I wouldn't ask, Chance, but it's truly a matter of life and death."

"You know I'd move mountains for you, doll. I'll meet you at Fauntleroy in forty minutes."

"Whenever you get there is fine. Don't get a ticket on your way. And thanks, Chance."

I stayed put, hunched over the rail, and watched the black water glide by. The storm front had kicked up some waves, and the ferry rocked gently in the swells. The lights of Vashon Island drifted into view and then slowly slid past until they retreated behind the vessel, growing smaller in the distance as the lights of West Seattle grew bigger. Already cool, the breeze over the sound picked up the water's chill, making my teeth chatter. I crossed my arms for warmth and wished for the first time that the heat wave hadn't ended.

When the ferry was five minutes from landing, I texted Reyna and told her to meet me at the bus stop by the ferry entrance. Before too many people returned to their cars, I headed toward the bow so I'd be one of the first passengers off. Two deck hands manned the bow and two others stood in front of the lead cars ready to direct traffic off the boat. The ferry glided in the last several hundred yards without power. At the last minute the pilot reversed thrust, and the deck rumbled underfoot from the power of the engine. The bow kissed the end of the dock without a bump, and the deck hands made the boat fast. In less than a minute, they lowered the ramp, pulled aside the cargo-net gate and waved the pedestrians off. Slouching, I disembarked with the first wave, staying in the middle of the small group, doing my best to remain inconspicuous.

Reyna caught up to me halfway up the dock and squeezed my arm. "You made it."

"Barely. Navy cops showed up and looked like they were going to check foot passengers, so I had to create a diversion."

"You did that? I wondered what was going on. Quick thinking."

"More like desperation."

"So, I figured we could call a cab, have him take us to get another rental."

"Already took care of it. A friend is bringing us a ride."

"You're kidding."

I shook my head. "Should be here soon."

By the time we got to the street, however, Chance was already waiting in the small parking lot next to the ferry entrance. He stood beside the open door of a white convertible dressed in four-inch stiletto heels, a short, tight cocktail dress and a sequined black shrug, and waved to us. I steered Reyna toward the familiar car, frowning.

"Chance?" I said as we drew closer. "What did you do?"

His heavily made-up face split into a wide grin, the brief illusion of femininity gone.

"You said you needed to get to Whidbey fast."

"Is this what I think it is?"

"What do you think this is?" Reyna said.

I faced her. "My ex-wife's car." Her pride and joy, a BMW M5. "I can't believe you asked Molly for her car, Chance."

"I knew she'd let me borrow it. So, what's the big deal? And who's the dish, doll?"

"Sorry. Reyna, this is my friend Chance Reno, one of my landlords. Chance, meet Lieutenant Commander Reyna Chase."

Chance's penciled eyebrows practically disappeared into his platinum wig. "*The* Reyna Chase?" Chance knew all about the last time Reyna had been in town, six months earlier. He straightened and gave her a mock salute.

Reyna laughed. "No need to be formal."

I looked around, suddenly nervous. "I hate to push, but I think we ought to get out of here."

Chance handed me the keys to Molly's car. "Top -secret mission, I suppose. You get to have all the fun, doll. Good luck. Don't go getting yourself killed like you almost did at Javier's."

"Oh, hell, I forgot to call him, too."

Chance waved airily. "He's fine. Restaurant's fine. Window's all fixed. He forgives you. Says the notoriety has actually helped business. Don't worry about it."

He turned to go.

"Do you need a ride?" Reyna said.

Chance thumbed over his shoulder. "Toji drove down in his car. He'll give me a ride back to the warehouse."

"You're not working the paper route dressed like that, are you?" I swallowed hard.

Chance laughed. "And ruin these fuck-me pumps? Hell no, doll."

He spun around and sashayed across the lot to a waiting car. Toji waved through the windshield. Chance rounded the front of the car and climbed in next to him, rolled down his window and leaned out as they drove past.

"Whatever you do," he called, "don't wreck that cute little car. Molly would have a fit."

They roared off. As they vanished in the line of cars heading up the hill, a parade of unmarked black SUVs with flashing lights swept down toward the ferry entrance.

CHAPTER 52

Langford moved quickly from room to room on silent feet, committing the layout to memory as he searched for a way to the basement. The high-ceilinged rooms in the old farmhouse were capacious and airy. While they all retained original moldings and dimensions, even in the dark he could see they'd been updated with recessed lighting on dimmers, a high-speed LAN connection to the Internet, and a multi-line telecommunications system. The living room and front parlor had been converted to conference rooms with multi-media projection capability. The dining room remained as originally intended, restored to a level of elegance likely not seen outside of Seattle when the home had been built. The kitchen had undergone a complete remodel with top-line commercial food equipment, the gleaming stainless reflecting the warm tones of rich cherry cabinetry even in the faint light from outside.

Time worked against him now, and he increased his pace. He spotted the door to the basement stairs in the kitchen. As he crossed the room his weight caused a spot on the bamboo floor to creak. He froze, barely breathing, and listened to the sounds in the house. A refrigerator compressor hummed quietly. A pirr of air whispered to him from the heating vents in the room. Water dripped outside the kitchen window. Faintly, he heard the wind's colloquy with the trees outside. Nothing else in the house stirred. Cautiously, he took a step. Still hearing nothing out of the ordinary he hurried to the door and down the stairs.

At the bottom, he pressed a wall switch, bathing the room in light. The basement also had been extensively remodeled. He stepped into a carpeted game room dominated by a billiards table in the center, a couple of pinball machines on one wall, and seating areas on another. He didn't pause, crossing the room to a door on the far side. Pushing through it, he turned on the lights and found himself in a large media room with more than a dozen plush movie -theater -style chairs facing a blank wall framed by heavy drapes. Beyond that he found a door into a mechanical room housing the furnace, water heater and air filtration system and a storeroom. There was no sign of the Wilsons, and he was running out of time.

Quickly returning to the game room, he scanned it again to see where he might have gone wrong. There were two other doors in the room. One was clearly marked with a restroom sign. He opened it and glanced inside. The only other door was narrower. He tried it anyway and discovered a small closet. Frustrated now, he went back into the media room. To the left, behind the rows of chairs was a door to a projection room. The glass pane between the rooms, he noted, was blacked out.

With a growing sense of exigency, he strode to the door and put his hand on the knob. *Locked.* He hesitated before bashing it in, worried about the noise it would make. He took a step back and removed his backpack. Quietly, he reached in one of the pockets and grasped the butt of the J.P. Sauer. He aimed it at the door while he slowly summoned his concentration. With as much power as he could muster, he kicked the door next to the handle, splintering the flimsy frame. He stepped back as it burst open, holding the pistol in both hands.

The room breathed fetid air, and Langford nearly gagged on the stale and ferrous odors of duress and dried blood. The light barely penetrated the deep gloom, but he saw the forms of two people in the corner prone on the tile floor. One of the huddled figures struggled to raise a head off the floor and turn a face toward the light. Langford shuddered involuntarily, momentarily repulsed by the sight of the man's ravaged face, almost unrecognizable from repeated beatings. The man stared at him from his one good eye, and lifted an outstretched arm, feeble as a baby.

"Help us," he rasped.

Langford swiftly pulled the door shut and turned away. He had what he needed. He shouldered the backpack and hurried back to the game room, pulling his cell out of his pocket. Gun still in his hand, he punched a speed dial number and heard it ring.

When a voice answered, his response was terse. "It's Langford. They're here."

He hit the wall switch and slipped the phone into his pocket as he raced up the stairs in the pitch black. Just a few feet more and he'd be out the door and on his way to true freedom. He faltered at the top when he heard muffled voices, a door closing and the tread of feet on the hardwoods. Pausing, he cracked open the kitchen door and listened. The voices belonged to one female and two males. *Security.* They'd find him in moments. He slipped through the narrow opening and ran for the back door, glass crunching loudly under the soles of his shoes. Footsteps thundered through the house after him. He yanked the door open, bolted onto the porch and threw himself through the screen door. As he leaped to the ground without using the stairs, a man the size of a freight train stepped in his path and aimed a gun at him.

"Hold it! Drop your weapon!"

Langford's arm started to rise of its own accord. For an instant he knew with deadly certitude that he could put the guy down before he got off a shot. But the clatter of shoes on the porch behind him stopped him. He pulled up, breathing hard, let the pistol slip from his grasp, and raised his arms over his head.

* * * * *

Letting the BMW have its head up I-5, we made the last ferry out of Mukilteo by just minutes for the short crossing to Whidbey. With little traffic at that time of night we cruised the main highway up the island at speeds most municipalities make money on. Reyna had grown increasingly quiet the farther we went. Now, with only a few miles to go according to her directions, tension filled the car like we'd driven into the ocean, water squeezing the air out and weighting us down until we couldn't breathe.

Reyna had spent part of the trip on her laptop, using a cellular modem to access the Internet. She'd researched everything she could find about Ross Industries and the facility on Whidbey. After putting the computer away, she'd spent another half hour taking apart her HK, cleaning and inspecting it.

She'd reassembled and dry fired it until she seemed satisfied, reloaded a magazine and rammed it home.

For the past twenty minutes she'd nervously chewed her fingernails and stared out the windows at the darkened scenery slipping past. The rain had eased to a drizzle and then stopped altogether, but we ran into occasional showers that slicked the roadway and coated the windshield with droplets. They fractured the oncoming headlights into a kaleidoscope of rainbow-hued halos until the wiper blades erased them.

"You better be right about this," she muttered.

I glanced at her. "Me? I thought we were in this together."

"You know what I mean. Jesus, Blake, I just threw away a pretty distinguished career."

"Not on my account, you didn't."

"Even if we're right, I bent or broke so many rules the past two days, they'll never give me my job back."

"If we're right, they'll give you damn medal."

She shook her head. "This is all wrong. You're a civilian. I'm wanted by the MAs on god-knows-what charges."

"We don't have a choice. You know that. You didn't do anything wrong. Well, except for that little matter of aiding and abetting a fugitive."

She said nothing.

"Reyna, look, it's all or nothing now. We find Keely. Either the Wilsons are there or not. If they are then this is all connected somehow. We figure that out and you'll have enough evidence to save your job *and* get a medal. We don't have a choice."

Wind rush and road hum filled the silence. Reyna's mouth was set in a grim line, the normally pouty lips thinned and taut.

"You *are* right," she said finally. "The only way they know that I helped you is through Baines. And if the brass is so scared of Baines they're willing to arrest me, then something's wrong. I'm not going down without a fight."

"That's the spirit." I wished some of her newfound confidence would rub off.

Ten minutes later we stashed the car off the road under some trees and approached the Ross Industries perimeter on foot. From what she'd been able to glean online, Reyna was convinced that the security overkill at the main entrance was designed to give the illusion that the entire facility was impregnable. The company was so confident in the precautions it had taken that the property even lacked a fence from the outside world. A liability in daylight, the open ground between the road and the compound wouldn't expose us as much at night.

In a low voice, she sketched out the rough plan one more time. When I assured her I got it, she moved thirty yards off to the right, crouched low and started running. I gave her a thirty-second head start, then ran a parallel path toward the compound, each of us stopping every hundred feet or so and dropping to the ground. We alternated that way until we'd made it within a hundred yards of the low outlying building and both lay prone behind some short scrub. Reyna was invisible against the dark ground, but I had a fix on the spot where I'd seen her dive into the dirt. I waited and watched.

Corner-mounted floodlights carved the outlines of the three low-lying buildings from the surrounding blackness and cast their shadows into the night. A small vehicle wheeled away from the parking lot in front of what appeared to be the main entrance of the compound. It sped toward the building closest to us, and when it disappeared on the far side of the building, a shadow detached itself from the bushes off to my right and raced toward the building. Visible in the light from the floods for only seconds, Reyna ran for the unlit side of the building and vanished in the dark. I followed moments later and picked my way along the side of the building in the pitch, momentarily night-blind. I saw no sign of Reyna.

Some large rhododendrons and smaller azalea bushes grew at the far end of the building in an attempt to soften the industrial appearance of the facility. Reyna crouched behind them, peering at something around the corner of the building. I came up behind her and craned my neck to see what she was looking at. An electric utility vehicle a little larger than a golf cart sat empty in a cone of light on the walkway in front of the building.

Reyna had her gun out. Motioning me to stay put, she scurried to the side of the door and pressed herself against the building. With a quick movement of her head, she glanced inside and pulled back. Like a runner exploding out of the blocks she raced to the other side of the entrance and plastered herself against the building again. I pulled out Charlie's semi-automatic and hefted it nervously. Reyna peered in my direction through the shadow's edge. I gave a short wave and saw her nod.

The blood rush in my ears sounded like the buzz of conversation in a tightly packed room. Sweat slicked the smooth steel on the butt of the gun. I pressed my fingers reassuringly against the knurly texture of the grip, then consciously relaxed my grip and inhaled deeply. *Dirgha pranayama.* From the number of times my heart beat I stood there a lifetime, but the wait couldn't have been more than a minute or two. A raindrop glanced off the side of my nose, followed in quick succession by more, plinking in my hair and on my shoulders.

A shifting of light in the entryway signaled someone near, and I tensed. The door swung open and a man stepped outside. He glanced skyward at the falling rain and pulled his collar up. Intent on making it to his vehicle without getting wet, he never suspected Reyna's presence until her pistol was pressed into the small of his back.

CHAPTER 53

The call came in when most normal people were asleep. He didn't mind despite the lateness of the hour. He was awake anyway. Sleep seemed to elude him most nights, but the lack of it never had a deleterious effect. He functioned just fine on the three or four hours that had become his routine. When he'd first experienced this pattern of sleeplessness, he's thought it might be due to stress, to thoughts of all the years he'd put in on the job and how little he had to show for it. He'd worried that it would take an edge off his game. In fact, the opposite had occurred. His mind was more agile, his acuity and insight into situations quicker and more unerring than ever.

He'd actually anticipated the call, had been lying on top of his bed in his skivvies waiting for the storm that had finally blown in to cool his bedroom below ninety degrees. When the call came, he eagerly reached for the phone in the dark. The man on the other end said only a few words, but they were exactly what he'd hoped to hear. As soon as the voice disconnected, he called his partner and woke him from a sound sleep. The irony both amused and annoyed him. When his partner gruffly indicated he was fully conscious, he passed along the message and told him to be ready in ten minutes. They had a long drive ahead of them, and no time to waste.

He wasn't sure how it would play out, but for the first time since he'd taken this path he was convinced he would reach his intended destination. Until the phone call, he'd bluffed his way into a position where he stood to reap millions. Now, he finally had confidence that he'd really be able to pull it off. One way or another, he'd get what he wanted. Tonight.

He opened the top drawer of his dresser and took out a disposable cell phone, punched in a number and sat on the edge of the bed. He let it rang twice and hung up, then called the same number. A voice answered with a simple "Yes?"

"It's tonight," he replied.

"Call when you have it," the voice said. "We'll give you coordinates then."

Fourteen minutes later, he pulled up to the curb in front of his partner's house and watched him stumble down the front steps while trying to zip a baggy windbreaker that billowed in the wind. Hunching his shoulders, his partner pulled the collar of the jacket up over his head as protection from the fat raindrops, and ran to the car.

"You ready?" he said when his partner shut the door.

His partner nodded. "About time. Let's go." Looking around with a small scowl, he added, "Why this car?"

He rammed the stick shift into first gear. "It's faster."

"Too small," his partner complained.

"Stop bitching."

He gunned the engine and popped the clutch. The black coupe roared away from the curb with a shriek of smoking tires.

* * * * *

I stepped into the circle of light and raised my gun. Both of us had the guard's attention now. He raised his arms over his head, expression wavering between nervousness and fear.

"Cover him," Reyna said.

I complied gladly, taking a few steps closer. The wink of a bright red eye on the overhang above the entry distracted me. I peered at the dark chiropteran shape hanging over their heads— a camera pointed at the walkway, the electric cart dead in its aim.

"Wait!" I said.

Startled, Reyna looked up at me and waited. I tucked the gun back in my waistband. The camera didn't move, and no light shone. I wondered if I'd imagined it. A second or two later, though, the light blinked again. With a couple of running steps, I went in for a dunk. Instead of an orange rim, I grasped the camera firmly at both ends. My weight brought it down easily, pulling the screws out of soft wood and yanking the wiring loose.

Reyna looked at it ruefully. "Damn, there's probably another one inside."

I tossed the camera in the bushes by the side of the building and took the gun out again.

"Looked like this one was taking stills every five or six seconds," I said. "Maybe the one inside didn't catch you in a frame."

The security guard looked even more nervous now. "What do you want? We don't keep money here."

Reyna snorted. "You're on rounds and you don't know why someone would break in."

"You're what, like industrial spies?"

"Shut up!" she said.

Reyna bound his arms behind his back with nylon ties from her pocket. She grabbed his arm and roughly jerked him toward the electric vehicle. He dragged his heels, so I encouraged him with a wave of the gun. Reyna spun him around and gave him a shove. Off balance, he had no choice but to sit, legs dangling over the steel armrest. She stuck her gun under his chin.

"Where are they holding the prisoners?"

His eyes widened. "Prisoners? What prisoners? This is a manufacturing plant, lady! Please, I don't know what you're talking about."

She cocked the hammer. "Let's try again. Where are they?"

"I swear! I don't know what the hell you're talking about! Please, you gotta believe me!"

I took a step closer. "Baines. Is he here?"

The guard turned his head warily, Reyna's gun barrel limiting his movement. He blinked rapidly.

"Mr. Baines? I don't know. Maybe."

"Which is it?" Reyna said, applying more pressure.

He winced. "I'm not sure. I heard he was here earlier, but I didn't see him, and he didn't sign in at the main desk. But he's the boss. He doesn't have to sign in if he doesn't want to."

"Have you noticed anything unusual on your shift?"

A thought stopped his head in mid-shake. "A couple of guys stopped in the security office earlier tonight. Said they were from the main office in San Jose. I was on my way out on rounds. I didn't talk to them."

Reyna and I exchanged a glance.

"Where would Baines go if not to the office?" I asked.

The guard shrugged. "Anywhere. The lab, one of the assembly buildings… But no one's been in any of those buildings tonight. Oh, could have been the conference center, too. There's a guest staying there, not sure who. But it's been pretty quiet. Guest turned in a while ago."

I studied the main compound. "Which one's the conference center?"

"The one on the left. Used to be the old farmhouse."

"The one with all the lights on?"

A tall Victorian house stood apart from the rest of the campus buildings in a stand of big oak trees from their size and shape. The house windows burned brightly.

He turned to follow my gaze and gawped. "What the—?"

Reyna placed the gun against his cheek and turned his head back until he faced her.

"Explain the layout," she said. "Start at the front door. Go room by room."

The guard rolled his eyes up to the black sky, envisioning the floor plan in his mind, and described the interior of the house for the next two minutes.

"Let's go," Reyna said when the words stopped tumbling out of his mouth.

I gestured with my gun. "Him?"

"He won't be any trouble," she said.

She pulled out her ID and held it under the guard's nose, angling it toward the light so he could read it. She spoke slowly, making sure he understood every word.

"This says I'm with the U.S. Office of Naval Intelligence. In Washington, D.C. That means I'm one of the good guys. What's your name?"

The guard swallowed. "Owens."

She grabbed a fistful of his collar and hauled him to his feet. Her strength surprised me. I was glad I wasn't on her bad side. None too gently, she dragged Owens to the back of the vehicle and fastened his wrists to a bar with another plastic tie.

"Okay, Owens, here's the deal," she said. "For your own protection as well as ours, you're staying here. If you so much as make a peep to warn these people, I'll bring the wrath of the U.S. government down on your head. We'll be back later to thank you for your cooperation."

She turned and motioned to me.

"What if you don't come back?" Owens said, plaintiveness in his voice.

She faced him and jerked a thumb at me. "Then he and I are probably dead, and you'll have to explain to the bad guys how you managed to get yourself tied up. Got it?"

He nodded vigorously.

Reyna loped into the darkness without another word.

Owens implored me. "You're coming back, right?"

I sighed and trotted after Reyna, catching sight of her silhouette in the light from the windows of the conference center. She skirted the pools of lamplight at the entrances to the other two low factory buildings. I followed her lead and hoped the maneuvers kept us out of camera range. She slowed as she closed on the house. I caught up to her just as she pulled up and dropped to one knee alongside some bushes at the edge of the yard. I crouched next to her.

The entire first floor of the building was ablaze with lights. Only one window upstairs glowed. My heart thumped loudly from nerves and the exertion, but Reyna didn't seem to notice. She stared intently at the house. I looked, too, but saw nothing out of the ordinary except the radiant gleam in the middle of the night. It finally occurred to me that what was missing was any sign of life amidst all that light. No sounds emerged, no shadows flickered across the window coverings.

"Circle left," Reyna murmured. "'We'll meet up by the back door and compare notes."

I pushed off and ran in a low crouch to a huge oak at the corner of the yard. Taking cover, I peeked at the house around the thick trunk. Nothing stirred. I dashed to the cover of another tree near the circular drive at the front of the house. No one stood guard by the front door. I caught my breath and listened to the night sounds. The wind had quieted to a light breeze that carried only the distant screech of a nighthawk, not any murmurs of human conversation.

The thin fabric of the shirt I'd bought in California provided little protection from the damp night air, and the chill had seeped into my bones. I shivered, and for a moment couldn't stop the tremors. Rubbing my arms fiercely to generate some warmth, I paced until they subsided. Exhaustion was a memory, and I wasn't sure what force still kept me on my feet. *Focus!* Taking several deep breaths, I sprinted back through the shadows to the rear of the house.

Reyna crouched by the steps. I joined her and shook my head silently. She nodded and tipped her head toward the door, then crept up the stairs silently, gun at the ready. She disappeared through the screen door at the top. I went up after her and found her squatting just inside the screen, staring at the door that led inside. A muted yellow glow came through a frilly curtain on the inside of the lattice. The pane above the doorknob sported a jagged hole. Reyna slid forward. I clamped a hand on her shoulder, wondering if the blink of red reflected in the glass had been my imagination. I twisted my head. A camera was mounted directly above us.

Slowly, I stood and stretched for it. Gripping it tightly, I waited for another red flash and twisted it sideways, aiming the lens at the ceiling. The relief on Reyna's face was palpable. She duck-walked across the porch to the back door and opened it. Light spilled out from a modern kitchen. She poked her head in quickly, then scooted inside and took up a position to the left of the door like a gargoyle sentry. Heart banging like a stick on the picket fence of my ribs, I slithered through the opening and bookended the other side of the door.

The soles of my shoes hummed with vibrations through the floor from the murmur of voices below. The dampened pounding of heavy feet on uncarpeted stairs reverberated through the kitchen. Reyna quickly sidled to the opposite wall, next to a closed door where the sounds came from. She frantically waved me off to my right. I scuttled behind an island in the middle of the room and crawled to the other side on all fours until I could peek around the corner. Reyna gave me a nod and focused on the door. It burst open.

Keely came through first, strode halfway to the back door and stopped. She folded her arms, stared at the back door, and tapped a foot impatiently.

"Let's not take all day," she called.

An out-of-uniform NFL nose tackle dressed in black fatigues emerged, backing through the doorway slowly, holding a gun on whoever came next. Reyna rose in a flash and jammed her gun in his ribs, holding a finger to her lips. He froze as Reyna twisted the pistol out of his hand. She motioned him back a few steps to make room. Though several inches shorter, he had thirty or forty pounds on me, and looked as if he spent spare hours bench-pressing large farm animals. He made me realize how big I looked to most people. He could have easily crushed Reyna, but surprise and a gun were great equalizers.

Next float in the parade was Clayt—his ponytail, at least—staggering backwards through the opening under the awkward weight of a woman's legs. Connie. Wink lumbered up the stairs with the rest of her, holding her under the armpits. Unconscious and limp, dead weight. Clayt lost his footing and stumbled into the football player, dropping Connie's legs to the floor. The guard grunted as Clayt fell into him and turned his face toward me. He was unrecognizable, the savagery of what they'd done bringing bile up into my throat. Wink lurched into the room under Connie's weight and sank to his knees, cradling her head so it didn't bang the floor.

Keely whirled at all the commotion and stared at Reyna. "Who the hell are you?"

Before Reyna could answer, the nose tackle's twin charged through the door, gun in hand, swinging it from side to side, not sure where to point it. I stood and aimed at his head.

"Uh-uh," I said. "Drop it, please, and kick it over here."

The jut of his chin begged for someone to swing at it, but the wild light in his eyes flickered out when he realized his twin was unarmed. The gun dropped to the floor with a solid thump. He nudged it with a toe and sent it sliding across the floor. I picked it up and stuck it behind my belt.

Keely wheeled and stared at me, mouth agape. "Oh, my god. *You're* here? Who in hell *politely* asks someone to drop a gun?"

She shook her head with a look of disgust. My face flushed, and my hands closed tighter around the pistol grip.

"She doesn't seem happy to see you," Reyna said.

"I don't know why," I said. "I pretty much did everything she wanted me to."

"Got that right," Wink muttered.

I glanced at him. "You knew she was using me to get to you? Why the hell didn't you leave?"

"I didn't think you'd put it together. And if I'd had a little more time, I would have been long gone before you led her there. One more reason I'll be dealing with you later."

Keely put her hands on her hips. "Not that the reminiscing isn't fascinating, boys, but save it for old home week." She turned to Reyna. "You're obviously in charge. What now?"

Reyna appraised her coolly. "I doubt everyone in this company is on your special payroll. Tweedledum and Tweedledee here can change places with those two and carry Mrs. Wilson. We'll head over to the security office in the main building, get her some first aid, and call in some guarded transport for you and your buddies."

Keely shook her head in disagreement. "Who are you again? Blake, this one of your cop friends? I don't know how you two got in, but I can guarantee you're not getting out as easily."

"Blake, would you escort Miz Radcliffe? Boys, you want to grab the patient? And please try something stupid. I'd love the excuse to shoot any one of you."

I circled around the island, giving the twins a wide berth. Keely's face was as dark as the windows. She glared at me defiantly. I tugged an arm behind her back and levered it up between her shoulder blades a little harder than was gentlemanly. She didn't even wince. Instead, she smiled at me over her shoulder. Then her eyes hardened like brittle shards of ice.

"Fool!" she hissed. "You have no idea what you're doing."

"Shut up. This isn't what you want. You want payback, turn them in. They'll go to jail."

"How the fuck do you know what I want? You're really going to regret this."

"Okay, folks, let's go," Reyna said. "Nice and easy. Blake, you lead. You big boys take Mrs. Wilson. Carefully! That's it. Langford, you want to help Mr. Wilson out, please? I'll keep an eye on these folks and you can follow at your own pace."

A piper—drab, not pied—I led the procession out the door and down the steps. Reyna and I herded the little group across the yard into a tree-covered parking lot adjacent to the main building. Halfway there, a pair of headlights sped down the drive from the main road toward the conference center. *Cavalry?* A black SUV passed us, but with a squeal of brakes, stopped, reversed and entered the lot. Reyna had frozen in a crouch, gun at the ready.

"Friends?" I said.

"I didn't call them," she said. "I think we're screwed."

The others stopped and stared as the vehicle roared up and stopped. Keely had a smirk on her face. What looked like the rest of the twins' defensive line piled out and surrounded us. Suited up in black fatigues like the others, these three came armed with assault rifles. Reyna and I dropped our guns and put our hands on our heads. Keely walked up to me smiling, and put her hand on my cheek. Her eyes were so baleful under the lot lights that I shivered at her touch.

A figure stepped out of the SUV and stood behind the door. I couldn't make out his features behind the glare of the headlights.

A disembodied voice bellowed, "Keely!"

The sound jerked her head around like a puppet on a string, her expression chary.

"Can't you—?" The voice was explosive with rage, but went on in a calmer tone. "Take them all to the lab. I'll be there shortly." The figure ducked back inside the SUV.

One of the men frisked me and relieved me of the gun in my waistband as well as the one I dropped. He frisked Reyna next, but Keely stepped away and picked up Reyna's pistol. Glancing over her shoulder to make sure the football team followed the playbook, she marched toward the boxy, windowless building on the other side of the main offices.

Tweedledum and Tweedledee continued to carry Connie, only because it was faster than letting anyone else do it. Clayt could barely stand. Wink had pulled one of Clayt's arms around his shoulder, sagging under Clayt's weight. I suddenly seethed with anger at the couple for putting us all in this predicament. I wanted to lash out. Instead, I grabbed Clayt's other arm and took some of his weight. He looked up at me blearily through one swollen eye. I couldn't tell if he recognized me or not.

A few minutes later, we crowded into a fifteen-by-twenty-foot room furnished with three rows of worktables littered with electronic equipment, computer monitors, circuit boards, oscilloscopes, and tangles of multi-colored wires snaking in all directions. Some were fitted with an overhead shelf loaded down with more gear. Empty stools crouched under the tables, waiting. Several gray, wheeled steel carts around the room held more racked equipment. The twins cleared a desk in a corner and laid Connie on it, unconscious. They herded Wink, Reyna and Clayt into the last aisle between the worktables. I ended up in the middle aisle.

"What now, Keely?" I said.

She strutted around the corner of the lab table into the aisle next to me.

"I'm sure you're smart enough to figure it out," she said. "Watch and learn."

The twins stood guard now while two of the others made their way around the room placing inch-thick black -plastic-wrapped bricks in different spots. About ten inches long and two inches wide, the bricks were imprinted with green letters, all caps. Too far away to read it all, I was able to make out the top line on the closest one—CHARGE DEMOLITION M112. The words didn't inspire my confidence. I suddenly noticed that none of the men in black had bothered to conceal their faces like before. The room suddenly felt colder than a meat locker.

"You're going to blow up your own lab?" I said.

"I can answer that," said a deep voice, the same one from the SUV.

An older man strode through the door with the kind of assurance that comes from years of unquestioning fealty from everyone around him. Tweedledee noted his presence from the corner of his eye with a nervous twitch of his lips. His mirror image straightened perceptibly. The other members of the team continued what they were doing, but seemed aware of him nonetheless. The boss, obviously. Baines himself.

I paid more attention, noting hooded eyes under dark brows, a sharply curved nose like a raptor's beak over a thin-lipped mouth. Silver hair lent him the air of elder statesman, but the kind who'd kept his place in power through backroom deals and efficient ruthlessness. Running a billion-dollar defense company would be good practice. Vaguely familiar, I tried to remember where I might have seen him, but I couldn't place him in context. Television news, most likely.

Instead of answering, he addressed one of the men setting charges. "Pete, you guys about done here?"

"Almost, sir."

"When you are, take Rocco and Kurt and make sure everyone in the facility evacuates. Shouldn't be anyone here but regular security, but double check. Tell them we got a bomb threat we're taking very seriously."

"Yes, sir."

Baines turned to Keely. "My timing was fortuitous."

Keely's nostrils flared, and the corners of her mouth whitened. "I would have handled it. *You* might want to have a word with your security chief up here. First, Langford, then these two... Getting in doesn't seem to be much of a problem."

"Even so, Keely, you nearly blew it, damn it! If it hadn't been for me, the compound might be crawling with feds right now."

She shrank from his anger, but parried one last time. "It wouldn't have happened if security was better."

Leaving only the twin linemen to ride herd, Pete and friends filed out the door past Baines in their black fatigues. The sight of

Baines's head behind them as they exited stirred a buried memory. It floated toward the light then drifted back down into the depths like a freshly washed sheet settling on a bed. I wished I could get a better look at it, but I was just so damned tired. I couldn't focus. My gaze bounced from face to face, eyes attracted by movements, sounds, voices as fast as thoughts caromed off the inside of my skull.

Baines gave an almost imperceptible nod, conceding Keely's point. "Nothing more from the Wilsons, I take it?"

She glanced at them. "What more could they possibly give us? They've told us everything they know."

He grunted, following her gaze. Connie's chest barely rose and fell, her breathing shallow. Clayt slumped on a stool, chin on his chest, unresponsive to events around him.

Baines turned to me. "To answer your question, the Wilsons are notorious radicals who have been wanted by the government for forty years. They initially claimed responsibility for the bomb that killed my daughter." He shrugged.

I glanced at Keely. She looked pained, like someone had poked her with a pin.

Baines went on. "Investigators will find their remains and assume they returned to their old ways. Langford, here, was convicted of my daughter's murder. If I'm not mistaken, he's violating conditions of his parole just by being here. The police will naturally assume he came here to wreak some sort of revenge on me, or the company."

"And us?" I motioned toward Reyna, who had been unusually quiet.

His jaw clenched. "You're trespassing. For all I know, you're in league with Langford and the Wilsons. Langford's your friend, isn't he? Or at least he was."

"She's with naval intelligence," I said. "You can't just kill off government agents."

Baines held up a finger. "If I'm not mistaken, Miz—Chase, is it?—Miz Chase is gainfully unemployed at the moment. I guess you two are domestic terrorists just like the others."

"You're forgetting something," Wink said quietly. Eyes turned and stared at him.

A vein in Baines' temple pulsed now, but he managed to turn up the corners of his mouth in a semblance of a smile.

"And what would that be?" he said, struggling to maintain a pleasant façade.

"What you've been looking for. The notes."

Baines frowned and glared at Keely. She looked confused, less self-assured.

"Kwan Ji, you mean," Baines said. He brushed aside an imaginary fly. "They don't exist. They never did. That's why I fired him."

"The notes exist, all right," Wink said. "At least they did."

Baines' eyes narrowed. "What do you mean?" he said sharply.

"I destroyed them."

"How? How did you get them?"

I piped up. "The Wilsons had them all along." I looked at Wink. "You found the Bible?"

Wink kept his eyes trained on Baines. "Fitch stole them when he helped set the bomb. He hid them in a Bible and gave it to the Wilsons for safekeeping."

"Impossible," Baines growled. "And even if he did, what good are they if you destroyed them? Seems to me you've lost your bargaining chip."

"He's got photographic memory," I told him. "The only way you'll find out what was in those notes is if you keep him alive."

Michael W. Sherer

CHAPTER 54

"Daddy?"

Keely's doleful voice had regressed to that of a querulous child.

"Daddy, don't they *all* have to be punished for what they did to Jill?"

"Not now, Keely! I have to think." Baines rubbed his chin, eyes on the floor. "This puts a different wrinkle on things."

He jerked his head up and his gaze lasered on Wink. "I could eventually get it out of you. Don't think prison made you so tough you can resist all the interrogation techniques those pansies in D.C. want to outlaw. Waterboarding works, Mr. Langford, I assure you. But it takes time. I assume you have something in mind?"

"We can probably work out an agreeable price," Wink said.

"And your friends?"

Wink shrugged. "The Wilsons deserve whatever they get. Do what you want with them." He looked at Reyna, then me. "Them? Up to you. The woman is pretty much screwed. You saw to that. She's got no credibility with her superiors. Him? Probably no threat to you, but it's no skin off my ass if you want to blow him up."

"How do I know the notes have any value?" Baines said.

Wink grinned. "Suppose I might have been able to tell if I'd finished college. Oh, that's right, I did—in prison." His expression turned serious. "If we agree on a price, why don't you give me half up front for half the notes. You can have your research team look them over and see if they're legit and hold promise. If so, you give me the rest and I deliver the other half."

Baines pinched the bridge of his patrician nose between thumb and forefinger.

"Daddy?" Keely whined. "I did this for you. I hunted them down for *you*. I found the Wilsons. I even found that harmless old man, Fitch's friend. You had *him* killed. You promised you'd punish them *all* for what they did! Don't you even care?"

The light in her eyes was alien. Something inside her had snapped, sending her over the edge. The suddenness of the change was unsettling. I wondered how long she'd managed to hold it all together, and shivered as I thought of how close I'd let her get to me. *Fitch's friend?* Jesus, I'd been right. I shivered again. Baines threw her a piercing look, face reddening with anger. He drew in a deep breath and looked away, as if mustering some force to quell the beast welling up inside. The motion put his features in profile, and suddenly the memory from earlier lurched back out of the muck and clawed its way into my consciousness. No fresh linen, this was a creature from a black lagoon of guilt I'd dammed up all those years ago.

"It was you!"

The exclamation out of my mouth surprised me as much as everyone else. I stared at Baines, seeing him not with silver hair and loose skin around his throat, but dark hair and youthful vigor. He blinked rapidly.

"You were right the first time, Keely," I said. "Wink didn't kill your sister. The Wilsons didn't even do it, though they might as well have. *He* killed her."

I pointed at Baines.

Keely's pout turned to confusion again. "Daddy?"

Baines' lips curled back in a snarl. "What the hell are you talking about?"

Giving voice to the truth, stirring up the muck, sent bits of what I'd thought were flotsam and jetsam floating into place like daubs of pigment in a paint-by-numbers picture.

"It all makes sense now," I said, wondering why I hadn't seen it before. "Kill two birds with one stone."

"You're babbling," Baines growled. He gestured to one of the twins. "Shut him up!"

Tweedledum took a step toward me, but Keely latched onto his arm and dug in her nails.

"Wait, just wait!" she screeched. "I want to hear this. What do you mean? What two birds?"

"Kwan Ji and Clayt—Colin Wilson." I watched Baines' face. "You suffered two blows to an ego that normally wouldn't stand for one of them. Kwan had been right all along. He had something, technology that could revolutionize battery storage. And you let him go. He was going to prove you wrong, and all his patents would have belonged to him and SIU, not Ross Industries. You bombed the lab to destroy his work, and then you had him killed, burned his house down."

Keely stared at her father, incredulity straining her features.

"Is this true? You set the bomb? To get back at someone you *fired?*"

"Keely!" he barked. "Don't listen to this. It's all crap!"

She cringed, but held her ground. "What about the other bird? What did Wilson do?"

"Colin Wilson had a fling with your mother. A long time ago. She didn't mean for it to happen, and it was a one-time thing. But Baines found out. Spent years trying to find Wilson and his wife after they skipped to Canada in the early '70s. They weren't there long. They managed to sneak back into the States and used Corinne Wilson's maiden name, Jones.

"Your father finally came up with a scheme to lure them out of hiding. He found Fitch, knew that Fitch had been close to the Wilsons during the Vietnam years, and told him that he wanted to make a statement, bomb a lab back in Illinois. He convinced Fitch to talk the Wilsons into sponsoring the mission. Figured they'd get blamed and eventually caught, and Clayt—Colin— would go to prison for a long time."

"But Jill. He wouldn't have done that to Jill."

"Of course not," Baines interjected. "It's bullshit, Keely. Don't listen to him."

"I'm not lying, Keely. Kwan didn't just take potential billions of dollars away from the company when your father fired him. He enticed your sister to help him work on the technology. He recognized her talent, and wanted to put it to useful work. Isn't that right, Baines? You couldn't stand the fact that Jill preferred working with Kwan than working for you. That's another reason you destroyed his work."

The veins in Baines' neck stood out and his face turned claret. "Someone shoot this bastard, goddamn it!"

"What happened, Baines? Too much explosive? Didn't realize it would take out the office next door and your daughter with it?"

"You son of a bitch! I'll kill you myself!"

Baines marched over to Tweedledum and tried to wrestle his gun away, but the big man pushed him away and held him off with a huge arm across his chest. Baines strained to push past.

"You realized what had happened," I told him, "went back in, and shot her. Only problem was Wink. You hadn't counted on anyone else being there. He got caught. The Wilsons went free. You've been looking for them ever since. Oh, and Kwan's notes were missing. The one thing you hoped to profit from. Besides revenge."

Keely stared at me with a growing look of horror.

"How do you know this?" she whispered.

"I was *there*." I watched my revelation home in on her heart like a heat-seeking missile.

Baines stopped struggling. "Not possible."

"I saw your whole team come out of the building," I said. "You waited for the blast. When the girl started screaming, you went back in. Less than a minute later I heard the gunshots, and you came back out. I was there, Baines. I saw your face, clear as day."

"Daddy?"

Baines turned slowly as if pushing against an enormous weight.

"You killed her? Daddy? All this time I tried to make you love me as much as her. I helped you find the people *you* told me were responsible. And you *killed* her?" Keely's voice rose to a shriek. "'*My* daughter, *my* daughter'... *I'm* your daughter, too, you bastard!"

"No," he said coldly, "you're not. You are the product of a generation that squandered its potential on recreational drugs and illicit sex, on making itself feel good without taking responsibility. Facts of life, little girl: The Vietnam War was a tragedy, but thousands of good men died for their country in that war while hippie faggots like Wilson stayed home, smoked dope and fucked whomever they felt like, including your mother."

Spittle foamed at the corner of his mouth as he spewed the words like cobra venom. "While I was off trying to *prevent* some of those soldiers from dying, the bitch went up to San Francisco to see how the other half lived. Like a trip to the zoo to see all the exotic animals. Smelling the sex on them and reverting to her basest instincts, an animal just like them. I never touched her after that. Your *father*? Take a look at him, Keely. Right over there. Sucking a comfortable living out the very system he tried to subvert and destroy back then. Big revolutionary. That pathetic never-was is where you come from. Not me."

For an interminable moment, a hush as solemn as a funeral fell over the room. Portentous as the eye of a hurricane, that brief calm carried tension that thrummed like high voltage through a transmission line and then exploded in a blur of motion and rage.

"You were *there*?" Wink roared from behind me. "All this time I thought you bailed, and you saw the whole thing?"

He jumped up on a stool and launched himself over the worktable before I could fully turn around. At the same time, Keely flew toward Baines with outstretched talons, mouth contorted in a snarl. Wink hit me full force, chest high. On the way down, I saw the twins jerk one way and then another in confusion. After that, all I saw was ceiling as Wink's weight bore me to the floor and he swung a fist into my ribs. Between the floor and his blow, most of the air in my lungs was expelled with a *whuff.* Shouting added to Keely's howls filled the room with dissonant clamor. Wink put me in a clinch, his mouth next to my ear.

"Gun, Legs," he whispered.

I struggled to break free, but he just clamped down harder, not even my height and weight advantage a match for his wiry strength.

"I've got a gun, asshole!" he whispered again. "Behind my back. Take it! On three. One, two, three!"

By the time I figured out what the hell he was talking about, he'd thrown himself to the side, taking me with him. As I rolled on top, I got an arm loose, reached around behind him and felt the hard lump under his shirt. *Tweedledee's gun from the conference center.* I got a grip on it and yanked as Wink rolled us again, putting me underneath him. I held the gun down on the floor close to my thigh, keeping it hidden.

"Get off me, butthead!" I said.

"Fuck you!" Wink yelled.

"Hey, knock it off!" someone behind me bawled.

Wink stifled a laugh and threw a punch at my face. I barely had time to block it. For a moment, the years were stripped away, reverting us to a couple of kids roughhousing in the backyard. I put a hand on his chest and shoved hard. He flew back on his rump and slid halfway under a lab table. Instead of charging at me, he leaned forward and dug a hand under his pant leg. He came up on one knee with a small pistol in his hand.

"Now!" he shouted.

He aimed over my shoulder and squeezed off three shots that sounded like firecrackers. I pointed my gun past his head, targeting on Tweedledum. The big man had his hands full prying Keely off her father. I fired twice, the echoing boom of the bigger pistol ringing my ears like a clapper tolling a church bell. Events happened so fast and adrenaline pumped through me in such quantity that I jerked the trigger. My first shot went high. The second flew wide.

Focus, damn it! What did Charlie tell you?

I sighted again as Wink scrabbled past me out of the aisle, and squeezed the trigger smoothly this time. The bullet slammed into Tweedledum's shoulder, forcing a loud grunt out of him and grabbing his attention. Moving faster than I would have thought possible, he pushed away from Baines and Keely and dove to the floor out of sight. I levered myself up on my feet and peeked over the top of the shelf above the lab table. With a loud *pow, pow, pow-pow-pow*, equipment and shelving exploded around my head in a shower of fragments.

I yanked my head back and folded to the floor like a punctured balloon. Heart racing on hummingbird setting, I tried to consider the options. *Think!* My breathed rasped in my throat, loud and fast. *Breathe!* My brain and body wouldn't cooperate. Part of me knew I had to pull it together and work it through quickly. But full-blown panic had set in, taking control, choking off rational thought. *Do something!* Gunshots reverberated in the enclosed space, jolting me out of the trance.

Among the stream of disjointed images filling my head flashed a picture of a high school ball player. A big power forward at one of Centralia's rivals. Like Jack's beanstalk, I'd shot up in those years, but nature had taken its own sweet time in adding weight to my tall frame. Every time we'd played that team, Coach had assigned me the big guy. After a lot of bruises and a chipped tooth, I'd finally experienced some success when I'd stuck out my elbows and ignored him, went into that zone where nothing else existed except ball and basket. Everything on the periphery had been an obstacle to avoid or bull through, including him. Fueled by the memory, I shoved aside the molten fear churning in my gut and focused.

Ball, basket. Get the ball. Go to the hoop.

I spun in a crouch and darted in the direction Wink had disappeared, rounded the end of the aisle and sprang up onto the last long lab table. Running down its length, I held the gun in front of me and halfway down started firing, aiming for the end of the table and what I suspected lay beyond it. Just before I got there, I changed direction and leaped over the shelf, firing in mid-air down toward the floor.

Tweedledum lay on his back clutching an assault rifle to his chest, legs churning like pistons as his heels scrabbled for traction on the tile floor, trying to push himself away from where bullets had been ripping through the lab table. His mouth opened to scream and his eyes widened at the sight of me looming above him. No sound emerged as a hail of slugs slammed into his chest, letting the air escape from his lungs before it could pass through his voice box. My momentum carried me into the wall, and I crashed onto an equipment cart in a heap.

"Legs, you okay?" Wink called. His voice sounded tinny and distant over the drone in my ears from the gunfire.

"I think so. You?"

"Never better."

Disentangling myself, I stood up and looked for him, doing my best to ignore the bloody corpse at my feet. The immediacy of death was messier, uglier, more personal and disturbing up close than at a distance.

Across the room, Wink's head popped up above a lab table. Quiet settled over us like the smoke from all the gunshots. Connie lay unmoving along the wall. Easing around the end of the worktable, I peered down the aisle. Clayt had slipped off his stool and lay curled up under the table. Baines and Keely were gone. Reyna, too.

"You're an asshole, you know," Wink said.

I nodded. "I should have told you. I should have come forward at the trial."

"You thought I did it."

"No one would have believed me, Wink. Mysterious men in black? Hell, they didn't believe *you*. I was scared. I would have lost my scholarship, and you still would have gone to jail."

"Maybe." He shrugged. "I figured you split before it happened. I was never mad at you. I would have done the same thing."

The admission barely registered. My train of thought had already switched down another siding.

"Wink? We have to get out of here. Baines…"

Just like the old days, he immediately tracked the weird way my mind shifted direction.

"Can you carry the Wilson woman?" he said.

I was halfway to the desk where she lay. "Already on it."

I scooped Connie up in my arms. Pale and pasty, she'd lost a lot of blood, but she hadn't lost much weight. Middle age and years of comfortable living under an alias had plumped her up like a holiday turkey, and I staggered under the load. I heaved her torso over my shoulder like a sack of cement and headed for the door.

"Wink! Let's go! He's going to blow this place."

"Shit! I'm coming. I can't convince this dickhead to move!"

I paused in the doorway and checked on his progress. Wink dragged Clayt across the floor by his ankles. Stepping out into the hallway, I waited for him to catch up. Clayt struggled feebly as he slid along on his back.

"Stop," he moaned. "What are you doing? Let me go."

Wink turned around and backed up between Clayt's legs, hitching himself to Clayt's wagon. With a leg tucked under each arm, he leaned forward and pulled. We shambled down the hall as fast as we could, a couple of draft horses pulling their loads. The building's front door beckoned, the potential threat behind us propelling us forward.

"Can't you drag his ass any faster?" I said. "Let's move!"

"I'm going slow so you can keep up. You out of shape?"

I straightened and slowed my labored breathing. "Candy-ass."

"Pussy."

I put my head down and broke into a trot, feet thudding heavily under the load. Wink leaned farther forward and raced me to the door. I won, banging into the door with my shoulder and bulled it open. Outside the entry I waited while Wink hauled Clayt into a fireman's carry.

The two of us stumbled onto a patch of grass out front just as the roar of an explosion blew a truck-sized hole in the side of the building. The concussion shattered the glass doors behind us. The building exhaled a thick cloud of smoke and dust through both openings. I fell to my knees and laid Connie on the ground. Sitting back on my haunches, I tipped my head up to the sky and let the soft rain pelt my skin.

Michael W. Sherer

CHAPTER 55

Wink stood over me and extended a hand.

"We're not done yet," he said. "They must still be close by. They couldn't have triggered the explosive otherwise."

I grasped his wrist and let him haul me to my feet. "Don't you think they're on their way out of here by now?"

Shots rang out behind me, proving me wrong. Wink motioned to the left, so I spun and ran in a low crouch behind a tree at the edge of the large parking lot in front of the main building. Wink leaned a shoulder against another tree fifty feet away. We both peered around them to see where the shots had come from. Across the lot, Baines was trying to get into the SUV. Keely had her arms around one of his legs and was pulling him back out. The man Baines had called Pete stood behind the open driver's door. He squeezed off a shot at someone off to his left.

Three other cars were scattered around the empty lot. With a boom, the blackness lit up in an orange flash behind one of them. Pete returned fire, three shots in quick succession that ka-*thunked* into metal. I looked over at Wink to see if he had any brilliant ideas, but he was braced against the thick tree trunk, cheek tucked near his shoulder, gun in his outstretched hands pointed at the SUV. He squeezed off a round, paused, squeezed off another. Paused and did it again.

Charlie once told me that big -city police forces like SPD don't require officers to target shoot from more than about twenty-five yards anymore. Too many cops are killed inside seven feet to warrant the extra training. Wink's dad had started Wink out at fifty yards, just like old-style competition shooting. His first shot punched a hole in the driver's door. The second punched another hole six inches above that. The third one shattered the window and drilled a hole in Pete. He dropped with a grunt.

Reyna's head popped up from the other side of the car Pete had been shooting at. She ran toward the SUV, holding a gun out in front of her with both hands.

"Baines!" she shouted. "Get away from the car! Now! On the ground!"

Baines still struggled to climb into the back of the SUV. At the sound of Reyna's voice, he looked over his shoulder. With renewed urgency, he yanked a leg free from Keely's grip and kicked her in the head, knocking her to the ground. He scrabbled into the back seat.

Wink ducked around the other side of his tree and trotted toward the SUV behind Reyna. I was slower to move, and suddenly saw movement low to the ground between the big vehicle's wheels. A black wraith stole around the front bumper, extending the barrel of an assault rifle past the wheel well.

"Reyna!" I bellowed. "Get down!"

I sprinted across the asphalt, arms and legs pumping, screaming like a banshee to distract him, hoping to get close enough for a shot that might not miss. The rifle muzzle spurted flames with a *pop-pop-pop* before the man's surprised face swiveled toward the sound and sight of me bearing down on him. He swung the barrel in my direction. I cut the same way, desperate to stay out of its field of fire, leading him as the muzzle flashed again. I heard both Reyna and Wink shouting. The shooter looked even more confused. In a panic, he swung the rifle back the other way. Keely staggered to her feet just as he fired, catching the burst meant for Reyna. She spun and dropped.

Screeching to a stop, I took three deep breaths while I peered down the sight, held the last one, and remembered Charlie's instructions: *"Slow and easy, like your first kiss."* The discharge when it came—*bang!* recoil—was almost surprising, the way it's supposed to be. The shooter grunted and sagged to one side, a hand instinctively going to the wound in his leg. With the other hand, he raised the rifle. *Breathe! In, out, in, out, hold, and squeeze!* The hammer felt on an empty chamber with a click. I pulled the trigger again. *Click.* The rifle barrel arced toward me.

"Drop it! Put it down! Now! *Do* it!"

Wink stepped into my narrowed range of vision and advanced toward the wounded man, gun pointed at his head. The rifle clattered to the pavement. Wink kicked it out of reach, leaned down and grabbed a fistful of fabric near the man's shoulder, and roughly forced him face down on the ground. He patted him down, removing a pistol from a holster on his belt and another in a pocket of his fatigues.

"Put the guns on the ground," a voice said. "Very slowly. Gently."

Wink and I turned toward the sound. Baines stood near the rear of the SUV, forearm locked tightly around Reyna's neck, holding a gun to her head. I tensed, felt my heart leap. Her jaw was clenched, but her eyes were narrowed in anger, not wide with fear. I stooped and set the empty, useless gun down. From the corner of my eye, I saw Wink slowly step away from the wounded man and lay down all the guns he'd collected.

Baines waggled his pistol to one side. "Move away. That's it. Far enough."

Keeping his eyes on us, he walked Reyna up to the open driver's door.

"Don't," Wink said. "Take me instead."

Baines stopped. "Why would I do that?"

"I lied," Wink said. "I still have the notebook. You want it. I can take you to it."

"You said you destroyed it."

"Hard to prove your motive for killing Kwan without evidence. Without the notes, Kwan's a scientific footnote, a guy whose research once showed promise in a new field."

"History's forgotten lots of people like that," Baines said. "Tesla and Edison. Tesla was the genius, but Edison secured the patents and made the money."

"I waited a long time to find the people who sent me to jail," Wink said. "Do you really think I'd trash the only evidence linking you and the Wilsons to the bombing?"

Baines considered it, and inclined his head slightly. "You drive. Get in."

I put a hand on Wink's arm. "You sure about this?"

He faced me and grinned. "No sweat."

Wink walked straight to the SUV, stepped over Pete's body and climbed into the driver's seat. Baines gave Reyna a hard shove, sending her stumbling toward me, and got in the back seat behind Wink, putting the pistol to his head. The engine started up. Wink slammed his door and shifted gears. The SUV inched forward, then stopped, pavement to the rear lighting up the color of blood. Wink leaned out the window.

"Remember that Caddy my dad used to work on?" he called. "Too bad this ain't no Escalade."

Before any of us could react, Wink put the SUV in motion again. It wheeled in a wide circle, drove out of the lot and headed down the lane to the main road.

I turned to Reyna. The sight of her face unharmed, framed in raven's wings blown askew by the storm, turned my legs to jelly. Shaking, I gathered her into my arms and held on for dear life.

"Are you okay?" I managed to get the words out before my throat closed up and my eyes filled. I blinked and swallowed hard.

"Just pissed," she said. "At myself, mostly. I let myself get distracted. Baines got out the other side, circled around behind me and had me in a headlock before I knew he was there. Took me like a damn plebe."

"Don't ever scare me like that again."

She wriggled out of my grasp and looked up at me. Her lips parted, but whatever she saw in my face changed her mind. She glanced in the direction of the vanished taillights.

"What did he mean about the Cadillac?" She faced me.

I frowned. "I don't know. Some memory he wanted to share."

She shook her head. "It's a message, Blake. Come on. *Think.* What was he talking about?"

"His dad had a big shop. Worked on all kinds of stuff. A real MacGyver type. Wink, too. I guess that's where he gets it."

She put her hands on her hips.

"Sorry. His dad had a bunch of old cars. One of them was a 'Fifty-nine Coupe de Ville convertible. He used to take us for rides in the summer with the top down. We'd sit on top of the back of the rear seat, try not to get bugs in our teeth."

"It's gotta mean *some*thing."

"'Caddy.' Golf caddy? Is there a golf course around here?"

"No, the message was for you, Blake. It was meaningless to Baines."

"Caddy," I muttered. My brain was fried, crispy. "Coupe de Ville. Escalade. Ain't no... Ain't nobody's—"

"Coupeville!" Reyna whooped. "That's it!"

She jumped on me, wrapped her arms around my neck, and kissed me hard.

"Excuse me?" The wounded man sitting on the pavement waved an arm anemically. "A little help?"

"What's your name?" Reyna said.

"Does it matter?" he said wearily. He grimaced. "Johnson, okay? Kurt Johnson."

"How the hell did you end up here, Johnson?"

Johnson bit back the pain. "Fuck you."

Reyna shrugged. "Bleed out if you want. Your choice."

He grimaced again, took a deep breath and let it out slowly. "Not a lot for a soldier to do out of the service. Baines pays well, and the conditions are a hell of a sight better than some mercenary job back in Baghdad. Didn't think it'd come to this."

Reyna reached down and pulled a combat knife from a sheath strapped to her calf. Johnson's eyes widened when the knife neared him, but Reyna sliced open a gash in his pants, exposing the bullet wound.

"Who the fuck are you, anyway?" he said, watching her work.

"Navy," she said simply. "He's civilian."

He shook his head. "All this for an ex-con?"

Reyna didn't reply. With a few more quick strokes, she cut away the rest of the pant leg and ripped it into long strips. She tied three of them together and knotted the length around his leg tightly. While she broke a stick off a dead branch that had blown down in the storm to fashion a tourniquet, I went and collected guns.

"Twist that tight," she told Johnson. "Hang in there. We'll get help."

She stood and did a slow pirouette, scanning the compound. Across the flat fields beyond the assembly buildings, the horizon had lightened to dull pewter. Daylight was approaching, but it would be muted and dreary. The air was calm, and the humidity after the week of drier heat was cloying and clammy on my skin. A robin's song somewhere in the dark broke the silence. Reyna caught me staring at what were once two living beings sprawled on the hard ground.

"It helps sometimes if you don't look," she said.

"You think they're both dead?"

Her forehead wrinkled. She stepped over to Pete, bent and put her fingers to his throat. Shaking her head, she moved a few feet to Keely and checked her for a pulse.

"She's still alive," Reyna said. She sounded surprised. "Barely. Lucky the idiot there was using the wrong weapon in close quarters."

Same mistake they'd made when they'd shot Charlie. Assault rifles are imposing, intimidating, scary as all get-out, but their small bullets launch at such high velocity they can pass right through a body at close range without fragmenting. Slower, bigger handgun bullets can do a lot more damage close in.

Typical of my thought process, a question sailed in out of left field.

"There were three," I said. "Pete and two others. Where's, um, whatshisname, Rocco?"

Reyna straightened. "Out cold. Caught him coming out of one of the buildings. How'd you think I got another gun?"

Without waiting for an answer, she took out her phone and dialed.

"Deputy Commander, please." she said. There was a pause. "I don't care how busy he is. Tell him it's Lieutenant Commander Reyna Chase. I'm in the middle of a situation here that he needs to know about. Immediately... No, he needs to hear it now. I'm two miles from Coupeville Nolf, and all hell has broken loose here... Ross Industries... Yes..."

There was a longer pause this time.

"Sir... Yes, sir, I know that... You can arrest me later... Sir... *Sir!* Shut up and listen! You and the section chief gave me a job, and I'm doing it. I've got at least three dead and multiple wounded here that need medical attention now! ... No, sir, just *listen!* Tucker Baines was responsible for the bombing at Southern Illinois, along with the death of his daughter and the murder of Kwan Ji... Yes, I know what I'm saying. He as much as admitted it in front of witnesses, sir. He just blew up one of his own damn facilities trying to get rid of us all... He left. Took a hostage... We think we know where he went... No, Sanders... And sir? The research notes still exist. There's definitely a connection to the back-chatter... Yes, sir... Thank you, sir."

She closed the phone and walked back to face me.

"What's Coupeville?" I said.

"Coupeville Nolf—naval outlying airfield. It's an airstrip about a mile or so east of here. An auxiliary field, part of Whidbey Naval Air Station."

"You think that's where Wink took Baines?" My brows knit in concentration, pain building behind my eyes.

"Why not? He was trying to tell you something. It seems logical."

I tried to make sense of it. "Maybe."

"We need to move or we'll never catch him."

"What about the others?"

"The naval hospital up at the air station will send medics, and some MAs to guard the bad guys." She looked around again. "We need to get the car."

A flash of light out by the road caught my attention. I watched a pair of headlights arc toward us as a vehicle turned off the road and headed down the long drive. I glanced at Reyna. She was frowning.

"Not one of ours," she said. "Couldn't get here that quickly."

"Someone heard the shooting and called in cops?"

"Possibly."

The twin beams of light swung back and forth on the gently meandering drive, catching us twice in its path. Enough, apparently, to attract the driver's attention. A small, black coupe turned into the parking lot and drove straight toward us, coming to a stop at the last minute with a chirp of rubber on pavement. Two men got out of the car with weapons drawn, their faces hidden behind the glare of the headlights.

"Hands on your heads!" one of them called. "Get 'em up where we can see 'em."

Reyna and I both did as he said. They advanced slowly, flanking us on either side.

"Where's Langford?" one of them said.

The voice sounded familiar. I cupped a hand over my brow to shield my eyes. Light reflected off bright four-inch -high yellow letters on their dark jackets—FBI. White teeth stood out against coffee skin hidden in shadows.

"Special Agent Drucker?" I said. "Is that you?"

"Don't fucking move, Sanders! We asked you a question."

"Lower your damn guns!" Reyna said. "We're on the same side."

Drucker moved into the light and sneered at her. "You sure about that, sweetheart? Now where's Langford?"

"Why?" I said. "You want him back in jail?"

Taylor stopped a few feet in front of me. "He called us. Told us he had a situation here. That wouldn't be you two, would it?"

"We're wasting time," Reyna said. "Baines is who we're after. Langford's his hostage."

"Tucker Baines?" Drucker sounded skeptical.

Johnson groaned softly behind us, bringing their heads up sharply. They peered into the gloom.

"You've got bodies back there?" Drucker said.

"Brilliant deduction, Agent," Reyna said. "What'd you think, we're having a early-morning picnic up here? We're going after Baines. Medics will be here soon to take care of the wounded."

"I want the Wilsons!" Drucker roared. "Where are they? I've been looking for them for forty years."

I jerked my thumb toward the lab. "Over there. They're not going anywhere. They're hurt pretty bad."

"Yeah, well, I'm sitting on them," he said. "They're not getting away this time."

"Suit yourself. MAs are on their way to take them into custody." Reyna grabbed my sleeve. "Come on."

Giving the two feds a last look, I turned away. Reyna bent over, scanning the pile of guns I'd collected, and picked out a semi-automatic pistol.

"Ah, here it is," she said holding it up. "That's the last time I let someone take my weapon away from me."

I pawed through the pile until I found what looked like Charlie's SIG-Sauer.

"Where are you going?" Taylor said.

"After Baines." I motioned toward Reyna. "Like she said."

Drucker sighed. "Okay, okay. You're right. We're on the same side. A little cooperation might be nice."

Reyna cleared her pistol, held the magazine up to the light, and traded it for a new one. She inserted it and smacked it home with the heel of her hand. Deftly, she racked the slide, clicked the safety and holstered the pistol.

"You're a little late to the party." She glared at him. "We broke this open. You wouldn't even be here if Langford hadn't called you in."

"Fine. You run point."

Reyna nodded and told them about Wink's coded message and the nearby airstrip. Drucker grunted and waved us toward the car.

"Come on," he said. "Where's your car? We'll take you there."

I wedged myself into the back seat, bending nearly double to do it, leaving Reyna a little space to squeeze in beside me. They drove us out to the road, and Reyna directed them to the spot where we'd hidden the BMW. We got out, and I tossed the keys to Reyna.

"You drive," I said. "I need to check something."

I climbed into the passenger seat and pushed it all the way back, reached into the back and retrieved Reyna's laptop. She started the car and reached for the shifter. I put my hand on hers and stopped her.

"Wait," I said.

"They won't just sit there," she said. The black coupe idled behind us. "They'll take off and assume point."

I shook my head. "Doesn't matter. Listen, why would Wink pick an airfield?"

"Coupeville is hardly used. There's no one there."

"Okay, but still. Did he fly in? How'd he get here? Why hide something at a naval airfield? Just seems too risky."

The screen on the laptop glowed brightly, lighting the interior of the car. I tapped the keys to pull up a map and aerial photo of Whidbey Island. Locating a label for Coupeville Nolf, I zoomed in a little tighter, and noticed a label for the town of Coupeville a few miles northwest of the airstrip. I zoomed in on the town, each click magnifying the photo and bringing features—roads, trees, buildings, cars, even tiny people—into sharper relief. A long wharf stuck out into the water from the center of town. I stabbed the screen with a finger.

"There! Bet he's got a boat tied up at the wharf."

"A boat? Come on, Blake. Why the hell didn't he drive? It's faster." Reyna swung her gaze toward me and froze, eyes on the mirror. "Oh, shit!"

She swiveled her head and looked out the rear window. I craned my neck and saw Drucker and Taylor pull away. Again, Reyna reached for the shifter. I squeezed her hand over it and pushed it forward so she couldn't put it in gear.

"Damn it, Blake! They're leaving!"

"Reyna, listen! Please. Remember at the cabin? Wink was out back when we got there. He was leading Clayt and Connie *away* from the cabin. Toward the water."

She bit her lower lip, eyes searching the darkness outside the windshield for the memory.

"He had a boat stashed," I said. "A family boat. For cruising the sound, weekend trips up to the San Juans. I'm sure of it."

Instinctively, I knew his family must have had a boat at a property like that. I just felt it.

Reyna swallowed and nodded once. I took my hand away. She backed the car out from under the trees, goosed it forward to the edge of the road and turned toward town.

Michael W. Sherer

CHAPTER 56

Reyna and I spotted the black SUV at the same time parked on the street two blocks from the wharf.

"Nice going, civvy," she said. "Smart guess."

She found an empty space at the curb down on the waterfront, jockeyed the car into it smoothly and shut off the engine. We got out, quietly shut the doors, and started walking. The street topped a steep bluff about twenty feet high. Several buildings were built into the bluff along the waterfront—a tavern, restaurant, gift shop, small inn and the like, all dark and closed up tight for the night.

Between two of the buildings, water the texture and color of slate stretched across a large cove under a bleak, fuliginous sky. The wharf waded more than four hundred feet from shore into deeper water on sturdy pilings as thick as my waist. A large structure sat at the end, the word "CAFÉ" painted in white letters on one red wall illuminated in a circle of light from a spot. Lampposts shaped like shepherds crooks stood at intervals along the right-hand railing of the pier. Old-fashioned metal warehouse shades reflected cones of yellow light down on the wooden planks. Shadow hid the left side of the pier.

To one side of the restaurant, a ramp led down to a floating pier that paralleled the shore. The pier itself extended two hundred feet from the wharf. Tied to the dock, six or seven boats bobbed in the rippling water. Two had the tall masts and rigging of sailboats, looking like a sloop and a ketch from a distance. The others all were powerboats, three of them too small for a cabin sizable enough to accommodate overnight sleepers. At least two appeared likely candidates.

"What's your plan?" I murmured as we strode onto the dock.

"Find the boat. Board it forward and aft, and surround the son of a bitch." Her expression was grim. "Be nice if we could get him to surrender, but I'll shoot him if I have to. You okay?"

I simply nodded, knowing she'd hear the lie in my voice. We stayed in the shadows, treading lightly, footsteps muffled by the soft soles of our shoes. At the end of the pier, we skirted around the side of the café and cautiously made our way down the gangplank to the dock. Rigging on the two sailboats creaked as they yawed gently at their moorings. A shackle swaying on a loose line softly tapped on an aluminum mast, sounding a hollow plink. Pennants rustled in a listless breath of air, and quieted. The sounds masked our approach.

I stopped Reyna halfway down and whispered, "What if Baines is already gone?"

"He's finished. We'll get him eventually."

"Should we wait?"

"For those two? They didn't wait for us. Screw them."

From our vantage point, I scrutinized the powerboats moored to the dock more closely. Two felt far too big, another one too new, and several too small to fit the image in my head. An older wooden trawler a little over forty feet suited better. Blackout shades covered the windshields, but side window coverings in the main saloon glowed a dim yellow. Someone was home. I pointed it out to Reyna. She nodded, pulled her weapon and crept toward it. I followed, looking for access points other than the sliding door to the main saloon.

Judging from the boat's shape, I guessed two staterooms, one with a V-shaped bunk in the bow and probably the master in the stern. Both sat more than halfway below deck. There was a hatch on the foredeck. Reyna stopped by the bow and motioned me on. I crept alongside until I had a good view of the stern. On the back of the rear cabin was a sliding hatch over shutter-style doors about three feet high.

I nodded to Reyna. She grasped the rail, bent her knees and vaulted up onto the bow, landing lightly as a cat. She crouched in front of the hatch, got her fingers under the edge and lifted. It opened soundlessly, and she gently lowered it until it rested on the deck. She sat on the lip and lowered her feet into the cabin below.

I took that as my cue and stepped over the rail at the stern, getting my foot as far onto the boat as I could before quickly transferring my weight from dock to boat. It rocked gently, and I froze, listening for a reaction. I heard the low murmur of a voice, but no one came out on deck. I tiptoed to the rear hatch and gave it a gentle shove. Wink apparently trusted the boating crowd; it wasn't locked, and it glided forward on well-lubricated tracks. I reached inside and eased the door bolt open and swung the little doors out. Tension squeezed my chest. With a hand on either side of the hatch, I stepped onto the ladder tread inside and slowly lowered myself into the cabin.

Light spilled from the main saloon into the dark stateroom. Varnished teak everywhere added a sepia tint to the yellow lamplight. I ducked under the ceiling's low headroom and started forward on the carpeted floor, making no sound. The four-step gangway up to the saloon was set slightly off-center. I leaned left and peered into the saloon. From the tight angle I saw Wink standing with his back to the helm, hands behind him. Duct tape bound his ankles, and a strip of it sealed his mouth shut. Baines wasn't in view, but I suddenly heard him speak softly. I couldn't make out the words, but his voice gave away his position.

Directly across the saloon another gangway led down to the stateroom in the bow. It, too, was dark, but dimly lit by the lamps in the main cabin. Motion in the shadows drew my attention. Reyna stepped down from the V-shaped bunk onto the floor and cautiously eased toward the gangway. I pointed to my right to let her know where Baines' voice had come from, but she didn't look my direction. Instead, she leaned to one side to get a better view of the cabin, as I had. Too short, she stepped closer and started up the gangway. The tread creaked, and she froze. I sucked in a breath.

Wink's eyes widened in surprise or fear, or both. He pressed himself against the wheel, flinching from whatever he saw. I had no time to wonder. A gun fired with a bang that nearly blew out my eardrums in the enclosed space. Reyna tumbled back into the forward cabin and disappeared from view. The suddenness, the shock, numbed my brain, already overloaded with sensory stimuli and racing thoughts. But the sudden noise of the shot touched off my temper like a match on gasoline. Red-hot anger flared and spread through me, flooding muscles with fat and glucose and accelerating my breathing and heart rate to NASCAR speeds.

I didn't think. I moved impulsively, bounding up the gangway in two steps and throwing myself to the right, where the voice and the shot had originated. Baines perched on a banquette behind a chart table, pistol in his hand. He shrank into the corner when he saw me hurl myself toward him and swung the gun in an arc. I grabbed his wrist as I crashed half on and half off the table, practically ending up in his lap. He pounded my head with his fist, bouncing it off the table and rattling my teeth.

His strength surprised me. He swung with his free hand again. I managed to block it, but he forced his gun hand at my face. I pushed back hard, straining with the effort, then yanked his arm toward me, using his own strength to pull him upright so he faced me. I butted him in the nose like I used to head a soccer ball for Cole. *Pay attention!* His head snapped back, nose spewing blood, eyes glazing. He recovered quickly, and punched me in the face. I turned at the last second and caught his fist on my cheekbone. Along with a few stars, I saw more red, fueling the flash flood of adrenaline surging through my veins.

I squeezed his wrist with a hand that once had easily palmed basketballs and heard a bone crack, felt it grind. His face went white with pain, but his fingers remained curled around the butt of the gun like talons. I pulled him close and head-butted him again, mashing his broken nose, ripping a scream from his throat. Getting my feet under me, I grabbed his other wrist and stood, pulling him up with me. Tipping my head under the low ceiling, I spread his arms and pinned his wrists to the ceiling, hanging him on an imaginary cross. He dangled there dazed, and I kneed him in the groin.

Wink hopped and skittered on the floor in front of the helm, grunting, woofing sounds coming from behind the duct tape. I glanced at him, saw him roll his eyes from one side of the cabin to the other. Suddenly, the companionway doors on both sides of the saloon slid open to what was left of the night. Men with guns burst through wearing navy blue windbreakers imprinted with those big yellow letters, "FBI." Taylor on one side, Drucker on the other. The good guys.

"Drop your weapon!" Drucker shouted. He aimed at Baines.

Taylor stood silently, his face grim. Something was wrong. He brought up the gun he'd been holding down by his thigh. The barrel was too long. He eased into firing stance and sighted down the long gun, his movements slow and deliberate. With muffled pops, the gun fired twice. Baines went limp in my grasp, two vinous flowers blooming on his jacket. His literally dead weight became too much to hold, and he slipped from my grasp in a heap on the deck.

"What the hell?" Drucker's eyebrows arched. He lowered his gun. "Are you nuts, Taylor? What the fuck did you shoot him for?"

Taylor didn't answer. He moved the gun a few inches to the left and fired two more shots, their sound dampened to hollow snaps by the suppressor screwed to the barrel. Both rounds hit Drucker in the chest. He staggered back through the doorway, lost his balance and flipped over the rail, disappearing. A muted splash followed a half-second later. By the time I looked at Taylor again, the long barrel of the silenced pistol pointed at me.

"Your gun," he said. "Two fingers, very slowly."

Confused for a moment, I realized Charlie's gun was still stuck in my waistband. With one arm in the air, I gingerly pulled it out laid it on the floor and shoved it with a toe. He stooped to pick it up without taking his eyes off me.

"Where's Chase?" he said.

Inclining my head, I said, "Down there. She's dead. Christ, Baines blew her brains out!"

With an expression of distaste, Taylor backed up a few paces and quickly glanced down the gangway into the dark cabin. He grunted and moved next to Wink, gun held level with my navel. Quickly glancing behind Wink's back, he returned his gaze to me and kept it there, while fiddling with something behind Wink with one hand.

He stepped away and told Wink, "Be a good boy. Hop over there and have a seat."

Taylor waggled the gun at the banquette. Wink nodded. Ankles and hands still taped, he hopped the few feet to the dinette table, lost his balance and tumbled onto the banquette. Now Taylor had us both in front of him, sitting ducks.

"I don't get it," I said. Simple logic was beyond my capacity by then.

He scowled at me, then turned his attention to something on the floor under the table. He bent and retrieved a small, dog-eared spiral-bound notebook with a faded blue cover. It must have fallen off the table during my scuffle with Baines. I hadn't noticed it. Taylor held it up so Wink could see it. Wink squirmed into a sitting position.

"This it?" Taylor said.

I got my mouth to work. "*That's* what you're after?"

Taylor ignored me. "You looked at it?" he asked Wink.

Wink nodded.

"Think the Korean was onto something?"

Wink hesitated this time, eyes flicking my direction before he shrugged.

Taylor nodded. "Right. How the fuck would you know, anyway? You're such a genius you spent twenty years in stir."

"What good is it to you?" I said.

He looked at me with the pitying expression of someone who considered the question moronic and sighed. "Okay, here's what we do. You're going to untie the bow and stern lines while I start this baby up. Call for help, try to run, I'll kill your friend. You've got thirty seconds. Go. *Go!*"

I ducked out the companionway and leaped over the rail onto the deck, brain working furiously. I saw no options other than doing exactly what Taylor said. I untied the stern line and tossed it on the deck. The big engines below decks rumbled to life, a cloud of smoke and throaty growl coming from the exhaust pipes at the stern. I sprinted to the bow and took the line off the cleat on the dock. Grabbing the rail, I put one foot on the bow and shoved off with the other, pulling myself onto the boat at the last second. I dropped the line on the deck without bothering to coil it and hustled back to the cabin.

Taylor had unsnapped the blackout cloths from the windscreens. When I stepped through the companionway, he backed away from the helm and motioned to it with the gun. "Step lively, matey," he said. He didn't smile.

I took the helm and steered out into the big cove, swinging the boat around in a wide arc to face east. The early morning sky lit up the water and landscape in depressed shades of gray, as if the storm had washed out all the color.

"Where am I going?" I said.

"I'll tell you as we go," he said. "Right now, you're fine."

Thoughts caromed off bumpers labeled "Reyna," "Baines," "Cole," "Molly," "Keely" and a dozen other faces. They zipped through spinners and shot up ramps and through gates, whizzing pinballs that rang bells and buzzers and tripped flashing lights. *Guns, and bad guys, and boats, oh, my!* The numbers on the scoreboard were going backward, heading for negative territory.

"It's about money, isn't it?" I said. I talked to fill the air in the cabin with something other than tension and dread. I talked to keep my mind on something other than thoughts of what lay in store for us. "You've got a buyer. Chinese military, if Reyna was right. You're selling out. Betraying your country. Ah, what the hell, I guess it doesn't make any difference. We already owe the Chinese so much money they'll eventually take over the country anyway, right?" I shook my head. "I can't believe you'd kill your own partner for this. You don't even know if it's worth it."

Taylor reddened, and a vein in his temple pulsed, but he said nothing.

"So, that's it. Now, what? We get far enough out, you shoot us and dump us overboard?"

Movement reflected in the glass windscreen caught my eye. Behind Taylor, Wink scooted his butt closer to the edge of the banquette. I needed to keep Taylor distracted.

"How'd you and Drucker find us, anyway?" I glanced at him over my shoulder.

He lifted a shoulder. "You didn't follow us right away. I knew Chase had to be pissed. When I didn't see your headlights, I knew something was wrong. Didn't even get to the airfield. I turned around right away. We were about a half-mile back, running without lights, when you got to town. It was easy enough to find you after that."

Wink's reflection launched itself at Taylor's back. With his hands and ankles bound, Wink had only one shot, and he took it with a bloodcurdling yell. Taylor was quick, but the split second it took for him to turn and react gave me enough time to whirl around in the small space. As Wink's weight knocked Taylor forward, I clubbed his gun arm with the heel of my fist, knocking it aside before he fired.

Taylor twisted at the waist, shrugging Wink off his back onto the floor, and stepped back. I widened my stance, crouching under the low ceiling, and balanced on the balls of my feet as the boat gently rocked in the swells. Taylor raised the gun again, but hadn't taken my reach into account. Longer than Sonny Liston's, it was a distinct advantage in the confines of the cabin. I knocked his gun arm away with a forearm block and landed an open-handed blow to his face, fingers leaving a white imprint on his cheek.

The muscles in his neck tensed and bulged, and his red face darkened a shade or two. He danced back out of reach, avoiding Baines' body on the floor, and shook his head.

"You should have fucking listened, asshole," he said. He raised the gun again, but pointed it down and to the side. "First, Langford. Then you."

His finger whitened on the trigger. A dozen voices screamed inside my head, all giving me different directions at the same time, the cacophony and confusion rooting me to the spot.

Blake Sanders! PAY ATTENTION!

I strained with mental effort, throwing off the momentary panic like ripping off a straightjacket at the seams, and charged him. His gun hand moved, tracking in slow motion up toward the threat I posed. Before I could reach him, two explosions ripped the air, and Taylor froze. I crashed into him and we went down together, sliding across the deck and down the gangway into the master stateroom. My head slammed into something hard, and an aerial fireworks shell burst inside my head.

The crackling stars slowly faded away. Through the ringing in my ears I heard a faint voice call my name. I pulled myself onto my knees. Taylor lay next to me, sightless eyes staring at the cabin ceiling, a large jagged red hole over his left eyebrow leaking blood and gray matter, shiny bits of white bone poking through the torn flesh. I clamped my jaw shut and turned away, swallowing the gorge rising in my throat.

Tiredly, I dragged myself up the gangway into the saloon. Reyna lay face down on the cabin floor, feet still on the bottom tread of the ladder up from the forward stateroom, gun in her outstretched hand. Thank god Taylor hadn't checked her more closely. Wink bucked and rolled on the other side of the saloon, trying to get to her. I rushed to her side.

"Reyna?"

She lifted her head and opened her eyes blearily, slowly focusing on my face.

"This really hurts," she said.

She closed her eyes and her head thudded onto her arm.

Her left side was covered in blood. I pushed and pawed and prodded, looking for the entry wound. Suddenly, I heard grunts and whimpers. I turned. The grunts were coming from Wink. He jerked his head, motioning me over to him. The whimpers, I realized, were coming from me.

"She's hurt, Wink."

He nodded vigorously, grunting louder.

I scooted over to him, grasped one end of the strip of tape over his mouth and yanked. He flinched, but didn't make a sound.

"Galley." He nodded to the side. "Knife in the top drawer."

I rose up on my knees, found the knife and sawed through the tape around his ankles. He sat up and turned so I could free his hands. He brought them around in front of his chest and rubbed his wrists to get the circulation going. I got to my feet and saw mile-distant shoreline scrolling past the windows. Startled we were still underway, it took me a few moments to figure out how to throttle down, shift into neutral and shut down the engine. The boat settled and drifted, the silence oddly discomfiting.

Wink kneeled next to Reyna.

"Left arm's a mess," he said, "but she doesn't seem hurt otherwise. She's lost a lot of blood. I'll get a tourniquet on it, but we need to get her back to shore pretty quick. Think you can pilot while I take care of this?"

I nodded. Turning back to the helm, I reversed what I'd just done, turning over the big twin diesel engines, moving both shift levers into forward and slowly easing the throttles up. I spun the wheel and turned the boat around until the bow pointed toward Coupeville, then I opened up the throttles even more. The only sound in the next five minutes was the loud drone of the engines. Wink finished what he could for Reyna and got up. He stood next to me and stared out the windscreen.

For a brief moment, I saw a glimpse of the two of us as we'd once been in the summers aboard his boat in Centralia. We were both a hell of a long way from that place.

CHAPTER 57

The shoreline sparkled with the pulsing lights of emergency vehicles parked on the quay above the pier. A small crowd of early risers had gathered at the foot of the long wharf just below them, gazing curiously out at the dock as Wink adroitly maneuvered the trawler into its former slot. I jumped down to the dock and made the boat fast. A small knot of people milled on the dock, watching me, not offering to help, possibly dissuaded by the presence of two sheriff's deputies standing with casual attentiveness, hands on holsters.

"Sanders!"

I turned. Two medics bent over a seated figure huddled under a blanket. The man struggled to get up, the medics trying to restrain him. He pushed away the hand on his shoulder and rose to his feet. In obvious pain, he drew closer, the question in his eyes outweighing it.

"Taylor?" His eyebrows arched.

"Dead," I said.

The deputies stiffened to attention like Dobermans behind a chain link fence. I tipped my head toward one.

"You in charge here?" I said to Drucker, my voice low enough not to be overheard.

He squared his shoulders. "I'll take responsibility."

"You okay? How'd you...?"

He shrugged and winced from the pain the movement caused. "Kevlar vest saved me. Don't think Taylor knew I was wearing it. Asshole never did like following procedure. Neighboring boater heard all the commotion and fished me out of the water."

I nodded and looked past him. Waving at the medics, I called them over.

"There's a badly wounded naval officer on board," I told them. "Unless you think this guy's gonna die any second, she's your priority."

One of them hustled back to grab a medical kit and they both climbed aboard. Wink came out of the cabin and let them pass, then joined us on the dock. Drucker nodded at him.

"I owe you, Langford. More than just an apology."

For a moment Wink looked as if he might deck him. He gave a weary shrug.

"Forgive and forget," he said simply.

Drucker shook his head, unwilling to let it go. "Officially, I can't advise you. But there are groups that will help you get a substantial settlement from Uncle Sam for what's been done to you."

"I've got enough money, special agent."

"Maybe a measure of moral restitution, then. Give you your good name back?"

"Maybe."

Drucker considered him for a moment, then turned and walked up to one of the deputies. I watched them confer.

"What now?" I said.

Wink stepped up next to me, gaze facing the same direction as mine. "Don't know yet. Big world out there."

CHAPTER 58

A figure sat on the steps of the house where I live, lounging in the early morning sun, not hunching. He had clipped grizzled hair, not tangled blond locks. As tired as I was from driving my paper route, there was little chance I'd mistake him for Cole. Or for Keely. He leaned back, resting on one elbow, and watched me silently as I came up the walk. I stood in front of him, waiting. He rose slowly and walked past me, then stopped.

"Come on," he said. "Let's get some coffee."

I hesitated. "It's been a long night, Charlie. I'm beat. Can't this wait?"

Wordlessly, he walked to the Toyota sitting at the curb and got in the passenger seat without waiting for an invitation. I followed slowly and climbed behind the wheel. We drove to our usual spot in silence.

Inside, when we'd both settled into a booth and a waitress had come by to fill the mugs already on the table, he rested his elbows on the table and cradled his coffee in both hands. He stared into the mug as if the brown liquid held his fortune.

"Look, I've never been much good at thank-yous or apologies," he said. "I just wanted you to know that if you ever want to talk about what happened up there you can call me, okay?"

I watched him for a moment, then looked away and rubbed my chin.

"Okay," I said quietly.

He looked at me then, eyebrows climbing up his forehead. "That's it?"

"What do you want me to say, Charlie?"

"I don't know. Nothing, I guess." He dropped his gaze to the tabletop, looking pensive.

"Sarah's still pretty upset," he said a moment later.

"Doesn't surprise me. Kind of a shock to discover what you thought you knew about your parents was all a lie."

His face colored.

"You seem to be taking it okay," I said.

He shrugged. "They've gotta take responsibility for what they did." A pause, then, "Your friend okay?"

I didn't know if he meant Wink or Reyna. I guessed Wink. "Better than okay, I'd say. For the first time in a long time."

Wink had his good name back, which was all he'd really wanted. But he'd also struck a deal with SIU to share the patent and royalties that might result from commercial development of the technology in Kwan Ji's notebook. He was smart enough to build on Kwan's research.

Silence fell over the table. It began to make me feel itchy. The events on Whidbey were two weeks behind me, but I still felt exhausted and listless most days. All that death, especially my part in it, had taken an emotional toll. I'd be working through it for a long time, maybe even consulting Jeri privately, not just at group meetings. And there was the nagging question of Reyna. ONI had reclaimed her, spirited her back to D.C. to recuperate at Walter Reed Medical Center. I hadn't heard from her and didn't know how to get in touch. Worse, I didn't know where I stood with her, what I wanted with her, what was even possible between people on different coasts.

I needed sleep, not coffee. I pushed it away and stared at Charlie until his eyes met mine.

"I appreciate your offer," I said. "I may take you up on it someday. You already know most of it from the reports. I'll tell you this much: I learned a couple of things. I learned that people aren't motivated by causes, or religion, or politics. None of that matters. It's all bullshit. It all comes down to what people themselves want, what individuals want. Money, power, sex…"

I shook my head and looked out the window at the sunshine spreading across the buildings on the other side of the street. I thought about the waste and destruction Baines's ego had caused. He'd killed two members of his own family pursuing… what? I didn't know anymore.

"What else did you learn?" Charlie prodded. "You said two things."

How could I explain what friendship meant to me? Or loyalty? Or what the fear of losing a friend ends up costing?

The past had caught up with all of us—Clayt and Connie, Charlie and Sarah, Baines and his family, Wink and me. What we'd done with the opportunity when it had made all the difference.

I gave another headshake and smiled at him.

"Nothing," I said.

Acknowledgements

People who don't know my work often ask if I write under a pen name (as if I'll assuage their feelings of guilt by admitting that, yes, I really write books under a name they've heard of—say, Michael Connelly or James Lee Burke). My pat answer, though, is this. I write under my own name. Since I did all the work, I'm taking all the credit. But we authors don't do all the work. Most of it, but not all. And here's where we get to thank those who helped.

Thanks to all those in uniform, both the police, firemen and EMS teams who protect us at home and the service men and women here and abroad who protect our freedom and that of others. Special thanks again for answering innumerable questions about policing in general and the Seattle Police Department in particular to Sergeant Deanna Nollette, Detective Kim Bogucki, Sergeant Joe Bauer, Detective Leonard Carver and Captain Neil Low.

I spent some time with Don Clifton, firearms instructor, at the Bellevue Indoor Range to understand not only basic handgun safety and differences among various arms makers' semi-automatic pistols, but also the effects of adrenaline on shooting ability.

If you found this book mostly mistake- and typo-free it's due to the terrific efforts of Peter Gelfan at The Editorial Department, who saw me through the first two drafts; Ed Stackler, my content editor who provided invaluable assistance on the final draft; and Craig Lancaster, who gave it a final once-over to smooth out rough spots and catch typos. The fabulous cover was designed by Anita Elder at Anita Elder Design.

It goes without saying, but thanks to my family, and especially Valarie, the love of my life, for supporting me and cheering me on. It's not easy living with someone who kills people for a living.

Finally, this is a work of fiction. Names, characters, places and events are the result of my overactive imagination and any resemblance to actual incidents, places or people, living or dead, is purely coincidental.

Also by Michael W. Sherer

<u>Blake Sanders Thriller Series</u>

Night Blind

Night Tide

Night Drop

<u>Emerson Ward Mystery Series</u>

An Option On Death

Little Use For Death

Death Came Dressed in White

A Forever Death

Death Is No Bargain

Death On A Budget

<u>Stand-Alone Suspense</u>

Island Life

About The Author

Michael W. Sherer is the author of *Night Drop*, *Night Tide* and *Night Blind*, the first book in the Seattle-based Blake Sanders series, which was nominated for an ITW Thriller Award in 2013. His other books include the award-winning Emerson Ward mystery series, the stand-alone suspense novel, *Island Life*, and the Tess Barrett YA thriller series. He and his family now reside in the Seattle area.

Please visit him at www.michaelwsherer.com or follow him on Facebook at www.facebook.com/thrillerauthor and on Twitter @MysteryNovelist.

Photo Credit: Valarie Kaye-Sherer

You've finished. Before you go...

Tweet/share that you finished this book.

Rate this book

If you enjoyed this book, please tell your friends. The most helpful thing any reader can do for an author is write a review. If you have time, please post your thoughts on Goodreads, Amazon, Shelfari or LibraryThing.

Turn the page to enjoy a sneak preview of **NIGHT DROP**, the third Blake Sanders thriller.

NIGHT DROP

PROLOGUE

The small boat rocked in the swells, tossed on the foam-flecked crests like a chip of balsa. Two men braced their knees against the port gunwale to keep their feet from slipping on the wet deck. They wrestled with a heavy net strung over the rail. Miguel Esparza stood in the tiny wheelhouse, knuckles white on the helm with the force of his grip as he fought to keep the boat on as even a keel as the rough seas would permit.

For a moment, he took his eyes off the boat's heading to watch the two men on deck haul in the big net hand over hand. From their effort it looked to be a good catch, an abundance of the small sea creatures that would put him one step closer to a bigger boat, a real boat. This was his third already. *La Diosa Fortuna*, he called her. "Lady Luck," though he would not tempt fate—or waste paint—by putting her name on the stern.

He'd started with an old, leaky dory, rowing himself out into the warm currents of the bays along the coast to cast his nets. Years of saving had led to the purchase of a motorized skiff, and now the small trawler under his feet. Soon, he'd have a boat to be proud of, a trawler to rival any of those in Magdalena Bay. Maybe in the summer, before the start of the new season. For now he felt content to work the coast south of there in *Bahia Almeja*, closer to his small village, or out on the ocean. It was worth the extra fuel to take his catch to San Carlos, sell it there, and return home rather than pay *la mordida* to dock his boat in San Carlos with the bulk of the shrimper fleet. But he had only a few weeks to bring in as much as he could before this season closed.

A wave sprayed over the bow, speckling the etched windscreen with rime, reminding him to make course corrections. A frown elongated his brown face, stretching his weatherworn skin into long furrows. A squall was blowing in from the southwest, a late winter blow. *Isla Santa Margarita* and

Isla Creciente protected the bay from the big waves and storms coming off the Pacific, but he and his men had ventured south along the outer coast of *Creciente*. The squall would overtake them before they reached the two-mile cut into the bay between the two islands. He eased the wheel to port, turning the bow into the strengthening wind. He glanced over his shoulder at Nacio and Felipe to check their progress.

"*¡Hola!*" he shouted over the wind.

Felipe raised his head, his gaze following Miguel's outstretched arm toward the ominous black clouds racing toward the boat.

"*¡Vamanos!*" Miguel called.

Felipe nodded and nudged his partner. The men on deck redoubled their efforts, but Miguel saw they struggled under the weight of the net on the pitching deck. He spun the wheel, turning the bow into the face of a rolling, cresting wave. The boat struggled up the face of the wave and tipped down into the trough. Miguel adjusted the throttle, watching the tachometer needle ease up another hundred rpm. He spun the wheel a quarter turn to starboard to take on the next wave, watching the curl of foam break at the top above his head.

"*¡Ay, caramba!*"

Miguel turned at the sound of Felipe's shout.

Nacio leaned out over the rail, grappling with the net. The water next to the boat churned and boiled. Something large thrashed in the net, drenching Nacio as it splashed.

"*¡Madre de Dios!*" Nacio cried as he pulled at the netting. "*¡Madre de Dios!*"

A dolphin, Miguel saw now. No, two. One caught in the net, the other frantically swimming alongside, bow to stern and back. Pacing, just as Miguel had outside the room where his wife Maria had delivered their child, his little Angelito.

With one hand, Felipe gripped the small boom that held the net away from the side of the boat. He leaned out and grabbed Nacio's belt with the other.

"*¡Es hecho!*" Nacio shouted.

The netted dolphin swam free flipping its flukes into the air as it dove under and broke the water again with an arcing leap. Felipe hauled Nacio back into the boat.

"*Bueno,*" Miguel called over the rush of the wind. "*Vamanos. La tormenta...*" He pointed again to the line of rain on the horizon.

"*Si, si.*" Felipe's head bobbed up and down.

Nacio pointed to the water alongside. "*¡Ay, dios mio. ¡Ay, Dios mio! Vistazo.*"

Miguel craned his neck. Both dolphins swam alongside the boat, each turning an eye up to the men on board, almost as if to offer their thanks. But it was their dorsal fins that caught Miguel's eye. Each animal had a strange mark about two or three inches high at the base of its fin, like a brand, unique to each—a Ω on the larger animal, and a ∞ on the one that had been trapped. Felipe and Nacio crossed themselves, as if to ward off the devil if the marks weren't a sign from God. Superstitious, both of them.

As soon as his two deck hands pulled the wriggling mass of shrimp aboard, Miguel spun the wheel and pushed the throttle as far forward as he dared, turning tail and running now before the oncoming storm, riding the crests of the waves toward the comparative shelter of the big bay beyond the cut. Both dolphins frolicked in the water ahead of the bow, their sleek gray bodies breaking the surface then running like ghosts just beneath it. They showed no signs of abandoning the boat. Even when the boat reached the calmer waters of the bay, the dolphins kept pace.

Miguel could see the wonder on the faces of his men as he throttled down and headed north toward San Carlos. Foolish men, the pair of them. The symbols on the pair of dolphins were not the mark of God, he knew, but the work of men. All kinds of scientists came to this part of Baja, some to count turtles, some to watch the whales. Why not dolphins? Suddenly, he throttled down and watched the dolphins slow and turn to swim back toward the boat.

"*Hola, Felipe,*" he called. "*Tírelos un pez.*"

Felipe nodded and pawed through the pile of writhing creatures on the deck. He raised an arm in triumph, a small yellowtail in his grip. He held it out over the side. The larger dolphin swam up to the boat and eyed Felipe and the fish with an open mouth. Felipe tossed the fish away from the boat. The dolphin rose halfway out of the water and deftly caught it in its jaws. Felipe plunged his arm back into the pile of shrimp and pulled out another small fish. He tossed it to the other waiting dolphin.

Smiling, Miguel changed course and headed for home. If the dolphins continued to follow, he had an idea who would know what to do with them. Someone who might pay him handsomely to trap and acquire them. The man from the mountains...

The stranger had shown up in the village a few months before to buy supplies. A hard man, brown-skinned like Miguel, but with features from a totally different part of the world. Definitely not Mexican, or Spanish, or mestizo, or like any of the pureblood Indians he knew. In time, word had filtered down to the village from the locals that the man came from a camp in the mountains, a camp where they trained men to fight. Revolutionaries, they said. Not like Zapata. These men had no interest in Mexico, they said. Only in the *gringos*, the *Norte Americanos*.

For them, they wanted only death.

CHAPTER 1

"I want to die."

Oh, to have a nickel for every time I'd heard that. I wondered how big a pile it would make, how much it would add up to. Not much. Fivers would be better.

"You're not even listening."

"I'm still here," I said. *Empathize. Put yourself in his shoes.*

"Dying would end the pain, wouldn't it?"

"Damn straight. Better than Ox. *Blam!* It's over."

The voice on the phone was bitter, morose. Male. Mid-teens, most likely. I imagined a crop of greasy, jet-black hair hanging over his eyes, one side of his head shaved. Silver rings through his left eyebrow and lower lip, studs in his nose and the crease between his lip and chin. Plugs through the holes in his earlobes, stretching them the way some African and Thai tribes do. Tats on his pale forearms. Nothing elaborate or colorful—that would be too expensive. A simple dragon, maybe. Or Chinese calligraphy that translated to something like "death is truth."

Focus.

"That's the pain talking," I said. "Think about it. Think about what life's like when the pain isn't there."

"Man, the only time the pain's gone is when I'm on Blue."

"Drugs?"

"Duh, yeah. Ox, man."

I ignored the sarcasm. *Take him seriously.* "Oxycodone. Got it. How long have you felt this way?"

"Like dying? Seems like forever."

"Have you ever tried to kill yourself?"

"No, man. I don't know. Once, maybe. I kinda OD'd one time. But I think that's because I was drunk and forgot how much Ox I'd already snorted. I was sick for days."

"What about now?"

Overhead fluorescents buzzed in a minor key, flooding the cramped room with light bright enough to scare shadows and thoughts of suicide into the deepest corners. A low murmur of voices provided harmony. The ticking of a large wall clock kept tempo. A paucity of windows rendered the position of the clock hands meaningless, even if they kept accurate time, which they didn't. Night, day, made little difference in here. No windows also meant a lack of ventilation, so the atmosphere in the room closely replicated the weather outside. Sweat speckled my brow and upper lip—definitely August.

Low dividers formed three sides around a battered metal desk in front of me, separating it from nearly identical cubicles, each occupied by an equally well-used secondhand desk and chair. On each desk sat a black, plastic multi-line telephone, ancient cathode ray tube computer monitor, keyboard, and almost prehistoric PC computer tower—a misnomer if there ever was one. Almost all of the furnishings and equipment had been donated.

An assortment of pens and dull pencils sprouted from a ceramic coffee mug on a corner of the desk, erasers on most of the pencils hard and blackened with graphite, worn down to the ferrules. The top desk drawer held a few scratch pads with most of the pages torn out, some with notes and doodles on the first several pages. I added my own to a pad on the desk in front of me. Over the top of the divider, the lights glinted off a huge amethyst ring hovering above wavy pumpkin-colored hair. The ring covered most of a forefinger. The flame-colored nail at the tip dug through the thicket of hair, revealing gray roots. Helen Olmquist, another volunteer.

"What do you mean?"

The kid's voice brought me back.

"How do you feel now? Sad? Lonely? Alienated? Hopeless? Helpless?"

"Jesus, how the fuck do you think I feel?"

"Pissed off, from the sound of it. That's a good thing."

"What the hell are you talking about, man?"

"If you're angry, you haven't given up hope. It means you care about something."

"I *care* about busting you in the mouth, that's what."

"That's a start. We can get to that later. Why don't you tell me why you want to die?"

"'Cause life sucks, that's why."

"Yeah, so?"

"What kind of counselor are you?"

Maybe it was his voice, nasal and high-pitched, that put me off. Not quite a whine, but close.

"Look, kid, we all have problems. What makes yours so bad you want to die?"

The mop of pumpkin hair in the next cubicle swiveled and rose in the air until the magenta raccoon mask of Helen's heavily shadowed eyes stared at me, wide with shock.

"I don't know." His voice broke into a sob, and he snuffled into the phone. "You just don't understand. Nobody does."

"Sure they do. There're lots of kids out there like you. Alienated. Angry. Feeling like they don't belong. You're not the only one. You're depressed. It's a treatable illness. You can fix it."

"You don't get it!"

The statement pushed a button into place with a click inaudible to Helen and the others in the room. Why did these kids call if they didn't think we understood what it was like to stare into a future fogged with misery and pain? Didn't they know that most of us were survivors? Family or friends of those who'd abandoned us by suicide? Some of whom even had experienced the metallic taste of a gun barrel themselves, or the bitterness of a handful of pills?

My son Cole's face flashed in my head. Cole, our golden boy, our only child. The good memories, so numerous, now usually outweighed the pain of his loss. But I still found the speed and force with which that loss could suddenly overwhelm me surprising. Like someone ripping a bandage off an open wound. Or a breaking wave that battered and rolled me over, pressing me to the sandy bottom with its weight and buffeting currents.

Despair was deadly. Rage seemed the only recourse, hot and primal, anger that fueled the blood with adrenaline.

"You think your family and friends would be better off without you?" I asked, my voice low, anger still in check, barely.

"Hell yes."

"Why? Think about it. Imagine yourself dead. Now imagine how all those people will feel. You think they *want* you dead? They want you happy, not dead. They want what you want, idiot: they want your pain to stop. They want you to get help."

"Hey! You can't talk to me—"

"Shut up and listen!"

Helen stood and toddled out of her cubicle, waving a plump arm in the air to attract attention. I didn't try to stop her.

"Do you have a plan?" I went on gruffly.

"Plan? What—"

"To kill yourself. How are you going to do it? Where? When? Have you thought about it?"

"Have I...? Sure I've thought about it. I think about it all the fucking time."

"So, what's your plan?"

On the far side of the room, Helen stood next to a tall, slender woman with short, dirty blond hair and gesticulated wildly in my direction. The tall woman listened attentively, head bent toward Helen, her gaze on me.

"Blow my brains out, man," the kid said in my ear. "Quick, easy."

"Got a gun?"

"Well, no. But I can get one."

"Got a back-up plan?"

"No-o." He drew the word out, unsure. "I don't know. I could take a bunch of Ox."

I sensed the kid was on the verge of tears again, but the anger welling up inside was too hot to temper before my mouth opened of its own accord.

"Bet you don't have any of that, either. Sure as hell doesn't look like you want to kill yourself to me."

430

"Fuck you, man," he sniffed. "I never said I did. I said I wanted to die. But I could do it. Where do you get off telling me shit like that? Who the hell are you?"

Whatever tattles Helen told worked. Our supervisor wended her way around the block of cubicles, Helen trailing in her wake like a pampered pooch. My anger drained away as quickly as it had appeared leaving me empty and weary.

"What's your name?" I said softly.

He hesitated. "Rory."

"Rory, I'm Blake. I'm going to make this quick. I had a son, probably a little older than you. He killed himself. There's not a day that goes by that I don't think of him, miss him. I guarantee there are people out there who feel the same about you. You don't want to die. If you did, you'd have a plan, and the means. You'd just do it. Like my kid did. And you'd leave a hole so big in some people's world that it could never be filled. So, here's what I want you to do. I want you to promise me you won't hurt yourself for the next twenty-four hours. Okay? One day, that's all I ask. Stick around one more day."

The tall woman stopped outside my cubicle and crossed her arms. Her blank expression spoke volumes more than any other she might have worn. She turned and shooed Helen back to her own doghouse.

"Okay?" I said again into the phone.

"Why should I believe you?"

"My kid's suicide? It's not something you lie about."

Suicide's a permanent solution to a temporary problem. I couldn't bring myself to voice the prevention group's mantra. The line went silent.

"All right," the kid said finally. "Sure, I promise."

"Good." I let out the breath I'd been holding. "Now here's what I want you to do next. I'm going to hand the phone to a nice lady named Jeri. I want you to let her make an appointment for you to come in tomorrow to talk to a real counselor, not someone like me. You hear me?"

"Yeah, yeah, I got it."

"Don't hang up. I'm handing the phone to Jeri now, okay, Rory?"

He didn't answer, but he didn't break the connection, either. I stood and gave the receiver to Jeri, letting her squeeze past me into the small space. She slid into the chair and put the phone to her ear.

"Rory, my name is Jeri Nolan," she said. "Blake says you're safe. Is that true?"

I walked out without waiting to hear the rest of the conversation, but I didn't go far. Jeri ran the organization. She'd want to lecture me before she sent me home. I checked my watch. Nearly time to head to the *Times* warehouse to pick up papers for my delivery route anyway.

In the break room next door, I poured myself a cup of tepid coffee from a nearly empty air pot and sat down. The table had a chipped laminate top and wobbled when I rested my arm on it. Emblematic.

Jeri showed up ten minutes later and eased into the opposite chair.

"Sorry," I said. "I screwed up."

Her eyes searched my face. "You're off your meds again, aren't you?"

"No, I..."

My sandcastle defenses quickly eroded. I tried to recall taking my last dose. I patted my pants pocket, reached in, and felt three small pills under my fingertips. Two doses and a spare.

"You got me."

I felt sheepish, but relieved, too. Though inexcusable, the way I'd treated the kid hadn't simply been the result of a bad mood. Or worse, a hereditary proclivity for being a jerk. But it *was* a result of genetics. A "developmental disorder," as the American Psychiatric Association's *Diagnostic and Statistical Manual* likes to call it.

"Blake..." Jeri tented her fingers.

Abashed, I shriveled under her disappointed gaze.

"We need bodies," she said gently. "As many volunteers as we can get. And I'm glad you're one of them. But not if you're going to be judgmental. I don't want to lose any of these kids."

"I didn't lose that one." I hesitated. "Right?"

She shook her head. "No, you didn't. But if he'd been closer to the edge…"

"If he'd said he had a plan, I'd have gotten nine-one-one on the other line. I know what to do, Jeri. And if he'd been closer to the edge, we might not have saved him anyway."

She inclined her head, but didn't say anything.

"He's coming in tomorrow?"

"We'll see," she said. "I'm hopeful."

"You're always hopeful."

"Can't do the job, otherwise." She touched her fingertips to her lips. "So, tell me what's really going on."

Jeri didn't miss much. I thought I'd only been put off by the kid's whining. She looked for the underlying cause.

"It's been nearly two years," I said.

"Since Cole's death," she said, confirming what I still had difficulty saying.

"We're not supposed to outlive our kids."

"No, we're not. It's a terrible thing when a child dies."

"People are impatient with me. No one wants to talk about it. They say, 'Move on. Move forward. Get over it.' I can't do that."

"Grief doesn't have rules, Blake. There's no timeline, no expiration date. We live in a culture that doesn't prepare us for death. It's okay to grieve still. Just try to find appropriate outlets for your grief." She paused. "Come to group more often."

I toyed with a tiny scrap of paper on the table, wadding and rolling it between my finger and thumb. I met her gaze and nodded.

She got to her feet. "Take the rest of the night off, Blake."

"Okay." I shrugged. "Almost time to go to work anyway."

She glanced at a watch on her wrist. "Witching hour. Damn."

Most suicides occur between three in the afternoon and midnight. The hotline tended to get busier in the hours just before midnight, and calls either increased or dropped off dramatically in the wee hours. It was impossible to predict which.

"I could stay," I said.

"That's okay. We'll manage." She hesitated at the door. "Blake, I'm glad you help out around here. You're a real asset. But you've got to follow the rules. You know that."

"I will. From now on." I held up two fingers. "Scout's honor."

A while back I'd pulled a young woman named Liz Tracey down off a bridge, but I'd committed a breach of ethics by contacting her afterward and forming a personal relationship. Nothing tawdry, or even remotely romantic. A simple friendship. Jeri would have expelled me from the program if I'd asked Liz for her contact information on a call into the hotline.

Suitably chastised, I walked out to look for my car, a challenge if I don't pay careful attention when I park. Close to where I thought it would be, the car didn't make me wander blocks to find it. I banged my head on the doorframe getting in, swore a blue streak, then jammed my knee under the steering wheel when I slammed the door shut. The old Toyota was designed in a country where the average adult male came up to my chin, but I'd gotten in the car thousands of times without injury. The times I didn't...

Pay attention, goddamn it!

I swallowed a dose of meds, drove to the *Seattle Times* warehouse down in Ballard, and spent the next hour or so assembling newspapers for delivery. I liked the predictability of the job, the comforting routine, the clear expectations. Nightly changes in the route—vacation holds, new subscribers, alternative products like *Barron's* and the *New York Times*—kept it varied enough to hold my attention. Most of my clients had never seen me, didn't know if I spoke English or Vietnamese, the native language of more than half the route drivers. Newspapers were dying right and left. But I often felt I provided as vital a service to the customers on my route as their doctors or postmen.

Night Tide

It wasn't one of those nights, but I loaded the papers in the car, swallowed another pill, and pulled out of the lot, determined to shoulder on.

www.ingramcontent.com/pod-product-compliance
Lightning Source LLC
Chambersburg PA
CBHW060339260626
47160CB00006B/2141